A Darker Shade
of Giemsa

A Darker Shade
of Giemsa

A J Donovan

A. J. Donovan

First edition independently published by A J Donovan in the United Kingdom 2022.
ISBN (Paperback): 9781739119904
Editor: Christine Beech
Typesetting: Matthew J Bird

A CIP catalogue record of this book is available from the British Library

For further information about this book, please contact the author at
ajdonovan.co.uk 07975 747570

Dedication

I want to dedicate this book to Biomedical scientists everywhere. Biomedical scientists save lives daily, performing their roles in haematology, biochemistry, microbiology, histology, cytology, and blood transfusion within our hospitals.

The Biomedical scientist works silently in the laboratory when others have gone home. Providing a 24/7/365 service has been the norm for many years, looking after all your diagnostic needs and providing appropriate blood and its components. Biomedical scientists work together as a team and also work closely with haematologists. Abnormal findings which require further investigation and intervention are passed to the haematologist to make a diagnosis. This generally includes additional blood tests, bone marrow biopsies, X-rays, scans, and genetic testing.

This book aims to bring to the forefront the essential and pivotal roles performed by Biomedical scientists, laboratory staff, and haematologists within the NHS.

1

Dr Sami Prakesh climbed out of his red Ford Mustang and bleeped the lock with his remote. He looked up at Lady Margaret's Hospital, the building which towered in front of him, and soon it seemed as though he had never been away on his three-week vacation to India to visit family members. Carrying his briefcase, he walked through the main doors and headed to the small coffee bar on his left-hand side.

"Good morning," said the assistant. "I haven't seen you for a while."

Sami raised his eyebrows in surprise. He didn't think he would be missed by anyone in this place, let alone a kitchen assistant. He replied to her in a flat monotone voice, "I've been on three weeks holiday, which is now a distant memory. A latte please."

He also selected a small box of cereal and picked up a small bowl. He paid the assistant and then strode along the corridor towards his office.

He bid good morning to Barbara, the night nurse on shift, then disappeared into his office and closed the door. Once in private, he placed his briefcase on the floor next to his desk and fired up his computer. After a three-week absence, there would be emails, hospital information, and patient details to familiarise himself with before starting the day ahead. He noticed some emails from Dr James Turnbull, the clinical lead of the department. He decided to read those first.

"Damn!" he tutted and rested his head on his right fist for a few moments before letting out a deep sigh.

He had forgotten all about the new female registrar who was due to take a position in haematology soon. It turned out that she was starting today of all days! He didn't relish the thought of working with a female at all, let alone having to share his office with one, as the desk opposite had been allocated to her. He found women difficult and was never at ease with them during conversations. He was very single too, with no room for a woman in his private life, not since his scheming former wife had taken all his savings in their divorce settlement. He would never allow that to happen again. He was married to his career.

He stroked his beard with his finger and thumb as he continued to read his emails and spotted another one requesting him to attend a monthly meeting that morning.

He sighed and rolled his eyes in despair. *What is the matter with people? he thought. A new woman is starting today. I am expected to introduce her to the job and attend a meeting at the same time. How ridiculous.*

He was about to get up from his chair and then remembered that Dr Turnbull never arrived until nine o'clock. Frustrated, he pushed the keyboard to one side and decided to eat his breakfast. When he had checked the rest of his emails, he left the office and knocked on James Turnbull's door before entering.

"Why have I got an email to inform me that a young woman is starting today? Then another one to tell me that I have to attend a meeting on the same day? Am I supposed to be a magician?" he snapped. "I cannot induct a new member of staff and attend a meeting at the same time. Who organises this nonsense?"

He slammed the printed emails on James Turnbull's desk.

"What is this place coming to? What am I supposed to do with this woman?"

James Turnbull sat in silence whilst Sami had his rant about the unfairness of his timetable that morning.

"Sami, the woman has a name. It's Dr Pemberton and I suggest that you treat her with respect. She gave a very good interview for the position and had good references and credentials. You are paid to decide what to do with Dr Pemberton today. I trust that your decision will be wise."

Sami shrugged, then stormed out of the office without a backward glance.

2

Dr Victoria Pemberton walked up the long hospital corridor and stopped outside the haematology ward. Looking at the door before her, she thought, *well, this is it.* She pushed it open and entered the ward.

She was a qualified doctor who had chosen to specialise in this field. She'd learned about the vacant position from an advert spotted by her mother who worked as a biomedical scientist in the hospital laboratory, closely connected with the haematologists.

After a successful application and interview, Victoria was offered the position three months ago. After confirming her identification, qualifications, and other security checks, her starting date was confirmed.

She reached a desk where two nurses were preparing for the day ahead.

"Can I help you?" the dark lady asked.

"Yes, I am here to see Dr Prakesh," Victoria replied.

"Have you an appointment?"

"No, he's expecting me. I am the new registrar, Dr Victoria Pemberton."

"Ooh! Welcome aboard!" the dark lady smiled. "Please take a seat and I'll try and find him for you."

She picked up the telephone and dialled a number. Just at that moment, a tall dark man appeared from the corridor that came from the outpatients' ward. He was smartly dressed but had a bushy beard and unkempt hair.

"Dr Prakesh, I've been trying to find you," said the nurse. "This is the new registrar who is starting today." She indicated to Victoria, who stood up and held out her hand.

"Dr Prakesh, I am Dr Victoria Pemberton. I'm delighted to meet you."

They shook hands. He hesitated to look at the woman in front of him. She had piercing blue eyes and a red streak down one side of her hair. He was transfixed by her eyes for a moment, then his attention went to her hair. He was a man of few words and simply uttered, "I'm Sami Prakesh. Welcome to haematology. Come this way."

He took her into his office.

"This is your desk and computer."

He indicated to the one opposite him and added, "Make yourself comfortable."

He went to his desk and took out a key.

"This is a key to the door of this room. Keep it with you at all times. You can leave your bag, coat, and personal belongings here. They should be quite safe, however, please lock the room if you leave and I am not in here."

Victoria went to her desk and placed her bags on the floor beside her, then placed her coat on the back of the chair. She took the key from Sami.

"Thank you," she said.

She continued to unpack her bag. She took out her three favourite photographs which had been part of each desk she'd ever had. One was of her fiancé Neil on the day he bought his first motorbike. He had the biggest grin on his face as she remembered. She placed that on the right-hand side. The centre one was a photograph of her and her pet cocker spaniel Bouncer and the third one was of her mother and herself on a night out with drinks.

Sami had taken his seat and continued to work on his computer whilst Victoria was happily arranging her desk. Suddenly she heard him tut disapprovingly at his computer and then take a big sigh.

"Oh, for goodness sake" he said, with his eyes transfixed on his screen, and then he slammed his fists down on his desk.

Then he got up as quick as lightning and marched out of the door.

He's not happy with something, Victoria thought. *I'm glad it's not me.*

She quietly chuckled to herself and took out her cell phone to check her messages.

Sami was away for some time before he finally returned to his office, then sat at his desk once more. He stared at the screen, rubbing his thick bristly beard with his index finger and thumb, deep in thought. He looked as though he wished that whatever was on his screen would go away.

He is a strange man, Victoria thought.

3

Finally, Sami looked over towards Victoria. He decided to keep quiet about her red hair for now and monitor her performance. He had more pressing things to consider, such as where to place her for the morning.

It's so embarrassing, he thought. She probably won't be very impressed.

Sensing she was being watched, Victoria looked up at him.

"Can I help you with anything?" she asked. "I gather your morning is not going as planned."

That's an understatement, he thought. He sighed.

"No, it's not," he said curtly. "It's always like this when I get back from holiday. Absolute hell!"

"Have you been anywhere nice?"

She tried to change the subject to help him forget the problems at hand.

"No," he replied abruptly. "India, to visit relatives. That's all."

"At least you got some time away."

Victoria was trying to calm the situation but wasn't having much luck.

"True," he replied.

Silence fell across the room again.

God, not someone else wanting to make small talk, he thought.

He could never understand why people wanted to chat amongst themselves about their private business instead of getting on with the job at hand.

If they concentrated more on what they were doing they would do a better job, he thought.

Then he remembered James' words. "Try and be kind to her, don't make her dislike you too."

The last registrar Dr Iqbal had left, as there had been a breakdown in their relationship and their dislike for each other was mutual. James Turnbull wasn't pleased.

"Look Victoria." He paused. "Sorry, may I call you that?" asked Sami, remembering his manners.

"Of course, that's fine," she politely replied.

"Well, it's like this. I found out this morning that you were starting today. The idiot sent the email two weeks ago when I was away. Then he sent me another email last Friday to say I had to attend the monthly meeting. So instead of giving you an induction, as would be correct, I have been summoned to a meeting, so I won't be around this morning. I feel I must apologise for this oversight, as this is not how things should be."

Victoria sat on her chair and didn't know what to say to him. She began to feel quite sympathetic towards him.

"It's just so frustrating and irritating when this happens," he continued, wondering what she could do, then a sudden thought entered his head. He remembered James saying previously that she had a connection with the laboratory. After a brief pause, he asked her a question.

"Do you know someone who works in the laboratory?"

"Yes, my mother works there as a biomedical scientist," she replied.

"Who is your mother?" Sami asked.

"Carol Reed."

"Ah, I see," he said. "Maybe you could go there for today? Your induction includes a day in the laboratory, observing and watching their work. Although that's not ideal, if I can arrange it, would you mind going there?"

"Not at all," replied Victoria. "It would solve your dilemma!"

"You see, we have a significant relationship with the laboratory staff, as we ask them to perform, or send away, lots of tests on our behalf.

They also look to us for advice and inform us of any abnormal results, highlighting any new diseases of the blood. The laboratory plays a vital role for the haematologist, as well as for the rest of the hospital with the provision of diagnostic results. I will make some inquiries."

Sami made the call and it had been agreed that Victoria would have her induction day in the laboratory.

Sami led Victoria from the office, down the corridor of the haematology ward, towards the laboratory. He introduced her to all the laboratory staff who were present.

"Hello, mum. It seems you cannot get rid of me," Victoria said, smiling as her mum Carol came into view.

"Are you sure you will be alright here today?" Sami asked.

He felt a pang of guilt about having to bring her here.

"I'll be fine," she replied.

"I'll call in when I can, to check everything is OK."

He felt very relieved that he had been able to arrange this. He suddenly turned around and then disappeared from the laboratory.

4

"So why are you spending your first day with us?" asked Jenny, a biomedical scientist who was a colleague of her mother.

"He's double-booked," replied Victoria, with a smile. "He has been summoned to a meeting on my start date which gave him a dilemma."

She continued to explain to Jenny about the emails and that he was quite annoyed that he wasn't able to do her induction properly.

"How do you find him?" Jenny asked.

"I've only known him a few minutes!" said Victoria. "However, he does seem to be an anxious man and is easily annoyed. I get the impression he likes to do everything by the book. And he doesn't half walk fast" she exclaimed.

"Certain people in here have had disagreements with him, with his manner in general and his attitude towards them," said Jenny.

"Well, he spoke very highly of everyone to me. He said you were all important and work very closely," Victoria informed her.

The staff members looked at each other in surprise, and Carol rolled her eyes.

"That's very interesting."

"Ok, Victoria," Carol decided that the chat about Victoria's new mentor should stop.

"Most mornings, in the laboratory, we are generally fairly quiet then the work gathers pace around ten o clock. The night shift does most of the equipment servicing however there are still a few tasks to complete."

"What's left to do?" Victoria asked.

"The quality control has to be performed on the machines to check they are in good working order. The liquids used to do the tests must be prepared before it gets busy, otherwise they will run out. The working area is cleaned too."

"I guess I'm doing the cleaning then. No different to being at home" Victoria teased her mother.

Victoria cleaned the workplace. Carol checked the machine controls and filled up the liquids. Jenny validated any work that came in for testing.

This continued until break time. Victoria went for her morning break with Carol whilst Jenny stayed and covered the laboratory. After the morning breaks were over, Victoria was introduced to the staff in the blood transfusion department. Hazel, who was in charge, explained how a sample was processed in the laboratory.

"It all starts here," Hazel explained, walking over to the sample receipt bench. "This is where samples are received into the laboratory. We need to check that the correct patient details are handwritten. We must have the patient's full name, date of birth, and a unique number on the request form and sample. If there are any discrepancies, the sample is rejected and the ward telephoned for a repeat sample. You also need to log the telephone call on the log sheet."

A sample came in at that point and Hazel unpacked it from its bag and checked it. She noted that the date of birth was different, so decided to reject it. She asked Victoria to make the phone call to the ward.

Victoria dialled the number and told the nursing staff about the different dates of birth.

"A repeat sample will be needed," she added, before noting the details on the telephone log.

"I didn't like doing that at all," Victoria smiled, "But I see how important it is for things to be accurate."

"It's all part of the job," explained Hazel. "You get used to it after you have done it a few times."

"Do you ever get people being hostile towards you when the samples are rejected?" asked Victoria.

"Yes, we do quite often," said Hazel. "You have to try and remain polite and professional and explain calmly why it cannot be accepted. You refer to the transfusion guidelines and people usually accept it in the end."

Hazel then showed Victoria the machines and explained how they worked. She showed her the blood fridges and freezers, where all the red cells and frozen products were kept, and also the platelet incubators. She explained about the temperature monitoring systems in place and the cold chain, which is an audit trail of the products in transport once they are removed from the fridges. It was a legal requirement that had to be kept for thirty years.

"The first practical thing anyone learns in blood transfusion is how to perform blood groups and antibody screens. They are generally done on machines, but they can be done manually too."

Hazel took Victoria to the manual working section of the transfusion laboratory. She took out some tubes and placed them in a rack, then took the reaction cards from the packet and placed them on the stand. The testing fluids were kept in the fridge in a white block, so she went to get them. She first demonstrated to Victoria how to perform blood groups in the tubes and then the antibody screens in the cards. She handed Victoria a results sheet.

"You need to write the sample numbers on here and jot down the reaction you see in the reaction tubes. These create a blood group pattern. At the side, there is a column in which to write the blood group." She selected ten random samples from those who had their tests completed and instructed Victoria to do as she had demonstrated, noting her patterns and groups on the sheet.

"We'll check them on the computer system afterwards."

Just as she started to practise the blood groups, Sami appeared.

"How's everything going?" he asked.

"It's all good, thanks. I'm just learning how to perform some blood groups. How was your meeting?"

"Boring, as I expected. I need to go back. Will you eat lunch with your mother today? I'll have everything properly arranged for tomorrow."

"Yes, that's fine," replied Victoria. "I think she was expecting me anyway." She smiled.

"OK, I'd better get back."

With that, he spun around and disappeared as fast as lightning.

Hazel and Victoria then checked the blood groups and all the reactions matched those validated in the computer.

Lunchtime came and went very quickly, then Victoria was back in the haematology lab once more with Carol and Jenny. Carol went through the result validation procedure with her and taught her how to search the database for the patients' history so comparisons could be made with the present results. A lot of samples had arrived to be processed, so Carol and her colleague Jenny worked tirelessly.

"They always come in big drops. Victoria, you could help by examining some blood films," said Carol.

"Yes, that's fine, wherever I can help out," she said. "I will need some help with the computer system though."

Carol briefly explained how to report the blood films and Victoria sat at the microscope to do the work. She processed the films competently and was examining one when Sami returned and stood beside her.

"Is everything still alright?" he asked.

He noticed that she was reporting films. Damn! He had wanted her to learn his method. Still, the laboratory had done him a favour today, so he kept quiet and flicked a switch which turned on the camera, showing an image of the film she was examining down the microscope.

"Checking up on me then?" she teased.

"Naturally."

He hesitated whilst looking at the image then to the report she was typing and continued, "All fine, except that you may want to check your spelling."

Victoria checked her report.

"Oh, my goodness!" she exclaimed. "Good job you spotted that!"

She felt quite embarrassed as she had missed the letter 'o' out of 'count', resulting in what would have been quite rude, and he'd seen it!

"I'd better correct it," she laughed.

Sami stood silently, with his finger over his mouth, hiding his amusement but Victoria had spotted his cheeky smirk. It was the first time she'd seen him smile.

"Right, I have some bone marrow reports to do in this side office. I'll be in there if you need anything."

Sami disappeared through the door.

"Oh no, that was so embarrassing," Victoria said to her mother and Jenny.

"Why? What happened?" asked Carol.

Victoria explained her spelling mistake and they all laughed.

"It's not the first time that has happened," said Carol, sympathetically.

Victoria finished the blood films and the laboratory seemed to have calmed down a bit, with not so many samples on the machines.

"It gets really busy again later," explained Carol. "The work from the GP surgeries is delivered by the vans and they all have to be processed by the late staff. The same amount of work again and often more, but only a skeleton staffing system to process it all."

"Seems a bit harsh," said Victoria. "Why can't they get them here earlier?"

"It's the way the system is," said Carol. "Often the blood is taken early in the morning but doesn't appear here until six o clock in the evening, or later. It's not a good system and is often very stressful for the late staff, especially if there is a problem that interrupts the flow of the work. Very often you finish work up to an hour later."

Jenny then mentioned a high INR result that needed attention.

"It seems that the result was raised before but it's now increasing," she said as she flicked the screen through the patient's history so that Victoria could analyse the results.

"I think it needs intervention to get the result lower," Victoria observed, and she went to seek advice from Sami. She gave him the patient's details and he entered them into the computer. He also flicked through various screens to get a proper analysis then said, "It looks like they haven't reduced her Warfarin medication."

He had a grim expression on his face.

"We need to go and see them."

5

Sami and Victoria left the laboratory.

"Can I reprimand them?" asked Victoria, eagerly feeling that she was getting the chance to take on her role.

"Be my guest," said Sami as they arrived at the ward.

Victoria approached one of the nurses and asked to speak to the doctor in charge of Mrs Jackson. The nurse went to find him.

"Hello, I'm Dr Brown, how can I help?"

The small brown-haired man with a moustache introduced himself to Victoria. He eyed Sami in the background, so was apprehensive about their appearance.

Victoria introduced herself. "Hello, I'm Dr Pemberton, Specialist Registrar in haematology. I have come to discuss Mrs Jackson's INR result."

"Ah yes, I'm aware it's rising. I was going to call you for some advice, but you beat me to it," he said, trying to smooth over the fact that he hadn't acted upon it yet.

"Well, it needs to be dealt with immediately," Victoria spoke in a firm voice. "She needs to be taken off the medication and given a dose of Vitamin K right now. This really should have been done earlier."

"Yes, I'm aware," said Dr Brown. "It's just been rather hectic in here today."

The young doctor has sweat on his brow and was feeling rather uncomfortable.

"It is no excuse," said Victoria. "If the patient fell and started bleeding, it could be very dangerous. I'll write it up in the notes, but can you please see to it that the patient gets the Vitamin K with immediate effect."

"I'll get on to that right now," said Dr Brown, and headed to the nurses' station. He gave instructions to a member of the nursing staff.

Victoria went to see the patient and introduced herself. She explained what was happening and updated her notes.

"I shall come back and see how you are tomorrow, Mrs Jackson."

"Thank you, Dr Pemberton," said the elderly lady.

Sami watched Victoria at work. Had this all been done to impress him, or was she always like this? He was impressed. She handled it like a professional and got her message across in a firm but calm manner. He always got irritated and annoyed with these people.

"How did I do?" Victoria asked Sami, when they had left the ward.

"You handled it well," he said, with a rather emotionless voice which did not express at all how impressed he had been with her. She decided to take it as a compliment.

They headed back to the haematology ward but did not speak again until they reached the door of the ward. Sami broke the silence.

"I expect your belongings are all in the laboratory? I hope your first day hasn't been too bad, despite the fiasco."

"It wasn't as I expected, but I have enjoyed the day," replied Victoria. "Are you doing anything nice this evening, Dr Prakesh?"

"Please call me Sami. I'm going to the gym. My first workout for nearly a month."

He didn't feel up to it after the return-to-work day he'd had.

"I will put a note on your desk regarding Mrs Jackson. I find it best to do that, so nothing gets overlooked. Enjoy your evening, Victoria. Doing anything nice?"

"I'm going out for a birthday meal with my family."

She'd let it slip out, despite not wanting anyone to know.

"It's your birthday? You should have said earlier. Happy birthday."

"I didn't want a fuss. Goodnight Sami."

Victoria walked towards the laboratory. She liked Sami. So, he seemed a bit abrupt, irritable, and got annoyed easily, but he seemed to give his best and liked to do everything correctly. She felt that there was a nicer side to his nature somewhere deep inside.

She thanked Jenny for her help as she collected her belongings from the laboratory and indicated to Carol that she was leaving.

Sami also headed home. What was he doing, making small talk with Victoria? He didn't exchange pleasantries with anyone. Yet, it was the poor woman's birthday and not the best start to her new job. He would get her a card and ask everyone to sign it tomorrow. It was the least he could do.

6

"How was your first day?" asked Paul, when Victoria arrived home. Paul Reed was Carol's husband and Victoria's stepfather.

"Interesting, as I ended up working alongside mother!" she replied.

They both laughed.

"How did that happen?" asked Paul.

Victoria told the tale, and then said, "It was different to what I expected, but I'm going to like it there."

"Good. That's the most important thing," replied Paul.

"Ok dogs, walk time," Victoria announced, walking through to the kitchen to get their leads.

The three dogs in the house bounded across the room after hearing the jingling noise of the dog leads. They were Meg and Reggie, her mum and Paul's two border terriers, and Bouncer, her cocker spaniel; a little dog that Neil had bought as a surprise for her when they shared the bedsit. She began to reminisce about the night Neil brought home the little bundle of fur …

"He's ours," he had said. "I thought he would complete our little family." He had paused, and then said, "At least for now, until we can afford children."

At the time, they were both young and money was tight. He told her that his grandmother's friend had a dog that had given birth to puppies. He'd gone to see them, fell in love, and ordered one of the dogs. The main reason was that a dog wouldn't need spaying in a few months, so no expensive vet bills. He'd had some money left from the insurance policy that matured on his eighteenth birthday, which he used to pay for the little dog. However, he kept it as a surprise for Victoria and came home one night, with him in a big box wearing a big bow.

"Oooh! What a lovely surprise. He's gorgeous," Victoria had exclaimed. "Thank you so much."

She had flung her arms around him and had given him a big hug and a kiss. Then she had taken the little bundle out of the box and cuddled him in her arms.

"He's called Bouncer," Neil had said, "but you can change the name if you want to."

Victoria had continued to stroke him.

"Put him down and let him walk around," Neil had continued, "then you'll see why my nana's friend gave him the name Bouncer."

Sure enough, as he pottered around, exploring his new home, his legs and hind quarters had an unusual bounce.

"I love the name. He's a Bouncer," said Victoria. "Let's keep it." She had flung her arms around him again and had given him a lingering kiss …

Tears sprung into her eyes as Victoria reminisced over those happier times. However, she quickly brushed them away. She didn't want to be sad tonight. She was going out later to celebrate her birthday and her new job. She attached the dogs' leads and headed out of the front door.

Sami made himself a coffee, and then quickly changed his clothes for the gym. He hadn't felt up to it earlier, but now he was ready to vent his frustrations on a few punch bags and do some weightlifting. Besides, he had not seen his friend, Richard, for a month and was looking forward to the meet-up.

After an hour's workout on the treadmill, bench presses, lifting weights, and boxing with punch bags, he felt a lot better and was ready for a drink. He ordered himself a lemonade-shandy at the bar next door to the gym and took a very welcome sip.

"How was the holiday?" asked Richard.

Sami sighed and said, "Ah you know, same old thing. Great when you first get there, then it becomes boring and the conversation changes to 'why don't you have a wife yet Sami', this and that, then I just can't wait to get back."

"So why do you go?" asked Richard.

"If I didn't go there to visit my family, there wouldn't be any other holidays, such is the dull and uninteresting life that I lead," said Sami, in his mundane voice.

"A barrel of laughs then?" laughed Richard.

"Indeed."

Richard then went on to talk about his family business and various aspects of his life at work.

"So how was work for you today?" asked Richard.

"Complete hell," Sami replied, and Richard laughed.

"Have you nothing happy to tell me? Everything is doom and gloom with you." Richard was used to his friend after all these years and found it rather amusing. Sami told Richard about the new registrar and how James had double-booked him so that he couldn't introduce the poor woman to her job.

"So, what is she like then?" asked Richard.

"She seems nice. It's just embarrassing having to palm her off onto other people."

Both men finished their drinks and then parted for the evening.

Victoria went to the Golden Fleece for a carvery that evening with Carol and Paul. She loved the food there, succulent meat with a variety of vegetables and trimmings. The house rosé wine was good too and Paul had ordered two bottles. "It's a double celebration tonight," he exclaimed, "as we are celebrating your new job too."

"I suppose we are," Victoria smiled.

"Let's propose a toast then." Paul lifted his glass and held it in front of him.

"Here's to Victoria. Wishing you a happy birthday and every success in your new position."

"I'll drink to that," said Carol, and they all clinked glasses and took a drink.

"And to Neil," Victoria added. Since his tragic accident, each year she raised a glass to remember him. If he was looking down from another world, he'd be thrilled that she had been given this opportunity. However, if he had still been alive, would she have achieved her present position? Originally, she was training to be a biomedical scientist, like her mother, as it seemed a good profession and it would have paid quite adequately with the shift work that accompanied it. She and Neil were always short of cash, and it seemed like the profession to make it possible for them to get married and then climb onto the property ladder. However, after his death, Victoria's priorities changed. She decided to continue studying and was interested in drugs used to treat cancer and leukaemia. Keeping busy, with her head engrossed in study books, was also a large part of her healing process, as her world had fallen apart after the accident. A place in medical school had been one of her major achievements. Now an even bigger step had been taken with her desire to specialise.

Sami returned from the gym and ate a pasta meal on his sofa. He had a large home cinema in his lounge, and he switched on his television to watch a film. He suddenly thought of Victoria, enjoying her birthday meal, and those bright blue piercing eyes he'd noticed when she introduced herself. He was impressed with her first day. She'd been patient about his dilemma and had handled Dr Brown well. *Maybe a female registrar wasn't so bad after all.*

Why on earth was he thinking about her when he was relaxing in his home? She was taking up far too much of his brain space.

7

Victoria Pemberton set her alarm clock early the following morning. She showered, dressed, and was ready to leave for work promptly the next morning. She was looking forward to working and getting started with her job in earnest today. She was also eager to arrive early to impress Dr. Prakesh.

Sami was also up early too. He needed to get to work an hour before his starting time, to get his paperwork and any reports completed without being disturbed, especially now as he was sharing his office with Victoria. As nice as she seemed, she was another person who liked conversation about things other than work and he would find that irritating when concentrating on work-related topics. So he showered, dressed, cleared the litter tray, and put a bit of food down for his cat Mitzi, giving her a little stroke and cuddle before he left.

On his way into the hospital, the little gift shop sold birthday cards, so he bought quite a pretty floral one for Victoria, before purchasing his usual coffee and cereal.

Once on the ward, he took the birthday card and signed it, then passed it on to Barbara, the night nurse.

"Could you sign this and ask the other nurses to write their names on it please? Found out it was the new doctor Victoria's birthday yesterday, on the day she started" he spoke rather uncomfortably as he never really bothered to get involved with peoples birthdays. Barbara gave him a knowing look and he noticed a wry smile tickling the corners of her lips.

"Will do, Dr. Prakesh" she replied. "I'll pass the message on to Sister Monaghan."

Sami went back into his office and turned on his computer to start working.

He had been engrossed in concentration for what seemed only a few minutes when he noticed the sound of footsteps coming up the corridor. He became aware of them stopping outside of his door. He sighed and slammed his hands on the table as he wondered who on earth could be disturbing him at this hour when he was trying to concentrate. Then he heard the sound of the key being inserted into the lock. It could only be Victoria. He looked at his watch. Eight-thirty, he thought. It's only EIGHT THIRTY!

"Good morning Sami" Victoria said as she breezed into the office. Frustrated, Sami rather reluctantly said "Good morning Victoria" as he sat staring at the work he now wouldn't be able to finish. He looked at his watch again.

"You're early" he muttered. He continued looking at his computer in the hope she would sit quietly and not want to disturb him.

"I wanted to be prompt today" she replied eagerly. "I'm looking forward to getting started with my job" then she sensed by his serious tone that he didn't want to be disturbed. She went across to her desk to put down her belongings.

"I'm just trying to get a few things done before work starts" he looked up as he spoke to her this time. He sensed her eagerness to get started and thought it was a refreshing change from others he'd dealt with in the past.

"That's fine, I'm going to buy a coffee anyway" Victoria got the message loud and clear that he wanted to be alone and left the office. She went to the little coffee bar near the hospital entrance and sat at a table with her refreshments and read a magazine. *Dr. Prakesh doesn't like being disturbed in the morning.*

Victoria returned to the office at nine o clock sharp. Sami looked at his watch. "Your timekeeping is impeccable," he remarked. Victoria was quite surprised he even noticed!

"Right, first of all, I should introduce you to all of our staff." She followed him outside of the office and closed the door behind her.

"Listen up everyone!" He had a very commanding and authoritative voice that made everyone quieten down and turn their heads.

"I would like to introduce you to Dr. Victoria Pemberton, our new Specialist Registrar" Sami made a gesture with his arm towards Victoria.

"Hello everyone," said Victoria. She smiled as she looked around at them all.

"We met briefly yesterday," said the dark-haired lady who had introduced her to Sami. "I'm sister Monaghan, but please call me Bernie".

"I'm Sister Stubbs, better known as Margaret Rose," said the grey-haired lady wearing glasses who was standing next to Bernie.

"I'm staff nurse Dawn Henderson," said the ginger-haired nurse who was with Bernie when she came in yesterday. "Welcome to our team" she added with a very pleasant smile.

"I'm staff nurse Susan Barrett," said the short dark-haired nurse. "Please call me Sue"

"Josephine Robertson," said the final person of the little group. "I'm the Healthcare assistant and you can call me Josie" Victoria couldn't help noticing her shorter skirt, immaculate blond hair, and bright red lipstick.

"Alright follow me Victoria" Sami quickly disappeared up the corridor. My goodness, that man was like greased lightning! He knocked and entered a room without waiting to be invited in. Victoria followed him.

"Dr. Turnbull, please meet Dr. Victoria Pemberton" Sami indicated to Victoria to enter the room. "Hello James," said Victoria. "James was on the interview panel which I attended before I was offered the job" explained Victoria to a baffled Sami. Of course! James had already met her. His opinion counted for nothing at all, even though he was expected to be the woman's mentor and have her share his office.

"Welcome to the team" continued James. "I hope you'll be happy here".

Sami left James' office rather abruptly and headed to another office on the right-hand side. He knocked on the door.

"Come in," said a female voice from the inside. Sami entered "Well good morning Sami" continued the voice. "To what do I owe this pleasure?" Sami indicated once more for her to enter the room. "This is our new Specialist registrar Dr. Victoria Pemberton. Victoria this is Dr. Verity Sinclair, one of our very valuable Haematologists.

"Hello, Verity" Victoria leaned over to shake her hand. "Nice to meet you"

"Welcome to our team," said Verity who seemed a very welcoming and friendly lady. It was plain to see why Sami seemed a lot more at ease with her. She'd sensed a lot of tension between him and James.

They left Verity's office and went to one other final room. The man was about to leave the room as Sami approached the door. "This is Dr. Andrew Bartholomew, another haematologist," he said to Victoria. The dark man looked across. "You must be Dr. Pemberton? I heard you were starting this week".

"Please call me Victoria" she replied also shaking the man's hand.

"Well, I'm off to see my patients. I guess we'll become more acquainted at another time." Andrew Bartholomew then disappeared along the corridor.

Back in the office, Sami explained their timetable for today.

"It's the ward round first. You will meet some of the patients and observe them today. Tomorrow you will be in charge and I'll observe. After coffee, I generally prepare for my afternoon clinic and see any patient's on the list that needs observing around the hospital. That will include Mrs. Jackson, the raised INR patient from yesterday. It's probably an idea to telephone them now and make sure they send the sample down, otherwise, they forget and the result won't be ready when you go to the ward. I'd let them know you'll be visiting mid-morning. Keep them on their toes"

Mrs. Jackson had completely slipped Victoria's mind.

"I'll telephone them now" which she did and spoke to Dr. Brown with whom she'd spoken yesterday.

As she replaced the receiver, there was a knock on the door.

"Come in," said Sami. A lady entered the room with greying hair tied back in a ponytail.

"Your patient notes for today Dr. Prakesh," said the woman who also wore glasses.

"Thank you Charmaine. By the way, please meet Dr. Pemberton the new Specialist registrar".

"Hello, Charmaine. Nice to meet you" said Victoria.

"Likewise," said the woman as they shook hands.

Sami explained that Charmaine was one of the Haematology secretaries, a pleasant lady, very old school. Very diligent always making sure the correct files were present and always in the appointment order.

"Alright time to get started" Sami jumped out of his seat like a rocket. "Follow me"

"So the object of the ward round is to undertake an assessment of each patient and plan the care which they will be given. We communicate verbally as a team and care plans are also documented in the patients' notes". He looked at his watch and tutted. "Where are the nurses?" he snapped.

"Sister Monaghan, we're ready," said Sami impatiently. He was a man who didn't like to be kept waiting. Bernie and Dawn hurried over.

"One of the sisters and a staff nurse accompany us" he continued. "They are the ones who generally care for the patients so it's crucial they know their treatment plans to perform their duties". Sami spoke in a serious monotone voice which did not change its pitch at all. Bernie looked across at Victoria and gave her a sympathetic smile.

Sami introduced the patients to Victoria. "This is Dr. Victoria Pemberton our new specialist Registrar. She will be involved with all your treatments and care from now onwards"

Victoria shook hands with each patient as they did the round. She liked to put them at ease bearing in mind that some of them may feel quite sick and frightened as the treatment for some of these diseases could be quite invasive and harrowing. She liked to give them some form of comfort in what could be a very dark place for them. Sami sighed and shrugged his shoulders as she chatted away with them, showing his impatience and disapproval, as he wanted to move on. Victoria did notice but she didn't care at all. Bernie and Dawn kept looking at each other and smiling. They pitied Victoria as they knew what a stickler he was for getting on with the job in hand. How refreshing it was to see someone come along and do things differently and they sympathised with her as they knew only too well, she would probably get a good grilling for it later, as they had all been there.

Upon seeing the fourth patient, a lady called Beatrice Delaney, Sami dropped his pen on the floor whilst writing up the notes the pen rolled under the patient's bed. He sighed in frustration as bent to pick it up. The lady liked to chat and told Victoria how she missed her husband of 48 years. "We used to go ballroom dancing together," she said.

"Really?" asked Victoria. "My grandmother used to teach ballroom dancing. It was her life. She was very successful and had many winning formation teams in her time"

"That's very interesting," said Beatrice. "I'd love to have met her"

Sami heaved a sigh, grimaced, and looked at his watch. Victoria got the message that she was taking too long and needed to move on to the next patient.

In a short, while the ward round had been completed and all the patient's Victoria had been introduced to, had their care plans decided for the day. Now it was time for the nurses and healthcare assistants to prepare and begin their duties for the day. Dr. Prakesh headed back into the office followed by Victoria.

"Right," he said in his commanding voice. "One thing you need to stop on the ward round is talking to the patients about things other than what is on their treatment plan. It ends up taking far too long. It should take eight to twelve minutes to assess a patient. So do you think you could try and do that tomorrow, and then we'll accomplish everything a bit quicker?"

Victoria felt a bit annoyed. She didn't mind at all listening to his advice and learning from him about medicine, but nobody was going to dictate her personality and manner with patients at the bedside! He stared straight at her without emotion, but the piercing blue of her eyes cut right through him. She told him politely.

"I'll try and do it quicker tomorrow if that's what you want. However, I disagree with your instructions not to make conversation with the patients. I need to talk to them, interact with them, put them at ease, and have empathy for them. After all, their treatments are quite intense and they are human. I think it's our job that, as well as being good Doctors, we show some compassion too".

He continued to stare at her, as though someone had dared to disagree with him and have their own opinion! She probably would go far. He sat and rubbed his beard with his forefinger and thumbs and thought carefully about what she'd said. He took a deep breath.

"OK. Talk with them if you want, if it's your way. However, can we just try and speed it up a notch tomorrow?"He looked at his watch. "It's taken an hour and a half today. Shall we see if we can finish in seventy-five minutes? In time you will see why I have said this. Once you have settled into the job a bit more, you will have more things to do and sometimes it's difficult to fit everything in"

"I would still never neglect the patient for the sake of getting the work done, even if I had to stay late or start early, as you do". He looked across at her. Of course, she was shiny and new at the moment but in time she would realise.

"Maybe it's time to go and pay Mrs. Jackson a visit? I'll let you do that alone as you are well capable".

"OK. I'll do that now" she replied, leaving the office and heading up to the ward. On her way there, she thought about the ballroom chat with Beatrice Delaney. It made her smile.

Bernie and Dawn Henderson were standing at the nursing station with Josie who had taken out a mirror to re-apply her lipstick

"We need to sign the card" mentioned Bernie. She retrieved it from its hiding place and they all took turns in signing their names.

"In all the time he's been here, I've never known him to do that before".

"Do what?" said Dawn.

"Buy someone a birthday card."

8

Sami checked his emails whilst Victoria went up to the ward. It would be coffee time upon her return so he hoped she wouldn't be too long up there. He sat thinking about her first ward round. There was no doubting she had a good bedside manner and it was noticeable how much the patients seem to like her. That red streak in her hair had not scared them. She was very opinionated too and he knew after she replied to him, that her having little conversations with the patients would never cease. He just hoped with experience, that she would realise it was important just to get on with the work. Victoria Pemberton had a quiet but confident character and she could be quite amusing. It may not be so bad having her around after all.

"Good morning Mrs. Jackson," said Victoria as she arrived at the patient's bedside. "How are you doing today?"

"Oh I'm alright, a little tired that's all" the woman replied.

"Have you had your blood taken this morning my dear?" Victoria asked.

"Yes, they came round earlier but I've heard nothing more"

"I'll go and find Dr. Brown," she said and headed towards the nurses' station at the bottom of the ward.

"Good morning Dr. Brown. Do we have an INR result yet for Mrs. Jackson? She said her blood had been taken earlier" asked Victoria directly.

"I don't know. I haven't checked yet as I have been busy with my ward round" he replied.

"Have you got a telephone somewhere, so I can call the laboratory?" Victoria asked.

"There's one just here" he handed it to her. "I wouldn't bother trying them yet as it often takes them a while to issue results".

Victoria was becoming very irritated with this man. "Once in the laboratory it's processed within thirty minutes," she said abruptly "unless it's still extended then they have to re-check it on the other machine to ensure the result is genuine". She dialled the number.

"Hi, it's Victoria Pemberton here. I'm looking for an INR result for Dorothy Jackson, date of birth four, seven, nineteen forty. It's the one that was raised yesterday"

"Oh yes," mother Carol replied. Victoria had someone with her as she didn't call her "mum" on such occasions.

"It's been through already, I remember it," said Carol tapping into the computer to retrieve the result. "It's five-point four today" she replied.

"Great! That's an improvement. Thanks".

"Well Dr. Brown, the result is there and it has improved," said Victoria. "Have you a spare computer?"

Dr. Brown showed Victoria around the corner. "This one is free," he said.

Victoria logged in and checked the patient's results doing a comparison with the latest result to previous results. As the new result is now much lower, the patient just needs to stay off the medication until it's back to normal.

Victoria instructed Dr. Brown to continue omitting the warfarin tablet for another two days and to continue with daily INR tests.

"I'll get that sorted, thank you," said Dr. Brown.

Victoria updated the patient's notes before heading back downstairs.

Victoria accompanied Sami to the coffee shop.

"I don't know what it is, but I find that man so irritating," she said.

"What man?" asked Sami.

"Dr. Brown. Do you know what he said? He said the sample would be still in the laboratory and not processed. That is not the thing to say to me when I have family working in there doing their best. If results are prolonged they have to be checked before they can be issued".

"I guess he doesn't know that," said Sami giving her a wry smile.

"I put him in his place" she replied. "He just hadn't bothered to look for the result"

Sami looked at Victoria and realised she was learning fast.

They had their coffee break and then made their way back to the office.

"We need to go through patient files and I will explain to you about each patient and what they are being treated for. I prefer to do that here, as opposed to when they are sitting in the room".

He read out the patients' names one by one their illnesses, their medications, and how often they attended the clinics. There were also a couple of new referrals and he explained why they had been referred.

After this had been completed it was almost time for lunch. Victoria made another note in the notebook about attending to Mrs. Jackson and the fact her results needed checking again tomorrow.

"OK lunchtime," said Sami. "It's up to you what you decide, but today I shall go for a snack and bring it back here to the office as I need to catch up with work on the computer".

Victoria decided to accompany him there, however, she decided to sit along there for a change of scene, and besides he didn't want her around when he was working so she felt uncomfortable about going back.

"Please be back by one o clock," he said as he left her at the food counter. Victoria chose a jacket potato and sat alone at a table with her magazine. When she'd finished eating, she made room for other people to eat and decided to find somewhere quiet to read. She found some nice lounging chairs near the exit and enjoyed the feel of the fresh air outside coming in through the doors. She was deeply engrossed in her reading and didn't notice Dr. Prakesh come back along to the small shop for another snack. He caught sight of her reading near the main exit and wandered over to her.

"Victoria. Why are you sitting here?" he asked. "You are welcome to sit in the office".

"I'm fine here" she replied. "I'm enjoying the fresh air. Besides I got the impression you wanted to do some work".

"That doesn't mean you can't sit in there," he said. He remembered being a bit moody about her early arrival yesterday and wondered if she'd sensed his irritability. He felt rather guilty about that now. "Come on, let's go back to the office," he said trying to coax her to go back there.

"It's fine. I'll follow soon" replied Victoria indignantly.

He made his way back to the haematology ward realising she was very stubborn too. He headed to the nurses' station and asked Bernie if they had all signed the birthday card. She handed it to him. "All signed," she said.

He went into his office, placing the card on Victoria's computer. He couldn't help noticing the display of photographs she had arranged on her desk. One of herself and her mother having drinks may be at a party somewhere, one with a cocker spaniel and her. *It must be her dog*, he thought rubbing his beard with his fingers. The third one was of a young man smiling with a motorcycle. He looked quite young. *Her boyfriend perhaps? Why shouldn't a nice young woman like herself have a boyfriend? She hadn't mentioned him.* Then he was aware of approaching footsteps so he walked over to his desk and sat down. One o clock exactly. He was impressed with her timekeeping.

Victoria entered the office and as she reached over to drape her handbag around the chair, she noticed an envelope on her desk with her name written on it. She picked it up and opened it. She took out a birthday card and saw that Sami and several other members of staff had signed their names inside. She was very touched.

"Oh my," she said placing her hand on her chest, then turning around to look at Sami. "Thank you all very much. It's lovely, but you really shouldn't have". She stood it on her desk.

"Why not," said Sami. "You're part of the team now".

Victoria left the office and walked over to the nurses' station. She hovered in the background, and then said "Sorry I don't know everyone's name as yet, but I just wanted to thank you all for taking the trouble to sign the lovely birthday card. It was indeed a nice surprise!" Victoria felt quite overcome with emotion at the kindness shown by people who hardly knew her.

"Thank Dr. Prakesh," said Bernie with a coy smile. "It was all his idea. It's the first birthday card I've ever known him to buy, so you must have made a good impression on him".

"Indeed I must" replied Victoria feeling a bit embarrassed.

At that moment, Sami opened the office door, pushing out the trolley of patient files. "Right Victoria, are you ready to come to the clinic?" he spoke in his doctor's voice again.

"Ready and waiting" she replied. "Do you need a hand?"

"No thanks, I'm fine" he replied as they both headed along the corridor towards the outpatient department. The door led to a small lobby with patient chairs on both sides and a reception desk on the right-hand side. The décor of the walls was blue; however, the floor was tiled with a mixture of salmon pink, blue, and cream. It seemed quite a cosy and peaceful little area. Sami introduced Victoria to the receptionist and also to the nurses there, who would look after the patients and take their blood for the clinic. Two patients were there already, having arrived very promptly. Sami indicated a room and Victoria opened the door so he could manoeuver the trolley inside. He flicked the computer to life and let it warm up whilst he took the files and stood them on the large desk in front of him. Victoria pulled over a chair behind the desk beside him and then went to fetch another from the lobby so a patient and their carer both had somewhere to sit, in the room.

"Right, I want you to observe today Victoria" Sami said as he sat in his chair. "I shall also need to ask the patients if they mind you being here, as a courtesy. If they have any objections, you'll need to take a seat outside".

"Of course" she replied.

"Right, could you call Mr. Johnson in please? We are ready to start". Victoria went to the door and called "Mr. Albert Johnson please".

The elderly gentleman with a walking stick slowly stood up and was helped by his wife who was wearing a maroon-coloured jacket. Slowly they shuffled their way into the consulting room. Albert Johnson and his wife did not mind Victoria being present in the room and as they were settling themselves into their seating, Sami quietly explained the process to Victoria. "The patient will have already had their full blood count done on the point of care machine before their appointment. The nurses take the blood upon arrival and the results can be printed from the small machine. It's much quicker than having the blood processed in the laboratory". Just then, there was a knock at the door. "Come in," said Sami in his usual commanding voice.

"Results, Dr Prakesh," said Louise the nurse, handing him a sheet of paper.

Thank you Louise" he said without looking up.

"So this print-out is the blood result" he continued. "Now I will examine this with the patient's previous history and compare". Victoria watched him from behind. "If there are any major discrepancies such as low platelet counts, any substantial changes, or raised MCHCs, the sample must be re-checked by the laboratory. We ask the laboratory staff to make a blood film on that patient and leave it in our tray, to examine later. Generally most of the time, they are acceptable but a little anaemic"

So a comparison of Albert Johnson's history showed that there were no real changes in his counts. Sami asked him a few general questions about his health and also filled out a general request form for the patient to have a few more generalised tests, before dismissing the patient, as his care plan would remain the same on this occasion. They both bid the man and his wife farewell and after he left, Sami updated the notes both in the patient's notes and the computer.

The clinic continued to proceed in the same manner. However, when the fourth patient entered the room, Victoria's mobile phone rang. "Sorry, excuse me, I'll take this outside," she said and left the room.

"Hello, Dr. Pemberton, Haematology Registrar, can I help you?" She took a seat in the lobby.

"Hello Victoria, it's me" Carol's voice was on the receiving end of the telephone. "Are you busy?" she asked.

"I'm in the clinic with Dr. Prakesh at the moment. What do you want?"

"We've found an abnormal blood film. The patient has come through the accident and emergency department feeling unwell. There's no history of any haematological disorders and there are immature white cells on the blood film. Someone will need to come and look at it" Carol informed her.

"OK mum, I'll sort it. See you soon"

She gave a quick knock on the door and re-entered the room. She waited patiently until Sami had dismissed the patient, before informing him about the abnormal blood film.

"Can you go down now and examine it?" he asked. "The patient will need admission to the haematology ward before accident and emergency discharge them. I trust you can do film reports, just watch your spelling" he smirked.

"My spelling is impeccable" teased Victoria as she left the room. Was that an attempt at humour from the otherwise very serious Dr Prakesh? Maybe there is some humour flowing through those veins after all.

9

"Right mum, where is the abnormal blood film?" said Victoria as she entered the laboratory. Carol handed her the slide and she took it into the side room to examine it. Upon examination, it was clear to see that it was going to be some form of acute leukaemia, so she typed in a report then telephoned the accident and emergency department.

"She spoke to a Senior Doctor called Nigel Cameron and discussed the blood film of Fiona Nicholson. "The patient will need admitting to the haematology ward as she has some kind of acute leukaemia. I'll come along and discuss my findings with yourself and the family" Victoria replaced the receiver and headed along to the accident and emergency ward. She introduced herself to Dr Cameron and spoke to the patient and her family in a small side room.

"Hello, I'm Dr Victoria Pemberton, Haematology Specialist Registrar. I'm afraid it's not good news". She took a deep breath and continued "I'm afraid it may be a type of leukaemia" she didn't like being the bearer of bad news. She went on to explain that Fiona would have to be admitted into the Haematology ward to undergo more blood tests and a bone marrow biopsy to investigate the haematological condition even further, to make a diagnosis. "Then, it will be necessary to begin some form of treatment. Victoria explained. "I think that's all for now. Are there any questions?"

The family nodded their heads in silence. At this point, people were often quite shocked at the news they've just received, so tend not to say much, however at a later time when the news has been absorbed, questions would spring to mind. She held out her hand to politely shake hands with them "Well I'll leave you to get settled in and will catch up with you tomorrow" she said politely as she left the side room and returned to the outpatient department where Sami was still doing his outpatient clinic. It was practically over when she returned, so she waited in the lobby until Sami had finished consulting with his final patient.

On the way back to the haematology ward, Victoria discussed the new patient with Sami, filling him in with all the details.

"Something new for you tomorrow Victoria," he said. "A bone marrow biopsy," he said with a wry smile.

It was almost the end of the working day. Victoria's final job was to go to the laboratory and report any blood films left on the tray by the laboratory staff as she didn't get the opportunity to do them earlier. So she completed those and had been permitted to go home by Sami. A bone marrow biopsy she thought. The thought of the procedure was scary.

10

That night at home, Victoria received a telephone call.

"Hello, Victoria. It's me, Sandra."

"Sandra! How lovely to hear from you. How are you?"

Victoria was delighted to hear from her old school friend who lived in America.

"I'm fine. How are you?"

"Good, thanks. Just to let you know, I'm here. I'm home!"

"Really? That's wonderful."

Typical that she should arrive now Victoria thought as she had just started a new job and probably wouldn't have much time to see her friend.

"I'm in Salisbury now, visiting my brother David, but hope to be up by Friday. Are you free at the weekend to meet up?"

"Indeed I am. Always for you," she said excitedly.

Sandra had moved out to America a few years ago when she met her husband, Micky. She had done a lot of voluntary aid work and met Micky at one of the places where she had worked. Victoria missed Sandra, but it was as though they had never been apart once they met up each time.

"We'll go for a trip out in the car somewhere. I'll think of something," Victoria said, excitedly.

She arrived promptly at the hospital the following morning and spotted Sami by the counter of the little coffee bar, buying his morning coffee.

"Good morning, Sami" she said, as she stood behind him.

"Good morning, Victoria. Very prompt as always. You make a refreshing change."

"Change from what?"

"Previous employees. Would you like a drink?"

"Cappuccino, please."

He ordered her drink and paid the assistant.

"Thank you very much," she said, and they headed toward their office to do various pieces of work before beginning their shift.

"OK then, we need to prepare for that biopsy first," he said, breaking the silence. "It must be performed under aseptic conditions, and the patient will need a local anaesthetic. Could you go to the laboratory and collect a tray with some glass slides, sample tubes, and a bone marrow biopsy needle?"

"All right, Sami, I shall go and do that."

He left the room slightly ahead of her. At the nurses' station, Dawn, Bernie, Sue, and Josie were getting organised for the day ahead.

"Good morning, Victoria. How do you like being part of our team?" asked Dawn.

"I love it. So far, so good."

"How about Dr Prakesh?" asked Josie, with her elbow on the counter, smoothing her fringe back with the fingers of her other hand.

"He is a great teacher."

"That's a glowing report," said Bernie. "We all reckon he must like you, as he has not complained, so you must be doing something good."

"Indeed, I hope so," Victoria replied, wondering why they wanted her to complain about him. "Anyway, I must disappear to the laboratory. I will see you all later. There's a bone marrow biopsy to perform on the new patient, Fiona."

Victoria headed to the laboratory and asked her mother, Carol, where the glass slides and biopsy needles were. She went to find them and handed them to Victoria.

"So we can expect one of those later then?" said Carol, with a resigned look.

The laboratory staff weren't too fond of bone marrow biopsies as they had a long and laborious booking in system, which was time-consuming, especially when other samples were going through the machines.

"Yes, I'm afraid so," replied Victoria. "The new patient, Fiona Nicholson. The blood film *you* found yesterday."

Victoria smiled and winked at Carol, then left the laboratory.

Sami closed the privacy curtain around the patient while Victoria collected the equipment. He showed Victoria how to arrange the slides and sample tubes before starting. Fiona was lying on her side, ready for the procedure. Victoria was quite nervous and started to feel nauseous. Sami waited patiently until she was ready.

"OK, you need to feel for the spot. You need the posterior iliac crest and you will feel a knuckle-like piece of bone near the dimples," said Sami.

Victoria felt the area with her fingers and found the spot.

"There?" she asked.

"Yes. Now inject the local anaesthetic right down to the bone surface."

His voice was calm, as he sensed Victoria was nervous. They paused for a few moments to allow the anaesthetic to take effect.

"Are you happy to proceed?" Sami asked.

"Yes, I need to learn."

She looked across at him and their eyes met and held for a moment before she turned away and prepared to start the procedure.

"Right, push through the skin gently and advance carefully until you feel the bone surface. Make sure you are in the numb spot."

Victoria proceeded until she reached the bone, as he had instructed.

"Is that all right?" she asked him, nervously.

"You're doing just fine," he whispered. "Now get the needle to bite and push firmly while rotating the handle. Stop when you feel a crispy crunching sensation, as you enter the bone."

Victoria was quite nervous about that part, so she allowed Sami to take over and demonstrate.

"OK, the bone marrow liquid is aspirated," he explained.

"Fiona, this part may give you some discomfort," he warned the patient.

Fiona nodded her head and stayed silent. Once the liquid was aspirated, Victoria placed it into the sample tubes.

"OK, the bigger needle is ready-assembled. Push it into the bone and remove the internal introducer," Sami instructed. "Now advance the hollow needle an inch into the bone, spin it a few times and then withdraw it."

Victoria listened carefully and followed his instructions.

"Now, use the rod device to remove the marrow from the hollow needle into the pot."

Victoria finished the procedure.

"I'll apply a dressing and some pressure. Could you label the sample tubes and pot, then make a few slides, please?"

He spoke so gently and had a calming influence on her.

"Fiona, you need to lie on your back for five minutes," said Sami.

They both helped the patient to turn over. Victoria was in a sweat. She felt relieved it was all finished. She took the slides, pot, and samples to the laboratory.

11

Sami sat in his office, rubbing his beard with his thumb and index finger. He was still trying to figure out why he felt a connection with Victoria out there, when she entered the office.

"The laboratory is in the process of sending it away now," she informed him. "So what's next?"

It was Victoria's third day at Lady Margaret's Hospital and already she had a few responsibilities. Sami informed her of the agenda for that day. There was still the ward round to do, Mrs Jackson to check up on, blood films to report, a clinic to observe and he wanted to introduce her to bone marrow reporting. Brushing off that feeling he felt earlier, he stood up to leave the office, with Victoria following behind.

Later that afternoon, whilst Victoria was upstairs checking on Mrs Jackson, Bernie asked Sami, "How is the new doctor settling in?"

"She's doing fine, Bernie."

He was a man of few words.

"We all like her too."

"Dr Prakesh, did you know she is single?" asked Margaret Rose.

"Is she?"

Sami seemed uninterested.

"You are telling me that because?"

"You're single too," said Bernie, with a wicked twinkle in her eyes.

"I'm not interested," he snapped, with that mechanical voice. "Please don't go around saying that, you'll frighten her away."

He turned and headed back into his office.

"I reckon he fancies her. What do you think Margaret Rose?" asked Bernie.

"Maybe he has a soft spot," she replied, and they giggled.

Sami sat in his office.

So she's single. I wonder how they got all their information. So who is the man in the picture? The smiling boy with his motorbike?

He reckoned that they must have misunderstood but, nonetheless, he felt an urge to get to know Victoria Pemberton on a more personal scale. At the same time, he didn't want to pry and ask her.

Why did he spend so much time thinking about her?

12

After being introducing to bone marrow reporting in the laboratory that afternoon, another day had finished. It had been a harrowing start for Victoria. However, she felt that she would be more confident the next time she performed a bone marrow biopsy. Sami had been very patient.

She remembered the moment their eyes met when the biopsy started. *Surely she must have imagined it?* She decided to put the whole matter behind her.

Upon reaching the car park, she saw Sami sitting on one of the wooden chairs, reading his newspaper. She headed toward him.

"Sami, is everything all right?" she asked.

"My tyre is flat," he said, with a resigned look on his face. "I'm waiting for someone to come and fix it."

"I'll change it for you if you want."

He looked up at her in surprise.

"You can change a car tyre?"

"Yes. Done mine a couple of times. As long as you have a jack, wrench and spare tyre."

"Yes, they're in the boot."

He folded his newspaper and headed towards his car.

"Wow. Is this yours?" she exclaimed in surprise, as he stopped beside a red 2010 Ford Mustang. "Nice car! Not sure I want to touch it."

Sami opened his boot. The car was immaculate inside with just his briefcase placed on the back seat and not a speck of dust to be seen. There was nothing in the boot, just the covering which he lifted to give access to the tyre and equipment below.

"Do you still want to do this?" he asked.

"I'll have a go," she said, although was feeling apprehensive. "It will save you waiting for the breakdown van."

Sami removed the spare tyre and equipment and placed them on the ground beside the car. Victoria began to loosen the tyre nuts by hand before removing what looked like expensive, hub caps. However, one was attached very tightly.

"Would you mind removing one of the nuts please, as it's rather tight?" she asked.

He looked at her and sighed, but she noticed a shade of crimson appearing above the collar of his shirt. He loosened it, wondering why on earth he was putting his trust in a woman he hardly knew to change his tyre.

Victoria jacked up the car and used the wrench to fully loosen the nuts so they could be removed and laid neatly on the ground. The flat tyre slid off easily. She then took the spare wheel and slotted it on and into the wheel studs. She fastened the nuts by hand first and then used the wrench until they were firm. She lowered the car and removed the jack, then completely tightened the nuts with a wrench.

"All done," she said, feeling quite pleased with herself. She stood up and tidied herself, rubbing her hands together to remove the grease.

Sami stood there, totally stunned.

"I don't know what to say," he said, as he picked up the flat tyre and placed it in his boot.

Victoria gave him the jack and wrench.

"You owe me a coffee," she replied, with a smile. "Don't forget to cancel the breakdown van."

"Thank you very much. You are a woman of many talents," he replied.

"I'm not just a pretty face Dr Prakesh."

She smiled across at him then said, "See you tomorrow."

She turned and walked towards her car. He noticed her bottom waggling as she walked, each cheek synchronised with the other, like two ripe plums. He sighed as he turned away. *He must stop having these thoughts.* He took out his mobile and waved to Victoria as she drove past.

"Where have you been?" asked Carol, as Victoria finally strode into the house. Victoria told her mother the tale about Sami's car.

"He keeps it immaculate," she said. "I must remember never to invite him for a lift in mine."

She giggled as she thought about how untidy it was, with dog covers, dog hair and other junk she carried around but hardly used. A car was just a means of travelling from place to place for her.

"I should maybe give it a bit of a clean before I meet Sandra this weekend."

Sami walked into the gym to do his workout.

"I see you made it," said Richard, in surprise, as he'd been notified earlier that his friend may not be there.

"A woman came to my rescue."

"A woman?" exclaimed Richard in surprise. "You don't do women," he laughed.

Sami told Richard the tale.

"So a woman fixed your tyre whilst you called a breakdown truck?" Richard said in disbelief.

"Something like that."

"You're unbelievable," Richard said, laughing. "It is men who are supposed to rescue women."

Sami knew that Richard would find it hilarious, so he just sighed whilst his friend laughed at his expense. Both men continued with their workouts and weight-lifting before going to the bar downstairs for a post-workout drink.

"So I think you like this woman, Victoria," teased Richard.

Sami spoke in his monotone voice.

"She's a work colleague, that's all."

"You could do with a nice woman in your life, Sami."

"Let's not go there Richard," said Sami, feeling exasperated. "I made a rule a long time ago about not dating women at work."

"Time will tell," said Richard, with a mischievous wink. He had noticed a slight change in his friend that week. He seemed more relaxed than usual. Once outside, they bid each other goodnight and set off to their respective homes.

The next morning, Sami was already busy in his office when Victoria arrived.

"Good morning, Sami," she said, as she entered the office.

"Good morning," he replied, but his voice was distant as though deep in concentration.

"I take it you got your new tyre?" Victoria continued, as she waited for her computer to load. Sami didn't reply. She shrugged, as she was used to Sami ignoring her when he was busy. She continued with her work.

He had a delayed reaction in realising what she had said.

"Er yes, I did," he replied, as he turned to look at her. "By the way, thank you for everything you did last night. It was much appreciated."

"Think nothing of it," she replied, sipping her cappuccino. "But I haven't forgotten you owe me a coffee."

She turned back to her computer. Sami continued to gaze at her. *She was quite an amazing woman who was, no doubt, going to become a proficient haematologist one day. Not only that, but she could change car tyres.*

Feeling a set of eyes boring into her, Victoria turned her head towards Sami and asked, "Is something wrong?"

"No," he replied, feeling rather embarrassed at having been caught. "You have another bone marrow biopsy to do this morning," he added. "A patient has been admitted overnight with a low platelet count."

"Splendid!" she replied, wondering why another one had come along so soon.

"I'll be there to supervise," he added.

Sami went to prepare the patient for the procedure whilst Victoria went to the laboratory to collect the implements.

"Hello, Mum. Bringing another present along for you later," she said. "Delightful," said Carol. "I can't wait."

Victoria arranged the slides as Sami had done, the previous day, before starting, and then she took a deep breath. Slowly, she began to perform the procedure and Sami stood behind her, with his arms folded, watching intently as she slowly recalled everything she had been shown yesterday. After a few minutes, and what seemed like a lifetime to Victoria, she had completed the procedure.

"Well done," he said. "I didn't intervene at all, so you're competent enough to do these unsupervised."

She turned to label the slides.

"I'll tidy up here if you take those to the laboratory," Sami suggested.

Victoria called to see Mrs Jackson on her way back from the laboratory to the ward. It seemed that the patient's INR result had normalised and she could be re-started on a small amount of warfarin. Next, it was the ward round and, early that afternoon, Sami had another clinic for her to observe. Her final job was going to the laboratory to examine the blood films left by the laboratory staff. As she left the office to go there, she overheard a conversation at the nurses' station.

"I reckon he must be in his forties," said Bernie. "What do you think, Margaret Rose?"

"I'm not sure. I don't think he is that old," she replied.

"That beard makes him look older," chimed in Josie, as she looked up from examining her nail polish. It became clear to Victoria that they were talking about Sami.

"Victoria, how old do you think The Iceman is?" asked Dawn, curious to know if Victoria knew.

"The Iceman?" asked Victoria. "Who's The Iceman?"

Of course, she hadn't heard them call him by his nickname before.

"Aww you know, Dr Ice. Dr Prakesh," said Dawn.

She paused.

"I don't know," she replied. "I'm not good at judging people's ages."

"Why don't you have a guess?" asked Josie, feeling very intrigued, as she brought out a compact mirror and topped up her lipstick. "We all think he's in his forties."

Victoria wasn't ready to answer such a question.

"Why do you call him The Iceman?" she asked.

"Isn't it obvious?" asked Josie. "He's cold, emotionless, miserable, grumpy, divorced. I'm not surprised he's divorced. Can't imagine how any poor woman tolerated living with someone cold like him."

Victoria disliked the way Josie spoke about Sami. Susan saw her look of disapproval.

"I'll go for age 46," she said, to break the awkward silence.

"I'll go for 47," said Dawn, with a giggle.

Everyone took a turn to guess an age.

"I think Victoria should be the one who asks him and finds out for us," said Josie, intent on her mission.

"I shall do no such thing," replied Victoria. "Now if you'll excuse me, I have films to report."

She walked down the corridor and left the ward. She thought of the nurses' conversation and, although they seemed nice people individually, they could be a den of vipers when together. No wonder Sami was aloof to them and didn't hold conversations that weren't associated with work. She had only known him for a week. He was a man of few words but had always displayed kindness and patience towards her. As for Josie, she didn't care much for that woman at all. Her uniform skirts were too short and she checked her makeup too often, instead of getting on with her job.

As Victoria returned to the office to collect her belongings, Bernie and Dawn were alone at the nurses' station and made a point of apologising to her about everything that had been said earlier. They said that Josie was a pain and difficult to get along with. Victoria certainly agreed, however, she didn't approve of the way they had all spoken about Sami behind his back.

Later, after bidding him farewell in the office, Victoria left the building.

It did make Victoria wonder about Sami's age. She agreed, after a great deal of thought, that he must be around the 40-year mark, or above. She hadn't realised that he was divorced. *She thought about his former wife and what had happened to make them separate. He was a very deep, dark and secretive man. There was so much she wanted to know about him and what exactly he had hidden beneath that doctor's coat.*

13

Victoria decided to go in later the next day, to allow Sami some time to concentrate on his work. Almost a week now, and she felt quite at home with her new position. She was also looking forward to embracing the additional responsibilities it would bring.

"You're late, Victoria," Sami mused when she entered the office.

"Late?" she exclaimed, "I may be late, but I'm also early."

They both laughed, and then Sami discussed the day's agenda.

"It's a case of wrapping up the loose ends of the week and deciding if any patients can be discharged, provided they return to Accident and Emergency if unwell. There's a small clinic to do this afternoon, the blood films, then we'll have a discussion over coffee about your progress for the week and plans for next week."

"Sounds scary," said Victoria. "Should I be worried?"

"I'm not saying," he replied.

"You're cruel," she said, with a wry smile as they both left the office.

It was the ward round first, and Sami decided to discharge two patients, who were delighted to be going home. He prescribed transfusions for Beatrice Delaney, who was often quite anaemic, and a pool of platelets for the patient who was admitted the previous day. Victoria checked Mrs Jackson's results on the hospital system and her INR result seemed to be doing OK.

After lunch, there was a small afternoon clinic which Victoria observed, as she had done all week, and then Sami instructed her to report all the blood films that remained in the laboratory. He followed her a bit later, to go through some bone marrow reporting before the weekend.

Once all the work was finished, Sami took Victoria to the coffee bar and bought her a cappuccino, before heading back to the office for the end-of-week discussion.

"OK Victoria, I think you have settled into your role well. How do you feel about it?"

"I've enjoyed it," she replied. "Everybody has been most welcoming and I already feel like part of your team."

"You ARE an integral part of the team. So let's discuss your achievements this week. Firstly, you spent a day in the laboratory, learning the essentials and the role they play in our work. You managed the raised INR patient, Mrs Jackson, and handled that well. You have been introduced to bone marrow biopsies and can now do those unsupervised. All of that is great progress in one week."

Sami seemed to be impressed with her.

"However, the only criticism I have, is that you talk to the patients for too long during the ward rounds so they take longer than they should."

She smiled and said, "I was waiting for that."

"I don't suppose I'm going to change that, am I?" he asked, with a resigned look on his face.

"Probably not," she replied. "I am who I am."

"They like you, that's what is most important," he said, then added, "One more thing. Whatever possessed you to get that red streak in your hair?"

Victoria looked at him in surprise and grabbed hold of the wisp of red hair.

"This?" she asked, puzzled. "It was just a bit of a mad thing I decided to do one day, just for fun. You don't like it, do you?"

"It'll grow on me, I suppose," he answered, before quickly changing the subject.

"Right, next week I want you to help make some of the decisions with the patients whilst I observe. Are you agreeable with this?"

"Yes," she replied, "as long as you think I'm capable."

"Absolutely," he replied, as he stood up.

"OK then, have a good weekend," he said, suddenly realising he wouldn't see her for two whole days. He had begun to enjoy her company.

"Any nice plans?" he asked.

"My friend, Sandra, is here from America with her son. We are going to go out somewhere, but I haven't decided where yet."

"Lindisfarne is nice," he replied. "Especially for tourists. They'll probably love that. Just remember to check the tide times. I know my mother loves going there."

"That's a great suggestion, Sami. I may just do that."

She had been there some time ago but not recently.

"Are you doing anything nice?"

"I'm going for a swim in the morning, then lunch with my parents on Sunday."

He realised that that sounded so boring.

"Have a good weekend, Sami," said Victoria, as she left the office.

"You too."

He realised that, within a week, he had talked to her more than anyone else he'd ever spoken to at work before, and that included Verity. There was something very appealing about her personality.

14

Sami set his alarm for half past eight the next day. It was Saturday and he had arranged to collect Richard at nine o'clock to go swimming. It happened every three months, usually when Richard's wife, Janice, visited her mother and took their daughter, Sarah, with her.

On the way to the swimming pool, Sami decided to buy petrol. As he approached the forecourt, there was a small queue, so he applied the handbrake and waited. On the opposite side of the forecourt, he noticed a woman refuelling her car. He thought she seemed familiar but couldn't place where he had seen her.

"Why are you staring at that woman?" asked Richard, with a cheeky smile on his face.

"She seems familiar, that's all," replied Sami, then suddenly he realised who she was.

"God its Victoria" he announced. He hadn't recognised her with her soft hair flowing loosely in the wind, but the red streak had given her away.

"The new registrar?" asked Richard.

"Yes."

As soon as Sami had answered, Richard leaned over and beeped the horn.

"What the hell are you doing, you idiot?" barked Sami, feeling annoyed and irritated. His face went bright red.

"Well, you fancy her, don't you?" said Richard, laughing at Sami's discomfort.

"No, I don't" Sami yelled. "She's my work colleague, that's all."

Victoria was refuelling her car when she heard someone sounding their horn. She looked up and thought she recognised the car at the opposite side. It was Sami's Ford Mustang. After paying the assistant at the counter, she walked over to his car.

"Hello, Sami. What a nice surprise," she said, brushing a strand of hair back over her ear. "You're up early for a Saturday morning."

"Richard and I are going for a swim before it gets busy," he said. He felt so embarrassed about Richard blowing the horn.

"I decided to take Sandra, her son and the dogs to Lindisfarne, as you suggested. Thanks for the brilliant idea."

"Did you check the tides?" he asked.

"Yes. As long as we leave by four o'clock this afternoon, all is good," she replied.

He glanced over and saw them waiting in her car.

"Enjoy your day."

"You too. Is your tyre OK now?"

"It's fine, thank you. I will see you on Monday."

She gave him a little wave as she walked back to her car.

That wave was sexy.

Sami watched her drive away from the forecourt and head along the road, in the direction of the motorway.

"You've got it bad," laughed Richard, disturbing his thoughts. "She seems a great woman. Why don't you ask her out on a date?"

"I don't know if she's single."

"I thought you said she was."

"The ward sister seems to think so, but I'm not sure."

"Stop looking for excuses!"

"I'm not, but she has a picture of someone on her desk."

"Well, you will have to find out," said Richard. "Why don't you ask her?"

"I'm not asking. Now let's change the subject. You are becoming annoying."

Richard despaired of Sami sometimes. He had seen a definite spark there a few moments ago but knew Sami would never want to follow it up.

"What about social media?"

"I don't like that nonsense. People find out too much about personal things."

"So you will find out about her."

Sami pulled forward to a pump, then got out and refuelled his car.

After he climbed back in, Richard said, "Today, after our swim, you are joining social media and I won't take no for an answer."

Sami sighed and rolled his eyes. He knew when he was defeated.

"Who are the guys?" asked Sandra, as Victoria climbed back into the car.

"The consultant I work with, and his friend," she replied. "They're going swimming."

"He seems nice. Maybe you'll do alright there," Sandra winked.

"He's a nice man but very single, I'm afraid."

"You'll work your charm on him."

"Not this one. He may be very nice, but I can't date men with beards."

"You're so fussy," said Sandra, laughing. "Still, it's great to see you and spend the day together."

"Just like old times," Victoria smiled.

Sami and Richard swam several lengths of the pool, but they both felt the effect of not having been for a while, so they tired quickly.

"We need to get here more often," said Richard. "I feel so unfit."

"Me too," said Sami.

They dressed and met in the café, where they ordered breakfast and took a seat.

"Now, about this social media," said Richard.

Sami sighed. "Not again. I thought you had forgotten about that."

"Not until you sign up, mate. You'll thank me one day."

"Why do I feel I'll live to regret this?"

Sami shrugged. It was an argument he wasn't going to win.

"Now, type in your profile."

Sami typed in his name and birthdate. He omitted his occupation, as he felt it attracted the wrong type of people, so he only added the hospital name.

"It'll keep them guessing," he smiled.

Then he added his likes, dislikes, favourite films, hobbies, television programmes and books. Then he needed a profile photo.

"Give me your phone," said Richard. "Now smile," as he quickly snapped a photograph of Sami before uploading it to his profile.

"That's awful," exclaimed Sami. "Look at me with my curly wet hair. I hate it."

"You can change it later," Richard said, having a good laugh when he saw it.

"Enjoy your moment. Laugh at me why don't you?"

Sami sighed, seemingly not having any control over his life anymore.

"Now we have to find you some friends," said Richard. "Do you know anyone who's on here?"

"My mother. She loves it."

"All right then," Richard laughed and typed in Anne Prakesh, whose profile appeared with her photograph. Richard sent her a friend request.

"That's all you do," he said.

Sami took his phone and typed in Victoria Pemberton. A few profiles appeared, but not of the woman he knew.

"I cannot find her."

"Does she use Vicki?"

"How the hell do I know?" exclaimed Sami. "I've just met the woman."

"OK. Let's find others. Anyone else at work she may have befriended?"

"Bernie Monaghan, the ward sister."

He typed in Bernie Monaghan, but there was no sign of her either.

"I knew this was a bad idea, but you would insist," mumbled Sami.

"Be patient. We'll get there. Let's try Bernadette Monaghan."

A profile and picture appeared of the ward sister.

"Success!" shouted Richard, sending a friend request to Bernie.

Other names began to appear, of people associated with Bernie. Dawn Henderson, Susan Barrett, Margaret Rose Stubbs and Josephine Robertson.

"Oh God, no, not them."

Sami was adamant that he didn't want the nurses on his profile. Margaret Rose Stubbs is OK and one there called Susan Vickers.

"She's my Auntie Susan."

So Richard sent friend requests, as instructed.

"Where is Victoria?" Sami asked, exasperated. "I know she uses it."

The phone beeped, as Bernie accepted his friend request and left a comment saying, 'Moving into the twenty-first century, are we?' with laughing emojis.

Richard laughed and said, "That sums you up, Sami."

"Where's Victoria?"

"Now that Bernie has accepted your friend request, you can look through her friends."

Sami scrolled through her friends' profiles and discovered Vix Pemberton.

"She's here," he shouted, as he sent her a friend request.

"That's definitely her. Gosh, I'd never have found that without you."

"There's also a Richard Thomas, who seems to have fallen to the back of your mind," Richard reminded him. "I'll send you a friend request."

Sami's phone beeped again.

"Now all you do is accept me as a friend."

"I don't know about that," said Sami, laughing. "You've opened a can of worms for me here."

They finished breakfast. Sami drove Richard home, before his shop at the supermarket. He hated shopping on Saturdays, as it was always crowded. Once home, he opened a nice cold beer and switched on the film channel. He wanted to have a nice relaxing afternoon.

Victoria and Sandra arrived at Lindisfarne and had a walk around the old abbey ruins, to stretch their legs, then they spread a rug out on some grass, at the side of the car park, to have their picnic.

"Isn't this great? Such a lovely day for a picnic," said Victoria, taking a sandwich and lying back in the sun, using her handbag as a pillow.

"I was a child when I last came here," said Sandra. "I'd forgotten how lovely it is. Such history."

She reminisced back to when she visited the island in her childhood. She had come up in the car with her mother and one of her brothers. It had poured with rain all day and they never even got out of the car. It was nice this time that she could experience the beauty of the place. Shame that little Martin was going to be too young to remember. She would have to come back one day.

Then they chatted about school and Sandra remembered Victoria's boyfriend, Neil, as she had often spent time together with them. Then there was Karen Bell. She was a character, very advanced for her years. It was because of her that Victoria had met Neil. Karen Bell had been with a few boyfriends in her youth and then, when they parted, it became Victoria's job to console her. She remembered one day when Karen had gone to the park, with her and Neil, to do their homework. Victoria had helped her with her homework and, the following day, the teachers were amazed at the good marks she attained. It didn't last long before another boyfriend appeared and distracted her from her work.

"Apparently, she had a baby at sixteen," said Victoria. "Not heard from her since."

"Wouldn't be surprised if she has other children now," said Sandra.

Just then, Victoria's phone beeped.

"My goodness, he's on social media," she gasped in surprise.

"Who?" asked Sandra.

"The guy we met at the garage," Victoria reminded her. "He told me it was all nonsense and didn't like it, now I have a friend request."

Victoria accepted the request.

"Maybe he's looking for you on there?" laughed Sandra.

"He's found me. I am difficult to find on there, as he doesn't know my nickname is Vix."

"He does now," giggled Sandra.

Victoria added a cheeky comment, 'No longer a dinosaur', with laughing emojis.

Sami was halfway through his first beer when his phone beeped. Victoria had accepted him as a friend. Success! He didn't seem to care if anyone else accepted him, as long as she did. *Was he going crazy?*

He noted the cheeky comment about him being a dinosaur and replied to say that he was now a computer whizz-kid.

Then he added, 'It was nice to run into you earlier. Hope you are enjoying your day'. To which she replied, 'I am, thanks'.

That was enough for him. Maybe he could get to like this social media. He scrolled through her profile, looking at her photos, then her birthdate and worked out that she was twenty-nine. He noticed her relationship status was 'Single'.

So who was Smiling Boy? He'd seen the same man on a few of her profile pictures. Was he an ex-boyfriend? Surely, if that was the case, his photograph wouldn't be on her desk at work. She was an only child, so he knew she had no brother. Maybe a cousin? It seemed odd. He needed to find out, as he was intrigued.

He scrolled a bit more and came across the following statement written across one of the pages.

I LOVE YOU, NEIL WILSON! ALWAYS AND FOREVER!

What did that all mean?

Victoria Pemberton was certainly a woman of mystery.

15

Before they all knew it, the weekend had disappeared with lightning speed and, already, it was Monday morning.

Sami arrived at the hospital at eight o'clock. He purchased his breakfast and latte from the assistant before heading to his office to make an early start on his work. He needed to get some documents printed before Victoria arrived.

Victoria headed down the corridor and entered the ward. It all seemed so familiar to her now, even after only a week. She arrived at the office door and stopped in her tracks.

"Oh, damn and blast! What is the matter with this ridiculous thing?" Sami yelled from inside. Barbara, the night nurse, looked across at Victoria and gave a little smile.

"He's on social media now. Did you see it?" she whispered.

Victoria nodded.

"Yes. Great, isn't it?" she whispered back and giggled. "Do you think I dare go in?"

"Not again, damn you!"

Then she heard papers being rustled and thrown about. She entered the office, just as Sami slammed his fists on the desk in despair.

"Is it Monday mornings you don't like, Sami?" asked Victoria, remembering last week when she started.

"Got a stupid paper jam," he snapped. "I cannot get the damned thing printed."

He picked up a crumpled piece of paper, which he'd rolled into a ball, and threw it into the wastepaper bin.

"Let's take a look."

She knelt at the bottom of his desk, where the printer was located. She looked in the paper drawer and said, "Sami, there are too many sheets of paper in here. We need to take some out."

She picked them out and laid them at the side of the printer. She spent a few minutes looking inside, picking out small strands of paper which were trapped in the workings, before finally assembling it again. Then she switched on the power button.

"Try now," she told Sami.

He bashed the keyboard with impatient hands and, in a few moments, the document printed.

"Thank you so much," he sighed, relieved that the document was finally printed. He reached over for the bowl and ate his breakfast, before picking up the document and darting out of the room.

Just then, there was a knock at the door. It was Charmaine, with the patient files for the clinic.

"Good morning, Dr Pemberton. How are you settling in?"

"Please call me Victoria. I'm doing just fine, thank you."

"How are you finding Dr Prakesh?"

"Different," she said, "but nice. He's a good man."

"Ah, that's good," she replied. "Not everyone has said that."

Not wanting to chat too long about Sami, Victoria smiled and said, "Thank you very much for bringing along those files."

"See you later," Charmaine said, as she left the room.

A few minutes later, Sami returned to the office and sat down to finish his latte.

"Remember Victoria, you are making the decisions today. Are you prepared for that?"

His voice had returned to the monotone she was growing accustomed to.

"Yes, I remember," she said. "That's fine." Although she felt rather nervous about doing it for the first time.

The ward round started. There were two patients Victoria thought needed transfusions, as they were anaemic. She prescribed the units and asked the nurses to take fresh blood for the laboratory.

"Double check the samples are correctly labelled and written in pen," she reminded them. "They are strict in there."

Another patient had a drop in their platelet count, so she prescribed a pool of platelets. A new patient with a low white count had been admitted to the ward over the weekend, so Victoria instructed the nurses to do a few different sets of bloods on him. She knew the patient required a bone marrow biopsy too, which she could do later.

At the end of the ward round, Sami took Victoria for coffee and to discuss the morning's work.

"There's nothing you did that I wouldn't have done myself, except talk less," he said, giving her a little wink.

Victoria took a deep breath and smiled at him.

"I bet the bone marrow came as a surprise too," he teased. "You can do it alone today. You are more than capable."

"I'll check on Mrs Jackson next, then I'll go and do it," she replied. "Anyway, how did your swim go?"

"Not good," he replied. "I found out how unfit I was."

"Unfit! But you lift weights in a gym," Victoria said, surprised.

"It uses different muscle groups. I told Richard we need to go more often."

"How about next weekend?"

"I'm on call."

Victoria headed to the ward upstairs, to check on Mrs Jackson, whose INR results had remained stable over the weekend. She instructed that the patient remained on the same dosage until re-checked at the clinic, as she was close to being discharged.

Sami headed back to his office and sat in his chair. He looked across at Victoria's desk and caught sight of the photograph of Smiling Boy.

He needed to drop it into the conversation one day and wondered how he was going to do it. He stood up and went over to her desk, picking up the picture and looking at it more closely.

Who are you, Smiling Boy?

He seemed very happy-go-lucky, much like she was. He was standing next to a motorbike.

Is he this Neil Wilson?

He placed the photograph back on the desk. *He needed to stop this, as it was taking over his thoughts. It was none of his business.*

He walked back onto the ward and saw that a privacy curtain had already been drawn around the new patient, Mr Pritchard, so he knew that Victoria would be doing the biopsy. He decided to remain there, just in case she panicked about it however, within a few minutes, the patient had been bandaged, the curtains opened and she emerged with all slides and samples in the tray.

"Managed OK?" he asked.

"Yes, of course," she replied with a smile. *Her smile was lovely.* He could never imagine her being upset or miserable.

"Let's take it to the laboratory," he said. "Then let's see how you manage with bone marrow reports."

After another introduction to the reporting of bone marrow films, Sami and Victoria went for lunch. He was hoping there may be a moment to drop a certain topic into the conversation, but the opportunity didn't become available.

Victoria chatted excitedly about her friend, Sandra, and their trip to Lindisfarne over the weekend. After lunch, it was time to prepare for the outpatient clinic. Between them, they wheeled the trolley containing the patient files to the clinic and settled into the room, before calling the patients.

The first patient, Mr Davis, entered the room, having been called by the nurse. Victoria introduced herself and said that she would be the doctor looking after him today. She looked carefully through his records and previous blood results, and then read the referral from his general practitioner.

"All right, Mr Davis, it appears you've been referred by your doctor due to a gradually increasing haemoglobin level. There are a few possible causes for this, and we need to establish which one. How do you feel about that?"

"Do whatever you need to do, Dr Pemberton."

"OK. Today is about taking a few different blood samples from you and running some tests. I see you're diabetic and that you also suffer from COPD, which could be a possible cause; however, we need to rule other things out."

Victoria gave Mr Davis a request form to give to the nurses and wrote the names of the tests on it.

"Please make a further appointment for six weeks' time at the desk. The results should be back by then, so we can discuss it further."

Mr Davis took the form.

"Thank you very much, Dr Pemberton," he said, holding out his hand to shake hers.

"You're very welcome. Take care now. See you in six weeks."

Mr Davis and his wife walked along to the phlebotomy area.

"What a lovely young lady," he said to his wife. "I'm sure they get younger these days."

"Did I do alright?" Victoria asked Sami, after the couple had left the room.

"You were fine," he said. "I will intervene if I disagree in any way or if anything is forgotten or omitted. Now make some notes on the patient record, and type it into the computer, before we call the next patient."

The rest of the afternoon clinic passed uneventfully and soon it was time for a quick break before going to report the blood films at the laboratory. Whilst in the small office, Sami mentioned that the results were back from the first bone marrow biopsy Victoria had performed, so she went over to his computer to read it.

"It's the initial result," he explained. "It will take a while longer for the others to be reported."

Victoria read the report.

"Seems Fiona does have AML," she noted.

"She'll need to start chemotherapy, so we will have to discuss it with her and any family, if they are there."

That was the worst part of the job, having to be the bearer of bad news. Victoria, being kind and compassionate, found that part of the job very difficult, although she knew that it was a weakness she would have to overcome. Sami asked Victoria to break the news to the patient that afternoon and inform her that she would need to start chemotherapy.

Sami and Victoria walked out to the car park together. He could sense that she hadn't been her usual confident self when having to give the patient's diagnosis.

"Have a glass of wine when you go home tonight, Victoria," Sami said, smiling sympathetically at her. "Goodnight. See you tomorrow."

"I may just do that," she replied, feeling a bit subdued. "Goodnight."

At home, Victoria decided that a nice long dog walk in the fresh air was the tonic she needed. All the dogs ran up to her, tails wagging when she arrived in the house.

"I reckon I must have WALK scribbled on my forehead," she laughed, as she gave each one a little fuss.

"Come on then, let's get your leads."

She took them on their usual walk up a path along the side of the house, then over some fields towards a big hill. There were other fields past the hill, where the dogs could run, and she threw a ball for them to catch and return to her.

Sami called to see his mother on the way back from work. She was usually getting the dinner prepared then, for his father coming in from the surgery. She would take half an hour away from the cooking to have a cup of tea and chat with her son.

As he drove out of the street it was a left-turn only, so he had to drive to the roundabout, then turn and go in the direction he needed, to head home. As he glanced out of the window to the left, he was certain that he caught sight of Victoria Pemberton, running in the fields with three dogs, or was it in his imagination?

16

L ater at home, Victoria gave all the dogs their food. Bouncer, her little cocker spaniel, wouldn't eat his. Usually, he gobbled up every morsel.

"What's the matter, little man? Are you not hungry?" she asked him, stroking his head with her fingers.

She thought he had seemed a bit subdued. She went upstairs to watch TV and sat with him on her knee, cradled in her arms, before going to bed.

She was woken up in the night by a strange thumping noise. Suddenly, she realised it was Bouncer, in his bed on the floor, and thought at first that he was scratching himself. However, it seemed to continue.

"Bouncer, what are you doing?" she whispered. "What's wrong?"

She reached over and switched on the lamp. Once the light was on, it became clear what was happening. Bouncer was fitting. He was shaking uncontrollably, with his feet hitting the bottom of his bed.

"Bouncer! Bouncer! Calm down, boy," Victoria whimpered, looking into his big brown eyes.

His eyes looked glazed and vacant, and he had to go to a vet. She took her mobile and telephoned the vet's number, hands shaking with panic. She scribbled the emergency number down from the recorded message and quickly dialled it. After speaking to the emergency vet, who advised her to take him there immediately, she pulled on some clothes, picked Bouncer up in her arms, and headed out of the bedroom. She noticed the light was still on in Carol and Paul's room, so she gently opened the door.

"Mum, Bouncer is fitting. I need to take him to the vet."

Carol could see that her daughter was upset and sprung to her feet.

"I'll come with you."

They left in Carol's car, with Victoria cradling little Bouncer in her arms and kissing him. The fitting had continued for several minutes, which Victoria knew was not good news.

The veterinary surgeon ran some urgent tests and gave Bouncer a thorough examination.

"Has he been like this before?" he asked.

"Yes," said Victoria. "He had a few mini seizures earlier in the year. He didn't eat his food last night."

He continued to examine the test results and then spoke to Victoria and Carol again.

"It appears that Bouncer has sustained brain damage during the fitting. I think euthanasia would be the best option, as there will be no quality of life for him now."

Victoria burst into tears. She knew the vet was right but couldn't accept it. He was her little pet. Her present from her lovely Neil. Now it felt like she was losing the last piece of him. Carol put an arm around her daughter and gave her a supportive hug. Tears were brimming her eyes too, but she needed to be strong for Victoria.

"I'll leave you alone for a few minutes to decide what you want," said the vet, as he promptly left the room.

"Maybe it's for the best, Love," said Carol. "You don't want the poor darling to suffer."

"I know he's right, Mum. I need a few last moments to say goodbye."

She leaned over to cuddle him on the table, tears rolling down her cheeks as she whispered to him, "See you on the other side of the rainbow bridge, my little darling. Will love you always, my gorgeous boy." Then she smothered him with kisses.

The vet re-entered the room a few minutes later and did the deed.

Victoria paid her bill, and they both left the emergency surgery. Carol placed her arm around Victoria as the tears flowed. It was the sheer disbelief of it all. Everything had happened so quickly, just as on that fateful night when Neil died. All the memories of that night came flooding back.

Victoria had been lying on the bed settee, watching a film, when she heard a knock on the door. She paused the remote and went to answer, thinking that Neil had forgotten his keys. She opened the door and was about to say, "Fancy forgetting your keys, you idiot", when she froze in total shock at the sight of two policewomen.

"Victoria Pemberton?" one of the policewomen asked.

She nodded.

"May we come in?"

Victoria invited them in by gesturing with her hand.

"Please sit down," she said, wondering what on earth was happening.

"Are you related to Neil Wilson?" they asked.

"Yes, I'm his fiancée," she said, showing them her engagement ring. "We got engaged last year," she babbled, as she was getting nervous.

"There's been an accident," they said. "Your fiancé, Neil, has suffered severe injuries and has been taken to the hospital."

She cried uncontrollably and then asked, "Can I go down and see him?"

"Yes, of course."

The policewoman paused.

"I have more to tell you. He was knocked from his motorbike by a driver whom we think was under the influence of alcohol and is in custody as we speak. Witnesses say he was thrown off the bike and hit a brick wall."

Victoria sat, shaking and feeling numb.

"Is there someone we can call for you, dear?" said the kindly policewoman.

"My mum," she said, her lip quivering.

The policewoman called Carol Reed and told her the news. "We will wait with you until your mother arrives."

Victoria busied herself by making a cup of tea, to try and eliminate what was going through her mind. It was as though she was in some bad dream and thought she would wake up at any moment, but that didn't happen. She was living a nightmare. Poor Neil. What had happened to him?

A drunk driver. I hope they lock him up and throw the key away for doing this to my lovely Neil.

Carol arrived and hugged her daughter. Victoria sobbed when she felt the comfort of her mother's arms around her. The two policewomen bid them farewell and left. Victoria and her mother then headed to the hospital.

Carol and Victoria arrived back home from the vet.

"I'll make you a cuppa, Love," Carol said gently to the numb distraught Victoria.

They both sat at the table quietly, staring at the tea in their mugs, hoping somehow that it would create a miracle and bring the dog back.

"Maybe you shouldn't go in tomorrow, Love. You'll be tired after being up all night."

"So will you, Mum," replied Victoria.

"I'll go and speak to Dr Prakesh for you. I'm sure he'll understand."

"I'll have to go in, Mum. Sami wants me to do all his clinics this week. I'll be letting him down if I don't go in. I'll see how I feel in the morning."

Very wearily, they both trudged upstairs to their bedrooms. Victoria fell straight to sleep, as she was exhausted after a very harrowing night.

17

Carol rubbed her eyes when the alarm rang at half-past seven. Last night felt like a dream; however, she had a thumping headache to remind her it had all been real. A shower was the only thing that would make her feel human. She also needed a cup of tea and some paracetamol.

"Come on, Paul, get up," she said, nudging her husband awake by pushing his arm.

"What do you want? I'm tired," he grumbled, stretching from tip to toe.

"You're tired," snapped Carol. "What about me? I've been up with Victoria all night and I have a full day at work. We need to get this done before she wakes up."

"Get what done?" yawned Paul.

"Do you ever listen to anything I say?" she scolded. "I'm going in the shower."

After her shower, Carol quickly dressed. Paul finally rolled out of bed and pulled some clothes on, knowing there would be no peace for him until he did as Carol wanted.

They went out to their cars and transferred Bouncer's body to the boot of Paul's car. He would go to the pet crematorium, and Carol had given him her bank card for payment.

Once done, they went back inside for tea and breakfast. There was no sign of Victoria, although her car was still outside.

"I'm just going to let her sleep as she's had a terrible night," said Carol. "I'll go in and explain to Dr Prakesh."

A few minutes later, they heard the bedroom door open.

"Did nobody think to wake me up?" Victoria shouted. "I've overslept."

"Go back to bed, Love. I'll go ..."

But she was interrupted.

"I can't, Mum! He's relying on me to do things today. I need to get ready."

She quickly showered, dressed, and dashed out of the house before either parent could say anything.

Sami was working at his desk, as was his usual routine. He glanced at his watch and noticed that Victoria had not arrived. She was usually there at that time. It wasn't her start time yet, but she prided herself in always being early to get organised for the day ahead, so Sami wondered where she was.

Victoria dashed into the little coffee bar and bought her usual cappuccino and breakfast, as Sami often did. He heard the heels of her shoes clattering along the corridor before she burst through the office door. Her hair was dishevelled, her handbag hung off her shoulder and her hands were full with the refreshments. Sami watched her, feeling amusement, and stifled a smile behind his index finger.

"Good morning, Sami," she panted, as she placed her belongings on the desk and floor.

"Good morning, Victoria," he replied.

He stared at the usually very organised and relaxed woman who had entered his office like a whirlwind. She sipped her cappuccino, poured her breakfast cereal into the bowl and started eating.

"Sorry, Sami, I overslept," she said, between mouthfuls of cereal.

"You're not late," he replied.

He noticed that she wasn't herself and continued to observe her.

"Victoria, are you sure everything is all right?" he asked.

"Yes, I'm fine. I didn't get much sleep," she said, and then caught sight of the photograph of Bouncer. It all became too much for her and she burst into tears.

"Whatever is wrong?"

Sami stood up and walked over to her desk. She was inconsolable. He bent down and touched her arm.

"Victoria. What is it?"

His voice was gentle and husky as he pulled a handkerchief from his pocket and gave it to her.

"It's my little dog," she said, then began to tell him the story between sobs, then threw her arms around him for comfort.

Sami hadn't expected that, and he jumped. He'd never had a woman's arms around him for a long time, except for his mother's.

What the hell do I do?

He looked at her tear-stricken face, then relaxed and put his arm gently around her shoulder to comfort her. He listened to her story about her dog.

She is grief-stricken and has had no sleep, so it is no wonder she came into the office in such a flurry.

Dr Andrew Bartholomew knocked on the door and entered at that moment, to discuss a patient with Sami. When he saw the scene before him, he said, "I'll come back later."

The nurses at their station heard the crying and started chatting.

"Do you think he's upset her?" asked Dawn, concerned. "She's always so pleasant. I have never heard her like that."

"I'm going to find out," said Bernie, heading towards the office door.

"Bernie, would you mind phoning the laboratory and asking Carol to come to my office, please?" said Sami, as Bernie arrived at the office door. Then he whispered in her ear, "Her dog passed away last night."

"Oh no! Yes, I'll do that right now," she said, trotting off towards the telephone.

Carol appeared at the door a few minutes later.

"I knew this would happen," she said to Sami. "I told her not to come in."

"You're going home," Sami whispered to Victoria.

"I can't. There's too much to do here."

"Not in that state. You're going home," he soothed. "Take a day, a couple of days, and get yourself sorted. I'm here, and I'll manage. Just let me know when you're coming back."

"I'll need your phone number," Victoria said, as she got her mobile out of her bag. "Can you type it in there?"

Sami entered his number and returned her mobile.

"Carol, are you able to take her home?"

"Yes, I'll call the laboratory and let them know."

"Thanks, Sami," said Victoria, in a squeaky voice.

She's had a horrendous night, yet she still wanted to come in, not to let me down. There aren't many women like her in the world. There is a kindness in her heart.

He noticed a little wet patch on the breast of his shirt, from her tears.

Victoria finally arrived home and composed herself. She felt like an idiot, bursting into tears in front of Sami, but his care and compassion had surprised her. He was known as The Iceman to everyone else, but she could only see a different side to him.

Paul had made her toast and coffee, which made her feel much better.

It was time to go to the pet crematorium.

18

Sami had been very busy without Victoria to help him, and he had missed her being around. He found half an hour over lunch to eat a sandwich and grab his favourite latte.

Word had filtered out about Victoria and her dog. Sami explained what had happened, and it started a conversation within the ward among the patients. All the staff knew, and Sami couldn't help but notice that even one of the patients, Beatrice Delaney, who had a great rapport with Victoria, was upset. She had obviously made a great impression on people in the short time she'd been there.

As Sami sat in the office, eating his sandwich, his mobile beeped. He took out his mobile and saw that the message was from an unknown number. He didn't do text messages very much. They were generally from Richard, Verity, or his mother, as he didn't give many people his number. He opened the message.

'Hi, Sami. I hope everything is OK there. So sorry to have let you down this morning and for being a blubbering fool. Here is my number in case you ever need it. Love Victoria x'

Victoria had sent him a kiss! *My goodness, that's not happened for a long time.*

He added her number to his contacts, as one of the privileged few, and then replied.

'Victoria, please don't apologise. Everything is OK. I hope you are feeling better now. S x'

He'd pressed the send button before he realised that he'd sent a kiss too. He sighed and thought, *My God, what will she think?*

Then another text came back.

'I'm a little better, thanks. I've no more tears to cry, love V x'

He finished the conversation with, 'You take care, S x'

He sighed. *He was losing his mind.*

Sami had replied to her text! She hadn't expected him to respond as he didn't strike her as a man who would send a text, but she had received two replies, and he'd even sent her kisses.

Not the thing an iceman would generally do.

The short conversation had cheered her up a bit, in the middle of her sad spell. The precious little spaniel Neil had bought her was gone. She and Paul had taken his body to the pet crematorium. She had chosen a nice casket for him. When everything was complete, she would bring his ashes home, back where he belonged.

"Damn, I need to buy some flowers and a card," Sami muttered, after gulping down the last of his sandwich and latte.

He decided to send Bernie over to the florist, as she would have a better idea of what a woman would like. He hadn't a clue about such things.

"Bernie, have you got a minute?" he shouted from the office door. Bernie walked over, as summoned, and he shut the door behind them.

"If a woman wants to be cheered up," he spoke very awkwardly, "you would buy her flowers, right? Some nice flowers and a card. I mean, from all of us to Victoria, from her work family. That's what we are, aren't we?"

"That's a very kind thought, Dr Prakesh," said Bernie, in surprise. "I'm sure she would love that."

He gave Bernie his debit card, then asked her to go to the florist, then purchase a lovely card for them all to sign. Bernie was only too happy to do this favour for him. She went back to the nurses' station, with a massive grin on her face.

"I'm going shopping," she said, flashing Sami's debit card. "See you all later."

She put on her coat and disappeared along the corridor.

"Where's she going?" asked Dawn.

"I don't know," said Susan.

At the florist, Bernie chose a lovely colourful bouquet and asked for some red roses to be added. After all, they would only be from Dr Prakesh, as he was paying for them, Bernie wickedly decided, as she knew that he had a soft spot for Victoria. It was obvious, as nothing like this had ever happened before.

The card they all had to sign was the second card in two weeks! She chose a blank card from the hospital shop, which said, 'Thinking of you' on the front and took it back to the nurses' station for everyone to sign.

"The flowers are beautiful, Bernie. Who are they for?" asked Susan.

"Victoria," she replied.

Bernie took the small card accompanying the flowers and wrote on it, 'Dear Victoria, thinking of you, love Sami Prakesh x' and placed it in the small envelope.

They all giggled.

"He fancies her," said Dawn.

"They do get along well. I haven't noticed it before with other colleagues, only Verity," said Bernie.

Sami finished his clinic. As he returned to his office, he caught sight of the bouquet.

"Ah, lovely," he said. "Thank you, Bernie."

"We've all signed the card," said Dawn.

Bernie handed the debit card back to him.

"Would someone mind taking it to the laboratory for Carol? She can deliver them."

"Consider it done," said Bernie, and off she went to the laboratory with the flowers and card. Bernie told Carol that the flowers were from Dr Prakesh and the card was from them all.

"Thank you," said Carol, taking the gifts from her. "I'm sure she'll be delighted."

19

Carol entered the house, laden with her bags, the bouquet, and card. "Be careful, Paul," Victoria said. "Looks like Mum has an admirer," she winked playfully across at Carol.

"It's you that has the admirer. These are for you, from Dr Prakesh."

"Really?" asked Victoria in surprise. "They're beautiful."

Carol handed her the card, with all the names on it.

"It's from them all. How kind of them," Victoria said, as she stood it on the table.

She then opened the little envelope attached to the flowers. They were from Dr Prakesh, but not his writing, so he must have asked someone to buy them on his behalf as he would have been busy. Still, they were beautiful and left a lovely scent in the house. They cheered her up enormously. She had missed Bouncer so much, especially his little footsteps, following her around the house.

Victoria waited until after they'd eaten their evening meal before she typed out a text to Sami.

'Hi, Sami. I just wanted to thank you for the beautiful flowers. Also, the card from everyone. So kind of you all to think of me, and they've cheered me up, love V x'

Soon afterwards, she got a reply. 'You are very welcome. How are you feeling? S x'

She replied to his text message. 'I'm a lot better, thanks. I shall be fine to come in tomorrow, love V x'

He replied, 'As long as you're sure, S x'

'Yes. Thanks for letting me have today. I think I did need it. Love V x'

'Cappuccino? S x'

'Yes, please. You know me so well already, love V x'

'See you tomorrow, S x'

He may not be the most popular man there, but she liked him. She enjoyed sending him messages and was glad she now had his number. He had shown her kindness.

Sami was sitting alone in the house, stroking his cat, when the text messages came through. He couldn't help feeling slightly excited by the text conversation with Victoria. There was something about that woman he liked.

The bed was a lonely place for Victoria that night, as she missed having Bouncer in the room. However, she slept well compared to the previous night. She was up promptly, and ready for work, the following morning. She couldn't be late as she remembered that Sami was buying her a cappuccino.

20

Sami remembered to buy Victoria a cappuccino, in addition to his breakfast, before heading to his office. A few minutes later, he heard Victoria's footsteps approaching the office door.

"Good morning, Sami," she said, as she entered the room.

"Good morning, Victoria. Your cappuccino awaits."

"Thanks," she smiled.

"Are you feeling better today?"

Sami wanted to be sure she was going to be OK.

"Much better, thanks," she replied. "I still miss Bouncer, but life has to carry on."

He took a deep breath.

"I suppose. It's hard sometimes. You need to be supported."

Victoria sat at her desk and decided to re-arrange her photographs. She moved Neil and the bike to the right-hand side, which was more in front of her. Bouncer's picture was moved to the left, making it more difficult to see. While things were still raw, she didn't need reminders to bring tears to her eyes at work. Sami handed her the cappuccino, and she stood up to reach it from him. She glanced down and noticed that his desk had no pictures, just a couple of pens, notepaper, stapler, hole-punch, and other stationery pieces.

"Why do you have no photographs on your desk?" asked Victoria, puzzled. "Your desk looks so lonely."

He gave her a strange look and frowned, before replying, "My desk is merely a piece of wood. Do I need to decorate it with photographs?"

"No. But I go everywhere with my favourites, and I know other people have them. You're the first person I have seen who has a lonely desk."

Sami sighed and gave a little smile.

"A lonely desk," he mused. "It's my place of work. Why do I need photos here?"

"To remind you why you're here. Or sometimes when things become stressful, you look at your photos and remember what's important in life," said Victoria.

"I live alone, so I guess my desk stays lonely," replied Sami.

"There must be someone. Your parents?" she asked.

Sami laughed and said, "Nobody puts photos of their parents on a work desk. It doesn't create a good image."

"My mum is on mine," she replied. "Any pets?"

"I have a cat called Mitzi."

"There we are then," she exclaimed. "Any photos of your cat?"

He rolled his eyes. Picking up his phone, he scrolled to a photograph of his pet. He showed Victoria a picture of a beautiful black cat with a red collar around its neck.

"Wow, she's gorgeous. How old is she?"

"I'm not sure. She is a rescue cat. She belonged to an elderly lady living near my grandmother. The lady died, and the cat needed a home."

"Sami Prakesh, you're a big softie at heart" Victoria exclaimed. "Will you send me that photo?"

"Why do you want it?" he asked.

"I'm going to sort out your first-ever desk picture," said Victoria.

Sami sent her the photo.

I have the strangest conversations with this woman. Now I want to ask her something I've been curious about for a while.

21

"Who is the man in the photograph? Is he your boyfriend?" Sami finally got the words out of his mouth. He noticed a change in her facial expression.

"No," she replied, then paused. "He used to be my fiancé but he was killed a few years ago in a motorcycle accident." Once she had spoken the words, he regretted opening his mouth.

"I'm so sorry," he said. "I should never have asked."

"It's fine, you weren't to know," she replied, with great understanding.

"I don't mind talking about him," she continued. "I met him at school when I was thirteen."

"Thirteen!" Sami exclaimed. "You started young," he said, giving her a mischievous wink.

"It wasn't like that," she said and began to reminisce about that day whilst relating it to Sami.

"Come on Victoria, we've got to be there in ten minutes," said Karen Bell, pushing her out of the school gate. "I don't want to miss Rob. He's the best-looking boy in St Peter's."

Victoria reluctantly followed her, wondering why it was her that always had to go with Karen on those occasions.

"I'm coming," Victoria said, running behind with her heavy school bag. They walked the half mile to St Peter's school gate where Karen got her makeup out and quickly applied it, and then she spotted the boy coming towards her.

"Rob!" she yelled, then jumped up and down waving. He came over to her and gave her one of those big kisses. Then they placed their arms around each other and

off they went, leaving Victoria all on her own. There was a boy who came with Rob and when the pair disappeared, he and Victoria just simply stared at each other.

"I cannot believe she's just walked off and left me here on my own," she said to the boy. "I'm not like her." The boy stared at Victoria and then said, "Hello I'm Neil, Rob's friend. I'm not like him either."

It all felt a bit awkward. Then the boy asked, "Do you want to go to Blacklands Park to do your homework? It's sunny and there's an ice-cream van there."

"Alright, sounds good," said Victoria, and that's what they did. They found a bench and he said he had some maths homework to do.

"I hate maths. I can't do it," he said.

"It's not so bad once you understand it," Victoria told him. "I'll see if I can help you." She explained the basic principles of the fractions and noted them on a separate sheet of paper, then he had a go at doing the sums.

"You're very clever. You'll do well in life," he said. He understood it a lot better after Victoria had explained it to him. She did her English homework and they sat quietly for a while, each getting on with their work. "

Do you realise they're having sexual intercourse?" Neil spoke suddenly and broke her concentration.

"Who?" asked Victoria.

"Karen and Rob. They go to his house and do it before his parents come home from work." He seemed to know more than she did.

"I thought only adults did that," replied Victoria. "Explains why she never does her homework."

"He doesn't do his either," said Neil. "He always gets into trouble but doesn't care. Do you want an ice-cream?"

"Yes, that would be nice," said Victoria. She gave him her bus fare to get her ice-cream.

"I'll walk home," she said.

"Where do you live, Victoria?"

"Newton Gate, what about you?"

"Brunton. It's been nice sitting with you. Can we meet again sometime?"

"Yes, I'd love that." They swapped telephone numbers …

"So that's what we did, and we kept seeing each other. Of course, as we got older, it developed into something more. He was my soulmate. When he was eighteen an insurance policy, paid by his parents, matured so he bought the motorbike. That photograph was taken on the day he bought it. He was over the moon with it. We got engaged then too. He bought me this ring with the money." Victoria swirled round a lovely ring, with a beautiful sapphire stone, on her third right finger.

"I still wear it, but on the other hand now. I will always wear it, as it has such sentimental value to me." Sami had sat quietly and listened to her story, realising that she had gone through a very difficult and sad time in the past. He felt guilty about asking the question, especially so soon after the passing of her dog.

Victoria continued with her story.

"We had a bedsit too. He paid the bond and first month's rent from his insurance policy. We both got part-time jobs to pay the bills. We had very little, but we were so happy. We were at college too, then university, trying to get better jobs. I wanted to be a biomedical scientist at the time, like my mother. It meant working long shifts but it would be better pay. The one night he wasn't working, he went to help a friend with his computer and got killed on the way home."

Sami sat with his thumb and forefinger on his beard. He wished he had kept quiet.

"I'm so sorry all that happened to you. You must have had a really difficult time," he said sympathetically.

"It was awful," she replied.

"What made you want to become a doctor?" he asked, intrigued.

"After being in the hospital when Neil died, I decided I wanted to help people. The subject of money was no longer an issue as I moved back in with my mother and Paul. I had an interest in cancer treatments and drugs so, after my degree, I applied to go to medical school. That, combined with my interest in what I'd already learned in the laboratory, is why I applied for this position, to specialise in haematology."

Just then, Charmaine knocked at the door.

"Your patient files for today," she said.

"Thank you, Charmaine," acknowledged Sami and she left.

Sami was puzzled.

"How do you manage to come in here with your big smile, always looking so relaxed and cheerful?" He had struggled with that, since his divorce.

"I hide behind a mask, Sami," she replied. "I often paint on the smile to conceal how I feel within. I take each day at a time. I feel like a widow; the widow who was never married." She gave a laugh. "My lifetime partner was taken too soon. I just try and get on with life in the best way I can."

"My goodness," he said, shocked by everything she had just told him.

"I'm guessing there has not been another love in your life?" he asked curiously.

"You guess right. There have been a few dates, but nobody has ever come close to him, or how he made me feel."

Sami looked across at her sympathetically. His question had been answered but he hadn't expected to learn so much about her life. He took a deep breath.

"I guess it's almost time for the ward round," he said, getting up from his chair.

"Indeed," she replied. They gathered their papers and notes, then left the office.

22

Victoria went over to the nurses' station and thanked everyone for the card and flowers. They were pleased to see her looking better. She conducted the ward round, accompanied by Sami, Dawn and Bernie. She signed forms for blood tests and prescribed transfusions of red blood cells and platelets. When passing the fourth bed, the elderly lady, Beatrice Delaney, handed her a card and some chocolates.

"It's from all of us," she said. "We heard about your bad news."

"Oh my!" said Victoria, in surprise. "How very kind. Thank you."

She excused herself and went to put them in the office, then returned and continued with the job in hand. After break time, Sami introduced Victoria to the Outpatients Ward. She hadn't worked there yet and it needed to be included in her curriculum. He also introduced her to another member of staff.

"Victoria, please meet Dr Maria Bright, who is another valuable member of our haematology team. Maria, this is Dr Pemberton, our new registrar."

"Pleased to meet you," said Victoria, as the two ladies shook hands.

Sami left Victoria with Maria who gave her an introduction and tour of Outpatients. Later, Victoria had lunch in the cafeteria with Sami.

"Hope you enjoyed Maria's tour of Outpatients," he said, as they sat down.

"It was most interesting," she replied.

"You will need to do some work in there too so I will arrange with Maria for you to accompany her, as you did with me on the Inpatients Ward."

Sami looked at the ring on Victoria's finger as he was speaking to her. Changing the subject, he said, "That is indeed a beautiful ring Neil bought you. He must have thought an awful lot of you." Victoria nodded.

"What about you?" she enquired. "You're divorced. What happened there?"

He looked down at the table, then said, "If you don't mind, I don't wish to discuss it," as he didn't want Victoria to think he was a failure.

"OK. I guess you haven't loved again either?" she asked.

"No," was his firm answer. "I have no intention of loving again. I'm very single, I lead a celibate life and I'm happy that way."

"So, no other dates then?" she asked, thinking she may be prying too much into his private life.

"There have been one or two, but nothing appealing," he replied. "My father invites new members of his workforce round to his home for lunch. My mother cooks a lovely meal and I am always invited. It's supposed to make them feel welcome at the practice but I feel it's a matchmaking process. None of them has ever interested me. I usually ask Richard to phone at a certain time and pretend to be the hospital calling me in." They both laughed.

"It irritates me," he continued. "My father wants me to produce a child to continue the family name and all that rubbish. Told him several times that we live in England and it's not happening."

He hesitated for a moment, then continued.

"The last one was a phoney," he reluctantly admitted.

"Really?" Victoria sounded surprised.

"Her name was Marianne and she lived in Leeds. We swapped a few emails. She looked quite pretty and wanted a serious relationship, possibly marriage. I wasn't sure so I decided to meet her. We arranged a date and I drove to a cafeteria in Leeds. I left early in the morning to arrive in plenty of time. When I finally arrived and parked, I received a text to cancel. She couldn't make it, as she had to fly out to Ghana as her father had suddenly died. She wasn't sure when she would be back as she had to sort everything out. I was angry as I'd travelled all that way for nothing. Had a meal in the cafeteria then drove back home."

"My goodness, that's awful," said Victoria. "Did you hear any more from her?"

"A few apologetic emails, as she knew I was furious. Then she started asking for money, so I blocked her. She was my last one."

"That's so unlucky. You know, not every woman is like that. There are still some genuine, kind ones left in the world."

"Well, I've never met one," he replied bluntly.

"Dr Prakesh, I'm sure that somewhere under that doctor's coat and icy exterior, there is a very kind and loving man waiting for the right woman to come along and steal his heart," she teased and gave a gentle smile.

He gave her one of those emotionless scowls, and then said, "Time to get back to work." They left the cafeteria.

23

There was another small clinic in the afternoon which Victoria had to do under the watchful eye of Sami. It was uneventful and afterwards, they returned the files to Charmaine as they went back to the ward. Sami called in to see James Turnbull and Victoria returned to the office. As she passed the nurses' station, the nurses were having a conversation.

"We are just talking about you," said Dawn, with a big smile on her face. "So, two cards and a bouquet in two weeks from dashing Dr Ice. We reckon he likes you!"

"No, he doesn't. He was just being kind, as you all were." Victoria hated these conversations.

"It was his idea. He gave me his card to go out and buy them," said Bernie. Victoria had already figured that out.

"Dr Prakesh is very single. He doesn't want a woman in his life. End of conversation," she said firmly.

"Time will tell," said Dawn.

"How do you feel about him?" asked Susan.

Victoria sighed. "He's a nice man and good doctor but, for the record, I tend not to choose men with beards as potential partners."

"Not sure I find them attractive either," said Dawn.

"I find it quite off-putting as far as intimacy is concerned, so end of story." Victoria took out her key and disappeared into the office.

She sat at her desk, deep in thought. She didn't like all this speculation at all. She liked Sami and it was very sad that someone had hurt him so much that he didn't want to love again. He had tried to move on and then got entangled with a phoney woman. She felt quite sympathetic towards him. The last thing he needed was any speculation between them. She decided to have a break, and then go to the laboratory to report the blood films. Sami returned to his office and was interrupted by Bernie on the way.

"By the way, Sami, she doesn't like beards." He didn't really have time for this.

"Who doesn't?" he shrugged.

"Victoria. She's not attracted to men with beards."

"Why are you telling me this, Bernie?" asked Sami, feeling irritated.

"Because she said so and you like her."

"Sorry to disappoint Bernie, but it's not happening," he said, disappearing into his office. After everything Victoria had told him today, he wasn't sure if she wanted to love again and that suited him. His phone beeped. It was Richard informing him that he was going to the gym tonight. He decided he would go too. After all, he had a lot to tell him.

Before heading home, he informed Victoria that he wouldn't be in the following morning. He was on-call that weekend and needed some rest time. "Dr Bartholomew will accompany you on the ward round," he said. "Just do exactly the same and he will observe you." Victoria collected her belongings and headed out of the office.

"Goodnight, Sami," she acknowledged, as she left the room.

"Goodnight," he said, whilst finishing off his paperwork before making an exit himself.

Sami went to the gym and did his usual workout with the weights and punch bags. Afterwards, he and Richard went to have a drink in the bar.

"Smiling Boy is dead," he announced. "He was her fiancé, then he was killed in an accident." He continued to tell the tale she'd confided to him that morning.

"I feel so bad about having asked her."

"My goodness," said Richard. "The poor girl. Sounds like she's had a hard time."

"Indeed," replied Sami.

"So she needs a man in her life to give her the love she deserves." Richard gave him a friendly punch. "So are you going to ask her on a date now?"

"No," Sami replied. "I don't know if I want that yet. I'm happy on my own."

"So if someone should come along and ask her out before you decide?" Richard asked.

"So be it," Sami shrugged.

"You're impossible, Prakesh. Totally and utterly impossible."

24

Victoria arrived at work a bit later the next morning as she knew Sami was not around. She met Charmaine in the corridor with the files and took them from her. She pushed them inside the office as she opened the door. A few minutes later, there was a knock at the door. Dr Bartholomew glanced inside.

"Hi, Victoria. How are you doing?" he asked with a smile. "I believe we're working together this morning."

"Indeed, we are," she replied. "Come on in."

Dr Bartholomew went to sit on Sami's chair, whilst Victoria continued with her preparation.

"You can call me Andy," he said. She had only seen him once or twice so didn't know him that well yet.

"How are you settling in, Victoria?"

"Good," she replied. "You have a great team here and I'm enjoying the work."

"Glad to hear it," he replied. "Sami mentioned you've been doing the ward round and he's been observing you."

"Yes, that's right."

"So if we do the same again today, is that all right with you?" he asked.

"Of course," replied Victoria, finishing her cappuccino. "Let's go." They left the office.

Andy Bartholomew used a slightly different approach. As Victoria analysed each patient, he asked her questions as she was in the process of deciding upon the patient's care plan which, of course, she politely answered. However, she much preferred Sami's approach of allowing her to do the job without distraction. Although Andy was a lot more talkative and joined in patient conversations, which Victoria liked.

After the break, it was time to check on Mrs Jackson again, prior to her discharge. There were other patients who she had received telephone calls about and needed advice.

Mrs Jackson's test results remained stable so she was referred to an outpatient clinic, to keep the INR monitored after discharge. Victoria then went to the laboratory, to polish off a few blood films before meeting her mother for lunch.

"So how was the ward round with Dr Bartholomew?" asked Carol.

"Rather different," Victoria replied. "He kept asking questions, which was rather distracting."

"I suppose everyone has their own flair. The laboratory staff find him a lot more approachable than Sami." Victoria raised her eyebrows in surprise.

"Really?"

"Anyway, how about a shopping trip tomorrow, just us girls? I need a new outfit for Hazel's birthday party next week."

"Sound's good to me, Mother," Victoria said, eyes open wide with excitement.

When Victoria returned to the Haematology Ward, the nurses were having another guessing game at Dr Prakesh's age, so she slipped into the office quietly as she didn't want to get involved. Sami was sitting at his desk when she entered.

"Good afternoon, Victoria," he said, in a breezy voice.

"Good afternoon," she replied.

"I've just been speaking with Andy. He was very impressed with your performance today."

"Oh good," said Victoria. She seemed surprised.

"So we have the clinic this afternoon, then we'll chat over coffee about this week and our plans for next week."

"Great idea," she remarked, as she prepared for the next clinic. They pushed the trolley of files to the Outpatients Ward.

"Did you have a good morning off, Sami?" Victoria asked on the way.

"Fine thanks. Just catching some sleep before my busy weekend," he replied.

The afternoon clinic passed quickly and unremarkably so before they knew it, it was time for coffee.

Sami told Victoria that she had progressed well that week. He had arranged for her to work alongside Verity Sinclair and Maria Bright the following week in the Outpatients Day Treatment Centre. Patients there were treated while sitting in a chair or beds could be made available, if necessary.

Victoria liked the sound of a different challenge and looked forward to getting started. She went to the laboratory to report the last of the blood films before collecting her belongings from the office.

"Have a good weekend everybody," she said, as she quickly gathered her belongings and made her escape. "Have a good shift, Sami."

25

Dawn Henderson wanted to see a film over the weekend. However, there was nobody to accompany her, as all her friends seemed to have plans. She messaged Victoria on social media to see if she would like to go, and Victoria agreed. Dawn promised to text the following day with the arrangements. The weekend suddenly seemed more exciting to Victoria with a shopping trip and now the cinema.

Carol always respected Victoria's opinion when buying clothes. Paul thought she looked lovely in everything. As complimentary as it was, it wasn't what Carol wanted to hear.

She tried on a lovely red dress and looked very nice in it. However, Victoria wondered if it was a bit too daring, which wasn't her mum's usual style. Carol then selected a sleek black outfit, which felt safer as it didn't show all the bulges. Victoria thought it suited her well, so she bought it.

"Now for matching shoes, Victoria," she said excitedly.

They looked around a few shoe shops. Carol didn't like heels that were too high as they were very painful for her feet. She always made sure she walked around the shop in them, for at least five minutes, to ensure they were comfortable. She selected her new shoes from a shop they had been in earlier. She was then able to look forward to the birthday party the following week.

"Are we going to have lunch, Victoria?" asked Carol.

"Sounds great," replied Victoria, so they headed to a favourite of her mother's in one of the little back streets, away from the central part of town.

"So who are you going to the cinema with tonight?" Carol asked as they sat at the table.

"Dawn, one of the nurses," replied Victoria, looking at the menu.

"It's great that you're making new friends there so quickly."

"I don't know Dawn that well, but she's very warm-hearted. She was struggling to find someone to accompany her, so I said I would. It will be a nice change."

The restaurant was relatively small but was a hive of activity. Victoria selected a jacket potato, with her usual cappuccino, and Carol chose the day's soup with a brown bun. There was a takeaway area at the front of the building with a selection of cakes, sandwiches, and take-out drinks, which seemed very busy.

After arriving home, Victoria took Meg and Reggie on their usual walk along the fields at the back of their house, and then she had a nice long soak in the bath.

She collected Dawn from her flat at seven o'clock and drove to the local cinema. Their film of choice started at eight, so they had enough time to head upstairs for refreshments. Victoria bought a Diet Coke, and Dawn selected an alcoholic option of vodka and lemonade.

"I'm so pleased you decided to come along tonight," said Dawn, gently brushing a stray hair away from her eyes. Her hair was long and auburn. At work, she always had it tied back. However, it was now flowing loose around her shoulders, accentuating her looks.

"It'll be good to get to know you more," remarked Victoria. "After all, there's never much spare time at work to chat."

"True," agreed Dawn.

"How long have you worked in the Haematology Ward?" Victoria asked.

"Two years and six months. I enjoy it there, and I'm very content."

"That's brilliant. I like it there too. We have such a good team. Haematology has always been a topic that's interested me, which is why I've chosen to specialise."

"You seem to work well with Dr Prakesh," Dawn mentioned.

"Yes. He's fine. He's an excellent doctor, and I'm just myself with him."

"He does seem to like you."

"I hope he does. Otherwise, I'm in trouble."

"Do you have a boyfriend, Victoria?"

"No. I've been single for a while now."

She told Dawn all about Neil and how she managed to cope with those following years.

"My God. That must have been terrible for you. I'm surprised you could concentrate on your studying."

"It helped me to cope. It was something to channel my mind upon, as my head in my books helped me to forget."

Dawn then told Victoria about her fiancé, Graham. They had been together for two years, got engaged, and then were together for four months before he suddenly decided he felt trapped and wanted to be back on the market. It left her feeling devastated for a while. However, now she was prepared to move on.

Victoria understood that it must have been an emotional time for Dawn.

Graham must have met someone else and let her down gently. Why else would he suddenly want to break off an engagement? Men could be ruthless sometimes. She had been lucky with her Neil.

"It must be time for the film now," said Victoria.

"I think we may have missed some of the adverts," said Dawn, with a giggle.

After watching the film, Victoria dropped Dawn at her flat before returning home and retiring to bed.

Sami wasn't at work at the beginning of the following week, as he had recovery time from his on-call shifts over the weekend. However, he had arranged for Victoria to work in the Day-care Unit with Verity and Maria, so she didn't spend much time with him.

The work there was interesting. Victoria dealt with the quick turnaround patients who came in for transfusions, where samples had to be taken early so that compatible blood could quickly be found.

Verity Sinclair and Maria Bright passed on a glowing report, about Victoria and her work, to Sami and remarked that she was a great personality to work alongside. He arranged for her to continue working in the Day Unit the following week, giving her more responsibility and a hand in the decision-making.

26

Sami rose early the following day. He decided that a trip to the barber's shop was well overdue. He needed to change his image if there was any hope of attracting Victoria's attention and putting an end to the nurses trying to guess his age incorrectly, adding years to his otherwise fit persona.

Victoria, not liking beards, felt like a wasp sting in his heart, so it was time for a change. He was going to have it all shaved off.

The barber shop he used wasn't in town. It had a suburban location near a petrol station. It was a very quaint building that used to be a post office, relatively small inside, and Sami wanted to be there early to avoid queuing.

"Take it all off, please," he said to Fred, the barber. Fred looked astonished as he had kept Sami's beard and moustache trim since he began growing them, six years ago.

"You are sure?" he asked, looking puzzled.

"Yes. Time for a new look," said an apprehensive Sami. He had got used to hiding behind it and not having to shave every day for a long time. "I need to impress a woman."

"Ah, that explains it," said Fred, looking amused. "So the doctor, who never wanted to take out another woman, has found a lady he wants to impress?" he asked, with a huge grin.

"Something like that," replied Sami.

Anne Prakesh went to Sami's house at ten o'clock, as she did most Saturday mornings. She went to do some cleaning for her son and iron his clothes to get ready for work the following week.

It was unusual to find him out unless he was on-call, but he'd never mentioned it and she was aware that he'd been on-call only last week. She was intrigued by his whereabouts.

She had almost finished the ironing when he walked through the door. She was stunned at the sight in front of her.

"Good grief," she exclaimed. "I have a new son."

She was so surprised. She and her husband, Imran, had told Sami several times to lose the beard and smarten himself up, but it always seemed to fall on deaf ears.

"Now he's gone and done it."

"Impressed then, Mother?" he asked, grinning.

"Yes, of course. You look so much better."

He hung up his jacket and then boiled the kettle to make coffee.

"What on earth made you change your mind?" asked the amazed Anne.

"Because you keep telling me to tidy myself up," he reminded her.

She didn't believe him. *He had never taken any notice before*, she thought. She knew Sami wouldn't do anything that drastic without reason. There had to be an ulterior motive. She was curious to know what it was.

Monday morning came quickly, as it often did. Sami set his alarm a little earlier than usual, as he had to allow himself time to shave.

He secretly wondered what the reaction would be at work that day. Often, he wasn't noticed by people there but reckoned he would be the talk of the ward. He wasn't interested in their thoughts. All that mattered were the thoughts of one person.

He went in early and heard footsteps approach the office door.

"Good morning, Dr Prak........"

Victoria stopped in her tracks and stared at him open-mouthed. At first, she thought it was an intruder. Then after a short pause, she recognised his face.

"Good grief." She stared at him in disbelief, placing her hand across her mouth.

"We have a new doctor." She gave a little smile and then made her way over to the desk. After putting down her belongings, she turned and looked at him.

"What made you do this?" she asked, looking at the transformed man opposite her.

"I decided to have it all shaved and start afresh with a new beard. I do it periodically," he replied.

"Well," she said, as she took her seat. "I think you look very smart." She took a sip of her cappuccino.

"Thank you," he said, feeling relieved. "Did I look so bad before?"

"Yeah," she laughed. She stood up and went across to him.

"Do you mind if I touch you?"

"No," he replied, as Victoria gently caressed her fingers down the side of his face and cupped them around the base of his chin.

"I can't believe it," she said. "You feel so smooth."

Her gentle touch felt good on his skin.

"You look so much younger, too," she said.

"All these compliments," he replied.

"You have a nice face," she continued, "Now that I can see it!" she laughed.

He could feel himself blushing. Her comments had made his day. He didn't care what the others thought now.

27

Dr Sami Prakesh was the topic of conversation for the rest of that day. There was complete silence when he emerged from the office that morning, and all the nurses could only look at him and stare.

"It's quiet out here this morning," Sami commented, as he sorted his papers ready for the ward round. Victoria slipped away to the Day Unit, where she was working alongside Verity. Later, when she returned to the office, she became caught up in the conversation.

"He's done it for you, Victoria. I told him what you said and, a couple of weeks later, it's gone," said Bernie, with a massive grin on her face.

"No, he hasn't," Victoria replied, indignantly. "Nobody would change their style, or how they express themselves, for someone else."

"Yes, they would, and he has," Bernie insisted.

"He has it done periodically to freshen up, so it's not for me." Victoria was beginning to tire of this now.

"Rubbish!" exclaimed Bernie. "He's never come in clean-shaven since he grew the beard several years ago. I know I'm right."

The other nurses all looked at her intently, dying to know the reason behind his sudden change of image. Victoria didn't have any clues at all. She hoped he hadn't done something like that for her but she would feel very flattered if he had. After all, he did look lovely and she could almost fancy him without that grotesque beard.

"He looks so much nicer," Josie piped up, "but then you remember his cold personality." She was holding up a finger, and she gently rubbed it with the forefinger of the opposite hand.

"Damn, I think I've cracked a nail." She reached for a small nail file she kept in her pocket and tried to smooth it down.

"Are you going to do any work today, Josie, or will you just stand there, filing your nails?" Margaret Rose shouted across, sharply.

Josie sighed, "All right," and reluctantly slipped off.

Victoria entered the office to grab her bag and headed to the laboratory.

Once back in the laboratory, Victoria saw the staff, including her mother, rushing about.

"They've activated the major haemorrhage protocol," Carol shouted across. "Can't do lunch yet."

An elderly lady had cut her femoral artery by falling on some glass. The senior staff member, Hazel, was taking and documenting the telephone calls. The four emergency blood units had been given to the porter in a box, while he signed the collection documentation. Another staff member placed the fresh frozen plasma into the thawing unit, and a third team member prepared emergency platelets and then ordered replacements from the blood service. It was all systems go.

Victoria went into the private office to report a few blood films. How awful it must be for all the staff to work like that. It happened regularly there too. At least she was aware in case any telephone calls came to her for advice, but none did.

A little while later, the major haemorrhage protocol was withdrawn. However, the laboratory still had a lot of work to do, as incident forms had to be completed and a backlog of work tidied. That could impact some of her patients as their transfusions could be delayed.

Her thoughts were distracted by a telephone call. It was Bernie, who sounded in a panic.

"Victoria, it's Beatrice Delaney. She seems to be deteriorating. Can you come and have a look at her?"

"Yes, Bernie. I'm on my way."

Beatrice Delaney was a patient on the haematology ward. Victoria liked the lady and often stopped to chat with her. She made no secret that Sami 'always had a twinkle in his eye' whenever Victoria was around and reckoned that they would make a great partnership. Victoria always laughed it off by saying it wouldn't happen, as he was single, but Beatrice thought she knew better.

Now the poor woman was running a temperature. Beatrice had asked Bernie to bring an extra blanket and wrap it around her, however Bernie said the bedclothes needed to stay off and she had opened the window behind her to allow the air to circulate. Victoria asked Beatrice how she felt and was told that she had aching muscles everywhere. She also felt dizzy. Her voice was weak, and she was struggling to speak.

"How long has she been like this?" asked Victoria.

"She pressed her buzzer, just before I called you, to say she didn't feel too good. Upon examination, I noticed her deterioration."

"Can you urgently take samples including a full blood count and CRP? I'll contact Sami."

Victoria phoned Sami and explained the symptoms displayed by Beatrice. She indicated what her suspicions were. He returned to the ward immediately to examine her. The blood samples had been taken, so Victoria rushed them to the laboratory.

The tests confirmed their suspicions that Beatrice had developed neutropenic sepsis, a complication of neutropenia. She would need to start antibiotics immediately. Sami decided that she should be transferred to Intensive Care to get the best treatment. Victoria was instructed to arrange that and call the patient's family, to inform them.

At home that evening, Victoria watched a television programme about ballroom dancing. It brought happy memories of her nana and she remembered Beatrice Delaney telling her that she used to have dancing lessons when her husband was still alive. Victoria thought about how she had deteriorated so quickly that day. She hoped the poor lady would improve soon but didn't have a very good feeling about it.

As the week continued, Victoria was working in the Outpatient Day Unit, so she never really got a chance to check up on Beatrice's progress. She decided she would check on her during her lunch break.

It seemed that Beatrice wasn't responding to the medication as well as they'd hoped. She lay in her bed, looking weak and pale. Victoria went over and spoke to her.

"Hello, Beatrice. It's Victoria. How are you doing today?"

"I've been better," she gasped. "I feel tired, so tired."

"You just get some rest, Love."

Victoria placed a caring hand on the elderly lady's hand. It felt cold.

"I'll look in on you later."

Victoria then called Sami, to tell him the news.

Sami was the on-call haematologist over the Wednesday and Thursday nights, and many of his calls were about Beatrice Delaney. The patient was getting weaker, had difficulty breathing, and the critical care doctor didn't think she would recover. He was informed that her family members were at her bedside.

Beatrice passed away peacefully on Friday morning. Sami had been notified of the situation. He knew that he would have to tell Victoria and that she would be upset. He didn't speak to her until lunchtime when she told him she would call and see the patient.

"Take a seat first," said Sami, in his calm, monotone doctor's voice.

"Oh, OK."

Victoria was stopped in her tracks and she sat on her chair, as he had requested. He decided to be direct.

"Beatrice Delaney passed away this morning."

He explained the calls he had received overnight and that her family had been at her bedside. Victoria burst into tears.

How can someone die that quickly? The poor old lady seemed to be doing all right last week.

Sami passed her a tissue. He went over, stood beside her desk, placed his hands on the table and then leaned towards her.

"That is why I told you not to become too deeply involved with the patients at the start. Because shit happens." He paused. "Actually, a lot of the time. Then we are expected to put it behind us and move on to the next patient. However, I've watched you and I know you'll never change," he said, as he gave her a sympathetic wink.

"You are damned right, I won't," exclaimed Victoria. "Beatrice was a legend, an absolute legend. It was a pleasure to have known her."

Victoria went to offer her condolences to the family and they thanked her for everything she had done for their relative. She could have easily left the building afterwards, but, as Sami had said, there would still be other patients to treat. She had to compose herself for work in the Day Unit and move on to the next patient. *One patient at a time, then the weekend* *she thought*. It was the death of a patient she'd been close to, and she knew it wouldn't be the last. It was tough, but she would have to learn to deal with it.

Sami was right when he said we have to move on to the next patient. The afternoon seemed like an eternity. Dr Maria Bright had noticed that Victoria wasn't her usual self. Sami explained why and then asked for permission to take her away for a coffee and end-of-week chat. After they'd had their discussion about her progress and the plans for the following week, Victoria headed to the laboratory to report any outstanding blood films. It was finally time to escape from Lady Margaret's Hospital for the weekend. She felt an enormous sense of relief.

"Any nice plans for the weekend, Victoria?" Sami asked as they walked to their cars.

"When I get home, I shall take the dogs for their walk. Then after that, I shall watch Summer Breeze and get totally and utterly drunk," she said, with a smile.

"You're watching Summer Breeze too?" he asked. "I'm up to Episode 5."

"I'm up to number 6," she replied, "but hoping to finish it this weekend. Have a good one. I'll see you on Monday."She bleeped her car locks and climbed into her motor.

Sami watched her drive away. He had wanted to invite her to his house to watch Summer Breeze, but he hadn't plucked up enough courage. They'd both had a tough day, and he would have welcomed the company. Sometimes life could be lonely. He'd given her a wave as she'd driven past, then decided to send a text message.

'Hi, Victoria, I wondered if you would like to come to my house tonight to watch Summer Breeze? I'll get some pizza and drinks. It's been a tough week. S x' He thought she'd read it when she got home. He started his car engine.

28

The two border terriers, Meg and Reggie, were always delighted to see Victoria when she arrived home. She always had to appease them with lots of love and attention.

"I guess it's time for your walk," she said, and their tails wagged as though they understood each word she'd spoken. Victoria took them on their usual route, over the fields behind her house, where she could let them off their leads, and they could have a good run. As they raced around, Victoria checked her phone and saw Sami's invitation. The idea appealed to her, especially after the sad day she'd had at work, so she promptly replied to his text.

'Hi, Sami. That's a great idea. What time shall I come over? V x'

'How about 7 pm? S x'

'Sound's great! See you then. V x'

Once back home, Victoria told Paul that she was going out for the evening and wouldn't want a meal. She decided to go in a pretty, but comfortable, pair of jeans with a classy blouse. She left her hair loose as she was aware that it looked more attractive. Before setting off for Sami's house, she added some extra perfume and light makeup. She had to quickly message him for a postcode, as she'd never been. His house was on a corner. She parked her car in front of his before entering the side gate and knocking on the door.

Sami had called at the supermarket on his way home, to buy wine and a few extra snacks for Victoria's possible visit. He was delighted when he received her text to say that she was coming. Once home, he unpacked everything and had a quick tidy around, to make his home presentable for her arrival. He fed Mitzi, then decided to go and change into something smart, but casual; splashing on some additional aftershave. He was filling the kettle and preparing the cups when he heard her knock at the door.

"Hi, Victoria. Welcome to my humble abode," he said. "Please, do come in." He was completely surprised at how gorgeous she looked.

"Good evening, Sami. Thank you for your kind invitation." She stepped into his kitchen, taking in the more 'normal' Sami, than the man she knew from work.

"I was just making coffee," he said. "I thought you may like one while we decide which pizzas we want."

He showed her into his lounge. It was spacious with a beautiful Houston leather chaise sofa and, what appeared to be, his home cinema. A huge TV was connected to the wall and a glass coffee table housed newspapers and remote controls.

"Wow! This is nice," she exclaimed, her eyes wide open.

"Please, take a seat." He placed her coffee on a coaster on the glass table.

"You have your own cinema here. This is fantastic," she remarked.

"Thank you," he replied. "I spend a lot of time watching films and TV while at home, so I may as well have the best systems." Then he turned to the takeaway pizza menu on his phone.

"What kind of pizza would you like?" he asked, passing the phone for her to look at the menu.

"I'm just a plain girl, so Margherita will be fine," she replied. "I will have a deep-pan base, please."

"I like Meat Feast, so I'll order both," he said. He placed the order and paid with his card. A message flashed across the screen saying that the pizzas would be delivered between thirty and forty-five minutes.

"All done," he said. "Should we watch an episode now?"

"Yes, OK. You need to catch up with me," Victoria replied, with a smile.

"Do you mind watching Episode 5 again?"

"Not at all. I'll try not to spoil it for you," she teased.

"You'd better not." He smiled back at her.

What is happening to me? I have never felt so comfortable around a woman in such a long time. She is great company.

He pressed 'Play' and the episode started.

Not long into it, Mitzi crept down the stairs and around the settee. She saw that Daddy had visitors, so she gave the couch a wide berth and then jumped upon his knee.

"Meow, meow!" She rubbed her head against his arm and purred.

"Hello, my lovely girl," he whispered affectionately, and she nuzzled into him as he scratched her head.

Who would have thought it? The grumpy consultant, a man of few words, known as Dr Ice, is sitting in front of me, stroking and kissing his cat! If only people could see what he can be like.

"Oh, she's beautiful," said Victoria, reaching over to give her a stroke.

"She's not too fond of guests," said Sami, as he continued to caress her.

However, Victoria was allowed to stroke her, just for a little while. Then she moved back, not wanting to invade Mitzi's space. The little cat promptly left Sami's lap and walked over the couch, towards Victoria, and curled up on her knee.

"Why don't you make a liar out of me, Cat?" he said in surprise, as Mitzi had never before curled up to anyone, on their first visit.

Victoria stroked Mitzi and told her she was beautiful, then said to Sami, "I'm surprised too, as I must smell of Border Terrier. Sit closer if you want, then we can both stroke her." Sami eased closer to Victoria and they watched Summer Breeze, fondling a delighted and purring cat.

Soon there was a knock at the door. Sami pressed 'Pause' on the remote and went to answer it.

"Pizza has arrived," he said. "I'll be a few minutes while I sort things out."

Soon he came through, with two big open boxes, and placed them on the glass table.

"Feel free to start," he said, then disappeared back into the kitchen.

He brought a kitchen roll, wine and two glasses. He began to pour her a glass, but she reached out to stop him.

"Not for me, thanks, Sami. I must drive home."

He surprised her by saying, "Surely one small glass will be OK?"

"I never mix the two," she said, vehemently. "Neil was killed by some idiot who mixed the two." She still got upset about people not making a proper judgment about drinking and then deliberately going behind the wheel of a car. They would all lose their licences if she were in charge.

"Please feel free to drink the wine yourself," she added, feeling as though she'd been a little rude. "I'll just have a soft drink."

He went into the kitchen and poured a Diet Coke.

You fool, he thought angrily. *You should have remembered.*

"Sorry, I just wanted you to relax and have a cheerful night, after Beatrice Delaney. I didn't think."

"It's fine. I feel very strongly about it, that's all."

"Understandably," he replied, realising that he had killed the mood slightly and, somehow, would have to try and get things back on course. Sitting closely on the couch together, stroking the cat, had been a rather special moment for him.

"Thank you for buying the wine," she said. "It was a very kind thought."

There was silence for a while as they ate their pizza, enjoying every mouthful.

"You could always stay," Sami blurted out. "Then we could share the wine." Victoria looked across at him, completely shocked.

Realising that what he'd said could be taken out of context, he quickly added, "I have a spare room, and I don't mind." He then said that she would be his first houseguest as nobody had ever slept in that room, then realised that he was beginning to sound like a bumbling idiot.

Feeling his discomfort, Victoria replied, "Thank you, that's very kind, but I have no pyjamas." They both laughed.

"Nor have I got my toothbrush or any clean knickers," she said, as they continued to laugh.

Then he disappeared upstairs for a few moments and reappeared with a rather large T-shirt and a new toothbrush, still in the packet.

"You have a nightshirt and a toothbrush now," he said, handing them across to her. "However, I don't keep ladies' knickers in my drawers, as they are not something I wear," he teased.

"I get worried about you sometimes," she giggled. She took a deep breath and replied, "Alright, I'll stay, and thank you."

She got out her phone to send a message to Carol to say she wouldn't be home, while Sami finished pouring her wine. He started Summer Breeze again, and they watched two further episodes, munching pizza and drinking wine, with Mitzi nestled between them on the sofa.

After Episode 7, Sami cleared the empty pizza boxes away and returned to the lounge with a couple of sundaes.

"Chocolate or strawberry?"

"Chocolate, please."

He then returned to the kitchen and brought through a plate of mixed biscuits, before pouring some more wine.

"You're spoiling me tonight," she said, smiling at him.

"I don't often have guests," he replied, "especially a lovely lady like yourself."

"So," she said, changing the subject, "what do you think then?"

"Think of what?"

"Summer Breeze," she retorted. "The series we're watching!"

"Oh, that," he replied. "Full of its twists and turns, isn't it?"

Summer Breeze was a series about a young doctor who left the city to work in a country practice, along with an elderly male doctor. She brought in fresh idea's while he was old-fashioned in his ways, so it caused a few disputes. She had caught the eye of the local restaurant owner, who took her out to see some of the local sights in the hope that she would settle there permanently. But he already had a lady in his life who had just announced that she was pregnant.

"What would you do if you were in his predicament?" asked Victoria. Sami sat there with his eyes wide open.

"You expect me to answer that?"

"Yes," Victoria replied. "You're a man. I'd be interested to know what decision you would make."

"If I tell you, you will disagree and probably slap me," he said, in fun.

"Of course, I wouldn't. I'm just interested. You're entitled to your opinion, and it would be good to hear your male outlook."

"OK," he said. "It wouldn't happen to me, as I wouldn't allow myself to get into that predicament. I would not partake in sexual activity unless I loved the woman." He thought, by saying this, that he would get away lightly, but no such luck.

"You still haven't answered the question. What would you do if you were him, not you?"

"I'd follow my heart and step out with the lovely doctor but, at the same time, I would be a proper father and support my baby."

"Man after my own heart."

"I thought you would disagree with me," Sami said, curiously.

"No. Could you imagine if the character did that?" Victoria was intent on the series.

"Resentment would build in the relationship and they would probably separate later anyway. By then, the doctor will have left town or she will be dating someone else."

"You old romantic," Sami said, smiling at her, even though he agreed with everything she'd said.

"Should we watch one more?"

"Go on then."

They watched another episode that involved a problem in the woman's pregnancy, so the young doctor had to treat her, which formed a complicated triangle. Exciting stuff!

"I want the doctor to get pregnant now," said Victoria. "That would put the cat amongst the pigeons!"

"You have an evil streak in you too," he laughed.

After finishing the second bottle of wine, they headed up to bed.

"I hope the room is comfortable for you."

"I'm sure it'll be fine," said Victoria, sleepily.

He allowed her to use the bathroom first. Then she said, "Goodnight, Sami," as she went into her room.

"Goodnight, Victoria," he said, as she closed the bedroom door behind her.

She undressed, sat naked on the bed, and then pulled the oversized T-shirt over her head. It made a great nightshirt as it fitted perfectly over her bottom. She climbed into the snug bed. It was so comfortable. Then her thoughts strayed to Beatrice Delaney. In death, the old lady had brought her and Sami closer. Bless her soul. She would have liked to have seen us together like this. Hopefully, she is watching from another world. It had been adorable sitting so close to him, with the cat. Yet he made no advances at all in any way. *Maybe he needs a friend to spend time with?*

All she knew was that she was ready to take things further with Sami, should the opportunity arise.

29

Sami lay in his double bed, thinking of Victoria lying next door. She was a female friend. That was something very new to him. He was never at ease around women, unless at work and in his professional role. They were challenging. Even his cat liked her. Animals could sense things so were good judges of character, in his eyes. There was still a part of him that didn't want to go down that road again, as he hated all the grief caused when things go awry. But he also felt stirrings inside that he hadn't felt for so long and maybe the day would come when he would want to touch her. The whole thing made him panic but, at the same time, he hoped that if Victoria ever stayed again, she would lie next to him, filling up the space in his double bed.

Victoria was woken by a knock at her bedroom door the following day. She rubbed her eyes and looked at her watch, suddenly remembering that she was at Sami's house.

My God, I've overslept.

"Can I come in?" said Sami's voice from outside.

"Yes, of course."

She brushed her fingers lightly through her hair to try and look respectable but knew she had failed miserably. Sami entered the room.

"I have some coffee for you. Did you sleep well?" Sami handed her the mug.

"Too well. I'm in a daze. Reckon it must have been the wine," she laughed, sitting up in the bed, taking the coffee.

"Thanks," she replied. Her pretty blue eyes sparkled in the morning sun and her messy hair spread over her shoulders. To him, she looked more attractive than ever.

"I'm sorry," she continued. "I hadn't realised it was so late."

"Victoria, it's Saturday. This is not late," he smiled. "I'll go and get my coffee."

He went to bring it in and sat on the bed beside her. They continued chatting.

"What are your plans for today?" she inquired, curious to know what time she would have to leave.

"Not much," Sami replied. "My mother generally comes around at ten o'clock to do some housework for me. While she does that, I tidy my car."

"What? Your already-spotless car?" Victoria was amazed, as it had been so immaculate when she had changed his tyre.

"There'll be dust there by now," he teased.

"Then my mother and I will have a drink, before she goes to her sister's house, my Auntie Susan."

"So I'd better disappear before your mother arrives then?" she quizzed. "Don't want her looking at us with suspicion." They laughed.

"No, there's no need to hurry," he replied. "At least have some breakfast."

They finished their coffee and he took the cups downstairs, leaving her to use the bathroom and dress privately. She made the bed before going downstairs into the kitchen.

"What would you like for breakfast?"

"Cereal, please," she replied, and he opened his cupboard so she could choose.

"Cornflakes will be fine."

After breakfast, Victoria suddenly remembered she had a little gift for Sami in her bag. She took it out and said, "This is for you."

"What's this?" he asked, before he unwrapped the tissue paper. In a small photo frame, was a photograph of Mitzi.

"What is it for?"

"I guess you won't have a lonely desk at work anymore."

"It's lovely, but you shouldn't have." He wanted to stand up, throw his arms around her and give her a huge kiss at that moment. However, he took a deep breath and controlled himself.

"Thank you for everything," she said, standing up and straightening her clothes. "It may be fun to do this again sometime." He promptly nodded and agreed. She walked down the path, looked back and gave him a wave.

She didn't notice the car that had just parked behind his car.

30

Anne Prakesh had noticed her. A woman was leaving Sami's house. Well, my days! That explains the mystery haircut for a start. She scrutinised the lady as much as she could without being noticed. She had long brown hair and a pretty smile. Please God, let this woman be someone special in his life.

After Victoria had driven away, Anne climbed out of her car and went into her son's house. Nothing was forthcoming from Sami about the mystery woman, so she decided to probe.

"Who was the woman I saw leaving the house just now?" she asked.

"Woman?" he queried, thinking Victoria would have escaped before her arrival.

"Oh, that woman," he said. "That was Victoria, the new registrar at work." He spoke very normally, giving nothing away.

"Here, on a Saturday morning?" Anne kept digging for answers.

"Yes, Mother," Sami sighed. "She stayed overnight in the spare room." He emphasised the last two words.

"Before you get excited, Mother, she is a female friend whose company I enjoy."

Sami felt irritated by his parents' constant interest in his love life. He was tired of them trying to match him up to different people and they didn't seem to understand that he was happy on his own. It was time they got used to it.

Anne knew by the tone of his voice that she wasn't getting anywhere, and he clearly wasn't saying any more on the subject. She still felt a little glow inside. Simply knowing that a woman had stayed there indicated a closeness not observed in a long time. Then there was the sudden change of image. She smiled inside as she quietly continued with her chores.

Anne couldn't wait to tell her husband, Imran, the good news when she arrived home. He was still annoyed that his son hadn't stepped out with the lovely Julie, from his practice, after she came to the family home for her welcome meal. He had given her Sami's mobile number, but Sami refused to talk to her and continually said he wasn't interested and blocked her number. Now Imran knew why. His son had his eye on someone else. He smiled and showed excitement, for the sake of his wife, but he was annoyed at Sami's treatment of Julie.

Anne made it her mission that week to find out about, and meet, the mystery woman who her son was showing an interest in. His 'female friend'. She called him at work on Monday, saying she had things to discuss and didn't want his father present. Usually that worked, otherwise it would be left until the weekend. By going into the hospital for lunch, she may get to meet the lady. So, it was arranged. Tuesday at one o'clock.

Sami wondered what his mother wanted to discuss with him that couldn't wait until the following weekend. It seemed strange but, nevertheless, he had agreed to meet her. He had grown used to having lunch with Victoria, however he did mention to her that his mother was coming in. Thinking he would be treating her to a meal in the cafeteria, Victoria opted for a takeaway lunch which she planned to eat in the office. However, on her return, the office door was ajar. She went inside and saw Sami, sitting at his desk, with a woman in the chair opposite him.

"Oh, I'm sorry to intrude. I thought you were having lunch in the cafeteria," said Victoria, feeling embarrassed.

"Don't worry, Love. I'm not staying long," said the woman, in a very gentle and soft voice. She had a lovely kind smile. Sami stood up and introduced them.

"Victoria, this is Anne, my mother, and Mother, this is Victoria, the new consultant registrar who shares this office."

"Well, hello," said Anne. "It's a pleasure to meet you." She recognised Victoria as being the woman who was at Sami's house the previous weekend.

"Likewise," said Victoria, as she went to shake the woman's hand.

"Please sit down, Love, and eat your food. Don't mind me. I have just come in to discuss Sami's birthday next week."

"It's your birthday?" asked Victoria in surprise. "You never told me."

"I've not had a chance!" exclaimed Sami, impatiently, as he suddenly realised what this was all about. She's been curious about Victoria and that's why she's here.

"I have some cake for you, Sami," said Victoria, removing it from a paper bag.

"Cake! Why do I want cake?" he sighed. "I need to keep my stomach trim."

"What?" exclaimed Victoria. "I have seen more fat on a skinny chip." Both women laughed.

"Share it with your mum then," she continued. "It's just you haven't seemed yourself this morning."

"Oh, he's not been in one of his moods?" asked Anne.

"Yeah," said Victoria. "You have it in one."

"Can I fit a word in edgeways at all here?" asked Sami, in exasperation. This truly was a battle he would lose.

"OK, Sami, about your birthday. Will you come round for a meal?" Anne asked.

"I guess so, if I'm being invited."

"What about Victoria, your female friend? Would you like to come too, Love?" Victoria looked across at Sami.

"Well, I don't want to intrude."

"You wouldn't be intruding at all. Any friend or colleague of Sami's is very welcome in my home." Victoria knew what Sami had said previously when his father's secretaries had been invited for lunch. She didn't want to feel like them. She hoped Sami would want her there.

"Don't look at him, Love. It's me that's inviting you."

"It's fine," said Sami. "I'd love you to be there." He felt that the whole evening would be so much more enjoyable if she was there and another opportunity for him to spend time with her outside of work.

"OK, then. I'd love to come. When is it?"

"Next Thursday, 4th November."

"There's one condition, Sami. I'll give you a lift to your mum's place, then you can have a couple of beers."

"It's a deal," he replied, smiling.

"So what was the other thing you wanted to discuss, Mother?"

His mother didn't reply. Sami knew perfectly well that she'd got what she wanted.

31

Victoria had to make a plan. Firstly, she must decide what to buy Sami for his birthday present. Then she needed to choose the right card. She also wanted to bake him a cake. It had been a while since she had baked anything, so she knew she would have to persuade her mother to help her. She would need to know his favourite too.

As for gifts, what do you buy the man who appears to have everything? He goes to the gym and lifts weights. He likes golf and has the occasional golfing weekend with a group of consultants from the hospital. She had no idea what golfers liked and presumed he would have all the kit anyway. He was always cleaning his immaculate car so probably had his preferences there. She could maybe get him something new to wear at the gym; however, she would need to know his size. How about a deluxe coffee set? That could be a possibility. Perhaps she needed to look online to see what she could find.

Sami was devising his own plan. He knew that Victoria's fiancé had his anniversary on Bonfire Night, which was the day after his own birthday, and she had told him how she'd kept the tickets for the fireworks display that year in memory of him, as they'd been bought in advance but not used. She had never felt like going since, as it brought back sad memories, whereas she had always loved going before that. So he decided he would purchase two tickets and take her. He enquired and purchased them online, then printed and hid them in his briefcase whilst she was out of the office.

Within a couple of days, Anne had become one of Victoria's social media friends, so she decided to send a message asking her opinion. Anne replied saying she thought the coffee set would be a great idea, however, she was baking the cake. Victoria wanted to bake one to take to work, so she was going to have a wild guess at the flavour and hope that he liked it.

At the weekend, Paul and Carol wanted to go to the cash and carry, so Victoria decided to accompany them and have a look around.

They were wandering through the bakery section when some cakes caught her eye. The carrot cakes, red velvet cakes and chocolate cakes all looked delicious. That was it! She needed to go midweek and buy one of those cakes. It would be perfect to share with all her friends and colleagues at work.

On the way out, after Carol and Paul had paid, they always stopped for a coffee. Whilst sipping her cappuccino, she noticed a small photography section advertising prints, photo books, cushions, mugs, phone cases, mouse mats, and the word that seemed to attract her most, 'Canvasses'.

She still had the photo of Mitzi on her phone. A canvas print of his precious cat to place on his wall would be far better than any coffee set. She went over to place her order and they said it would be ready midweek.

Online, she selected a 'special friend' card with the illustration of a man, just like him, holding a beer. She would need annual leave to get everything prepared.

Sami was playing golf that weekend. It wasn't often that his consultant colleagues and he got a weekend together, however, this was indeed one of those times. So, they had travelled to a nearby hotel, with spa facilities and a golf course, to make a weekend of it. They had just eaten a light lunch and were heading back to the golf course when Sami's phone beeped. The message was from Victoria about annual leave. He told her to request it by email on Monday morning, as he needed to have an official record. Then another text came back.

'How is your weekend going? V x'

'Fine, thanks. It's a refreshing change.' Then, thinking he had been rather mean, he asked her, 'When do you want the annual leave? S x'

'Wednesday.'

'It should be OK. Please email me officially. S x'

Victoria was excited as she started work on Monday morning. She was going to be busy with work and preparing things for Sami's birthday. She sent the official email first thing, as he'd asked, however, he didn't reply until later to confirm it.

Wednesday arrived and, after a short lie-in, Victoria decided she needed to go to the cash and carry, first of all, to get the best choice of cake and also collect the canvas. She asked Paul to accompany her, as she needed his card to make her purchases since she wasn't a member.

Once there, Victoria went straight to the cakes and decided upon a red velvet one. She placed it in the trolley. Paul enjoyed wandering about, to see if he could bag any bargains. He stood in the distance, beckoning Victoria to go over to where he was standing.

"You'll need paper plates if you are taking the cake to work for your colleagues," he said, pointing to some in a box. Victoria hadn't even thought of that.

"Good job I'm here to keep you right," Paul laughed.

"Suppose I need some serviettes too."

Paul filled the trolley with some more provisions before they headed for the checkout. Victoria paid the bill, as a way of thanking Paul for coming. On the way out, she collected the canvas.

She called into the shopping mall on the way home as she needed a card, wrapping paper and labels. Then she had to go to the florist.

"You're going to a lot of trouble for Dr Prakesh, aren't you? Is there something you haven't told us?" Paul teased. Victoria scowled at him.

"He doesn't normally celebrate his birthday so I just wanted to do something nice," she sighed.

"Have you considered that he may be a private bloke who doesn't want any fuss?"

"Oh, it's only a piece of cake between colleagues," Victoria said impatiently. "It's hardly an all-night party."

"Are the flowers his too?" asked Paul with a wink. She sighed.

"No, they're for Neil's grave."

The online friendship birthday card had arrived when they got home. Having ensured that the cake was placed safely in the fridge, Victoria went upstairs to write the card and wrap up the canvas of Mitzi. She was delighted with it and was certain he'd love it. She put them aside as they were for the following night, however, the serviettes and paper plates would go into work, with the cake, the next morning.

Sami had his own plans. It was busier on the work front, with Victoria not being there, but he used the time alone in his office to compose a letter to accompany the tickets for the fireworks display, which he would then place in an envelope and leave on Victoria's desk. If she agreed to accompany him, that would be two evenings in one week that she would spend in his company. He smiled as he thought about it.

He made a couple of attempts to write the note but ended up screwing the paper into a ball, and then throwing it into his wastepaper bin. He took a deep sigh.

He was happier with the third attempt, so he sealed it in the envelope with the tickets and placed them in his briefcase until the next day.

32

Victoria was up promptly the next morning. She had a lot to organise and needed to be at work before the very prompt Sami. She had set everything on the dining table the night before and only had to remove the cake from the fridge.

At the hospital, she decided to take the cake in first as she had planned to hide it in the nurses' room. Then she returned to her car for the other bag with the serviettes, plates, knife and wax candle.

Next, she asked the night nursing staff to sign the large card and pass it on to the day staff. Finally, she went to purchase cereal and coffees for herself and the birthday boy. It wasn't long before she heard his footsteps coming along the corridor.

"Good morning, Victoria, you're in early," he remarked, raising his eyebrows in surprise.

"Good morning, Sami. Happy birthday."

"Thank you," he said, as he put down his briefcase. "How was your day off?"

"It was good, thanks. The dogs had an extra-long walk," she shrugged, then changed the subject. "How's your birthday so far? Any gifts yet?"

"From Richard and family. Saw him at the gym last night. I tend not to make a big fuss over it. Generally, it's my parents and that's it." *It'll be different this year,* thought Victoria, trying to stifle a smile.

After the ward round, Bernie made sure that everyone had signed the card and handed it to Victoria as she approached the nurses' room. She took out the cake and lit the candle.

They headed to Sami's office and crept inside. Then they began to chant, "Happy birthday to you, happy birthday to you, happy birthday dear Sami, happy birthday to you."

Sami glared at them in surprise. No medals for guessing who is behind this.

"Victoria, did you really have to do this?" he sighed.

"Come on, blow your candle out," Victoria said, ignoring his question. He blew out the candle.

"Are you cutting your cake, Sami?"

"No, I'll leave that in your capable hands."

Victoria cut slices of cake and placed each one on a paper plate. Everyone else filed out of the office to eat it during their tea break. Sami and Victoria were finally left alone.

"What is the meaning of all this?" he asked her curiously, but annoyed that everyone in the ward now knew his well-kept secret.

"It's your birthday and we needed to do something special to celebrate," Victoria said calmly, oblivious to the fact that he didn't like to celebrate birthdays.

"Do you like the cake?"

"The cake is lovely," he replied, not really wanting to eat it, as he knew his mother would have a cake ready too.

"It is delicious," Victoria said. "Best coffee break I've had in a while. I'll ask the nurses to keep the rest of it in their fridge, so you can take it home later."

"I couldn't possibly," said Sami, as he felt full to the brim. "Take it to the laboratory and see if your mum and her colleagues would like it."

After cutting a large piece and leaving it for the night nurses, Victoria carried the cake to the laboratory and placed it in their staff room. They were delighted to have cake to accompany their lunch.

Whilst Victoria was at the laboratory, Sami took the envelope out of his briefcase and left it on her desk. He enjoyed a few minutes of peace before returning to work. He made his way across to the nurses' station and made a point of thanking all the staff for the lovely surprise. Of course, Bernie couldn't resist her reply.

"It was all Victoria's idea. It's her you need to thank." She paused.

"I think she likes you," she said, as her eyes twinkled mischievously.

Sami sighed, "Not that again." He turned heel and disappeared as he had a patient to attend to.

Victoria had examined the blood films whilst in the laboratory, then she briefly returned to the office before going to the Day Treatment Unit.

She paused as she noticed an envelope on her desk. It had her name in Sami's handwriting on the front. She opened it. Inside were two tickets and a note.

'Dear Victoria. I would like you to accompany me to the fireworks display on Friday evening. I took the liberty of buying two tickets, however, if you would rather decline, I will understand. Love, Sami x'

Wow! She used to love going there when Neil was alive, but she hadn't been since he'd died. It had somehow felt inappropriate and she never felt any desire to go. Suddenly, there were two tickets from Sami. It was so kind of him. She looked at the tickets again and felt a tinge of excitement. Yes, she would accept his offer.

She sent him a quick text message, 'Hi, Sami. Thank you for buying the tickets. I'd love to accompany you. V x'

33

Victoria left work a bit earlier that evening as she needed to go to the shopping mall to collect the flowers. She stopped at the cemetery on her way home and placed her posy in the grave vase at the side of Neil's headstone. She always stayed and talked with him for a little while.

"Happy anniversary, Darling," she said, as she put her arms around the side of the headstone as though she was hugging him. "I can't believe it's nine years since you left me," as tears and a sob came forth. She sat quietly, remembering the events of that dreadful night like it was only yesterday.

"I'm going to the fireworks display tomorrow. A kind man has bought me a ticket. I've never wanted to go without you. We always had such fun." She paused again as she cried a bit more.

"I will go again this year." It had been June since she'd last paid him a visit.

"I'm training to be a consultant now," she went on. "We could have done so many things together, had many adventures, now I have a bit more money." She paused for another few tears. He had been robbed of so much, having cruelly been taken so soon.

"The kind man invited me to dinner tonight, so I must go. I will visit you again soon, Baby. I love you, always and forever." She kissed the gravestone as she got up and waved him goodbye, blowing a few kisses as she left.

Her tears dried as she drove home. It always felt as though Neil was still there when she visited his grave and she believed that he was watching over her. They would meet again when her time on this earth was done. However, she had to live this life first. Suddenly she remembered that she hadn't visited Neil's parents for a while. She must visit them.

At home, Victoria wrote the small card on the bouquet for Anne, then left the flowers in the boot of the car. Once inside the house, she ran a bath and had a relaxing soak. As her body was enveloped by the fragrant bathing bubbles, she rested her head on the base of the bath and closed her eyes. Her heart began to speak to her first.

'Why am I having a birthday meal with Sami tonight? I can't love Sami, as Neil was always my love.'

Then her head interrupted, by saying, 'It's his birthday and it was kind of them to invite you. Neil is in the spirit world and is not coming back. You need to start living your life again.'

Of course, the head is always right, as the heart is full of sentiment. She tipped her head back into the water to wash her hair, just enjoying the peace and serenity of being alone in that room and having time to reflect. What should she wear? She massaged the shampoo into her hair. The little black dress, she decided. Sami has never seen me in a dress.

She picked up the nicely wrapped canvas and card before leaving the house. "Have a good night," said Carol, as Victoria left.

She placed the canvas and card in the boot, swapping it with the bouquet which was then placed on the back seat. She headed round to Sami's house to collect him. He was ready and waiting when she arrived. He cast his eyes over her figure. "Wow! You look stunning," he remarked, as he stepped into her car.

"You don't look so bad yourself, Birthday Boy."

"This is a refreshing change," he said, as he sat in the passenger seat.

"What's that?"

"To be chauffeured, as opposed to driving somewhere," he replied, as he clicked the seat belt into position. They arrived at Sami's parents' bungalow.

"This is nice," said Victoria, as they pulled up outside. She opened the back door and lifted out the bouquet.

"Who are those for?"

"Your mother. She was kind enough to invite me to dinner." Anne had already seen them arrive and came to open the door.

"Hello, Victoria. How lovely to see you," and she hugged her.

"Hello, Anne. These flowers are for you."

"They're beautiful, thank you," Anne replied, then placed them in the centre of a small table.

A man sitting, reading the newspaper, looked up at the flowers and acknowledged them.

"Ah, very nice." His voice was quite deep and gruff.

"Dad, I would like you to meet Victoria. She is a consultant registrar, working on my ward."

I wish he would put down the newspaper and not be so rude.

Victoria offered him her hand, and said, "Nice to meet you."

"His name is Imran," Sami continued. They shook hands.

"Another doctor, eh?" Imran smiled across at her as she took her seat. She felt his smile wasn't natural, more painted-on. Sami had mentioned that his father wasn't fond of female doctors, however, she wanted their first meeting to be polite and give a good impression.

"Please take your seats at the table," Anne said. "Dinner is ready."

"What will you have to drink, Victoria?"

"A Diet Coke, please," she replied. "I'm the driver."

"Surely one glass won't hurt," said Imran, as he walked to the table. Sami sighed and rolled his eyes. He knew how Victoria felt about that, however, she kept her composure.

"I prefer not to, thanks."

They all sat down to a beautiful roast pork dinner. It was rather like having Sunday roast midweek.

"Well, Victoria," asked Anne, breaking the silence. "What made you decide to become a doctor?" Victoria took a deep breath.

"Life events, if I'm honest," she replied.

"I was doing a degree to become a biomedical scientist, like my mother, and during my second year at university, my fiancé at the time was killed in an accident. I was in a very dark place for a while and, for several months, I struggled to concentrate on my course. I got some great support from my mother and the university, who allowed me to take my exams at a later time. Then my mother suggested that I apply for a sandwich year, as there was a position in the laboratory. After a successful interview, I took that position for a year which helped me a lot."

"Ah," exclaimed Imran, "so you got that position with your mother working in the laboratory, right?" He smirked, then concealed his face with his hand as disapproving looks were directed at him by his family.

"Imran, don't be so rude," said Anne, feeling very annoyed with him. Sami tutted and rolled his eyes, as if to say, 'Carry on Victoria, ignore him.'

Victoria continued.

"I worked at Central Hospital for a year. I enjoyed the work but something was missing. I felt the desire to get out there and help people. I became interested in cancers and the medications that treated them so, after passing my degree, I went on to medical school."

"That's marvellous," said Sami, laughing. "I needn't have given you the day in the laboratory, as you knew it already."

"No, it was helpful as a lot of things are different now."

"So you wanted to specialise in haematology," said Imran. "Why?"

"My interest in cancer treatments, combined with everything I'd learned in the laboratory."

"So you hope to be a consultant one day?"

"With your son as my mentor, I hope to be successful one day."

"How long ago was it since your fiancé was killed?" Anne asked, changing the subject.

"Nine years."

"That must have been a difficult time for you."

"It was, but I had a lot of support. How about you? How did you both meet?"

"We worked at the same hospital," replied Anne. "I was his nurse."

"How romantic," she smiled. "I didn't know you were a nurse."

"Yes. I gave up once we were married, as I wanted to concentrate on raising a family, but that never happened. I had several miscarriages before Sami," she continued, with sadness in her voice. "Once Sami came along, my family was complete. We didn't try anymore."

"I'm so sorry," Victoria replied. Anne stood up to collect the empty plates.

"I have my son and, for that, I am thankful."

"That was a lovely meal, thank you," said Victoria. "Would you like some help?"

"No thanks. You're a guest here. Imran will help me."

They went into the kitchen and left Sami and Victoria alone.

"I'm so sorry that my father has been rude. I don't know what's been the matter with him lately," said Sami, feeling exasperated.

"Don't worry, it's fine. It's probably his idea of a joke and he thinks he's funny."

"Well, he's not," said Sami, crossly.

"Stop worrying. It's your birthday."

Just then, Anne came in with more drinks, a beer for Sami and a Diet Coke for Victoria. After rinsing the dishes and placing them in the dishwasher, it was time to give Sami his presents.

Anne came into the room bearing gifts. It reminded Victoria that her gift was in the car, so she excused herself and went outside to get it. When she returned, Sami began to open his gifts. The first one, from his parents, included two shirts, one white and one blue, exactly like the ones he wore for work. Victoria wondered if he wore shirts in any other colour.

"Thanks, Mum and Dad," Sami said unenthusiastically, almost as if he knew what was going to be inside the wrapping paper. He picked up his next gift. Navy socks. Victoria watched Sami's face and could see there wasn't much of a reaction. She guessed that he got the same things each year. The next gift was a pack of underpants. There were three pairs, one navy, one blue and one white. Victoria giggled behind her hand but stifled the laugh as she didn't want him to see. Parents could sometimes be so embarrassing. He tried to cover them with his hand so that she couldn't get a glimpse.

"They're pants, Sami, I can see them," Victoria giggled. "You know, we all need pants." Sami's face went scarlet. She could almost feel his embarrassment.

Imran burst out laughing too. He had a cackling laugh.

"Unless you don't wear any," he joked.

"Dad!" Sami scowled. "Leave it."

If he had wanted to embarrass someone in front of a nice lady, then he's just succeeded, thought Sami crossly. Victoria picked up her parcel and handed it to Sami.

"Why don't you open this?"

"What is this? I told you not to buy me anything."

"I can't go to someone's birthday meal without a gift," she said impatiently. "Now open it."

He began to open the large present, wondering what it was. When he saw it, his eyes immediately twinkled in excitement.

"Wow! That's beautiful," he exclaimed, looking at the wonderful picture of his cat. "It's awesome. I love it. Thank you." He leaned over to give her a big hug.

Why do I feel as though I want to kiss her?

Anne leaned over to get a better view.

"That's gorgeous, Sami. It'll look great in your lounge," she said, with a big smile on her face. He stood it against the table and then proceeded to open the final present.

"Some golfing polo shirts," he said. "These are nice."

"Ideal for your next golfing trip," said Victoria, with a smile.

"Thank you, very much, everyone," said Sami. "They are all lovely."

Of course, the canvas is my favourite.

"Come on Imran. Time for dessert," said Anne, as she ushered her husband into the kitchen.

"I am very surprised by the picture. You didn't have to spend so much on me," said Sami.

Victoria shrugged and said, "It wasn't very much, and I knew you'd love it."

"You know me too well," he replied.

"She's a great woman," said Anne, who was excited about Sami's interest in Victoria.

"She's OK, I suppose. I was just annoyed that he showed no interest in Julie," Imran mumbled.

"Why would he? He was interested in someone else!" They took the cake and fresh cream through to the table for dessert.

"I hope you like strawberry cheesecake, Victoria."

"I love it."

That is the second piece of cake I've eaten today. I really must reduce my food intake.

After dessert, Anne made coffee, which was lovely, made with cream. Victoria felt stuffed. Anne had been very busy that night and it was obvious to Victoria that it was something she did often, perhaps every time Imran employed a new member of staff. She offered her help once again, but Anne declined, as she was a guest.

She cut a large slice of the birthday cake and wrapped it in foil for Victoria and her parents. The other half was shared between Sami and his parents. After coffee, Victoria and Sami bid their farewells. Victoria thanked Anne for her hospitality, then helped Sami carry his gifts to her car and they waved as they drove away.

Once alone in the car, Victoria thanked Sami for inviting her and said she'd had a lovely time. He had enjoyed it too, more so with her company. He could see that his parents liked her but his father could be so rude at times, that it made him feel embarrassed. As she reached Sami's, she helped him with his gifts again.

"Goodnight, Sami," she said. "See you tomorrow."

"Goodnight," he replied, then closed the door behind him.

He decided to hang the canvas that night, on the right-hand side of his TV. He took out his tool set and got the job done. The picture of Mitzi did look good. It was the best birthday he'd had in a while. Victoria had been the highlight, of course, arranging all the surprises at work, and then accompanying him to dinner. He knew his feelings were deepening towards her, as he felt a chemistry that he hadn't experienced for a long time.

"That went well," said an excited Anne. "You can see he's quite fond of her."

Imran sighed and replied, "OK yes, I suppose she is nice, but don't start getting too excited."

"Why not? He hasn't shown an interest in anyone for years."

"She's not his girlfriend yet."

"Only a matter of time."

"Don't forget that you invited her."

"He wanted her to come."

"If he wanted her here, he should have invited her himself," he retorted, aware that Sami hadn't had another girlfriend since the divorce from the miserable Angela. She had let him and his family down big-style. English people could be strange sometimes. They lacked the commitment and family values evident in the land from where he came. He knew Anne had been different and he had been lucky to meet her.

He had never liked Angela much. Sami needed the stability of a good woman and, in the back of his mind, he often thought that an Indian girl would be more suitable. He hoped his little plan would materialise before things became too serious.

34

Victoria lay in her bed that night, thinking of Sami's birthday. She had enjoyed the evening. It had been a welcome distraction from Neil's anniversary, and Anne Prakesh was a lovely hostess. She had noticed the glint in her eye which told Victoria that she was hopeful of Sami and her forming a partnership one day. Maybe she didn't realise he didn't want marriage or she just lived in hope that he would change his mind.

Imran was a strange character too. There was something she didn't like about him but was uncertain of what it was. He was quite unusual in his ways. She did think that Anne could not have had the easiest life, living under the same roof as Sami and Imran.

As for Neil, it was his anniversary soon. Nine years ago, he died. She looked at her watch and remembered travelling to the hospital, not expecting the sight she would encounter. Each year, she lit a small candle and said a prayer to remember him. She was tired after the evening out, however, she still placed the candle on her bedside table, beside his photograph. She watched it flicker as she recited a few precious memories of their times together. It was as though he was in the room.

"I still have the tickets for the fireworks display from the day you passed, and we weren't meant to go," she stared at the burning flame, feeling the tears brimming her eyes again.

"I hope you don't mind me going with another man this year," she said in a shaky voice. "You're no longer here with me and I need company." More tears rolled down her cheeks.

"I miss you so very much, my love."

The small candle began to flicker and burn out, just as Victoria closed her eyes and inadvertently dropped off to sleep.

She was in a deep sleep when her alarm rang in the morning. She rolled over and switched it off, with her wrist, before dozing again. When she finally woke up properly, she realised that she was running late. She got up and quickly dressed, then dashed to the hospital. Sami was waiting in the office with a cappuccino for her.

"Good morning, Victoria. I was getting a bit worried about you."

"I overslept," she explained, as she scrambled into the room in a disorganised fashion. "Thanks for the cappuccino, much appreciated."

"So I take it you slept well?" he asked, thinking that it must have been a difficult night for her.

"I went to sleep late, as I lit a candle for Neil and sat there reminiscing. I must have fallen asleep as the candle burned out."

She took out her brush and bobble and began straightening her hair. Once finished, she took out the deodorant and perfume and sprayed that on. Sami looked on in amusement. At one time, he hated women spraying their perfumes and potions in his room, but he had become accustomed to it.

"So are you wearing your sexy underwear today?"

"Excuse me!" he turned his head in shock at her words.

"The underwear you opened last night," she teased.

"That is none of your business," he replied, with a wry smile.

"I reckon you are wearing them, as you are in denial," she giggled.

"Come on, it's ward round time," said Sami, changing the subject to hide his embarrassment.

Victoria watched him walk in front of her. She thought he had the perfect bottom. Perfect size, quite peachy and it waggled quite attractively as he paced the hospital corridors. She was amused to think of that underwear covering it. She thought a more modern and sexy design would be much better. Then she collected her thoughts and brought her mind back to the job at hand.

Throughout the day, when an opportunity arose, Victoria teased him about the underwear, grinning broadly at his uneasiness around the subject. Later, she went to collect her belongings before setting off home. Sami was sitting at his desk.

"So you think you deserve to go out tonight, after your performance today?"

"Of course," she replied. "My performance as a doctor has been second to none. Besides, a gentleman should never break his promise."

Sami took a deep breath, and said, "I'll pick you up at seven o'clock."

"OK, see you then. Don't forget your warm underwear, as it can get quite cold," she giggled, as she left the room. Sami picked up some paper, screwed it into a ball, and then threw it at her as she left.

He was very excited about meeting her that night.

35

True to his word, Sami collected Victoria at seven o'clock and she excitedly breezed out of the door.

After driving to the venue, he managed to park on a side street near the display venue. Victoria and Neil had often walked there when they were young. There was a queue forming already outside the entrance. There were lots of excited, eager faces waiting to enter the large grassy area. It was a cold, but clear, night and Victoria wore a warm sweater with jeans, a jacket and boots with a matching scarf, pom-pom hat and gloves. She did look very attractive. Sami was in his usual navy blue jeans, sweater, jacket and scarf, also wearing a pair of walking boots. He opened the passenger door of the car.

"Shall we?" he asked, giving Victoria his hand and helping her out of the car. After locking up, he turned and looked at her glowing face, then took her hand in his.

"Do you mind?" he asked. "I just think it's good manners when I take a lady out."

"Not at all," she replied, as they walked along and joined the end of a queue.

She had been excited about going there that night and felt like a child again. After Neil had suddenly died, those special years had been snatched away from her. She looked through the railings and could see a few stalls, eating places, a small Ferris Wheel, a Waltzer and some rides for smaller children.

"This is great!" she said, excitedly. "I can't wait to get inside."

Her childlike eyes glistened in the dark. It wasn't Sami's idea of fun, but it pleased him to see her bursting with happiness.

Once inside, they strolled around the different stalls. Sami played a game where he had to throw three balls into a hole to win. He won a large pink fluffy teddy bear which he gave to Victoria. She loved it.

"I think I'll call him Samibear," she said, her eyes widening with excitement. Sami rolled his eyes as he realised it was his mother's baby name for him.

"Well, he will remind me of you and how you won him for me."

"Should I feel flattered that a pink teddy bear is a reminder of me?" Sami sighed.

She is so different to anyone I have taken out before. There is a big child within her and I love that. She is just herself and doesn't pretend to be anyone different.

"Come on. Let's buy some food. I'm hungry."

They found a nice burger stall that also sold coffee. Sami bought a burger with chips whilst Victoria was happy with a hot dog and onions. They both had their usual coffee drinks. They found a wooden bench to sit on to consume their refreshments.

"So when was the last time you came to anything like this?" Victoria asked Sami.

"Years ago," he replied. "Probably when I was a child. It's not my thing."

"Then why are we here if you don't like it?"

"I wanted to make you happy."

"You are so kind. Thank you for bringing me here. We'll not stay long if you're not enjoying it."

"I am enjoying it, more than I thought," he said, wondering if he could ever become childlike again. His ex-wife, Angela, had managed to destroy all that.

Later, Victoria wanted a ride on the Ferris Wheel and almost dragged Sami on with her. His face was white as he didn't like rides at all but wanted to be brave. As the wheel started whirling around, he felt sick as Victoria shrieked.

"Wooh! It's so good to be a child again. Weeee!" she squealed. As it slowed down to stop, Victoria looked across at Sami and saw that he wasn't sharing her fun. He looked ashen.

"Are you alright?"

"Yes, fine." He staggered off the ride, walking forward so that she couldn't see his face.

"You're not, are you?" She grabbed his arm and looked at him with concern.

"Well, I'm not keen on rides."

"Then why didn't you tell me?" She gave him a sympathetic look as he seemed to be suffering a lot for her happiness.

"Once the firework display is over, we'll go."

Just then, there was an announcement over the loudspeaker, saying that the fireworks were due to begin in a few minutes. As they stood waiting, he placed his hand on her shoulder. Suddenly the air was filled with bangs and whistles, as rockets and Catherine Wheels shot up into the night sky, in an array of bright and beautiful colours.

"Wow!" exclaimed Victoria. "They're glorious."

The fireworks continued for several minutes. When it was quiet, everyone in the crowd gave loud cheers and applause. Once finished, Victoria and Sami headed back towards the car. She held his hand, while Samibear was cuddled into her opposite shoulder.

Sami is probably glad to be going home, she thought.

There was a short delay as all the cars exited the area, and then Sami drove her home and parked the car outside.

"Thank you so much for tonight. I appreciate what you have done," said Victoria.

"The pleasure has been all mine."

"There were times when I didn't think you liked it."

"I did," he said, as he touched her wrist to reassure her. They looked across at each other and held each other's gaze for a few moments. Then Victoria leaned forwards and hugged him. He hugged her in return and smelled the scent of her hair.

She decided to give him a kiss of appreciation and, as she turned her head, he sensed what she was about to do. Their lips brushed together as they met and the kiss, although just a gesture of affection, was held for a moment with their lips together before Sami decided to pull away before it became anything more.

"Good night, Sami. Thank you for a lovely night," Victoria said, as she climbed out of the car. He watched her as she took out her key and entered her house. She gave him a wave as he drove off.

My goodness, what happened there? Did he want to kiss me? Does he fancy me? She had just had the most wonderful night for a long time, and it didn't matter whether he just wanted a friend. It would be nice to have more but his words, when they first met, remained in the back of her mind.

'I am not interested in a relationship.' She noticed that he had pulled away rather abruptly as if it had been a mistake.

Sami drove home, annoyed with himself for not controlling his feelings.

You fool. You nearly kissed her on her fiancé's anniversary. How disrespectful was that?

What shocked him, even more, was how easy and natural it would have been to have kissed her passionately. It had so nearly happened. He hadn't felt like that for a long time. He began to feel alive again but, at the same time, he was panicking inside.

He had not intentionally set out to embark upon a relationship, but this was now happening. The feelings had simply overtaken him and were very real. He hadn't wanted another relationship after his disastrous marriage which almost made him a recluse.

As fond as he was of Victoria, he knew he was going to have to distance himself from her somehow, without hurting her feelings.

36

Victoria had a long lie-in on Saturday morning. After two reasonably late nights and a lot of socialisation, she felt drained and needed to catch up with some much-needed sleep. She opened her eyes, looked over at Samibear, the pink bear, and smiled. She thought about Sami and wondered what he would be doing over the weekend. She decided to send him a text message.

'Hi, Sami. Thank you for last night. I had a wonderful time. I hope you are OK this morning. What are you up to today? V x' No reply was forthcoming, so she turned over and began sleeping again. Later, a knock on the bedroom door woke her. Her mother entered the room.

"Coffee?"

"Ooh, yes, please," said Victoria. "That's just what I need." She sat up and leaned against the bedhead before taking the cup from her mother.

"Thanks, Mum."

"Did you have a good time last night?"

"Yes, I did; thanks, Mum."

"OK then, I'll leave you to it."

Carol left the room. She was intrigued by how much time Victoria was spending with Sami away from work. However, she decided not to pry. She knew that Victoria would tell her if there was anything she needed to know. There was still no reply from the earlier text.

Is Sami ignoring me? Maybe he has other plans.

She had other plans too, as she had agreed to meet Helen and Cathy for a skating session at the local ice rink. She had kept in touch with her two friends on social media for a while, and it had been years since they had last skated. They had skated competitively in their youth, travelling around to various competitions and events but had since moved on to very different lives. Helen worked in a supermarket and Cathy had become a schoolteacher.

I don't even know if my skates will still fit.

She raked around in the bottom of her wardrobe, where she had last seen them. She got them out and looked at them. A bit dusty and faded over time, but they held many memories. She decided to try one on. She struggled to get her foot inside but gave one big push and her foot slotted in comfortably. They were a bit tight, but OK for that day.

If it becomes a regular outing, I'll buy new ones.

She placed them back into the bag and, after finishing her coffee, it was time to take a shower and get dressed.

Sami also had a lie-in. He wasn't used to having two consecutive late nights either. He got up, made some coffee and then took it back to bed, intending to stay there a while. He drank the coffee and got himself dressed, when he suddenly remembered it was Saturday and that his mother would be coming. He had heard his phone beep earlier and looked at the message from Victoria. He couldn't see her that day. The situation was moving too fast, and he needed to get his head sorted. He decided not to answer it immediately. In the meantime, Anne breezed into his kitchen, and he went down to make more coffee and have breakfast.

Victoria dressed in jogging bottoms and a thick jumper for the ice rink, and then tied her hair back in a ponytail. She checked her phone and saw that there was still no reply from Sami. It was strange, as he usually replied straight away. Still, she had other arrangements and didn't have time to worry about him. She headed downstairs for a late breakfast before heading off to the ice rink. She was looking forward to meeting her friends.

Anne talked about Victoria while she was at her son's house.

"She's a lovely girl, Sami. You need to invite her out on a proper date and make it official." Sami thought it was best to nod in agreement but, as she continued, he rolled his eyes and sighed. He was tired of her interfering with his life.

"I'm too busy at the moment, Mother. I'll get around to it sometime."

"Sami, she won't be around forever. If you take too long, someone else will step in before you."

Sometimes he can be so infuriating! It is clear to see they like each other. Sami knew there had been no other man in Victoria's life for a while, so he wasn't worried. It was a relief for him when his mother finally left.

Victoria, Cathy, and Helen met on the leisure centre concourse. They hugged each other.

"My goodness, it's been so long," said Helen.

"Too long," said Cathy.

"We must make it a regular thing," said Victoria. They chatted excitedly as they entered the ice rink and sat on a form to put on their skates.

"God, these are tight," said Helen. "I can't remember how old I was when I last wore them."

"If we make this a regular thing, I reckon we shall all need new ones," said Victoria.

"Come on, hurry up. I'm going on the ice," said Cathy, and off she went.

"Ooh, it feels weird."

They went on the ice, and it did feel strange after not having skated for all those years, but the feeling gradually came back and, before long, the three girls were skating around the ice rink as though they had never been away from it.

"Oh, this is great!" exclaimed Victoria, as she pulled them around in a chain. Helen screamed, not expecting that move, and they all giggled.

"Let's see if we can still do some tricks," Victoria said. "I'm going to try a spin." With her arms held out to one side, she pushed herself into a spin with the other leg.

"Weeeee," she screamed, then stopped with her toe pick. "Ooh, I'm dizzy."

"I'll try a three jump," said Helen. She stood back to give herself some space, then went for the jump.

"Ouch, my ankle, it's not as easy as it used to be."

"I think we should just stick to normal skating around the rink," said Cathy.

"Good idea," the others agreed. The afternoon flew by and the girls felt tired and ached as they left the ice rink. They had coffee together on the concourse and arranged to meet the following month. They said their goodbyes.

Victoria checked her phone and saw messages from both Sami and Dawn. She read Sami's first.

'Hello, Victoria. Sorry for the late reply. I went swimming with Richard this morning, and then we went for lunch. I have only just seen this. Please feel free to call round later, if you wish. S x'

He has lied to me.

When she had sent the message earlier, she'd noticed a tick, and the word *read* beside the message, so she knew he had read it earlier.

Why has he lied to me?

She read Dawn's message, which asked if she would like to go and see the latest James Bond film tonight. She messaged back and said she'd be delighted to go. She also messaged Sami and told him she had other plans. If he is going to be dishonest and mislead me, he can spend the evening alone. He can forget about having a relationship.

37

Sami received the text from Victoria to say she had other plans. Part of him felt disappointed as he was missing her. However, another part of him felt relieved as he knew he still needed some space. Perhaps not seeing her over the weekend would give him the space he needed, as he had felt guilty about ignoring her text that morning and making an excuse for her not to come round.

Victoria had an early meal at home as she needed to get ready and wear something more suitable for a night at the cinema. She chose jeans, a white blouse, and a pale blue sweater. She and Dawn had arranged to meet a bit early, have drinks and chat before the film, like last time. Victoria spoke of her skating adventure that afternoon and how she used to compete as a child. Dawn was amazed as she knew very little about Victoria's past. Then she asked another question.

"How are things between you and Sami? People have noticed you are quite close." Victoria had to choose her words carefully, knowing that whatever she said would be talked about at the nurses' station.

"I wouldn't be so sure. I've spent two lovely evenings with him, but then he was rather evasive earlier."

"What do you mean?" Victoria showed her the texts, with the times visible, and Dawn's pupils widened with surprise.

"Oh, my goodness," she said. "What's that all about then?"

"I don't know, but I intend to find out next week."

"Are you going to confront him?"

"Not straight away. I will see how things go and wait for my opportunity."

"I've never known anyone confront Dr Ice before. People are usually too scared."

"Not me."

They finished their drinks and went to watch the movie. The James Bond film was excellent. The action and special effects were second to none. On the way home, Dawn asked if Victoria had plans for Sunday.

"No. I'm having a relaxing chilled day tomorrow, just walking the dogs and catching up with TV programmes. What about you?"

"I'm going to my parents for lunch and then much the same as you," she replied.

"Relaxing before another busy week."

"Tell me about it."

Victoria pulled up outside Dawn's apartment. They said goodbye, and then she drove home and went straight to bed. She looked at Samibear and felt sadness and disappointment in her heart at how things could change so much in twenty-four hours. Last night, she had felt on top of the world; tonight, she felt disconcerted.

She did not share any other texts with Sami that weekend.

38

Monday morning came and Victoria still felt somewhat sad as she sat in bed and rubbed her eyes. The niggling thought of why Sami wasn't sincere was still on her mind. She didn't get up and dress for work with her usual vigour and enthusiasm. She left a bit later than usual and couldn't remember if it was her turn to buy the coffees, or even if she wanted to buy him one. As she turned off her ignition, a text message came through.

'Your cappuccino awaits. S x' That answered her question. She entered the hospital and made her way along to the office.

"Good morning, Sami," she said politely.

"Good morning," he replied, in his doctor's tone. "Did you have a busy weekend?" He looked up at her and raised an eyebrow.

"Been catching up with sleep," she struggled, taking a sip of her waiting drink.

"After all that skating," he grinned, then made some gestures and poses, of the balletic kind, with his arms. Victoria wasn't in the mood and scowled at him unimpressed, then gave a wry smile.

"Stop extracting the urine," she said calmly.

He sensed a difference in her mood today, so he began to talk about work. He explained that he had to go to the monthly meeting today. Every second Monday of the month, there was a meeting for Sami, James and Andy, which generally lasted for two to three hours. There was a bone marrow biopsy to do on a patient who was admitted to the ward last night, and the usual ward round was her job that day. Verity was aware that she would be in charge of the Outpatient Area. After leaving his instructions, he gathered his files and left the office.

Victoria had a busy schedule. Bernie and Dawn accompanied her on the ward round. She spoke to each patient and wrote the treatment plan in their notes. She realised it had taken her considerable time to do the round, so she took a quick break before attending to the bone marrow. She had phone calls to deal with in-between work. One was from a GP wanting advice on a patient; another was from Accident and Emergency regarding a patient with a suspected intracranial bleed taking Warfarin. She advised them to contact the laboratory for some Beriplex. Finally, she made it to the laboratory to prepare the bone marrow. While there, a message appeared in her inbox.

'Sorry, I won't be able to make lunch today. I'm meeting a lady. I will catch up later. S x'

"Mum, what time are you doing lunch? I may accompany you."

"Probably never, if you bring one of those down," Carol laughed.

"I'll get this done and be ready to go."

"Where's Sami?" asked Carol.

"At meetings, then lunch with a woman," she replied, nonchalantly. There was no doubt in her mind that he was behaving strangely. She went to the ward and performed the biopsy, and then took the aspirates, slides, and trephine to the laboratory.

Victoria and Carol headed to the cafeteria. Victoria chose a jacket potato with tuna and salad, while Carol opted for a lasagne. After settling at one of the tables, Victoria saw Sami having lunch with 'the lady' at another table. Considering he was a man of few words and didn't speak to many people, he seemed engrossed in conversation.

"Who is she?" asked Carol.

"I don't know. He didn't say."

"Maybe it's his ex," said Carol with a giggle.

"I doubt it," replied Victoria. "She looks too elderly for that, unless he was a toy boy." They laughed. The woman was dressed in a white blouse with a plum-coloured cardigan and had shoulder-length greying hair.

"You'll have to ask him later," said Carol, growing very curious.

"I wouldn't give him the satisfaction. He'll tell me if there is anything to tell. Otherwise, it's not my business."

But Victoria was curious to know the mystery woman's identity. She watched as they both stood up, and he shook her hand as they said their goodbyes. No doubt he would go back to the office, and she wasn't in any rush to join him. She returned just in time for the clinic.

As she entered the office, he asked if she could start the clinic alone as he had some paperwork to do. Victoria nodded and wheeled the trolley of files, which Charmaine had left earlier, out of the office and along the corridor towards the Outpatient Department.

It seems as though he is trying to avoid me.

39

As it happened, Sami didn't get his paperwork done. He had to assist Verity in the Day Treatment Unit, as a patient had reacted severely to their treatment. The infusion was stopped and the patient was admitted for observation. It was unfortunate that Victoria was doing the clinic, as this would have been a good learning experience. Later, when she returned, Sami explained the afternoon's events and exactly what they had done to rectify the situation.

Victoria then had a quick break before going to the laboratory to finish the blood films. When she returned to the office, she noticed Sami's briefcase had disappeared. He had gone home. He'd been behaving strangely ever since that near-kiss the previous Friday evening. She'd hardly seen him all day, which was unusual as she had always worked with him at some part of the day. It was as though he was trying to avoid her.

Maybe he is embarrassed about the near-kiss? Or perhaps it is just my imagination?

She picked up her belongings and went home for the evening. There was no exchange of texts between them.

The next couple of days passed similarly. By then, she knew that she hadn't imagined it. Even their conversations were strained and not as relaxed as usual. She decided that she needed to discuss it with him and clear the air. She got her opportunity to do so on Wednesday afternoon. Sami was doing his paperwork, but his thoughts were disturbed by the most surprising words.

"You know that kiss?" she blurted out. Sami looked up in bewilderment and stared at her.

"What are you talking about?"

"That kiss we had last Friday night, in the car."

"What about it?" he muttered.

"It was different somehow; did you not think?"

"Not really." He was starting to feel uncomfortable.

"So you didn't notice?" Victoria kept on with her questions.

"OK, it doesn't matter." She picked up her bag and started walking towards the door.

"What didn't I notice?" Victoria stopped and turned around.

"Well, it felt different; it sort of lingered." He knew she was right. His eyes were wide and attentive now, but he was panicking inside.

Shit, he thought.

"Ever since that moment, you've been different. You have been cold and distant towards me, even lied to me, and I need to know why."

"Whoa, hang on a minute," he interrupted. That word stung him like a wasp.

"Lied to you? I haven't done that," he exclaimed.

"You have." She walked over to his desk and showed him the evidence.

"This text was read at 10.30 am. There's your reply saying you had just read it at 14.30."

His heart sank as he knew he had dug himself a deep hole. That had never been his intention. He'd never wanted to hurt her feelings. He was ashamed and stared at his paperwork, not wanting to look at her.

"You can't tell me things are not different, because they are," she continued. "So, if the kiss was no different and you felt nothing, then fine, but please do not be dishonest with me. I thought we were colleagues and good friends." Her voice quivered as she held back the tears.

"We are," he said, reaching out to touch her arm, but she snatched it away.

"Friends show each other mutual respect and honesty. Decide whether you still want me as your friend or just a colleague. Tell me. Don't pussyfoot around, avoiding me and being economical with the truth." She turned and stormed out of the office, clashing the door behind her.

"Good night, everyone," she said to the nurses, who stood there gaping at her. It seemed that they had overheard the conversation.

Sami sat with his head cupped in his hands. He hadn't handled things well, and he'd hurt her feelings. He needed to apologise as he had felt scared, knowing that his feelings had run out of control. She was as sharp as a needle and hadn't missed a trick. He discarded his paperwork as he could no longer concentrate.

Later at the gym, Sami vented his frustration on the punchbags.

"What on earth is up with you tonight?" asked Richard.

"I think I've ruined everything with Victoria," he replied, and told Richard the tale. Richard rolled his eyes in exasperation.

"You need to apologise and buy her some flowers. She'll come around." Sami wasn't as convinced.

40

Victoria decided to go to work at her usual time. She felt relieved after confronting Sami yesterday but, at the same time, thought she shouldn't have spoken to him in the manner she did. It was her turn to buy the coffees and Barbara, the night nurse, gave her a sparkling smile as she approached the office.

"Good morning, Barbara," she said, as she entered the office.

Sami was sitting in his usual place, and it was as though he hadn't moved since the previous night.

"Good morning, Sami," Victoria greeted him politely and placed his latte beside the desk.

"Look," she said, breaking the silence. "I apologise for how I spoke to you last night and for leaving the office the way I did." He didn't reply. She continued to her desk and spotted a bouquet.

"Oh! Who sent these?"

"Why don't you read the card?" Sami said, calmly.

She opened the card, which said, 'Dear Victoria, I apologise profusely for being a fool. I hope you will still be my friend as I value our friendship. Love, Sami x' She stood speechless as she hadn't expected them to be from him.

"Thank you, they are lovely." She placed the card in the flowers and hugged him.

"I've missed being your friend."

Her sweet perfume intoxicated his nostrils with a powerful desire. He felt relieved that she had forgiven him. Victoria realised that Sami only wanted a friend. It had been foolish of her to get excited and think otherwise. She must compose herself, act professionally and treat him as a friend and work colleague. She needed to set her sights elsewhere for a romantic connection. Finding someone else, after the special times she'd spent with Sami, would be challenging, but necessary.

I need to get fit again. Maybe lose some weight. That way I'll look more attractive. Could I maybe join a gym? I might even meet someone there.

They all seemed like good ideas. She decided to consider the gym options online during her break. She grabbed a sandwich and a coffee at lunchtime and returned to the office. She fired up the computer.

I could also go skating. However, once a week won't be enough.

She looked at Body Heaven gym, which wasn't far from her home. It was £18.99 per month for unlimited usage, open 24 hours, and it could be cancelled at any time without being held to a contract. It sounded ideal, although she'd need an induction to learn to use all the equipment.

Sami walked into the office with a sandwich and sat at his desk. He was about to switch on his computer when he glanced at Victoria's screen and saw the website for Body Heaven.

"Are you thinking of joining a gym?"

"Yes," she replied. "I need to get fit."

"I thought you were going skating at the weekend?"

"It's not enough," said Victoria. "I need to exercise more than once a week."

She flipped onto a contact page to send an email about booking an induction session. Sami watched her.

"Why don't you just join? You can easily cancel if you don't like it."

"I need a trainer to instruct me on how to use the equipment. It all looks so sophisticated," she said, as she continued to type her email.

"Why don't you come along with me? I'll show you how to use the equipment."

"You go to Jimbo's. I'm signing up for Body Heaven as it is closer to where I live."

"Well, sign up for Jimbo's. You can book for one day only, and then I will show you."

After the fireworks display, she didn't want to become involved with him outside of work again. She wanted him to stay as 'work Sami'. Warning bells began to ring in her mind. That was the Sami she was seeing now, professional at work and friends in the office. Not the complete Dr Ice, which her other colleagues saw, but also not as loving as the Sami she'd seen at the fireworks display. He noted her hesitation and then said, "At least think about it," as he turned to his computer to catch up with some work.

Victoria considered his offer.

Is it so wrong to meet him once, outside of work? He could show me around the equipment during one session. When I get home, I can sign up with Body Heaven and start going alone.

It all seemed very civil, so she decided to accept his offer. Before leaving that evening, she informed him that she would like to go to the gym with him sometime, so they arranged to go after work on the following Monday evening.

41

On the following Monday evening, Sami left work with a spring in his step. They had arranged to meet inside Jimbo's at six o'clock. Victoria needed to go home first and decide what to wear. She chose some grey jogging bottoms and a plum-coloured polo top. Upon her arrival at Jimbo's, she saw Sami's red mustang in the carpark, so she headed into the building and typed in her PIN.

The gym was airy and spacious with different equipment; a particular area for lifting weights, and a side room for aerobics and spin classes. There were a few people, all of whom must have come straight from work. She spotted a sign saying 'Ladies' and headed there, hoping to place her belongings in a locker. As she looked across the gym, she noticed Sami in the weight-lifting area with a blond-haired man. He waved when he saw her, and she promptly waved back.

"That's Victoria," said Sami to Richard. "I said I'd help her to get fit."

"You must take her on a proper date."

"All in good time, my friend," said Sami, knowing that they'd already had that conversation. Victoria appeared out of the changing rooms and walked towards them.

"Hi, Sami," she said politely. Sami introduced her to Richard, his lifelong friend, whom he had known from school. Victoria had already heard Sami speak of him and remembered seeing him at the garage that day. She took out her hand to shake his and said, "Nice to meet you."

"Likewise," Richard replied.

"Sami, you didn't tell me you had company tonight. I don't want to interfere with your time with your friend ..." She was interrupted.

"Don't mind him. He's a big boy and can look after himself." They smirked at each other, and then Sami indicated for Victoria to follow him.

"Come on. I'll show you how to work the treadmill." He took her to a free treadmill and switched it on. He showed her the settings and how to alter them. Victoria climbed on and started her workout. She decided to do fifteen minutes and see how she felt. Sami returned to the weight-lifting area while she continued her brisk walk.

He kept glancing across at her and his eyes became aware of her bottom as she exercised. It wobbled very attractively as she stepped, making him smile as it reminded him of two large, sweet plums moving in synchronisation beside each other. She was certainly very attractive.

He spent the evening showing her how to use the rowing machine and the cross-trainer, and she also went on the exercise bike. Then she went to an area to do some floor exercises, which she had learned from her skating days. By that time, she had broken into a sweat and was feeling tired. Sami and Richard looked as though they were calling it a night too and they came over to where she was sitting.

"Have you enjoyed it?" asked Sami.

"It's been great."

"Would you like to come to the bar for a drink before you go home?"

"No thanks. I don't want to intrude on any more of your time."

"You're not intruding and, besides, it would be nice to get to know you," said Richard, before Sami could reply.

Victoria hesitated then said, "OK then, just one as I don't want to be home late." She could have kicked herself for giving in and not sticking to her decision. *But then she thought, what harm can one drink do?*

The problem was that he was being nice. Sami all over again like he was at the fireworks display. She had to be strong and not fall into that trap again. The time was cheerful and pleasant, with Richard doing most of the talking. It was a more neutral situation having him there, and he seemed lovely. However, when the offer came for a second drink, Victoria politely declined and insisted that she needed to get home as she hadn't eaten her evening meal. She thanked Sami for his help and then bid them goodbye before disappearing through the door.

"It's going to be a while before I gain her confidence again," Sami said to Richard, as he sensed her eagerness to leave. He wondered if she would come there again or sign up at Body Heaven.

"Continue to be your charming self, and you will win her over. Don't go cold on her again. If you feel something nice happening, you need to follow it and see where the journey takes you."

"You're right."

Victoria felt stiff while eating her evening meal, so she decided to have a bath. Once submerged up to her neck in warm fragrant bathing bubbles, she laid her head back on the ledge and relaxed. Her mind floated to the events of that evening.

She had enjoyed her time at the gym and the drinks afterwards. Sami was an excellent instructor as far as showing her the equipment had been concerned, and she'd noticed he had a few solid weight-lifting muscles which she'd never seen at work under his shirts and jackets. He had a nice torso. She felt pleased that he had a lovely friend like Richard. She had learned, in the bar, that Richard was married to Janice, and they had an eighteen-month-old daughter, Sarah. Sami was so relaxed in his company, and they teased each other, as good friends do. She had never seen him like that before.

She realised that there were many sides to his character which people didn't see. What she saw that night was the 'real' Sami, yet he earned the name 'Dr Ice' because of how he was at work. She wished she could see the 'real' Sami more, as he was so damned nice. However, the 'work' Sami seemed to be the way she would have to accept him.

She had a dilemma. Did she sign up with Body Heaven, and go it alone with her fitness regime, or did she sign up at Jimbo's and continue her exercise plan in the company of Sami and Richard?

She knew what her heart wanted but decided to give it a few days of careful consideration.

42

The following day, Victoria ached all over. Her thigh muscle was sore, so she rubbed ointment into it before leaving for work. She hobbled into the office she shared with Sami.

"Good morning, Sami."

"Good morning, Victoria. Feeling a bit stiff?" He stifled a smile.

"I ache everywhere. I've found muscles I didn't know existed." She sipped the cappuccino he'd bought for her. He could not hold back any longer, and he burst out laughing.

"Why are you laughing?" Victoria was puzzled as he rarely laughed at work. He got up from his chair and mimicked her painful walk.

"Excuse me, Madam, I just need to take your blood pressure," and he mocked what he thought she would be like, working on the ward.

"So you think this is funny?"

She picked up a pen and playfully threw it in his direction. He laughed as he picked up the pen and threw it back towards her.

"Did you hear laughter from that room?" Dawn asked, at the nurses' station. "I'm sure I heard Dr Prakesh laugh."

"Laugh? He's incapable of that," mocked Josie, as she straightened her uniform and flicked her hair to one side with her long fingernails. Just then, laughter rang out again from inside the office. They all heard it that time.

"I wonder what's going on?" asked Bernie.

The door opened, and out limped Victoria.

"What's the matter?" asked Bernie. "Is everything alright?"

"Just a bit sore from the gym," explained Victoria.

Sami walked past in the direction of James's office and uttered, "Wimp," in a low voice as he passed her.

"I feel as though I've lost my horse," she said, to which everyone started chuckling.

As the day continued, Victoria's muscle pain eased slightly. However, she could not wait to get home and have a long hot soak in the bath. Sami asked her if she was going to go back.

"We are going on Friday after work if you'd like to join us again?"

"I'd love to. I might be less sore by then."

She had found herself saying the words before she'd even thought about the situation. She had made up her mind. She would become a member of Jimbo's and improve her fitness with Sami and Richard.

43

Two weeks passed, with Victoria continuing her fitness regime at the gym, following work, with Sami and Richard. Their friendship had blossomed, and Victoria had lost some weight. She checked the bathroom scales one morning and discovered she had lost half a stone, due to doing more exercise and reducing her consumption of cakes. She felt very pleased with herself.

As Victoria walked past the nurses' station that afternoon, Charmaine was selling some tickets.

"Would you like to come to the Christmas party, Victoria?" she asked. "There will be a buffet, disco and drinks."

"Yes, that sounds great. I'll buy a ticket. How much are they?"

"Thirty pounds."

Victoria got some money out of her purse. She wondered if Sami had purchased any tickets. Probably not, so she would buy him one.

"I'll have two, please." Victoria offered sixty pounds to Charmaine.

"Ah, it's just for staff, I'm afraid. You cannot bring friends," Charmaine said sympathetically.

"The other one is for Sami."

There was a sudden silence.

"Sami?" queried Charmaine.

"Yes, I presume he hasn't bought a ticket."

"No," she continued. "He never goes."

"I'm sure I can persuade him," said Victoria.

"Good luck with that then."

Charmaine took the money and gave her the tickets.

Victoria knew that Sami liked to enjoy himself away from work. She had seen a different side to him. He wasn't the Dr Ice they all seemed to think he was. She took the tickets into the office and placed them in her purse.

Sami entered the office and saw Victoria rummaging in her handbag.

"Silly lot," he grumbled, as Victoria looked up at him, puzzled.

"They all started giggling as I walked past. No doubt, some joke at my expense," he muttered, and sat down, not looking up. Victoria had learned to keep a straight face since working with him, but sometimes he made that difficult as he could be so funny without realising. She guessed the nurses were still gossiping about the likelihood of his appearance at the Christmas party.

"Oh, I forgot to mention," said Victoria, suddenly, "that Charmaine came in earlier, selling tickets for the Christmas party, so I've bought one for you." She rustled in the back of her purse, pulled out the ticket, and offered it to him.

"I don't go to the Christmas party," he said, looking at the ticket.

"Why not? It will be fun" said Victoria, enthusiastically. He took a deep breath.

"I'm not fond of mixing with staff outside of work."

"You mix with me," she retorted.

"You're different," he paused, choosing his words carefully. "You're the exception to the rule."

He gave a small laugh but felt guilty about her having bought him a ticket.

"So you're not coming?" Victoria was disappointed as she had thought it might have been an ideal time to get closer to him. Sami sighed again.

"I don't know. Now you have bought the ticket, I'll wait and see how I feel."

So it's not a NO, she thought.

"I'll keep your ticket in case you change your mind," she said, putting it back in her purse.

On the days leading up to the weekend, the ward staff speculated whether Sami would go to the party. Most people thought he wouldn't appear. However, Victoria remained optimistic. It would be good for the other staff to see 'real' Sami and not the cold, brusque person they saw at work daily. Victoria had another plan up her sleeve, as she wanted to buy a new dress and look good. She arranged to go to town with her mother on Saturday. She would send Sami photographs of herself, in the dresses.

So Carol and Victoria set off into town around lunchtime. They had pre-booked a table at Leonie's restaurant, as Carol knew the owner and had been there several times. They served good food and had waitress service. Leonie was an older lady who had retired, but one always felt her presence. She was generally there on weekends.

A waitress escorted them to a table and handed them both a menu. The restaurant had an older style décor with linen tablecloths and stylish wall lamps.

"I think I'll have my usual ham omelette, but I'll ask if I can have a jacket potato instead of chips," said Victoria.

"You are taking this fitness regime seriously, aren't you?" asked Carol.

"I've got to look good in my new dress."

"Carol!"

She heard the familiar voice of Leonie approaching the table.

"How are you, my darling? How lovely to see you."

The woman gave Carol an affectionate hug.

"Everyone is OK, thanks, Leonie."

"No Paul today?"

"Ah no, this is a ladies' shopping trip."

Both ladies laughed. Leonie was unmistakable with her dark hair combed back into a bun and large sparkling rocks on her fingers She took their order and gave it to the waitress.

Of course, any friends of Leonie got the best service. Their meals were ready quickly, and Leonie returned to sit and chat with them.

"Carol, you haven't been in for a while," said Leonie.

"I generally don't get much time to come into town on the weekend. I work many Saturdays too, and it gets quite difficult to swap them."

"You must be retiring soon?"

"Hopefully, in another couple of years."

Leonie couldn't persuade them to eat dessert, so the two friends hugged each other again and said their goodbyes.

In the department store, Victoria looked at several dresses. She selected three to try on and asked Carol to take photographs of her in them so she could send them to Sami. A pale blue silk and lace dress with a full skirt, a black lace dress, and a stunning red dress. She sent them to Sami and awaited a reply.

Sami was at the supermarket doing his shopping when the photographs came through. He was shocked to see pictures of Victoria in the three dresses. She had mentioned something to him about moving on in life and, if there were any potential men at the party, she wanted to look attractive.

So why is she asking me?

He returned a message telling her to go for the red one as she looked stunning in it. He struggled to continue shopping and felt quite hot under the collar. His phone pinged again, with a photo of a red underwear set.

'Do you think these will match the dress?'

Jesus.

He felt his face going crimson. He was distracted by the thought of her wearing those under that dress.

My goodness, perhaps I could be the lucky man peeling those off next week.

He had to take deep breaths to keep calm, as he realised if he did get that far, he wouldn't be able to stop the inevitable. Another text arrived.

'Have you changed your mind about going to the party next week, V x'

'I'm still not sure. Will see how I feel, S x'

Having seen Victoria in her dress, he was becoming more eager to attend the party.

Maybe it's what I need. To go and see Victoria enjoying herself with friends and drinking an alcoholic beverage. Her guard may be down just a little, then maybe I could gently make my move.

44

On Monday, Victoria entered the ward to start her working day and noticed Dawn was in early.

"Hi Victoria, did you have a good weekend?" she asked, with an excited cheery voice.

"Yes, thanks. I bought my outfit for the party." Victoria took out her phone and showed her the photo she'd sent to Sami.

"Wow, that's gorgeous! I got a black lace outfit last weekend. I'm getting so excited, and I can't wait!" Dawn had a big smile, and her eyes opened wide at the thought of the party on Friday.

"Do you know if Dr Prakesh is coming yet?"

"I don't know," replied Victoria. "He sent a text over the weekend saying he'd see how he felt on the night."

"I reckon it's a no," said Dawn.

"Probably," said Victoria, "but it won't spoil our fun."

She then turned and entered the office. Sami was, as always, sitting at his computer.

"Good morning, Sami. Did you have a good weekend?"

"Good morning, Victoria, My weekend was quite boring until I received a photo of a stunning woman in a red dress," he mused.

Victoria was surprised at his words.

"Oh! So who is she?"

He didn't reply and just nodded his head with a wry smile. He changed the subject to work talk and gave her instructions on the tasks she needed to do that day as he had a meeting with James Turnbull.

The atmosphere in the ward was buzzing with excitement at the impending party, and the conversation kept drifting towards Sami, and whether or not he would appear. Victoria decided not to ask him anymore as she wanted to enjoy herself.

She remembered her disappointment after the firework display. She didn't want to feel that over Christmas. She remembered that he only wanted a friend at the end of the day, and she would accept his earlier comment as a compliment. Friday came around very quickly. Sami gave Victoria two hours of annual leave to prepare herself for the party and said he would finish off work. Andy Bartholomew was also keen to leave early as he was attending the party with his wife.

"Will I see you later?" she decided to ask before she left.

"You may, but probably not," he said before she left the office.

She couldn't help feeling a pang of disappointment as she had hoped that maybe she could move closer to him that night and see how he reacted. She guessed it wouldn't happen.

"However, if you want a lift home, give me a call," he said suddenly. "I won't be in bed until late anyway."

"I can't possibly do that if you're not coming out."

"You can, and I want you to be safe. The offer is there."

"Well, thank you. That is kind."

"Have a good time," he said as she left the office.

Sami didn't like parties. They weren't his thing at all, and he intended to give Victoria the money back for the ticket. That was until she sent him that photograph last weekend. He'd kept it in his photo gallery and had looked at it several times during the week. He knew he was falling for her in a big way and wanted to see her in that dress.

He thought he might secretly go later, when she wouldn't expect him.

45

Victoria had a nice long soak in the bath and washed her hair. She took it slowly to get dressed in her silky underwear and tights before finally slipping into her dress. She had to ask her mother to fasten it. She wanted her hair to remain loose as Sami had liked it that way at his birthday party, but she decided to curl it to give it more body. Finally, the taxi arrived at half past seven and then headed to Dawn's flat and Susan's home to take them all to the venue.

Sami had a shower that evening. On the off chance that Victoria should come home with him that night, he wanted every part of his body to be squeaky clean. After all, it had been a while since she'd had a boyfriend. He'd even bought condoms in case Victoria didn't use contraception. He pulled on a pair of Calvin Klein underpants and black trousers that fitted quite tightly around his buttocks, enhancing their shape. Then he sat and watched TV with his shirt ready to pull on later before he left.

Once at the party, the girls found a round table in an alcove at the back of the room. They bought drinks and chatted excitedly as the disco music thundered in the background. Gradually, people started to appear on the dance floor. Soon, there was an announcement saying that the buffet was serving food.

"Let's go and grab some food. I'm starving," said Victoria, and they trooped to the buffet while Bernie and Margaret Rose guarded their belongings.

Victoria stood in the queue at the back of their little group when she sensed a presence behind her. She turned around and saw a blond man, with a smiling face, holding a piece of mistletoe above her head.

"Happy Christmas, lovely lady."

He was quite charming with his smile and a twinkle in his eye. Victoria looked at him, then the mistletoe he held above her. She shook her head.

"What the hell are you doing? I don't know even know you and I'm about to eat," she snapped.

"OK, I'll come back later," said the man and put the mistletoe back in his jacket.

What a cheek.

"Who's he?" whispered Dawn.

"I've no idea," replied Victoria. "Let's get our food and return to the table."

The experience with the blond man had unnerved Victoria. It was true she wanted to meet new people, but when they were too confident and wanted to kiss without speaking first, that was too fast for her. It made her think of Sami and how she wished he would come to this party. He had been a perfect gentleman taking her places and inviting her to his home, taking the time to get to know her. Then there was that near kiss. Maybe he had just been nervous. If only he had come tonight, she could have tried to gain his confidence. She realised she wasn't interested in the blond man or anyone else. Sami had her heart.

She sat at the end of the round table and, a bit later, the blond man approached her again.

"Hello," he said, with his quirky smile and sparkling eyes.

"Hello," said Victoria with some reluctance. "I don't take kindly to people trying to kiss me before I even know them."

"Are you going to move along so I can sit down?" he asked. Victoria refused, as there was little enough room without him adding to the equation.

"I apologise. I should introduce myself. I'm Chris," he said, as he held out his hand for an introductory handshake.

"Victoria," she said, mustering up some enthusiasm to return the handshake. *At least I know his name now.*

"So you work in haematology?" he continued.

"Yes," she replied. She wasn't going to say she was a doctor; she never did upon meeting someone.

"I'm a foundation year one doctor in the Accident and Emergency Department," he informed her. "Can I buy you a drink? What are you drinking?"

"Gin and tonic, please," she replied, and he disappeared off to the bar.

At least that will get rid of him for a bit.

"Looks like you've stirred up an interest, Victoria," smiled Dawn. "You should go for it. It'll teach the Iceman a lesson for not coming." Victoria nodded and gave a little smile, but her heart wasn't interested.

At least Chris had taken the time to introduce himself and offered to buy a drink, but I wish Sami had come to the party. It seems he doesn't want a relationship. I must try and move on.

Sami was sitting at home, debating whether to go to the party or not, when his phone beeped. It wasn't Victoria as he expected; it was a text from Bernie.

'If you have any interest in Victoria, then you need to get here quickly. Another man is chasing her, love Bernie.'

"Damn," he muttered.

I should have gone earlier.

He hadn't heard from Victoria, as he'd expected, at some point in the night.

No wonder, if she's interested in some other guy.

He got up, pulled on his shirt, zapped the remote to switch off the TV, topped himself up with deodorant and aftershave, and promptly left the house. On the way, he began to panic about what he would see inside the venue.

Would Victoria be in the arms of another man? He couldn't handle that at all. *She's my Victoria.* He'd worked long and hard to build up the friendship, hoping it might lead to more even though he was scared at first and, after all, he helped her choose her outfit!

While Chris was at the bar, Victoria and her friends headed to the dance floor. After finally being served, Chris saw them dancing, so he raised the glass so that Victoria could see that he had bought it for her. Victoria indicated a 'thank you' with her hand and continued to dance with her friends, in the hope that he would disappear off somewhere else.

Instead, he came over to dance with them. He put his arms around Victoria as he danced. He was indeed a good mover. After a while, they all decided to go and have a rest and consume their drinks. Chris suddenly kissed Victoria passionately before leaving the dance floor, which surprised her.

He's not so bad, she thought, so she decided to let him sit at the table and chat. Eventually, she took a sip of the gin and tonic and scowled.

Ugh. That's awful.

It was very strong, like he had bought a double or even a treble. She continued chatting but began to feel a bit hot and dizzy.

I don't know this guy. Is he trying to get me drunk?

She quickly excused herself, got up, and headed for the toilets. Once inside, she sat and rocked back and forth. The taste was still in her mouth and made her feel nauseous. As she left the toilet, she slipped to the bar and explained to the barmaid that she felt sick and asked for a glass of water with a slice of lemon. She stood behind a group of people to remain unseen by her party. She felt rude, but she needed to slip away. She wasn't enjoying this party. She had begun to trust Chris but not now. She no longer wanted his pursuit. She was panicking.

I even kissed him and thought he was OK. Now I don't trust him. I need to escape. Why doesn't Sami want a relationship? He did offer me a lift. Maybe I should phone him. None of my colleagues seem to be missing me.

She decided to slip out unnoticed and dashed down the stairs in tears. As she turned the corner into the lobby, in her haste, she ran straight into the arms of Sami Prakesh.

"Victoria, are you alright?" he asked, as the encounter was unexpected. She looked up in surprise.

"Sami, you came," she said, as she flung her arms around his neck. "I've never been so pleased to see you."

"You look stunning," he said and grabbed her hands, holding them. "But are you alright? Where were you running off to?"

"I was just going to phone you."

"Why? What's the matter?" He placed a concerned arm around her shoulder, and she told him the tale about the guy who had been chasing her. At first, she danced with him and then kissed him. He had bought her a gin and tonic.

"It tasted foul, and I don't feel well, Sami."

"Well, I'm here now," he soothed, and she suddenly felt much safer in his arms. "Let's take you back to my place."

He left her arm around his shoulder and walked her back to his car. Before she got in, she started to retch and vomited on the grass outside. There was sweat on her brow. After a few moments, she felt better and climbed into Sami's car.

"Why did you decide to come?" she asked him.

"I changed my mind. I wanted to see you in your red dress." He decided not to mention the text from Bernie. He was glad she'd sent the message, or he wouldn't have come and found Victoria running down the stairs.

She took out her phone and sent Dawn a text.

'Hi, Dawn. I don't feel well, so I'm getting a taxi home. Please don't drink the pink gin, V x.'

Dawn replied, 'Wondered where you were. Hope you are better soon, D xx'

Victoria sent another message to her mother to say she wouldn't be home that night.

When Sami arrived outside his home, Victoria put her arm around his neck and kissed his cheek and said, "Thank you for rescuing me tonight."

"The pleasure is mine. How are you feeling now?"

"A little better, thanks."

When they got inside, he made her a coffee and placed it on the coffee table. She had taken off her shoes and tights, before sitting on the settee. She felt very foolish telling Sami about the evening.

He probably thinks I'm immature and cannot look after myself. But I feel so safe in his arms and his house.

He went upstairs, brought down the pillow and duvet from the spare bedroom, and tucked her up on his settee.

"Now have your drink," he said.

"I'm sorry I spoilt the party for you."

"What party? I didn't get that far," he laughed.

"I know. You decide to go to the party, and I spoil it for you."

"I don't care," he replied. "All I care about is that you're safe."

Victoria drank her coffee and promptly fell asleep on the couch.

46

Sami liked watching Victoria sleep. Her heavy breathing and little snores made him smile. He gently ran his fingers through her soft hair, further dishevelling it. She gave a sigh and then closed her eyes again.

Sami took the remote and switched on his TV. He flipped through the channels, but nothing interested him, so he left a music channel playing in the background. He looked at Victoria again. She was sound asleep. He decided to go upstairs and change into his night boxers, then he returned and lay on the couch with her. She looked so sexy in her dress, and he could smell the intoxicating scent of her perfume. He placed his arms around her body and had the best sleep.

Victoria woke him. She was trying to get up as she needed the bathroom. He sat up and rubbed his eyes.

"Would you like a drink?" he asked.

"Water, please."

He got up and filled two glasses. On her return, they drank the water and promptly lay down again.

"Do you mind me being here?" he asked.

"No," she said. "I'm sorry I fell asleep. I must be such boring company."

"*You?* Never," he said, as he put his arm around her. "I've enjoyed listening to you snore."

"I don't snore," she retorted.

"Yes, you do," he laughed playfully. "A bit anyway."

He turned off the TV and leaned over, to place the remote back on the table. An overwhelming desire overcame him again to kiss her, but he decided against it after the night she'd just had. He needed to earn her trust. He loved her. He wanted to touch her but was afraid, after having ruined things the last time. He needed to be patient. At least she was with him.

At that moment, she took his hand and squeezed it. He could feel his heart racing, as he felt an erection in his boxer shorts.

Christ, what is she doing to me?

He hoped she wouldn't notice.

She had noticed. She'd seen how Sami had become very hot and that his breathing had become rapid, yet still, he lay there!

She was going to have to make the first move. She knew he must want her, and she wanted him badly too. She took the plunge and pressed her lips against his. Their kiss became deep and passionate. He moved on top of her and searched the back of her throat. He pushed his hands behind her back, feeling for her zip. He wanted her clothes off.

"Hmm," she gasped. He stopped and stood up. He indicated for her to stand up too. He unzipped her dress and let it fall to the floor, revealing her matching bra and panties. *Jesus.*

"I'll be back in a minute."

He darted upstairs to get one of the condoms, then came back down. He took her in his arms and laid her across the settee. He kissed her again and slowly worked his way down, starting by kissing the swell of her breasts and teasing the edge of her bra. She reached behind her back to loosen it, and give him access to her whole breast.

He soon had her breasts enveloped in his mouth. She groaned with pleasure as he licked them with his tongue. His kisses became more profound as he devoured her skin, moving down toward her genital area. His penis was throbbing as he placed the condom on it before inserting it deep into her vagina, where he drew immense pleasure from being enveloped by her vaginal wall. As he thrust deep inside her and rubbed against her clitoris, her gasps and cries became louder until she uttered a cry of joy when she reached her climax. He continued thrusting into her until he felt his release. His hot juice flowed inside her, and pleasure rippled through his body. He gave his cry of ecstasy.

As their breathlessness calmed, he spoke.

"I love you, Victoria Pemberton."

"I love you too."

They fell asleep in each other's arms.

47

"What happened last night?" she asked, coming straight to the point.

"What do you mean?"

"Between us?"

"Do I need to explain?" He laughed and smiled at her, pushing a strand of hair behind her ear. She paused, collecting her thoughts, then continued.

"I remember a conversation we had in the office once. I distinctly remember you saying you weren't looking for a relationship. Then after the events of 5th November, we ended up falling out. I don't want you turning weird again."

"That won't happen this time. Last time I shocked myself with the depth of feeling I have for you, and I didn't know how to handle it. I'm sorry."

"What happened to the man that said he didn't want love?"

"A strange woman breezed into his office one day, bringing joy, laughter, and sunshine into his life. He changed his mind and developed feelings he could no longer control. Victoria, I cannot explain it at all. It happened, I desire you, and we're here. End of story."

"So I melted the Iceman?"

"You did," he replied. "Let's see where the journey takes us. There is just one thing. I can't offer marriage as I cannot commit to anyone else after Angela. If you want more and you meet someone in the future who will commit, I shall stand back and let you go."

"That doesn't bother me. I'm happy for us to stay as we are," replied Victoria. They kissed again, and then Sami looked at his clock.

"My mother is coming this morning," he said.

"Oh well, I'll go and make myself scarce …"

Before she could get up, he pushed her back onto the settee, and said, "There's plenty of time yet," he whispered. "Enough time to do this."

He climbed back on top of her and began kissing her naked breasts, exploring each cell of her skin with his tongue. She gasped in delight as she felt the passion growing within her again. His desire for her was immense, and his heart beat faster, as he moved further down and felt her body writhing in pleasure below him. He pushed open her thighs, and her vagina was wet and waiting. He inserted his erection with expertise and propelled it back and forth within her, listening to her gasps become louder and louder until she cried out in ecstasy. He continued to thrust within her until he felt his orgasm ripple through, giving him his release. They then lay awhile in each other's arms, before Sami turned and spoke.

"My goodness, what have you done to me? I haven't felt like this for a long time."

"Neither have I."

Victoria had reached a point where she needed someone to love her physically but hadn't found anyone suitable. She could hardly believe that it had happened with Sami. She secretly hoped that she could spend more time with him that weekend. They got up, as Anne's arrival was imminent. Victoria wanted to disappear before she arrived, but Sami wanted her to stay. He looked forward to telling his mother the news about Victoria. He poured some cereal into a bowl for her, and they were eating breakfast when Anne arrived.

"Mum, I have some news," he said, as Anne walked in. "Victoria has agreed to be my girlfriend."

"Oh, that's wonderful news!" She embraced Victoria and the joyous look on her face was evident.

"I'm so happy that you're together at last. I feel like all my Christmases have come at once. I'm delighted!" The poor tearful woman could hardly contain her pleasure.

"Sami, no present for me this Christmas. You have just given me the best present ever! Welcome to the fold, Victoria.

48

"Your mother is overjoyed," said Victoria, once they were in the car.

"Yes, they've been trying to pair me with someone for ages, but it hasn't worked. I think they'd given up hope," he laughed. "Will you come back later? Bring your overnight bag and stay all weekend. I want us to be together."

"Yes, I'd love to," she replied.

"I'll send you a text when I return from shopping. Just come anytime you're ready." He parked outside Victoria's home, took her in his arms, and passionately kissed her. She gave him a wave when he drove off.

Victoria went indoors and saw her mother ironing.

"Did you have a good time last night?"

"Yes, it was great."

Victoria headed up the stairs and had a long shower. She packed her overnight bag and slipped on a comfortable pair of jeans and a blouse, before drying her hair. She took her time, knowing that she would have to break the news to her mother. She entered the kitchen to make some tea. She took some biscuits and cups into the lounge and sat down.

"Mum, Paul, I have some news." Carol and Paul suddenly looked up and frowned.

"News?" enquired Carol. Victoria paused and took a deep breath.

"Sami and I are together now," she announced. There was silence for a moment, and then Carol spoke.

"Oh, that's great!" It hadn't surprised her, as she had noticed their closeness recently.

"I'm pleased for you, Love. I'm glad you have found someone that will make you happy." She knew that Victoria had not settled with anyone since Neil had died, so it was a relief that she was finally moving on.

Then she added, "I hope he does make you happy."

As I know how miserable and frosty he can be.

"He does, Mum," Victoria replied.

"Are you here for dinner?" replied Paul, as he was the household's cook.

"No, I'm going back to Sami's later. He's invited me to stay for the weekend. I'll walk the dogs and go there later this afternoon."

After finishing her drink, Victoria got up and fetched the dog leads. The sight and sound of the leads meant a walk. Suddenly the place was full of life, with two dogs barking excitedly.

She took Meg and Reggie for their usual walk up the hill, behind their house into some playing fields, where they could have a good run. She threw a ball and they tore off, racing each other to fetch it and bring it back to her. She looked at the road below, as the traffic rumbled by. She could see the road that led to Sami's parents' bungalow. Knowing that Anne was with Sami, Imran would be there alone. She wondered how he would react to Anne's news.

She missed Sami and ached for him during their few hours apart.

Sami was in the supermarket, doing his weekly shopping. He wasn't the best cook but got by, living on his own, and pasta was one of his favourite dishes. He could make a good Pasta Alfredo. He decided to buy ingredients for that and a few other things to accompany it. He purchased a tub of ice cream and some chocolate cake for dessert. Once outside his home, he sent Victoria a quick text.

'Hi, Victoria. I'm back at home. Come anytime you're ready. Love Sami x' He had missed her like crazy when they'd been apart.

Imran Prakesh was sitting in his lounge, reading the newspaper when Anne returned home.

"Imran, Imran! You'll never guess what's happened," said Anne, in an excited voice. Imran continued to read his newspaper as though he hadn't heard her. He never knew why his wife had to visit their son and do his housework every Saturday morning. The boy was an adult. If he couldn't manage, he could pay for a cleaner. At least it gave him some quiet time to read his newspaper undisturbed.

Anne came bursting into the lounge, beaming from ear to ear.

"I have some wonderful news," she said excitedly. "Sami has got a girlfriend! Remember Victoria, who came for dinner on his birthday?"

How could I forget?

"He just announced it to me earlier. I think I'll invite her for lunch tomorrow. We need to welcome her into the family."

"Steady on, Woman," Imran snapped. "They are just dating. They are not getting married."

"It's a start," she replied. "It's taken him seven years to get here!" She didn't understand why Imran wasn't sharing her excitement.

"It's fine, do whatever you want," Imran replied, wanting some peace to finish reading his paper. He didn't share Anne's enthusiasm as he had a plan for Sami, and this turn of events would likely destroy his agenda.

49

Later that evening, Sami set the table for dinner. He was cooking the Pasta Alfredo which he made regularly, so it didn't take him long to prepare.

"Do you need help with anything?" asked Victoria, walking into the kitchen, and glancing towards the cooker.

"Hmmm, that looks nice," she said, as she watched Sami stirring the sauce with a spoon.

"No, it's all under control. You can get out the glasses and pour the wine." Victoria took a couple of glasses from the shelf and placed them on the table. Then she took the cold bottle out of the fridge and poured a serving into each glass. Sami poured the sauce into the pasta and continued stirring until it was the correct consistency.

"Hmmm, it's lovely," praised Victoria, as she took her first mouthful. "You are an excellent cook." That was something else she would never have thought possible, on the first day she had met him.

"Thank you," replied Sami, feeling pleased that she was enjoying his food. "I cook well enough to get by with living on my own."

"What else do you cook?" Victoria enquired, taking a sip from her wine glass.

"I make curry sometimes," he replied. "However, I remember you saying once that you are not a fan of curry."

"A mild curry like Chicken Korma is fine. I don't like anything too spicy."

"We will eat that another time, now that I know."

"I guess we still have a lot to learn about each other," Victoria said, as she smiled and added more wine to their glasses.

"I guess we do," Sami laughed. "So, how did your parents react to the news?"

"They were fine," Victoria replied. "Although, not as excited as your mum. However, they did say that they hoped we would be happy together. It's about the best I could expect."

"At least it was positive."

"My mother will be fine with everything. However, if you ever hurt me, she will intervene," laughed Victoria.

"That's an instinct for parents," he said, smiling.

Victoria placed the dishes in the dishwasher after they had finished their meal. She was happy to have the vanilla ice cream alone for dessert, while Sami had a slice of chocolate cake with his.

"Not watching your figure today?" Victoria teased.

"Your memory is far too good," Sami retorted. "Besides, it's a special weekend."

"Special?"

"Yes. Our first weekend as a couple," he said, looking at her longingly with his deep dark eyes. They ate their dessert and cleared away.

"Now go upstairs into my bedroom and undress. I will follow you in a few moments."

Victoria was surprised, but she didn't argue. Giving him a cheeky smile, she left the kitchen and climbed the stairs. She went into his bedroom, which smelt of his gorgeous aftershave. Anne had made the bed perfectly with a silver grey duvet cover with a black striped pattern. After taking off her clothes, she climbed under the duvet and waited.

Sami came upstairs and saw Victoria under his duvet. The thought of her naked body under it aroused him. He undressed and pulled back the duvet. She was a beautiful sight.

"I want to make love to you. I want to show you how deep my feelings are for you."

Her heart raced as he knelt on the floor at the bottom of the bed. Clasping her leg with his hands, he started to nibble her toes with his tongue and continued with a trail of kisses inside each leg. She moaned as every nerve in her body tingled as he moved higher up her leg and found her clitoris. He swirled his tongue on it as he manipulated her thighs. She gasped at his touch.

Then he moved further up, placing another trail of kisses along the length of each arm before tasting her gorgeous breasts, placing kisses around each one before sucking on her nipples. He wanted her just as she wanted him.

He ran his tongue down her stomach, placing his fingers on her clitoris. She was wet and waiting for him. He took a condom, put it on his erection, and entered her, slowly at first. Then he began to thrust deep inside her, in and out, harder, kissing her cheeks, lips and forehead as he did so.

She moaned. She rocked her hips, taking him deeper inside, feeling his penis rub against her inner walls. He noticed her moans getting faster and her passion building within. He continued pulsing into her, releasing a cry as a bolt of pleasure rippled through his entire being. She moaned as she felt her orgasm wash over her.

He collapsed beside her, and they lay in each other's arms until their breathing slowed. He suddenly felt dehydrated, so he fetched two glasses of water. Victoria took a huge gulp.

"I needed that drink," she gasped. They lay with their bodies entwined and fell fast asleep.

The following day, Sami woke up to a vile smell.

My goodness, what is that smell? He suddenly jumped up, as realisation hit him. Then he saw something move. Mitzi was in her litter tray. Victoria was still sleeping but had turned to face the opposite way.

"Oh no, you haven't?" he whispered. "Of all mornings, you choose today, you smelly little cat."

"Meow, meow." Mitzi jumped off the litter tray and nestled back onto the bay windowsill where she always slept.

Victoria woke up at that point and heard Sami say, "Smelly little cat." Then, noticing the intense aroma that filled the air, she sat up and said, "When a girl has to go, a girl has to go."

"I really must apologise for this, Victoria. I'll go and clean it up. It stinks."

He picked up the cat litter tray and went downstairs with it. Victoria thought it was hilarious that his cat had caused him so much embarrassment. She looked over at Mitzi on the windowsill. It was as though the cat gave a little smile, knowing what she had done.

With the litter tray cleaned, Sami returned and placed it back on the floor. Then he went to the bathroom to get the air freshener. Victoria giggled again.

"Why are you laughing?" he asked, still annoyed with his embarrassing cat.

"It's you! You are just so funny," continued Victoria, still laughing. Sami shook his head.

"I'm glad I've provided the morning's entertainment."

"Animals do poo, Sami. It's a fact of life," she said, as she continued to laugh. "It's your reaction to it!" She leaned over to hold his arm.

Sami stared into space in utter disbelief. "It's not very romantic. The first lady I have here, and she goes and does that. I'll go and make us some coffee." He disappeared back down the stairs. Victoria got up and went to stroke the disgraced creature.

"I think you've embarrassed and upset your daddy, little one," whispered Victoria, continuing to snigger.

At least Victoria has seen the funny side, Sami thought, while he was downstairs.

He would move the litter tray into the spare room as he didn't want that to happen again.

"Coffee served by a naked man. I could get used to this," Victoria said, with a smile, as he returned to the bedroom. Sami shook his head. She loved to make him feel awkward. They sat and drank their coffee, but there was something on Victoria's mind that she needed to ask him.

"I want to know what happened with your wife, Sami." Sami had a feeling that the subject would raise its ugly head again.

"You pick your moments, Victoria," he sighed, not wanting to broach the subject.

"I can't understand how such a gentle and sensitive man like you, who is so caring and passionate, especially in bed, could be divorced. I can't understand why someone would want to let you go," she said, as she nuzzled up against his luscious torso.

It is a part of my life I want to forget. I have blocked it out for so long, but I expected Victoria might want to know at some point since our relationship has progressed.

He took a deep breath and chose his words carefully, telling her part of the story but not everything.

"I met Angela at a friend's house party. I spent time with her that evening, and we swapped phone numbers before going home. I later asked her out on a date and enjoyed her company. I was trying to escape from a possessive relationship at the time, with someone at university. After eighteen months, we got engaged and married a year later. It was the longest relationship I'd had at the time, but we were too young. Not long afterwards, I knew things weren't right. She married my title, not me. The reason we broke up was that she was unfaithful."

Victoria sat and listened, feeling shocked. She had always felt it hadn't been because he was cold and unaffectionate, as everyone at the hospital thought. She had seen a different side to him, from day one. However, an unfaithful wife? No wonder he didn't want to trust anyone again. She pulled him closer in a tight embrace.

"My God, I'm so sorry," she said. "That must have been traumatic for you. Did she have many affairs?"

"I don't know. Just the one I know of but, looking back, I reckon there were others."

"Did you ever try and work things through?" she asked.

"No," he said, adamantly. "From that moment, something changed within me. It was like a light switch moment. Any love I had ever felt, was gone in a flash." He clicked his fingers to indicate the power of his feelings, before saying, "I loathe the woman."

"Do you ever see her?" asked Victoria, remembering the mystery woman in the hospital.

"No. Angela has another partner and has moved further north," he replied.

"So you still hear about her?"

"Yes. Her mother, Cathy, attends the chest clinic. We usually meet for lunch when she has an appointment."

So that's who the mystery woman is.

"I can understand why you don't want another relationship," she whispered to him, sympathetically. He kissed her.

"At least not until you sneaked into my heart, through the back door," he laughed, stroking her cheek with his index finger. She leaned over to kiss him again.

"Her loss is my gain. I have the most wonderful man in the world lying here with me. He is kind, considerate, and loving. He has the sexiest body in the world and is a passionate lover. I can't understand her wanting to leave all that behind."

She massaged his pectoral muscles and ran her hands further down his stomach. She left a trail of kisses on his chest and then downwards towards his tummy button, when he squealed and let out a huge laugh.

"I've found your weakness too," she giggled. "You're ticklish."

Victoria touched his penis by manipulating her hand up and down its length. He laid back and gave a moan, his breathing suddenly becoming faster. She tickled his length with her tongue as he became harder and continued to moan. He sat up and flipped her over onto her back, taking in the sight of her breasts and hard nipples. He kissed them gently, giving each one a slight sharp nip.

"Oh," she moaned, at his touch. Her heart was pounding, and her face was flushed as she felt his naked skin rub against her flesh. Momentum gathered as they continued to kiss and caress each other, and then Sami placed his fingers on her clitoris, massaging it in a circular motion. She gasped with pleasure as he entered her again, thrusting vigorously until she cried with delight as her orgasm washed over her. He experienced a bolt of pleasure ripple through his entire being. They collapsed and lay on the bed with their legs entwined, each gently caressing the other's skin.

Later, Sami got up to make more coffee and poured some cereal into two bowls. He took their breakfast upstairs on a tray.

"What time are we going across to your parents?"

"About one o'clock this afternoon, so we have plenty of time."

50

At eleven o'clock, Sami climbed out of bed.

"I need a shower," he said, as he stretched, then slowly wandered towards the bathroom. Victoria gazed at his glorious body with the perfect buttocks she had previously admired at work.

He is so attractive that I can hardly believe he is the same man I met when I started my job. I could never have imagined then, that I'd end up in his bed.

Once showered, they got dressed. Victoria had taken a nice pair of dress trousers, and a blouse, to wear for lunch at Sami's parents. He had informed her that his mother wanted to make a special lunch to celebrate their union.

As they entered the house later, Anne greeted them with a lovely smile and hugs.

"Hello, my darlings," she said. "Do come in and take a seat."

Imran decided to be well-behaved as his wife was so delighted about their son acquiring a new girlfriend, and he didn't want to spoil her moment. When he saw them together, it was evident to him that his son was very fond of the young woman.

"Lunch is nearly ready, so please take your seats at the table," said Anne, bustling around doing what she did best. Victoria sympathised and offered her help. However, she refused, insisting that Victoria was the guest.

"You just sit and relax; it's all in hand," she said.

Anne served a lovely roast pork joint and carried through tureens, filled with various vegetables, for them to help themselves. She opened the bottle of wine and poured a serving for everyone except Sami, who was driving. He had a lime soda.

Anne picked up her glass and said, "I'd like to propose a toast. Here's to Sami and Victoria, for a long and happy relationship together." Everyone raised their glasses and clinked them.

"I shall certainly drink to that," said Sami, with a massive smile.

As they ate, Imran chose to ask Victoria how she was getting along with her registrar position.

"I love it," she replied. "It's a great place to work. I have a great team and a wonderful teacher."

She moved her hand across to touch Sami's and gave it a little squeeze.

"You will indeed be the best, having been trained by my son," Imran added, giving his cackling laugh. Then he paused and asked, "How will this affect you at work?"

Victoria didn't understand and looked puzzled, so Sami intervened and asked, "What do you mean, Father?"

"Well, now that you are in a relationship. Will that affect how you work together on the ward?"

"It won't make any difference," replied Victoria. "I still know my place there; we are both professionals."

"Ah, it's just that you women get fond of giving your orders," Imran said, wagging his finger; then gave his little laugh again as though he was only joking.

"Imran, leave them be," scolded Anne. "I'm sure they will continue to work together as true professionals."

"Are your parents pleased that you have found a nice consultant for a boyfriend?" he continued. Sami sighed and scowled at his father, wishing he wouldn't speak.

"They are delighted," said Victoria. "They only want me to be happy. I think they have been quite worried about me since Neil's death."

"Of course, that must have been such a difficult time for you," Anne soothed.

"Yes, it took a long time."

Not wanting to dwell on that subject, Victoria commented on the spread in front of them. "The food is gorgeous," she remarked. "The pork crackling has an exquisite taste. What did you add to it?"

"Mustard," Anne replied. "Two teaspoonfuls of Dijon mustard with three teaspoonfuls of grain mustard, and I spread it across the top of the joint with a knife before placing it in the oven."

"Wow! That's tasty," remarked Victoria.

Anne was pleased to receive such compliments. She could serve the pork with concrete as far as Imran and Sami were concerned, as they never seemed to notice. They just gobbled their food like hungry tigers.

"It's strawberries and cream for dessert. Is that all right with everyone?"

"It's perfect," said Victoria.

Anne began collecting the dinner plates, and Victoria got up to help carry the tureens into the kitchen. Thankfully Anne had a dishwasher, so the crockery was easily rinsed and placed inside it. Following the strawberries and cream, everyone went to sit and relax on the more comfortable sofa and armchairs in the lounge, while Anne made some coffee.

Imran spoke first.

"Sami, I am thinking of retiring soon, within the next two or three years." He paused, then asked, "Would you consider giving up your current job and taking my place at the practice?"

Sami sighed and took a deep breath.

"I haven't given it any thought, Dad."

He paused and continued, "There's a lot to consider, and I enjoy doing my job."

"I know, Son," said Imran. "I want to leave the practice in capable hands."

"Surely, if you advertise, you will find someone good. Or maybe someone already there can take your position and then advertise for a new doctor," Sami reasoned with him.

"Will you at least give it some thought, Son?" Imran asked. "Let me know either way."

"Yes, I'll think about it." It wasn't the first time Sami had spoken to his father about the subject, Anne explained to Victoria.

"It has always been a dream of Imran's to have Sami run the practice with him. It's not that he isn't proud of what Sami has achieved, but I think he hoped he would join him one day."

"How would you feel about bringing in more wages than your boyfriend, Victoria?" Imran asked, with a laugh.

He seems to keep asking odd questions.

"It wouldn't bother me in the slightest," she answered, sincerely.

Sami was getting annoyed.

"Why are we talking about this when Victoria is present? It is not very nice for her," he snapped. He felt that his father disapproved of Victoria and didn't understand why. After all, he had nagged him for long enough to find someone.

Imran didn't dislike Victoria. He just hoped that she would disappear of her own accord, as she was interfering with his plan. Of course, he could see that his son was smitten.

He would have to email Masood in the hope that he could cancel their plans.

51

Victoria and Sami called to see Carol and Paul on their way back after the lovely meal. This pleased the two excited dogs as, when Victoria entered the house, they gave her such a greeting, licking and pawing her and generally making a huge fuss. She put on their leads, took the ball, and headed on their usual walk. She threw the ball, and they ran to fetch it, bringing it back to her. From the field, it was possible to see Sami's parents' street, as Sami had pointed out.

"Your dad's proposition may be good for you," said Victoria. "After all, you do get stressed a lot at Lady Margaret's, don't you? Working at a GP surgery may be more relaxing and calmer."

"It won't be relaxing and calm with my father there," laughed Sami.

"I thought he wanted to retire?"

"He will not retire. He will keep going there, part-time perhaps, but if I wanted to modernise or change anything, he wouldn't budge. It would end up driving me nuts!"

"He'll not be able to work forever," said Victoria. "If he gives a definite retirement date, I would consider it, if I were you."

"He'll never do that. He thinks the place will fall apart without him."

Victoria threw the ball, and the two dogs ran excitedly towards it again. Reggie picked it up and ran back to Victoria, wagging his tail and dropping the ball in front of her. She threw it again. Next time it was Meg who got there first.

"Don't you two ever get tired?" Victoria said wearily.

"I get tired just watching them," laughed Sami.

Once back at Carol and Paul's, the two dogs had a long drink, then collapsed on the floor and fell asleep.

Later on, at Sami's place, he and Victoria ate a light tea of crackers with cheese after feeling a little full from Anne's lovely meal.

"Fancy watching a film?" asked Sami.

"Let's see what's on," said Victoria.

They chose a film about a teenage girl who went to a party and had a one-night stand. She discovered she was pregnant but was too afraid to tell her parents. So she packed her things and went on the run. It showed her adventures trying to keep one step ahead of those trying to find her. It was quite gripping and kept you on the edge of your seat. Mitzi came down the stairs and jumped in the middle of them, and Victoria gave her a little cuddle.

Sami got up to make more coffees and then settled onto the settee, moving closer to Victoria and putting his arm around her neck. He gazed into her beautiful blue eyes that had captivated him when they first met.

"This has been the most wonderful weekend of my life," he whispered gently. "Thank you so much for being here and agreeing to be my girlfriend. I know I'm not the easiest person to get along with."

"I always knew that, underneath the cool icy facade, there was a gentle soft person inside waiting to escape," she replied.

"You melted me," he laughed.

"I melted the Iceman."

"Such a pity the weekend is almost over."

"There will be others, and there's still tonight."

He kissed her lips tenderly, then with more intensity and passion. When they paused, Sami whispered in his husky voice, "It's time for bed."

When they both stood up, he flipped Victoria up in his arms, and she yelped.

"What are you doing?"

"I'm carrying you upstairs."

Once there, he laid Victoria on the bed and undressed her, kissing her gently at first, then becoming more passionate. He removed his clothes and continued, his soft caresses on her skin making her quiver in delight. Her heart raced as he began to suck her breasts and work his fingers down below.

She moved her hands up and down his muscles, caressing his buttocks with her fingers and then digging her nails into them. She moaned as he opened her thighs and swirled his finger on her clitoris. He felt very aroused and hard. Slipping on a condom, he inserted his erection into her vagina and propelled back and forth, gently at first, then more vigorously, the pleasure building inside her until she cried in ecstasy beneath him. Overwhelming pleasure washed over his whole body. He rolled over and collapsed beside her, wrapping his arms around her body.

"I love you, Victoria Pemberton."

"I love you too," she replied, nuzzling into his chest. Before long, they fell asleep in each other's arms.

52

Sami's alarm tinkled a tune at the side of his bed. He rolled over sleepily and knocked on the snooze button. He stretched himself, then thought, *fairy tale weekend over, and now it's back to reality.*

He looked at Victoria, sleeping peacefully, and gently kissed her lips. She stirred, stretching her body and opening her eyes.

"Good morning, Gorgeous," she said to him with a smile.

"Good morning," he whispered. "We have to get up, unfortunately."

"I'll let you shower first," she replied, rolling onto her side and snuggling back into the duvet. He stroked her soft, shiny hair.

"I thought *I* was bad in the morning," he said, smiling. Being a creature of habit, he did his usual check of the litter tray in the other room before disappearing into the bathroom.

As Victoria heard the shower water running, she got up and wandered into the bathroom. Sami was standing before her, naked, wet, and beautiful.

"What do you want?" he asked.

She walked over to the shower and climbed in beside him.

"I want *you*," she replied, taking the sponge out of his hand and continuing to lather his biceps, pectoral muscles, and his back.

Putting more gel on the sponge, she continued along each arm, then down towards his perfect buttocks, planting a gentle kiss on each. She gently bathed his legs and feet before returning to wash his penis. She dropped the sponge and manipulated the soap into it with her hands. Then she placed her mouth around it, leaving a trail of kisses on his length. She swirled her tongue along, then around the tip.

He grabbed the side of her head and cupped her face in his hands. He kissed her passionately. She knelt, then pushed his erection into the back of her throat and continued running her lips up and down, licking each part of him. The pleasure was quickly building within him, and he gasped and found his release.

"Oh God," he moaned.

"You are very naughty," he whispered, wanting to take her back to bed but knowing there wasn't the time as it was a work morning.

"Your turn," she smiled, handing him the sponge.

He threw it down, and she moaned at the feel of his strong hands kneading soap into her skin along each body contour. He embraced her in his arms and kissed her passionately under the running water.

"Our first shower together," she whispered.

"The first of many," he replied, "however we really must get ready."

53

They arrived at work later than usual; however, they still had time for their coffees and a quick check of their computers for any weekend news about the patients. Sami discussed the plans for the morning ahead and decided that Victoria needed to assist with the ward round. He then gave a big yawn.

"My goodness, I'm completely exhausted."

"Was the weekend too much for you?" Victoria giggled. He rubbed his brow and took a deep breath.

"A weekend of sex has not been part of my life for a long time, if ever. I'm out of practice."

Victoria giggled even more.

"It's all right for you!" he continued. "I'm on-call for the next two nights."

Victoria still chuckled at him as they gathered their papers and headed out of the office.

As they had shared their news on social media, it was the morning's gossip. Sami had guessed that would happen and kept his distance.

"Congratulations, you two," said Bernie, as they came out of the office. Dawn also came over and hugged Victoria. She quickly told her the other news of the night. The guy Chris, who had chased Victoria, eventually went back to sit with his department and ended up leaving with his arms all over another woman. It seemed that Josie had found herself a man too, which didn't surprise Victoria. After catching up with the news, she headed toward Sami.

"I wonder why he's attracted to *her?*" Josie suddenly spoke, looking across at Bernie and then Dawn. "She's no oil painting. Dull, boring, plain, and no make-up."

"She has a nice personality, unlike others around here," said Dawn.

"Josie haven't you got some duties to do?" snapped Margaret-Rose. Josie tutted, then strutted away like an irritated peacock.

It was a busy morning at Lady Margaret's. Sami found out that two additional patients had been admitted to the ward over the weekend. They needed blood tests and bone marrow biopsies.

As news circulated about the romance, other colleagues, such as Verity and Andy, came to convey their congratulations. Only one person wasn't amused at the information, and he called Sami to his office that morning.

"So I hear that you and Victoria have embarked upon a relationship," said James Turnbull, as he sat at his desk, scratching one side of his head with his fingers.

Sami took a deep breath and answered, "Yes, we have."

"I'm aware it's not my business, but you are in the position of being in a supervisory role to guide Victoria as she trains to become a consultant. Do you think it's a good idea?"

"You're right," said Sami, annoyed. "It's not your business." He stormed out of the office.

Victoria had gone to the laboratory to collect the slides and kits for the biopsies. While she was otherwise preoccupied, Sami went to see Verity in her office.

Damn! he suddenly remembered.

As he was so annoyed with James, he'd forgotten to submit an annual leave request.

"Do come in, Sami," Verity said smiling. "Congratulations on the wonderful news. I'm very pleased for you both." Verity was someone he'd always had a good rapport with. They often spoke about cats, as Verity had four of them, so there was a lot of common ground.

"Thank you. It's nice to hear someone say they're happy for us. James was miserable this morning. He's not at all happy about it."

"Oh, ignore him!" said Verity, throwing her hands in the air. "If he smiled, we would all wonder what he'd been doing." They both laughed.

"I was wondering if you could take Victoria under your wing this Wednesday. I want to take some annual leave to buy her a Christmas present."

"Of course," Verity replied. "Have you decided what to buy for her?"

"I have no idea," said Sami. "I'm hoping I'll see something which Victoria will like."

"What about some jewellery? Or some clothing?" Verity suggested, trying to give him a few ideas.

"I may call the laboratory later and ask Carol for ideas. If I buy clothes, I shall need to know her size."

"Yes, of course. That would help," laughed Verity. "I shall make sure she's fine in your absence."

"Great," Sami said, as he left the office.

He went to sit at his computer and typed an email.

'Hi James, Would it be possible to book a day of annual leave on Wednesday, following my on-call shift on Tuesday night? I have already spoken to Verity, who is happy to keep an eye on Victoria in my absence. Regards, Sami'

He pressed the 'send' button.

As Victoria was still busy doing the biopsies, Sami headed to the laboratory to speak to Carol.

"What does Victoria like?" he asked. "I'd like to buy her a Christmas present."

"What do you have in mind?" asked Carol.

"I'm not sure," he replied, as he placed his fingers on his chin, trying to think.

"I may buy her an item of jewellery," he said at last. "Or items of clothing, but I am unsure of her size."

"What type of clothing do you mean, Sami?" Carol asked. "A new top, or are you wanting to purchase underwear?"

Sami could feel himself turning a deep shade of crimson. He hadn't thought of underwear. Although Carol's suggestion was great, as he realised that sexy underwear would be a great present.

Carol sensed his embarrassment and tried to contain her smile.

"I will write down all of Victoria's sizes and bring them to you."

"That would be great," he said, then entered the side room to finish some bone marrow reports.

Carol entered the room, a few minutes later, to give Sami a piece of paper.

"It's much appreciated," replied Sami, as he placed it in the top pocket of his shirt.

Some nice underwear would be the perfect gift for Victoria. He remembered her red matching lace set, under her red dress last Friday, as he had undressed her for the first time. He needed to stop thinking such thoughts. He was on-call that night.

As Victoria prepared to go home, the haematology ward seemed quite busy. Sami bumped into her as she left the office and locked the door. He was in a sweat as he had been dashing around.

"Sami, is everything all right?" she asked.

"Sorry," he gasped. "It's just been rather busy."

"Do you want me to stay and help out for a while?"

"No, it's fine. You just get yourself home. I may be around for a while yet. I don't know when I'll get home to feed the cat."

"Do you want me to call in and feed her?" she asked. "I don't mind, and you won't be worrying."

Sami paused.

"Are you sure you don't mind?" as he placed his hands on her shoulders, feeling immensely relieved.

"Not at all, but I will need your key." Sami entered the office, took out his house key, and gave it to Victoria.

"Thanks," he said. "Call me when you get back, and I'll tell you my whereabouts." He gave her a quick kiss on her forehead, then spun around and disappeared into the ward.

Mitzi was asleep in her usual spot on the bay windowsill in Sami's bedroom. She was used to seeing Victoria now, as she was Daddy's friend. As long as Daddy liked her, she wanted her too.

"Mitzi!" called Victoria. "Come on, little cat. Come and eat your dinner."

The little black cat jumped from her bed, swishing her tail, then tiptoed down the stairs. She dived into the delicious cat food which Victoria had placed in her dish.

While she was eating, Victoria went round and closed Sami's curtains and decided to leave his lounge light on. She sat and drank coffee to keep Mitzi company for a while and gave her a stroke on the settee. Mitzi purred in delight and rubbed her face into Victoria's side. Sitting there, she wondered what Sami would eat for his tea. Had she been staying that night, she would have prepared a meal for him.

After a while, Mitzi jumped off the settee and headed upstairs to her favourite place. Victoria decided to head back to the hospital since Mitzi felt settled.

Sami's phone rang as he walked along the corridor.

"Hello. Dr Prakesh, haematology consultant," he said as if it were a recorded message.

"Hello, it's your sexy registrar here, ready and waiting for you," she giggled. She felt the relief in his voice, as it softened.

"Hi, Victoria. Come to the ward. I'm heading there now."

"Ok, see you soon," she replied and hung up.

Victoria saw Sami at the nurses' station, leaning over the desk, making some notes.

"Thank you for doing that," he said, taking the key from her hand. "I appreciate it. Is Mitzi ok?"

"Yes, she's fine. She ate all her food, and I've closed your curtains. Will you be long now?"

"Hopefully not," he replied. "I will see you around lunchtime tomorrow." Victoria leaned over to kiss him.

"See you tomorrow, Darling," she said as she went to leave the ward. Before she left, she heard a comment from one of the patients.

"Come on now, that's no good. Kiss the girl properly!"

Sami and Victoria smiled at each other, then he gave her a lingering kiss before she finally went home.

"That's more like it!" said the amused patient.

Later that evening, Victoria was in bed watching TV when her phone beeped. It was a text from Sami.

'I'm missing you like crazy. S x'

She messaged him back.

'I'm missing you too. What time did you get home? V x'

'Around 7.30 pm. I'm having my tea now. S x'

'I hope you get some sleep, Darling. V x'

'I can't sleep without you. It's crazy. I slept alone for seven years without a problem. Then, after a weekend with you, I miss your touch, perfume, taste, and presence. S x'

'I shall cuddle my pink bear tonight and pretend it's you, V x'

'I love you. I will let you sleep now. Good night. S x'

'I love you too. Good night. V x'

54

Sami slept until noon on Wednesday. He needed to get up promptly as he was going into town. It was a place he rarely ventured. However, he needed to buy Victoria some Christmas gifts.

He ate lunch at the department store in town. It seemed an excellent place to begin. He had already decided on underwear, but the thought of going into a ladies' underwear department made him feel self-conscious.

After he'd eaten, he decided to go there first. He looked around at the array of different coloured sets and tried to imagine Victoria in each one. *She would look sexy in them all, he thought.*

"Can I help you, sir?"

The assistant made him jump. He could feel his face turning crimson.

"I'm looking for some nice underwear for my girlfriend," he blurted out. "As a surprise for her Christmas present."

"Come this way," said the assistant, as she took him to a rack and handed him a lovely black lace set.

"This set is made of elastic lace and mesh material. It is a comfortable, lightweight fabric smooth against the skin, bringing comfort while still looking sexy and stylish."

"That's nice. My Victoria likes her comfort. I'll take it," said Sami.

He followed the assistant over to the desk and purchased the item. He felt quite relieved to leave that department.

Next, he looked at women's tops. He knew she liked animal designs. He came across a novelty T-shirt in black with the logo 'Just a girl who likes dogs' and the picture of a dog, which looked similar to the border terriers she walked for her parents. They had it in her size too. So he took it to the payment desk.

He then headed towards the novelty section and browsed a variety of items. He found some fluffy pink slipper bedsocks and a novelty coffee mug with chocolates inside, which he bought as smaller gifts.

He left the department store, feeling pleased with his purchases, and headed for the jewellers. Verity had suggested getting her something special, like a piece of jewellery. It was trying to decide on something she'd like. He stood rubbing his chin, with his forefinger and thumb, deep in thought. There was a necklace with the initial V on one side. Then he saw a tree of life pendant but decided against it as it was in sterling silver. Then a silhouette pendant caught his eye. It was a leaf design with some quality sparkling diamonds.

That's the one, it looks special.

He went inside to pay for it and had it specially gift-wrapped.

He also needed to wrap the other gifts at home that afternoon and hide them before Victoria arrived. He felt happy that he had been able to find those lovely items, and he looked forward to seeing her open them on Christmas Day.

He now needed to go to the supermarket to purchase the ingredients for a Chicken Korma, as he remembered Victoria saying that she liked that dish on the previous weekend.

55

Victoria had been in the Outpatient Department, working with Verity, as arranged. She finished promptly and arrived at Sami's house around five o'clock. Sami was busy in the kitchen, preparing the Chicken Korma, some plain basmati rice and naan bread.

"Wow. You're spoiling me," she said as she noticed that he had already set the table with wine glasses.

"Can I do anything to help?"

"No, it's all under control."

She noticed the coconut milk on the bench.

"Are you using this?"

"Yes, it gives creaminess without calories, and it's also rich in vitamins and minerals."

"You're a man who knows his curries."

"Not really. I don't often make curries, just on special occasions. I hope you enjoy it," he said, placing the dinner on the table. Victoria took her first mouthful.

"Hmm, it's delicious," she said, with her eyes open wide. "The wine is good too."

They chatted and Victoria told him about her working day with Verity.

"James mentioned my on-call duties, which start on 8th January," she said. "However, he needs to arrange my second on-call rota, so I think he will be speaking to you."

"I could do that. After all, you will be staying here most nights."

"I think he prefers the rota to be fair."

"I'll have a word with him tomorrow."

They cleared the dishes placing them all into the slimline dishwasher. Sami made some coffee, and they went to relax in the lounge.

They spent the evening wrapped in each other's arms, watching a film. As the credits rolled down the screen at the end, Sami stroked Victoria's cheek gently and kissed her passionately.

"I have missed you like crazy. I can't bear to be apart from you. Please come and stay again tomorrow."

"Yes, I will. I've missed you so much too." They kissed again more passionately.

"Come on. Let's go to bed."

Once upstairs, he was like a hungry wolf. He pulled her close and kissed her deeply, his tongue searching her throat. He unbuttoned her blouse roughly and threw it on the floor. He loosened her trousers, and they fell to her ankles. She pulled him closer and ripped off his shirt. He removed his pants and gently pushed her onto the bed.

Red-hot passion blazed from his lips. He tucked his arm under the small of her back and then pushed his hand down to squeeze her bottom. He gently nibbled her breasts with his tongue. Her heart raced, thumping hard against her chest wall as she dug her fingernails into his back. Then he left a trail of kisses down her stomach and towards her clitoris.

She moaned as her nerve endings tingled at the feel of his touch. He teased her, then turned her onto her stomach, nipping her bottom with his teeth. She grabbed his erection and rubbed her hand up and down his length. He moaned as he kissed her again and flipped her over onto her back. She arched her hips forward as she wanted him. He thrust himself inside her, pounding into the walls of her vagina, ensuring every part of him was inside. He released his hot liquid within her, groaning as he found his release. She gasped as she felt the pleasure of her orgasm ripple through her body.

He collapsed on the bed beside her, breathless, then he gently kissed her lips.

"I love you," he whispered, brushing his fingers through her messy hair.

"I love you too," she replied. They kissed softly again, wanting the night to last forever, sleeping in each other's arms.

56

It was the last weekend before Christmas. Sami was on call, so Victoria stayed at home and went to town with her mum to do some Christmas shopping. The city was bustling with shoppers, and the festivities were in full swing.

They started in the underwear department where Sami had stood only a few days earlier. Victoria decided to buy a unique item for him.

She then purchased a novelty bottle holder for Sami and a new dressing gown for Paul. Carol bought a few gifts for family members and a circle of friends.

Before leaving town to go home, they went to Leonie's restaurant for lunch. Leonie was surprised when Carol had called to reserve a table so soon after the last visit. She was delighted to hear that Victoria had a boyfriend and wanted her to bring the young man in for lunch sometime. They had a beautiful meal and exchanged Christmas greetings before leaving the restaurant.

Victoria spent the afternoon wrapping her Christmas presents and then organised them tidily in her wardrobe, ready for distribution the following week. She had arranged to visit Neil's parents that evening to give them presents and have a chat. Sami messaged Victoria while she was in her bedroom.

'Are you coming to visit this weekend? I miss you. S x'

'I have arranged to visit Neil's parents tonight. I'll come tomorrow after lunch.'

'I can't wait, Darling. I love you. S x'

'I love you too. V x'

Victoria ate her Sunday lunch and then helped Carol load the dishwasher. Then she took Meg and Reggie out for their usual walk on the fields behind the house. As she walked further along, she looked at the housing estate where Sami's parents lived. Victoria wondered if Sami was still there and whether he would ever break the habit of going there for Sunday lunch. She loved Anne, who cooked some delicious food, but wasn't keen on Imran and his awkward questions. She would love to cook Sunday lunch just for them one day; then they could have a glass of wine without the worry of someone having to drive. As she returned to her house, she felt a familiar cramp pain in her stomach. Her period had started.

She left to drive to Sami's in the early evening, as planned. He was taking a call when she arrived, so she made some coffee and took it through to the doctor's room in his house. Once the call finished, he circled his arm around her shoulders and kissed her passionately.

"Hello, Darling. I've missed you."

"Been busy?" she asked.

"I've taken a few calls today. A lot seems to be happening there." They sat and drank their coffee.

"I don't know if you want me to stay as I have my period."

"Of course, I want you to stay. I've been lonely without you, my darling. A quiet night watching TV is the perfect medicine."

Christmas Eve arrived, and Victoria had taken a half-day of annual leave. She made an appointment to renew her hair colour and remove the red streak, even though Sami hadn't mentioned it for a while. Then she had to buy gifts for her mother and visit the florist before the shops closed.

She visited Neil's grave on her way home and got everything else prepared for the next day. Then she had to place Sami's gifts in a large Christmas bag and pack her overnight things.

She had arranged to meet Sami at his home around seven o'clock. He had cooked a beef lasagne for their dinner, with ice cream for dessert and rosé wine cooling in the fridge. On his lounge table, he had filled a bowl of sweets for them to munch as they watched Christmas Eve television.

"Gosh, you've been busy," Victoria said.

"Of course. Only for my best girl," he replied.

Christmas this year was going to be very different for Sami. His usual plan was to stay with his parents for two days, so he felt very excited about doing something different with the special lady in his life. Victoria's plans would have followed a similar path too.

"So, what has happened to your red streak?" Sami asked.

"I had it removed and just wanted my natural colour this time. Besides, I know you weren't keen on it."

"It had grown on me," he replied.

After dinner, they took the glasses and the remainder of the wine to the lounge. One of the Christmas films was on TV, so they lay in each other's arms watching it. Sami had more wine cooling in the fridge, so he went to get it during the advert break. Later, once the film had finished, Victoria asked, "Can we open one of our presents tonight?"

"Tonight?"

"Yes."

"You are like a small child," Sami laughed. "You can't wait to dive in."

"No, I can't," she laughed too.

"Go on then," he said, relenting.

He went over to get the present he wanted her to open. She unwrapped it, pulled out the black t-shirt, and saw the picture of the border terrier, then the logo which said, 'Just a girl who likes dogs.' She held it up in front of her.

"Wow. That's wonderful, Sami. I love it. Thank you," she said excitedly, kissing him.

"Now, your turn," she said, as she jumped up and rummaged through his present bag.

She brought out a small present and gave it to him. He unwrapped it and took out a piece of clothing, holding it up in front of him. He looked puzzled.

"You want me to wear this?" he asked, looking at the black and red lace basque.

"No. It's for me to wear."

"So why have you wrapped it up for me?"

"Because when I wear it, you can have whatever your heart desires. It's for special occasions."

"I see," Sami said, but still looked rather surprised.

"Would you like a demonstration?" she asked.

"OK."

Victoria went upstairs and quickly got changed. She walked downstairs provocatively and struck a pose by the handrail.

"Dr Prakesh, what would you like this evening?"

He stared at the beautiful sight before him, not knowing what to say.

"Are you glad you're not on call?"

"Oh yes," he whispered, as she climbed onto his knee, straddling him. She unbuttoned his shirt and smothered his chest with soft kisses. He could feel her silk panties squirming on top of him, and her touch made him feel aroused.

"I want you to take it off so I can make love to you," he whispered in that husky voice.

"Not yet," she teased, as she pulled his lips towards hers, and then they kissed passionately.

"It has to stay on a little while," she said, as she slid her hands down to undo his trousers. She rolled onto the settee as he slipped them off.

"Let's go to bed," he said. As they stood up, he took her around the waist and lifted her over his shoulder. She gave out a cry.

"Eeeeh."

Upstairs, he threw her onto his bed.

"I feel like all my Christmases have come at once," he said, as he kissed her lips and then searched her throat deeply.

The silk of the garment against his skin felt erotic, as his hand traced the contours of her body. Then he pushed the garment to one side and teased her breasts with his tongue.

She manipulated her hands into his lean muscles, then dug her fingernails into his perfect buttocks. As he moved lower down, he realised he could undo the garment, and did just that. As he massaged the area with his fingers she melted in his arms.

"Kneel in front of me, my darling," he whispered.

She did as he asked, and he took her from behind. She felt his warmth sink into her and she heard his loud groan of satisfaction.

Breathless, they then lay beside each other until their breathing slowed.

"So that is your fantasy then?" Victoria asked.

"What?"

"Taking me from behind."

"No, it was just different."

"What is your fantasy, then?"

"Sex in the wild."

"You devil," she laughed. It's rather cold for that at this time of year. They lay with their bodies entwined, eventually falling asleep.

57

Mitzi jumped onto the bed, as though she realised it was Christmas and that she would get some extra treats. Victoria climbed out of bed, went downstairs, and got the Christmas bag.

Mitzi purred and pawed against Sami, waking him.

"What do you want, sweet girl?" he asked, stroking her fur. Victoria appeared with the presents.

"What have I got, Mitzi?" she asked, waving a present in the air.

She went back to bed and helped Mitzi open her present. It was a packet of treats which she opened and took two out. Mitzi wolfed them down.

"Don't be so greedy," said Sami, as she ate a couple more.

"That's enough," he said. "You'll need to hide them."

"Merry Christmas, Darling," Sami said, leaning over to kiss her.

"Merry Christmas to you too," she replied, and they kissed again.

She passed his next present out of the bag to open. He removed the packaging and looked at the box.

"Take it out," said Victoria.

He started to remove it and realised it was a wine bottle holder in the form of a golfer.

"That's lovely," he remarked. "It's very unusual. Thank you." He replaced it in the box.

"Now I need to get your presents and I'll make coffee too."

He disappeared for ten minutes and came back with the goods. As he sipped his coffee, he took another gift out for Victoria. She opened it. It was a novelty mug with chocolates inside.

"I love that," she said. "Thank you."

Victoria handed Sami the next package. She was interested to see what his reaction would be. He opened the package and took out the three shirts in different colours; lemon, green, and salmon.

"Will you wear those colours?" she asked.

"They're different," he remarked. "But no harm in trying. My parents only ever buy me blue and white."

He passed over her next gift, and said, "This one is special."

Victoria opened it and took the pretty necklace from its box.

"That's beautiful," she said, looking at the leaf pendant with sparkling diamonds. "I want to wear this today."

"Now for the last presents," said Sami.

They opened them together. Sami loved his coffee set, and Victoria loved her black lace underwear. She wanted to wear that today too.

After opening the presents, Sami and Victoria lay together for a while. They had both decided to visit their respective parents for lunch and meet again in the evening. In between, Victoria would walk the dogs, and they could meet in the field for some exercise.

Victoria wore her black lace underwear, new necklace, and black t-shirt. Sami wore his lemon shirt. He dropped her off at her parents' house, so she could have a drink on Christmas Day.

"See you later, Darling," he said. "Text me when you walk the dogs." She kissed him and then waved as he drove off.

Victoria presented her mother with a luxury smartwatch, which she was delighted with, and Paul loved his grey dressing gown with matching slippers. She went to help Paul with the vegetable preparation, and then indulged in some wine with Carol, as Sami was coming to collect her.

The roast turkey was delicious for Christmas dinner, with various vegetables and cranberry sauce. Then they consumed Christmas pudding with custard.

She came over tired and slept before gathering the energy to take the dogs for their walk. She messaged Sami as she left the house. He was waiting in the field as she approached. They held hands and walked, as the dogs bounded across the field.

"Are your parents having a good Christmas?" she asked.

"Yes. Mum enjoys every minute, of course, and Dad mentioned his proposition again."

"So what did you say?"

"I told him maybe in a few years. I'm not ready yet. I have a good position now and need to build a nest egg for the future. That has been so difficult since my divorce from Angela."

"Why is that?"

"The settlement took all my savings. That's why I'm reluctant to marry again."

"I'm not surprised."

Victoria liked the way he had opened up about Angela without being prompted.

"I'm glad I have my inheritance," she confided in him. "It was left to me by my father when he died."

"Your father is dead?" he asked.

"Yes. A few years ago. He had cancer. He wanted me to use it for travelling, but it has never happened since Neil died. I only went to America once, to visit Sandra."

"You are best keeping it in the bank," said Sami.

Victoria took the dogs home and, an hour later, Sami called to take her back to his home. As enjoyable as it was to see one's parents, they were both pleased to be able to relax together, and Sami was glad to have a Christmas beer. They sat watching films together, and ate crackers and cheese for supper.

"I've had a wonderful day," Victoria said.

"It's not over yet," replied Sami as he leaned over to kiss her.

"Then I need to put the basque on."

"Your surprise tonight," he said.

She went upstairs to change, then came down and straddled him on the settee. Their kiss was long and passionate.

"What do you want me to do to you?" he whispered in that husky voice.

"I want you in the doctor's room."

"As you wish."

Sami slipped his arm around her waist and hoisted her over his shoulder. He placed her on his bed, pulled aside her lace basque, and began to kiss her nipple. She gave a small gasp, then caressed the contours of his back. She undid his trouser button, aware of his erection inside. He wriggled out of his trousers and underpants and lay beside her. His tongue searched her tonsils as she grabbed his erection, massaging her hand up and down its length. He laid back and gave a moan, his breathing suddenly becoming faster. Then she tickled his length with her tongue as he became harder and moaned more.

He sat up and flipped her over onto her back, taking in the sight of her beautiful breasts. He kissed them gently, giving each one a slight sharp nip. She moaned at his touch. Her heart was pounding, and her face was flushed as she felt his naked skin rub against her flesh. Momentum gathered as he entered her, thrusting vigorously against her vaginal walls until she groaned as her orgasm washed over her. He experienced a bolt of pleasure ripple through his entire being.

They collapsed into each other's arms and lay together, eventually falling asleep.

58

Victoria woke to find Sami wasn't beside her.

Maybe he went to the bathroom, she thought.

However, when he didn't return, she got up to investigate. She found him upstairs in bed, asleep. She placed her arm tenderly around his shoulder and planted a kiss on his cheek. He opened his eyes to find her staring down at him.

"I missed you," she whispered.

"I couldn't sleep. That bed is too uncomfortable for two of us," he smiled and returned her kiss.

"I'll go and make coffee," she said, getting up and leaving the bedroom.

Auntie Susan had invited Victoria and Sami to her house. She always liked a family buffet on Boxing Day, and Anne always helped her prepare the food. Susan was Anne's younger sister, divorced with two grown-up daughters, Beverley and Karen. Beverley had children, Mark and Chloe, who were Sami's niece and nephew. Sami's grandmother, Rosy, would also be there. Victoria felt very apprehensive but looked forward to meeting them. It was her turn to drive so that Sami could have some beers.

The whole family was eager to meet Victoria, the woman who had captured Sami's heart. They knew that would never be an easy feat since his divorce from Angela. None of them had liked Angela, as she was above her station. Being married to Sami gave her the lifestyle she craved, with holidays, gym membership, and always out lunching with friends. A total opposite from Susan, who was also divorced, but had to work hard to bring up her daughters alone. She was pleased when Angela left, although horrified by the fact that her sister had to lend Sami money for the divorce settlement, as Angela had taken all his savings. It was no surprise that Sami had been adamant about remaining single. So they were intrigued about Victoria.

She dressed in some smart jeans, a long white blouse, and a thick jumper to meet Sami's family. They stopped at the supermarket on the way as Victoria never liked to visit people empty-handed. She purchased a bottle of wine and a box of biscuits to give to Susan.

Sami introduced Victoria to his Auntie Susan, cousins, nephew, and niece. She handed over the goodies. Everybody then poured drinks, and Victoria chose lemonade.

Susan and Anne had laid a generous spread over the table in the kitchen. They all took a plate and helped themselves to food.

Afterwards, they all wanted to know more about Victoria, so she sat and told them her life story and how she had accepted the registrar's job, where she met Sami. "What attracted you to Sami?" asked Susan.

"It wasn't instant," replied Victoria. "However, we connected as friends, and things developed from there. I always knew that, under his ice-cool exterior, there was a big softie," she laughed.

"Did removing his beard make a difference?" asked Beverley. "We all hated that beard," she laughed.

"When I finally saw his face, yes, it did," replied Victoria.

"We all know he did that for a reason," Beverley said.

Sami went crimson. *Not all this again, he thought.*

Victoria, who was sitting on his knee, turned towards him.

"Did you do that for me?" He took her hand in his and squeezed it.

"Yes, I did."

The other family members laughed, knowing they'd always been right. Victoria smiled but didn't laugh. She lay against his shoulder, hugging and squeezing him, realising Bernie had been right. He had been trying to woo her.

"Why didn't you just say you liked me?" she whispered.

"Rumour had it that you didn't date men with beards. Besides, I was nervous."

"Nervous? Why?"

"In case you didn't feel the same."

"So, come on, Sami, what about you? When did you feel the attraction?" asked Karen.

"Straight away," he replied. "I was instantly drawn to her baby blue eyes."

It was Victoria's turn to feel embarrassed. She hadn't known that the bearded straggly-haired man she shook hands with that day had felt an instant attraction. Then she thought about the cards and flowers she'd received quite early in her employment, and it all made sense.

It was clear to them all that Sami loved this woman. They had never seen him so happy, and it was as though he had withdrawn from a shell. They were impressed with Victoria too. She appeared to be genuinely kind. The type of person Sami needed in his life.

Later, after more drinks and food, Susan got the old family albums of Sami, Beverley, and Karen when they were young. Sami turned crimson again as Victoria was keen to look at them. There were ones of him pouting when he didn't get his way.

"That hasn't changed at all," Victoria laughed. There were others of him running around naked. It seemed he was fond of doing that when he was younger.

Imran sat in the corner, feeling very sheepish. He couldn't watch the TV as Mark and Chloe were playing computer games. He sat with his head in a newspaper but not reading it. He was half-watching and listening to the conversation around him, observing his son's happiness and realising he had made a terrible mistake with his plan.

He hoped and prayed he could cancel it.

59

It was back to reality the next day for Sami and Victoria as they returned to work and continued with ward rounds and patient care plans. Since the festivities were over, Sami took his Christmas tree and decorations down in the evening, assisted by Victoria, who also helped him tidy the place afterwards.

Victoria realised that her on calls were starting soon and began to get anxious about them. Sami comforted her and said that he would be by her side if anything was untoward. She felt relieved but realised that if she was going to be a consultant in the future, she would have to manage them alone.

"I have every faith in you," Sami said. "I'm on call over the New Year if you want some practice."

Since Sami was on call on New Year's Eve and New Year's Day, Victoria decided to spend New Year's Eve with her parents. They invited Sami for an evening meal. He was pleased as he didn't want to be alone.

As the chimes of Big Ben rang out on TV, Victoria, Sami, Carol, and Paul all clinked their glasses and gave each other a toast for the New Year.

"You're welcome to stay if you wish, Sami. Victoria has a double bed upstairs."

As much as he wanted to stay with her, he declined, as he didn't want his phone disturbing them all if he got calls. They arranged to have lunch with their respective parents the following day and spend the evening of New Year's Day together.

Victoria woke up late on New Year's Day, after the celebrations of the night before. She went to help Paul prepare lunch which they were having early, as Carol had to go to work at the laboratory at two o'clock. After a very filling roast pork lunch, Victoria felt the need to exercise the dogs, and once they heard the sound of their leads, they were as excited as ever. Sami was waiting at the field as Victoria walked towards it to take the dogs for their run.

"I'll be so glad to get back to the gym," she said.

"Me too," said Sami. "I've overindulged this year."

"I bet I've gained the half stone I lost," she laughed.

"You'll lose it again if I chase you round this field," he laughed, as she ran away and he chased after her. Of course, Victoria couldn't run fast, so she was no competition for him. He caught her, and they fell on the grass together, breathless.

"I've got a stitch now," she giggled.

Their lips met, and he kissed her long and passionately.

"Victoria Pemberton, you have made this the best Christmas ever."

Just then, a ball fell beside Sami's head, and the two dogs looked down on them, wondering what on earth they were doing. Victoria got up, lobbed the ball into the distance, and off they scampered again.

Later, Victoria drove to Sami's house with her overnight bag. Sami was still working, so they sat and watched TV in the doctor's room. She snuggled into his chest and caressed her fingers down his leg. Sami allowed her to answer a couple of calls for practice and she easily gave the correct advice.

"You see. You'll be fine," he said.

"I'm not looking forward to being disturbed overnight. I need my sleep."

"You get used to that," he replied. "And you don't need to go in until lunchtime the following day."

Victoria unbuttoned his shirt and placed some soft kisses on his torso.

"Please don't, in case the phone rings."

Victoria continued undoing his belt and unzipping his trousers. She placed her hand inside and touched his erection.

"You are naughty, Victoria Pemberton."

"You like naughty," she laughed, as he lay on his side and unbuttoned her blouse.

Victoria wriggled out of her clothes, succumbing to his gentle touch, and he teased her breasts gently with his tongue. She gasped with pleasure, and her heart began to race as he moved and touched her below. He felt her wetness as he moved on top and thrust his erection deep inside her. It propelled back and forth, rubbing against her vaginal walls until she cried in ecstasy. She felt his hot liquid release inside her as he groaned with pleasure.

The phone rang, and he reached over to answer it, feeling breathless. He got up, as he needed to check something on the computer. He gave the doctor his advice and then hung up.

"Just managed to fit that in on time," Victoria laughed.

"You're a tease," he said as he lay beside her again. They watched some TV, and later Victoria headed up to the main bedroom for the night.

60

It was the New Year.

Imran Prakesh left early to go to his GP practice in early January. He was one of the partners there, and it had always been his dream to work alongside his son one day. However, Sami was a consultant at the hospital and, although very proud of his son's achievement, Imran was disappointed that Sami never seemed keen to go into partnership with him.

Sami's private life had never been easy. He married Angela far too young, and it ended in divorce. No matter how hard he tried to introduce Sami to women, he never showed any interest.

He was particularly disappointed about Julie, as she had felt an attraction to him, but then he had met Victoria. While they had common ground, since she was a doctor and a career woman, she was not good family material. However, it seemed that Sami was in love with the woman, so Imran would have to cancel his plans. He decided it was a good time to send the email.

Dear Masood,

It is with regret that I have to cancel our arrangements for March. My son Sami has found a girlfriend and fallen in love.

I look forward to seeing you on our next visit to Bangladesh.

Kind Regards

Imran.

Victoria booked an appointment at the family planning clinic, as she needed birth control. She managed to get an appointment within four days and was given some birth control tablets. She was instructed to start taking them on the first day of her next period. She placed them in her bedside cupboard as that would be at least another two weeks away.

8th January arrived. Victoria felt rather apprehensive about her first night on call. She finished dealing with the patients for the evening and returned to Sami's place. He had gone home earlier and cooked some pasta for their evening meal. Victoria was thankful as she was hungry.

Her first phone call came through after the evening meal when she was relaxing in the lounge with a coffee. It was Jenny from the laboratory.

"I have an abnormal blood film for your attention. There are abnormal white cells and immature blasts on it."

"Can you send a digital photograph to my email, please?" asked Victoria. Jenny agreed and hung up. A few minutes later, a couple of photographs arrived. They were slightly blurred, so Victoria couldn't quite decide what the cells were. She showed the photo to Sami.

"They look a bit suspicious," he said. "Why don't you telephone the laboratory and ask Jenny to send another?"

She did that, and the following photograph was similar.

"I'll go in. I'd rather have a good look and make a better judgment."

"Call Accident and Emergency and ask them not to discharge the patient," Sami said.

Victoria entered the laboratory to look at the blood film and make her report, then she asked Jenny to prepare the sample to go to Central Hospital for flow cytometry, the following day.

Next, she went to the Accident and Emergency Department, to speak to the doctor with whom she had spoken earlier. As she walked along the corridor, she saw a familiar man but couldn't place where she had seen him before. As she got closer and saw his face, she realised it was the man from the party. He stared at her too, as though he was thinking the same thing.

"Chris?" she asked, as she looked at him. He frowned, then suddenly he realised who she was.

"The girl that disappeared from the party"

"Yes," she replied. "I'm sorry, but I didn't feel well."

"Even your friends didn't know where you had gone."

"I messaged one of them later."

"Well, once a girl stands me up, she gets no more chances," he said, shaking his head.

This guy has a large ego.

"I'm already spoken for," she retorted.

"So what brings you here?" he asked.

"I'm looking for Dr Chris Rogers."

"Why do you want to see him?"

"Are you always like this?" Victoria was getting irritated, and said, "I need to speak to him about a patient."

"Who?"

"That's none of your business," she said and continued to walk towards the central part of the ward.

"I am Dr Chris Rogers," he introduced himself. She turned and stared at him.

"And I am Dr Victoria Pemberton, the haematologist."

He looked at her, shocked.

Shit. I nearly pulled a consultant that night, he thought.

"I need to meet the patient, David Stoker, and his family," she continued. "I'll also need a private room to discuss my findings."

Two nurses were giggling at a workstation nearby, no doubt at Chris's expense. She gave them a wry smile.

Chris took Victoria to a room the F1 doctors used. It was empty as they were all busy with patients. He introduced Victoria to the patient and showed him and the family into the room.

"Some tea would be nice if you don't mind," she said to Chris.

Bossy bitch, he thought, but he did as she asked. At least it kept him away from the front line.

After making everyone tea, he asked Victoria and the family if he could sit and listen, as a learning experience for his studies. They agreed.

"OK," said Victoria, as she sat and faced the patient.

"Has anyone explained the findings to you?" she asked.

"Not really" said David "although I'm aware my white cell count is high."

"Would you like me to share my findings with you?"

"Yes, I'd like to know what's happening."

"All right" she paused. "I think you may have a form of leukaemia. We need to run some further tests to make a complete diagnosis. This will include further blood tests, bone marrow biopsy, and genetics testing to study your chromosomes, genes, and proteins. It may be best to admit you to hospital in order to carry out these investigations.

"What is the prognosis?" asked one of the relatives.

"It's too early to say as we need to do the testing first." There was silence in the room as the family tried to absorb the news.

"Are there any further questions you would like to ask?" There was no reply. It seemed a lot was going through their minds and they were processing emotions.

"You will be going onto the haematology ward and one of my colleagues will do the assessments tomorrow. In the meantime, if you think of anything at all, note it down on some paper and ask at a later time." She shook hands with them.

"I'll catch up with you tomorrow."

Chris Rogers listened, impressed with her knowledge. He made the necessary arrangements to get the patient admitted, while Victoria headed for the corridor to leave the Accident and Emergency Department.

"Going home already?" asked Chris Rogers, from behind her.

"Yes. I'm finished now."

"Part-timer," he joked.

Victoria made a cheeky face at him before she left.

When she got home, Sami reminded her to type notes into the computer so that he would receive them when he arrived at work the next day. They swapped over from the previous week, with Victoria occupying the doctor's room as Sami relaxed in his bed.

Victoria had handled her on-call week well, although she found it tiring being disturbed by the telephone. Sami was her second on-call person, which seemed more manageable as she stayed with him. He was there to help, but she hadn't needed to disturb him overnight.

The weekend came along, and they were a bit different. She had to go to the hospital in the mornings and see the haematology patients, as well as patients from other wards needing help and advice. It generally took the morning and part of the afternoon to complete those duties, sort out their treatment plans, and report any films left by the laboratory. Once finished, a Saturday afternoon seemed an appealing time to catch up with some of her administrative work with no distractions. Besides, Sami would still be out shopping.

As she switched off the computer and left the room, Carol stopped her.

"Would you mind not going yet? There's a baby sample here with a platelet count of two, and I'm just checking it."

"Ok. I'll wait." The repeat analysis was the same, and there was no clot in the sample, so Carol examined a blood film.

"No platelet clumping," she said, handing the film to Victoria.

Victoria returned to the side room to examine the film and make her report. She telephoned the ward with the result, asking for an urgent repeat to confirm the accuracy. Next, she phoned Sami and asked for his advice.

Sami suggested that they test for NAIT and transfer the infant to the Central Hospital. In the meantime, if the result was the same, to ask the laboratory to order neonatal platelets.

The second sample gave the same result, so Victoria made the necessary phone calls while Carol ordered the neonatal platelet pack on the online ordering site.

"Samples will be coming at some point to test for NAIT. Can they be stored and sent to the Central Hospital on Monday?"

"Yes, I'll deal with those."

"So can I go now, mother, before you find anything else?"

"Don't know about that," she replied. "I think you should stay until eight o'clock, like me." They both laughed.

"I'll go and walk the dogs."

Sami and Victoria ate lunch in the doctor's suite on Monday. Victoria had completed the ward round and sorted the patients' treatment plans for the day. Sami had his long monthly meeting with James and Andy. He was never a happy soul when he came out of those meetings. In his opinion, they were a waste of time when there were patients to be treated.

"James is just a paper-shuffler," he continued. "He was asking about your on calls and wants me to make a report on how they went and the situations you had to handle. I told him everything was fine, but that's never enough for that man."

"I can't remember every single call," said Victoria, astonished.

"We'll do it back at the office."

Victoria's phone rang in the office while she was in the bathroom, and Sami answered. It was Carol. He heaved a huge sigh and then said, "I'll pass it on."

Victoria saw his frustrated face as she returned to the office.

"What's up?" she asked.

"There's a positive malaria screen in the laboratory."

"Guess James will have to wait for his report," she smiled, as she left the office.

What's up with Sami? He didn't sound too happy on the telephone," said Carol, as Victoria entered the laboratory.

"He never is after those monthly meetings."

Carol was beside the laboratory sink. The blood films had been stained and were drying. The giemsa stain, used to identify the malarial species, had been specially prepared.

"So he's in a dark mood today?" asked Carol.

"Yes. It's darker than the giemsa stain you're using," Victoria laughed.

"So he's a darker shade of giemsa?"

"Exactly," they both laughed.

"Are the thick and thin films ready?"

"Yes, they're in the side room."

Victoria examined the films. The patient had travelled around Africa and returned home with flu-like symptoms. Victoria could see parasites. They looked like ring forms with the crescent-shaped gametocyte, diagnostic of plasmodium falciparum. She counted the parasitaemia to be 3%.

Carol entered with the giemsa films for Victoria to examine, which confirmed her findings as she saw the Maurer's Clefts, some membranous vacuoles which are sack-like structures in the red cell. They have the appearance of blue dots on the giemsa film.

She spoke to Dr Cameron in the Accident and Emergency ward, to discuss her findings. The patient was to be transferred to the Central Hospital for treatment, and the slides would have to be confirmed by a specialist laboratory.

Sami and Victoria met for a coffee and chatted about the positive malaria screen.

"Have you reported it to the CCDC?" he asked.

"No. It will need to be confirmed by the specialist lab."

"Ask the laboratory to do it. They keep a particular form." Back in the office, Victoria phoned Carol and, finally, she and Sami were able to sit and discuss the on calls.

Later, they went to do their work out at the gym. Victoria hadn't been since before Christmas and had gained some weight, so she felt stiff and unfit. She wanted to lose a stone, so she reduced her cake-eating and increased her exercise. They met Richard there and, after the workout, they had their usual drink accompanied by some dinner before going home.

Victoria took a deep, weary sigh as she sat on the settee.

"Do you fancy a holiday, Sami?"

"Holiday?" he looked at her in surprise.

"Yes. I feel exhausted from the on calls and the disturbed sleep. I could do with a break away somewhere."

"Where do you have in mind?"

"Scotland."

Sami hadn't been to Scotland before. However, Victoria had been as a youngster, with Carol and her father several times and more recently with Carol and Paul.

"Scotland?"

"It's beautiful up there," she said. "Magical."

"It'll be cold. Freezing," he grunted.

She spent the evening scrolling through potential cottages and found one in Aviemore.

"Aviemore," she said, excitedly. "It takes me back to my childhood when I used to do skating competitions up there. I'd love to go back."

"One thing you've forgotten," he mentioned. "We both need to be off work together, which means the others will need to cover the clinics and on calls."

"We can go when neither of us is on call," she said. "Let's ask James tomorrow."

"OK, we'll both ask him."

Victoria's big blue eyes were open wide with excitement. She was like a young child; something Sami loved about her.

The next day, Victoria was perhaps more eager to speak to James Turnbull, as they entered his office and enquired about a week off during the middle of February. He sat at his desk and scratched the side of his head with his forefinger.

"I will have to get back to you. I will need to arrange cover for the clinics." Later in the afternoon, he confirmed with Victoria that the annual leave had been approved as he had managed to get cover for the clinics. She could go home and book the cottage she had found called *Two Collie Dugs*.

Imran Prakesh checked his emails at work and looked at one with horror.

Dear Imran
I'm afraid we have booked our flights for 16th March and I'm unable to cancel as I cannot get a refund. I look forward to seeing you then and watching my daughter meet your wonderful son.
Kind Regards
Masood.

61

The weeks until 15th February passed very quickly. The alarm was set for six thirty the following day. Victoria leapt out of bed with joy.

"We're on holiday," she shouted excitedly, at the top of her voice.

"Do you have to make so much noise?" grunted Sami from under the duvet. He was looking forward to the trip but not with the same enthusiasm as Victoria. Holidays had always been mundane experiences for him. Travelling to India with his parents over the years, to visit family, always started well, but after a while he became bored. His former wife liked Spain, and holidays lounging in the sun, which also bored him. The Scottish Highlands had been Victoria's idea, but it was a whole new entity for him. She pulled the duvet off him and slapped his bottom.

"Don't be so grumpy," she said. "Get up while I go and make some coffee." If nothing else, she knew coffee would be the one thing to get Sami moving.

"You are such a child," sighed Sami, as he sat rubbing his eyes.

After coffee, they both showered and then Victoria packed the remainder of their belongings.

"Should we get going and then stop and have breakfast on the way?" she asked.

"Sounds a good idea," he replied, pulling on his trousers.

Sami packed the last bags in the car and saw that Victoria had a few things already stored in her boot.

"You have enough baggage to last for a month," he laughed.

"You never know what you may need, Sami. It's a varying climate up there. You need different types of clothing for all weathers."

They headed north and stopped at a restaurant to eat breakfast after an hour of travelling. There was a supermarket nearby where they collected a few provisions for the first night.

Soon they had crossed the Scottish border.

"Now I feel like I'm on holiday," said Victoria.

Sami merely nodded in agreement.

Victoria drove through Edinburgh via the port of Leith. Edinburgh was a busy city, and it always took a little while to navigate to the other side and head for the Forth Road Bridges.

The Queensferry Crossing is the gateway to the north and east of Scotland. It is 1.7 miles in length and the most significant three-tower cable-stayed bridge in the world. It is indeed a breathtaking sight. Sami took some photographs and recorded a video of the crossing.

"Wow! It's stunning," he remarked, looking upon it in awe.

"I guess you're in holiday mode now," Victoria said with a smile.

She had been to Scotland more recently with her mother and Paul and had watched the whole project during its construction.

Once the Queensferry Crossing had faded into the distance, the views on the roads ahead were stunning. They passed an array of colours, various shades of green, from the striking pine and spruce trees to the yellow gorse bushes and the contrasting purples and whites of the Scottish heather. The mountains were magnificently regal and stood bold in the background with exquisite charm. Different varieties of sheep and cows dotted the fields in the distance.

Victoria stopped at another coffee bar near Perth before making the final ascent north towards the Scottish Highlands.

Aviemore is a town in the Cairngorms National Park. During the mid-winter, it is a top-rated ski resort and a popular tourist spot all year round, particularly in the summer.

Following the satellite navigation directions, their holiday cottage was easy to find.

Two Collie Dugs was a cosy bungalow, nestled beneath the mountains in a peaceful setting, central to Aviemore. It was in a cul-de-sac of other cottages, each of which has its unique design.

The interior was delightful. It had a spacious lounge with a TV, two leather settees, and a dining table with four chairs at the rear. A large mirror took a dominant position over a fireplace. There are various pictures on the wall of collie dogs and other small animals. The bedroom had a nice double bed, with a view of the back garden and woods to the rear of the cottage.

"It's like being in the middle of a magic forest," said Sami. "You're right. It's stunning up here."

"It is," replied Victoria with her eyes open wide. "We will have a great time here away from it all."

They unpacked their belongings and settled into the cosy cottage. They decided on pizza for their evening meal from a place nearby and the cottage owner had generously left a complimentary bottle of wine. Sami placed the order by telephone, and they took a short walk to collect it half an hour later.

Sami was in the lounge, opening the pizza box and sorting the glasses for the wine when, suddenly, he heard Victoria call for him, but in a whisper.

"Sami, Sami! Come here now. Come quickly."

Wondering what was happening, Sami dashed through to the bedroom. Victoria was standing beside the window, moving the curtain to one side so she could see out.

As he entered the room, she whispered, "Look out there, Sami," and she pointed towards the window.

A pair of young fawn deer were in the field behind the cottage. They were eating the grass and then looking up at the surrounding area before taking another mouthful.

"Wow!" whispered Sami. "That's unbelievable. I've never been this close to deer before. I'm going to fetch my camera."

Victoria had already taken some shots with her phone. Sami came back and took some more photographs.

"My mother would love this place," he said. "It's incredible."

The deer remained for a few minutes before disappearing through the trees and into the woods.

"I'm going to be looking out for them all the time now," said Victoria. Sami understood what Victoria had previously said about loving nature and wildlife.

They returned to the lounge to eat their pizza and drink the wine. Afterwards, they just relaxed and watched the TV, allowing all the tension to seep out of their bodies. Later, Sami headed towards the bedroom, and Victoria sat in the lounge and read a book for a while, before following him to bed.

"How do you like it so far?" she asked him.

"I love it. It's a wonderful place."

She undressed slowly and climbed into bed next to him. His eyes settled on her bare breasts, filling him with desire. He kissed around their perimeter, softly at first. Then he nibbled her nipples playfully with his teeth. His touch felt electric.

She groaned with pleasure as he slid his fingers past her belly button to the inside of her thighs, touching her clitoris. She returned his deep kisses and their passion grew deeper as his tongue searched her tonsils.

"Oh," she moaned beneath him.

He flipped her over, kissing her. She was on top of him, her luscious breasts dangling in his face, and he placed his head between them, kissing one and then the other. Victoria grabbed his penis and manipulated its length, making him groan with pleasure. The condom was ready, and he slipped it on before entering her. At first, it was soft and gentle, then faster and deeper, increasing the rhythm while pushing his length within her, until she felt her release and cried out with pleasure. He continued pulsating deeper and deeper until he released his hot juices, with pleasure rippling through his body. He continued to kiss her lips softly and then gently cupped her face in his hands.

"I love you, my darling."

"I love you too," she replied, wrapping her arms around him before falling asleep with her head against his chest.

62

The next day, Victoria looked out of the bedroom window, but there were no deer outside.

It was quite a windy day, but the sun was shining, so they decided to take a drive up to Inverness, a city which is the gateway to the north of Scotland, then drive across the Black Isle to Chanonry Point, where it is possible to see dolphins swim. Victoria had checked online, and the best time to visit is one hour after the tide goes out, as they often come in to feed then.

Once they arrived and parked, they found a small beach area. They walked further along to where there was a gathering of people who had spotted dolphins swimming and doing backflips in the distance. Some had come prepared with binoculars and camera equipment to get a good view and the best photographs. However, Sami and Victoria were too far away to get good pictures on their phones.

"It is exciting to watch them in the distance," exclaimed Victoria. "Paul would love it here. He has a professional camera."

Sami inhaled the fresh air and looked at the scenic green countryside overlooking the Cromarty Firth. It was exhilarating and more refreshing than other places he'd visited. It was much more his style.

They headed away from Chanonry Point and found an ice cream shop nearby. Part of a holiday was sitting on a bench with ice cream and watching the world go by.

Victoria then took the Highland Tourist Route towards Elgin and Aberdeenshire. She turned off and took some scenic country roads known as the Snow Roads Scenic Route, where they could stop at specific points to take photographs of the spectacular views. The mountains proudly stood on each side of the road, boasting a mottled patchwork effect of green grass and purple heather. Sheep and cattle dotted the lower fields, and some even stopped at the roadside. Pretty gorse bushes added a spray of yellow. There was also the Malt Whisky Trail, but that was for another day.

They approached the village of Tomintoul, where Victoria stopped. They bought some water in a shop at the corner of the village green, which still boasted an old vermilion post box and telephone box. They then took the road leading to Braemar and passed through the Lecht Ski Centre with chair lifts. All was quiet there and it appeared to be closed, due to maintenance.

Braemar is a pretty village but rather expensive. Sami and Victoria stopped for coffee and snacks there and walked around before heading towards Pitlochry. Then it was back up to Aviemore.

Victoria was happy with the photographs she had taken of the Scottish countryside. She loaded them onto her laptop, which was on the table in the cottage, and sent the best ones to Carol, along with a text, 'You seriously need to come for a holiday, Mother.'

Back in the northeast of England, Carol was watching the TV when her phone beeped. She looked at the beautiful photographs Victoria had sent her of the Scottish Highlands and the deer behind their cottage.

"Look at this, Paul," she said, passing her phone to him.

"I think we must go there sometime," he replied.

63

Victoria felt a bit strange the following day. She sat on the bed and felt dizzy and nauseous. Getting up slowly, she wondered if there were any deer, but she couldn't see them. She went to make a coffee but found that the smell of it made her more nauseous. She ran into the toilet, at the front of the cottage, so as not to disturb Sami, and vomited. Just a little bit. Then she felt alright again after a few minutes and returned to the kitchen. She couldn't drink the coffee, so she opted for a water bottle.

Later on, in the town of Aviemore, they visited the Tourist Information Centre. Victoria was informed about Green Lochen, a beautiful loch where it is said the fairies wash their clothes. She immediately fancied the walk, thinking the fresh air would be good after her morning episode.

She parked the car at Glenmore Visitor Centre. They began to walk along a gravel path, adjacent to a stream. They walked a while before coming to a gate and continued past a small humpback bridge which crossed a babbling brook. It was so serene and calm, with only birdsong and the sound of falling water every so often.

The walk continued for a while then, on the right side, there it was. The most fantastic loch they had ever seen. The water's unusual green appearance is said to be due to the reflection of light from the surrounding trees. The mountains form a backdrop in the distance. They found a seat, rested their legs, and gazed at the view.

"This is stunning," said Victoria. "I could sit here all day."

"So this is where the fairies are supposed to wash their clothes?" asked Sami.

"Yes."

"You bring me to some strange places," he laughed. "But it's a truly magical world."

There were a few people in the distance at the other side of the loch and another family not far away on a little beach area with a dog. Mallards were swimming in pairs, making a trail of movement in otherwise perfectly still water.

"I wonder if we'll see any fairies?" asked Victoria.

"I'm beginning to believe anything is possible here," replied Sami.

"They may come at night when nobody is around," she said.

They sat quietly, holding hands, enjoying the wintry sun. Then Sami leaned over and gave her a passionate kiss. For the first time in his life, he felt happy and peaceful.

The walk back to the car park took an hour and twenty minutes. They decided to have some refreshments at a small café before returning to the car.

Victoria drove further up the Cairngorm Mountains and came to a large car park at the top. From there, you could see for miles around.

"Stunning," said Victoria, looking down over Aviemore and Loch Morlich. They sat and admired the view from the mountain for a while before returning to the cottage.

Victoria had a sudden thought when she lay down in bed that night. *Could I be pregnant? When was my last period?*

She realised that it was a while ago.

64

It was an early start on the Friday morning as they had to leave the cottage by quarter past seven for the journey to Fort William. The shaky feeling and nausea Victoria had suffered over the last few days continued. While Sami was in the shower, she vomited in the other toilet and sipped some water and ate a few digestive biscuits she had purchased at the supermarket. They seemed to settle everything down.

She took it slowly as the road was winding. As it got lighter, they could see a stunning view. Farm animals, such as sheep and cows, were already in the fields. As they headed west, the countryside became more dominated by the command of the mountains, which were much more rugged.

The station at Fort William was easy to find. Once parked, they found a small café and purchased some breakfast. Victoria still couldn't face coffee, so she opted for a fruity tea.

"It's unlike you not to drink coffee in the morning," noticed Sami.

"I prefer fruit teas on holiday," she remarked.

She had been trying to hide her symptoms as she hadn't done a test yet. She would have to purchase a testing kit discreetly.

Sami went to buy tickets for the Jacobite train. However, it didn't start running until April. He was disappointed as it was something he wanted to do in Scotland as he'd heard about its reputation as a tourist attraction and had been voted the best railway journey in the world.

"There is a ScotRail train that runs to Mallaig," said the man in the ticket office. "You still see all the sights, and it is much cheaper."

Sami waited for Victoria to return from the supermarket, as she had called there to get some water bottles.

"We are here now. Let's go for it," said Victoria, enthusiastically.

So by ScotRail, it was. As the train pulled away and passed through various places, Victoria took photographs of the fascinating countryside. It travelled across the magnificent Glenfinnan Viaduct and gave way to some rugged but beautiful countryside. There were a few different lochs, running wild deer, and golden eagles. Sami also tried to capture as many photographs as he could.

Once at Mallaig, it was good to get some fresh air and exercise exploring the small town, designed for tourists with many restaurants, cafés and souvenir shops.

Sami took Victoria's hand and led her away from the direction of the town.

"Where are we going?" she asked.

"Somewhere different," he replied, as she continued to follow him into the countryside, away from the town. There was a gap behind a big oak tree, and he pulled her in behind it. He began to kiss her passionately.

"What are you doing?" she asked.

"Kissing you," he laughed and before she could say anything else, he began to kiss her again.

Then he stopped and said, "Thank you so much for this beautiful holiday. It has been truly magical." He kissed her once more.

"I knew you'd like it," she said.

"There's something that would make it perfect."

"What's that?"

"Wild sex. Sex outside in the open, with you now, behind those rhododendron bushes."

"Have you lost your mind? What if someone comes?"

"Nobody will come here, except maybe some sheep," he teased, taking her hand and moving towards the place he had in mind.

He kissed her again, and she yelped as he pulled her to the ground. They rolled under the hidden bushes, as Sami loosened her blouse to bare her breasts.

"You are crazy. You know that?" Victoria gasped and moaned between breaths as he kissed each breast and sucked at her nipples.

"I'm crazy about you."

He continued to tease her nipples with his tongue. He heaved down her panties and began to manipulate her clitoris with his fingers. She moaned with pleasure. His touch was like electricity. His erection grew next to her leg, so she released it from his trousers and sucked it hard. He groaned and then thrust it deeply into her waiting vagina. They rocked in unison together and Victoria gave a cry as her nerve endings screamed with passion.

As she was about to come, he stopped and kissed each breast before retaking her hips and pounding inside her once more. They both cried with ecstasy at their joint moment of orgasm.

They were breathless and panting heavily beside each other in the Scottish undergrowth. Sami smiled at her.

"I have never done anything this crazy in my life before. It must be your influence," he laughed.

"This was your idea" she giggled.

Sami moved away and zipped up his trousers. Victoria pulled up her pants and dusted herself off, as her clothes were covered in woody undergrowth. She then brushed her fingers through her hair.

"I guess we'll eat and then enquire about a train back," said Sami.

Unnoticed by Victoria and Sami, a ScotRail passenger train had slipped past. They could have been visible to anyone, seated higher up, who had glanced out of the window at the time. Whether they were seen or not is left to the imagination!

65

Victoria awoke, after arriving home from Aviemore the day before. She had filled the washer with clothes and hung them up to dry before going to bed.

While in the supermarket on Friday morning, she had discreetly purchased a pregnancy testing kit. It was time to do that test.

She took a urine sample in the bathroom and left the kit beside her bed while she went to eat breakfast. When she went back upstairs, she discovered that the test was positive.

Sami texted mid-morning to tell her that he was having lunch with his parents alone, as there was some family business to discuss. He said he would text when he got home, and then she could go and stay.

She wondered what they wanted to discuss without her being present. She guessed it would all be down to Imran. He had never liked her.

She happily ate lunch with her parents and chatted excitedly about the holiday in Aviemore. In the afternoon, she took Meg and Reggie for their usual walk. As she was in the fields near Sami's parents' bungalow, she noticed Sami's car drive out of their street and up to the roundabout to turn around. However, she didn't face the main road. She wondered how long it would be before she heard from him.

"We have some friends coming from India to visit soon," said Imran. "Masood Ahmed is an old friend of mine, and they have a daughter who is looking for a husband." Sami glared in disbelief.

"I hope you are not expecting me to be the potential husband," he snapped.

"Well, it's like this, you see ..."

"It's not like anything," Sami yelled, slamming the palm of his hand on the table. "I have a girlfriend called Victoria, and I love her. Does that count for nothing?"

"It's a long time since there's been anyone, and when you refused to speak to Julie ..."

"So that's what this is all about, is it?" Sami raged. "I turned Julie down because I did not fancy her! I love Victoria. I refuse to marry anyone else. End of story."

"You don't have to marry the girl," Imran said. "We spoke of the idea before you were with Victoria."

"Nice of you to inform me," Sami stormed. "It's all about you. Did you even stop to think about how I would feel?"

"Sami, I ..."

Anne interrupted. She had predicted this would happen.

"I've only just found out about this, too," she said, in a tearful voice.

"More fool you, Mother. You'll have to cook for, and clean up after, this family while he swans off to work out of the way. It would help if you stood up to him. He is treating you like a doormat."

"Stop shouting, both of you." Anne wept, and she asked Imran, "Why do you always have to interfere?"

"Stop taking his side. You are supposed to support me," Imran shouted.

"OK, let's solve the problem," Sami said. "Get on the telephone to them now, Father, and tell them that your son has now got a girlfriend and is unavailable, so it won't be possible to come."

"I've already tried that. The Ahmed family have booked their flights."

"I don't believe you," Sami said as he slammed his fists on the table. "What am I supposed to say to Victoria?"

"Explain to her that it's just for two weeks, and you won't be marrying the girl," said Anne. Sami slammed his fists on the table again.

"So you think pushing someone into the background for two weeks is acceptable? I won't be staying for lunch, Mother. I've suddenly lost my appetite." He stormed out of their house and slammed the front door behind him.

As he drove his car around the one-way system, he saw Victoria up in the field with the dogs. The tears that threatened to water his eye sockets spilt over and began to roll down his cheeks.

What am I going to say to her? he thought.

He needed time to calm down before inviting her over.

Victoria received a text from Sami at five o'clock, inviting her to go to his place. She wondered why he had waited so long as she had seen him leave his parents' much earlier. On her arrival, he was in the kitchen preparing hot drinks.

"Hi, Darling," he said, kissing her.

She noticed that his mood appeared relatively subdued. She reckoned there must have been an argument with his parents. They sat in the lounge drinking their refreshments.

"There's no easy way to say this, but I need to tell you," he said, in a low voice.

"Tell me what?" She began to feel worried.

"My father, in his wisdom, has arranged for an Indian friend to visit." He took her hand and held it.

"His friend is looking for a potential husband for his daughter." Victoria remained silent as she tried to take it all in.

"I can assure you that I won't be marrying her," he continued. "I'm not ready to marry anyone."

"So why is she coming?" Victoria asked. "Surely your father has told them about me?"

"My father arranged it in secret. Nobody knew but him. I'm furious."

"Why?"

"Because he's an interfering old sod and cannot keep out of my private life. My choices matter very little to him." Victoria sympathised but couldn't understand why he had agreed to follow his father's wishes.

"He's never liked me," she snapped. "He always asks me strange questions. It seems I'm not good enough to be your girlfriend." She was struggling to keep her composure.

"Look," he said, as he rubbed her wrist with his thumb. "Nothing will change between us. I won't be marrying her."

Victoria jumped up.

"It does change things. I'm your girlfriend. Suddenly I must be pushed into the background while she comes to parade at the forefront of your life! You could stand up to your father and say no. That way, I would know at least you care about my feelings." She picked up her overnight bag.

"I'm going home," she said, and marched through the kitchen, slamming the back door behind her.

"Victoria, please listen!" He ran out of the house behind her but Victoria had driven off and didn't look back. Sami sighed and went back into the house. He had a feeling that would happen. How he hated his father.

Sami sent Victoria a text message later.

'I must go through with it as they expect it of me. I'm not happy at all either. I love you. S x'

Victoria did not reply to his text.

66

Victoria didn't rush into work the following day. She wasn't in the mood to make small talk with Sami. She was annoyed with him for succumbing to his father's wishes. She didn't know how she felt about this girl, knowing she was trying to win her man.

Sami had bought her the usual cappuccino. She was still off coffee, so she didn't want to drink it. They were both subdued, and there was an awkward tension between them.

"Victoria, I'm sorry," said Sami, breaking the silence. She just shrugged.

"My father has put me in this impossible position," he continued. "I want to assure you that I love you very much, and no other woman will take your place. We have just had a beautiful holiday, as I have never experienced before. Look, it's just two weeks, and it will all be normal again. Victoria, I need you to trust me."

"I need time to think. It's time you stood up to your father," she replied, as she left the room and threw the cup, with the cappuccino, into the bin.

Victoria took her breaks alone that day as she needed the time to process Sami's words. He wanted her to trust him for two weeks, then the girl would go home and they could resume their relationship. *It didn't seem that bad, did it?* She just hated being pushed aside for someone else.

She ate lunch with her mother and asked for her advice. Carol didn't agree with the situation either.

"You have to decide whether he's important enough," she said. "Do you still want him? If the answer is yes, you will have to trust him over the next two weeks."

She had important things to do, as she needed to visit her GP and confirm her pregnancy. She decided to give Sami the benefit of the doubt. Maybe the news of a baby would distract him from the woman and make her disappear home early. She smiled at the idea.

When the family arrived, Sami explained the situation to the young woman, Zarina. Marriage between them was impossible as he had a girlfriend whom he loved. Still, to be polite, he had taken a week of annual leave to show her around.

Victoria was disappointed at the news of his annual leave. She wanted the visit to be over so that her life with Sami could return to normal. She decided not to see him over the next two weeks.

She contacted her GP and made an appointment. He confirmed her pregnancy the following week, so she decided to visit Sami that evening to tell him the news.

Sami opened his kitchen door.

"Come in," he said. "I thought you didn't want to see me."

"I have something important to tell you," Victoria said.

"OK, I'll make tea"

Victoria sat in the lounge but, after a few minutes, she needed the toilet so she ran upstairs to the bathroom. As she came out, she noticed Mitzi was hissing.

"What's the matter, sweetie?" she asked, walking across to the bay window to comfort the little cat.

"There, there," she soothed.

Suddenly, she noticed a movement out of the corner of her eye. She looked around and saw Zarina sitting up in Sami's bed. She stood and glared at the girl, feeling numb. Furious, she marched down the stairs and confronted Sami.

"What the hell is going on?" she yelled. Sami turned around, bewildered.

"What's up?" he asked.

"Don't play innocent with me," she stormed. "That woman is in your bed ... I wasn't born yesterday."

"Victoria, what are you talking about?"

She burst into tears and screamed, "Why did you lie to me? You asked me to trust you, and foolishly I did. It didn't take long for you to start sleeping with her."

"Victoria, I'm not sleeping with her," he said, as he reached out to hold her, but she shook him off.

"Don't touch me," she snapped.

"Leave me alone. We're over." Victoria stormed through the kitchen and left the house.

"Victoria, come back."

Sami chased her, but her foot was already on the throttle, and she didn't look back as she drove off. Sami put his head in his hands.

Why did she think I was sleeping with someone? She was fine when she entered the house, then he remembered her words.

He went upstairs and found Zarina in his bed.

67

"What the hell are you doing in my bed?" he boomed in a thunderous voice. "Do you realise what you have done? Get out, you little slut."

Sami reached over and grabbed her by both wrists. He tried to tug her out of his bed but she resisted by arching her back and then kicking wildly with her feet.

"No, no!" she cried. "It is me who is going to be your wife."

"Never in a million years," he yelled. "Now get out!"

Zarina resisted again. It took Sami all his strength to wrestle with her and get her off his bed. He then threw her over his shoulder. Beaten, she kicked and screamed as he marched her out of the room, and then she began to punch the small of his back. He took her into her bedroom, dropped her onto the bed, then left the room and locked the door behind him.

"I will telephone my father," she wailed, behind the door. Sami didn't care. He closed his bedroom door and cupped his head in his hands, wondering what he had done to deserve this.

Meanwhile, Zarina telephoned her father, and said, "That man has hit me. I'm frightened. I don't want to stay here any longer."

Sami lay on his bed contemplating his life when he heard a knock at the back door. He ignored it as he was in no mood for visitors. The knocking continued and was getting louder. He went down to answer the door. It was his father and Masood.

"What have you done to my daughter?" shouted an irate Masood. "Where is she?" His father followed him inside, looking straight through Sami, as though he didn't exist.

"Your daughter is upstairs in her bedroom. I have done nothing to her, except remove her from my bed."

"She's been in your bed?" Masood exploded.

"I didn't invite her there." Sami began to lose his cool again. He went upstairs and unlocked the bedroom.

"Father, Father," Zarina sobbed, running downstairs past Sami. "Take me away from here. Please, Papa."

She threw her arms around Masood and sobbed.

"I did not bring you up to behave like this, Sami," Imran shouted. "You should apologise to my friends."

"Apologise for what exactly?" Sami raged.

"You were never brought up with violence …"

"Violence! I never touched her. I pulled her out of my bed because I didn't want her there. She punched me on my back!"

"My daughter said you hit her, and she doesn't lie," yelled Masood angrily.

"Your daughter is a proper little madam. I am not marrying a woman who acts like a spoiled brat. Now, get out of here," Sami raged.

"How dare you!" raged Imran, as Sami turned to face his father.

"This is all your fault. You have ruined my life. I've lost Victoria because of your meddling, and she is the only girl I've ever loved." Sami broke down in tears and continued, "You brought this family here, knowing that I was in love with her …"

There was a knock at the door.

"Who now?" he muttered.

"Good evening, Sir," said one of two policemen at the door. "We've had reports of a disturbance from this address."

"They were just leaving," said Sami.

Masood and Imran were shocked to see the police. They walked through the kitchen towards the door. Masood had his arm around his weeping daughter. Imran stopped before the police officers and turned to Sami.

"This is not over."

"It is over. I want nothing more to do with you."

Sami locked his house, relieved that he was alone at last. He poured a neat whisky, gulped it down in one shot and then sat on his settee, cupping his head in his hands.

His phone beeped. It was social media. Victoria Pemberton had just changed her relationship status to single.

68

Sami woke with a thumping headache. He thought it had all been a dream, then realised it had been real. His life had become a living nightmare. He phoned in sick from work and learned that Victoria had done the same. James's manner was very abrupt as no doubt he was under the impression that he had been unfaithful to her.

He called his GP to make an appointment. He couldn't face his work colleagues, nor did he want to upset Victoria. He needed to speak to her privately, apologise and sort out the mess.

A knock at the door disturbed his thoughts.

It was his mother. He was so delighted to see her that he flung his arms around her and began to sob uncontrollably.

"It was complete hell when Masood and your father came home last night. I almost walked out," Anne said. "Sit down. I'll make coffee."

Sami felt better, getting everything off his chest, as he explained about Victoria and the events of the previous night.

"Your father isn't at work today. Masood threatened to go to the police about you hitting their daughter."

"I didn't hit her. It happened as I explained."

"I believe you, Sami, but unfortunately Masood believes his daughter. Your father is arranging early flights home for them to save your skin."

"She's a spoiled brat," he continued. "She created that scene to upset Victoria. As for my father, I want nothing more to do with him. He caused all this."

"He's your father, Sami. You can't say that."

"I can. He has ruined my life. I will no longer come for Sunday lunch. I will take you out on Saturdays instead if you want?"

Anne nodded in agreement. She also agreed to accompany Sami to the GP and take his sick note to James Turnbull.

Victoria woke up feeling numb. A wave of nausea swept over her, and she headed for the bathroom. The morning sickness was getting worse. Her mother brought her a fruit tea and two digestive biscuits.

"Here, have them," she soothed, pushing a strand of Victoria's hair behind her ear, and tried to reassure her by saying, "Everything will be all right." Victoria burst into tears again.

"I should have been here with you rather than staying at his place," she sobbed.

"You need to lead your life," Carol replied. "Never forget that there's always a room here for you and the little one." She felt Victoria's tummy as she spoke.

Victoria went back to bed and drank her fruit tea. She wondered how she could have gotten things so wrong. Not long ago, she and Sami were having their dream holiday, and they broke up three weeks later. *What had happened?* Things hadn't been right since they got back. She wondered if his father had planned this, while they were away, to encourage Sami to leave her. It had worked.

Sami hadn't been in a relationship for seven years. Suddenly, there were two women within three weeks. She couldn't understand it.

Her mother had said he had always been strange. So did her work colleagues. *Had she been entirely blind?* Another wave of sickness washed over her, and she rushed into the bathroom again.

In the afternoon, Victoria needed some fresh air. She decided to take a walk to the supermarket. Carol gave her a list of provisions to purchase. Her head still felt fuzzy as she walked around the store looking for the items. As she looked at the different flavoured yoghurts, she was aware of a voice behind her saying, 'Hello', but she didn't turn around. He spoke again, "Hello. Fancy seeing you here." She jumped and looked around.

"Hello, Chris. How are you doing?"

"I'm good. You look rather peaky. Are you OK?"

"Yes, I'm fine, thanks."

But he could see that she wasn't her usual bubbly self.

"You're not alright, are you?" he asked, placing his hands on her shoulders. She was close to tears.

"Sami and I broke up," she said.

Chris was quiet for a moment, then said, "You should have chosen me at that party."

He winked, giving a playful smile, but Victoria didn't respond.

"I tell you what, give me ten minutes. I'll meet you upstairs in the café and buy you tea and cake. Then you can tell me all about it."

She didn't want to bother, but she needed friendly company. Maybe she should have chosen him, and then her heart wouldn't be breaking.

He was upstairs before her, with the tea and chocolate cake waiting.

"Thank you. This is most kind."

"Think nothing of it."

Victoria poured her tea and explained the events that had happened a few nights previously.

"The dirty rascal," he said, thinking of the burly-looking miserable consultant that appeared so squeaky clean. He wondered what Victoria saw in him.

"His father never liked me. The ironic thing is that they want him to have a family, and I am pregnant." Chris burst out laughing.

"Does he know?"

"No. I went there to tell him that night. Now I'm not sure how he will react."

"Will you go out with me?" asked Chris. Victoria sighed.

"I really can't go out with anyone right now. I'm not in a good place."

"Well, if you change your mind, you know where I am." He took her phone and typed in his number, then sent himself a text so that he would have her number.

"When you feel ready, get in touch with me. I will support you, and if you decide to have your baby, I will marry you."

"What?" Victoria remarked in surprise. "I thought you liked playing the field."

"If I were lucky enough to have you in my life, I would give it all up."

"You can't be serious?"

"I am. Deadly."

Victoria took a deep breath and wondered why she was wasting her energy on Sami.

They got up to leave the cafe.

"Thank you. I feel better after our chat," said Victoria.

"You have my number. Anytime you need to talk, get in touch. I hope we can at least be friends."

"We certainly can." She smiled as he walked off in the direction of the main road.

Later, he sent her a text.

'You looked very sexy today, even with a miserable face, love Chris xx'

She replied, 'You are a flatterer! V x.'

69

After an exhausting weekend, Victoria decided to dust herself down, lift her chin and return to work. It was time to forget Sami and move on with her career. It was eerie without Sami in the office, but she was glad he had taken some time off. It would give her time to settle back into her role without him.

Early in the morning, she entered James Turnbull's office.

"How are you, Victoria?" he asked.

"I'm fine," she said. "Things are tough at the moment, but I will be OK. I need to tell you something, James."

"What is it?" he asked.

"I'm pregnant." There was a short silence.

"Does Sami know?"

"Not yet. I haven't seen him since that eventful night, and I'm not ready to face him yet. I will tell him when I'm ready. I would appreciate your confidentiality regarding this matter."

"Your secret is safe with me," he added, "but the sooner he knows, the better."

"I've had terrible sickness too, so I don't know how it will affect my work."

"We'll play it by ear," he said. "Verity will take you under her wing in Sami's absence."

"Thank you, James," said Victoria and she left the office.

Victoria continued professionally with her work and appeared to get along fine without Sami. Emotionally, things became more manageable for her in the following weeks. However, she was aware of Sami's impending return. She needed to see him before then and, at least, tell him about the pregnancy. Her twelve-week scan was due the following week.

Sami felt very depressed over the loss of Victoria and her presence in his life, which was all down to his father's interference. He had not spoken to him since. He had no relationship with Zarina, but how could he prove it? He had never wanted to hurt Victoria. He had tried to phone her to explain, but she didn't answer. Her stepfather, Paul, answered the last call and said she needed more time to think.

So he sat, hoping that every day would be the day she would call, but it didn't happen. Anne was worried about him. He spent days watching films as an escape from the real world and began drinking heavily.

The departure of the Ahmed family had left a trail of disaster. Imran was angry that Sami refused to see him, and he felt that Anne didn't support him.

Sami kept in contact with Verity regarding work. Victoria was back working, like the true professional she was. She appeared to have moved on without feeling hurt by the situation. His looming start date would be much more difficult as he would have to share an office and work with her. He wasn't sure that he could do it so he began looking for employment elsewhere.

The week before he returned to work seemed to be a good time to drink less and get out and about. Richard tried to persuade him to return to the gym as he had not been for over a month.

When he returned, he was surprised that Pauline had gone back to the gym. He had previously asked her for a date, but she had a boyfriend, so it had all been quite embarrassing. But she had broken up with him and had renewed her membership.

Sami chatted with her and told her that he had just ended a relationship. They exchanged telephone numbers and, later that evening, he sent her a text to invite her on a date.

70

Victoria took a day off on Friday. She decided to go into town as her clothes were getting rather tight and she needed to buy maternity wear. Visiting the department store, she remembered the last time she had been there, she was buying Sami some Christmas gifts. Tears began to well up in her eyes. She had to forget him and move on.

She purchased maternity trousers, a couple of dresses and tops, then headed downstairs towards the restaurant.

Lost in her thoughts, she didn't notice Anne, Susan and Rosy, looking at comfortable shoes nearby, until she was practically beside them. She darted along another aisle, pretending not to see them, but they had spotted her.

"Victoria. I'm so glad I have run into you," said Anne, with a big smile. "I'd like to talk to you. Will you have some tea with us?" They went to the café and Anne bought tea and a slice of cake for everyone.

"It's lovely to see you, Victoria. How have you been?" she asked.

"Not good," she replied in a subdued voice. "I suppose you heard about the argument I had with Sami?" as she hadn't seen Anne since the breakup.

"Oh. That was a dreadful night," she replied. "I was at the end of my tether. There were two grown men shouting at each other. Amira was crying and Zarina just sat staring into space with her arms folded. She caused it all."

Victoria listened with interest as she knew none of that.

"I cooked meals and cleaned up after that family and not a word of thanks. I was exhausted. It was as though they expected it. Imran insisted that I brought Sami round the next day to apologise, so I went to see him and he was in a terrible state. I listened to his version of events. He refused to apologise. They haven't spoken since."

Victoria knew they weren't speaking.

"Imran was furious that I hadn't brought Sami back. He yelled at me in front of his friends, and I was so hurt. I lost my temper and left them all to fend for themselves. I've been staying with my mother ever since." She picked up her serviette and dabbed her tears.

"They've gone home now, surely?" asked Victoria.

"Yes. Imran had to organise early flights home or they were going to report Sami to the police," she said.

"What for?" asked Victoria.

"Zarina accused him of hitting her."

The Bitch, thought Victoria.

She sat in silence, feeling shocked. Imran had not only ruined her relationship with Sami, but his own too. She didn't blame Anne for walking out at all, shouting at her like that. What a dreadful man.

"I knew Imran never liked me. I don't know why," Victoria said.

"Imran isn't keen on career women, and that's how he saw you. Career women are generally reluctant to have children."

If only he knew!

"I'm sorry you've had to go through all of this," Victoria said, gently taking her arm. "You don't deserve it."

"He's an idiotic bumbling buffoon," exclaimed Rosy, showing her frustration at how Imran had treated Anne. "He may be a doctor, but he has no common sense."

Victoria laughed at how forthright and blunt Rosy was.

Maybe I should have been more direct with Imran, rather than trying to be polite and impress him she thought. If I do get to see him again, I will tell him exactly what I think of him. Pooh! A career woman indeed. Wait till he finds out the truth. Victoria began to feel rather smug.

"I'm concerned about Sami too," Anne said. "He's been in a deep dark place and drinking heavily. He loves you, Victoria. Zarina created that scene deliberately to upset you. I know Sami wouldn't have done that to you. He walked in on his ex-wife sleeping with another man, and I know how much that hurt him. Don't lose faith, Victoria. I know he'd do nothing to hurt you."

Sami had never told her that he had walked in on his ex-wife though she knew she'd been unfaithful.

"I never knew that," she said.

"Oh, yes. Sami finished work early one night and went home with a bottle of wine and food for a romantic meal, only to find Angela in bed with a bald man. The man ran like a frightened kitten and Sami told Angela to leave. She came back two days later with a solicitor's letter. It said she was still entitled to live there as it was a shared house. So Sami had to buy her out, even though he paid all the bills. It took all his savings to buy her out and we had to lend him money. He sold that house and moved into the one he lives in now, so he was able to repay us."

Victoria was shocked as she knew none of that. *Maybe she'd been too harsh on him. Maybe she shouldn't have ignored him.* She decided she would call and see Sami that night. It was time to talk.

She left the department store and walked across the market square, deep in thought. A long dark-haired woman, with round gold earrings in each ear, stopped her. Victoria noticed that the woman was pregnant, almost due.

"Would you like to buy a charm from a lucky gypsy?" she asked. "I'll tell your fortune, and it will bring you luck."

Victoria thought she could do with some luck, however, she already knew her future. She was a doctor and would be a single mother raising a child on her own. That was her life, and it wouldn't change. The gypsy took her hand and looked at her palm.

"I see you have a broken heart, my dear."

Not hard to guess, thought Victoria, as she nodded.

"Well, you will be lucky in love," she said. Victoria rolled her eyes.

"I see a dark man, strange, but he has a good heart."

Yeah, that's him.

"You need to lose your anger, my love. I sense anger within your heart. It will help if you let it all wash away. Take some deep breaths. When you do that, my love, everything will become clear."

Victoria paid the woman ten pounds and thanked her.

"Thank you, my darling," she replied. "Remember to lose the anger."

It's true. She had been angry. Maybe it was time to forgive.

71

Victoria parked her car outside Sami's house. She sat for a few minutes to compose herself. In the past, her visits there had always brought happiness. However, she hadn't been since that fateful night, so she felt apprehensive. She knocked on the door.

She could hear footsteps inside as he approached the door. He was taken by surprise when he saw her. They both stared at each other before Victoria broke the silence.

"Hello, Sami," she greeted him.

Before, he had always opened the door to invite her in, but there was no such gesture on that occasion.

"What do you want?" he asked. She could smell the whisky on his breath.

He is drunk.

"I thought we should talk."

"Talk?" he asked.

"I'm ready to talk now. Besides, we have to work together from Monday."

"So you're ready to talk, huh?" he leered.

Victoria sensed that it wasn't going well.

"What about all the times I wanted to talk during the last weeks? Each day I woke up, hoping today would be the day I would hear your voice, but that never happened. The unanswered calls, then your stepfather told me to leave you alone. I was in a dark place, Victoria. I thought you loved me, and that we had a friendship. Yet when I needed you, you ignored me."

"I'm sorry, Sami. I just needed to sort my head out. I saw your mother in town, and she told me some things. She's concerned about you, Sami."

"She's the only person who cares," he said, as he felt a lump in his throat.

"She says you've been drinking a lot."

"What I do here is no longer your business," he said, raising his voice. "You've made that very clear. Now leave me alone."

He slammed the door shut in her face.

Victoria returned to her car with tears streaming down her face. He still didn't know she was sorry and that she was pregnant.

'His mood is a darker shade of giemsa.'

Monday came around quickly. There was no need to get to work until nine o'clock. Victoria felt that familiar nauseous feeling as she got up, so she took her time. She wasn't looking forward to that day.

Sami regretted his outburst when Victoria visited his house. He decided he would apologise that morning to get things on to a sound footing, but she didn't show up until later, no doubt avoiding having to spend time with him in the office.

They had barely managed to speak before James Turnbull announced that he wanted to talk to them both in his office.

"I appreciate things have been difficult for you both; however, I cannot allow things to spill over into this hospital. Victoria, I have rostered you to work in Outpatients this week, to keep some distance between you. Are you happy to continue sharing the office?"

Victoria's heart lurched. She couldn't imagine not sharing the office with Sami, as much as she had tried to avoid him that day.

"I want to stay where I am and see how things go. It won't be a problem for me. We are professionals, and we both put the care of the patients first." James then turned his head to look at Sami.

"Yeah fine," he said.

"Good. Now I need to speak with Victoria alone," James added. Sami left the room.

"Does Sami know that you're pregnant yet?"

"No, he doesn't," said Victoria.

"You need to tell him as soon as possible. Things are getting awkward."

"I wanted to tell him last Friday, but the meeting didn't go well. I shall do it this week."

"Good."

Work continued as usual, with Sami and Victoria working in their separate areas and only using the office when necessary.

Sami sat alone in his office in the mornings as James Turnbull had been lenient with Victoria arriving late, owing to struggles with her morning sickness. Sami picked up on her timekeeping as it had slackened in recent months.

"You're late," he snapped, as she arrived one morning. He didn't look up from his computer.

"I'm sorry. I didn't feel well this morning. You're lucky to have me at all."

"Your starting time is nine o'clock sharp. Make sure you're here by then in the future."

Sami detested a lack of punctuality with any staff member. Victoria ignored him, collected her things, and left the office. There was a spare computer in Verity's room that she could use.

Sami presumed that she spent lunchtime with her mother, as she often had in the past when he was unavailable. Not wishing to use the restaurant, he decided to step into the doctor's suite for a change. It was new, and he had heard that it was good but he had never tried the food there.

As he purchased his takeaway and walked through the suite, he noticed Victoria sitting at a table with Chris Rogers. They appeared very relaxed together and her eyes sparkled as she engaged in conversation. He remembered that it used to be like that between them once and he missed those times.

It looked as though she had set her sights on Chris. She had never mentioned it, but then again, why would she? He was jealous and loathed Chris since he had chased Victoria since the Christmas party.

Sami needed to move on and banish the terrible pain he felt inside. He had arranged a date with Pauline even though Richard thought it was too soon.

Victoria caught him in the office before leaving work that night and asked, "Can I arrange a time to meet you outside work sometime? I have something I need to discuss with you."

"Discuss it now if you want," he replied.

"I'd rather it was in private."

Sami got up and locked the office door.

"Now we are in private. What do you want to discuss?"

"As I said, I don't want to discuss it here," she insisted.

"Meeting you outside of work is no longer an option. I am dating someone else." Victoria stopped in her tracks, totally shocked. She took a deep breath and said, "I guess it can wait." She left the office without speaking.

She went home, lay on her bed, and sobbed like a child.

How could he be dating someone else so quickly? I obviously didn't mean anything to him at all.

Victoria messaged Verity. She explained what had happened and wanted to find out if he had mentioned a girl. Verity confirmed that it was true. He had a date that evening, with someone he had met at the gym.

Victoria was despondent that evening but managed to pick herself up again over the weekend. She decided to announce her pregnancy to all the staff who would be present at the nurses' station on Monday morning.

72

Victoria entered the office with her head held high. Today she would drop her bombshell. Sami was sitting at his computer, catching up with his administrative work. He looked across at Victoria, sitting opposite.

"Are you not going to ask how my date went?" he asked.

"No. I'm not the least bit interested," she replied.

"It went well. I'm meeting her again on Thursday." Victoria ignored him, knowing that her announcement might change everything.

"How does Wednesday evening sound?" he asked. She looked across at him, puzzled.

"For whatever it is you want to discuss. I'll go home, change, then meet you at the coffee shop near me at six-thirty."

"OK," Victoria nodded.

The announcement would have to wait.

James had rostered Victoria to work with Sami that week. She went to the nursing station and exchanged pleasantries, as usual, and then she and Sami just got on with the job.

She ate lunch with her mother but, during the afternoon, she began to feel tired and dizzy. She needed to sit down and take breaks between visiting patients.

Victoria took a bath that evening and decided on an early night. As her head sank into the bath bubbles, she wondered how Sami would react to her pregnancy.

The next day, the morning sickness was back with a vengeance. Again, Victoria had to take it slowly and eat her digestive biscuits until it settled. The dizziness remained. She decided that if it continued, she would call her doctor. The morning sickness made her late and, once again, she faced the wrath of Sami.

"You're late again, Victoria. It must be at least three times in the last week."

"I'm sorry. I'm not well," she snapped, irritated by his lack of compassion.

"You were never late all through last year. You were here at eight o'clock, like me. I know things have changed between us, and you may not want to be here early, but at least be on time. If this continues, I shall have to inform Dr Turnbull."

"He already knows and is much more understanding than you," she snapped again.

Sami cupped his head in his hands. It was Dr Iqbal happening all over again. Victoria felt a wave of sickness sweep over her again and hurried to the toilet. As she came out, Sami was ready to start the ward round.

"I need a quick cup of tea first and I'll catch you up," said Victoria.

"What the hell do you think this is? A holiday camp?" he yelled at her, in front of all the nursing staff. "Not only are you late coming in, but you now want a cup of tea!" Victoria took a deep breath.

Keep calm.

She thought of the gypsy woman telling her to let her anger wash away.

"Sami, I've told you that I'm not feeling well," she said, trying to stay calm. A wave of dizziness came over her, and she placed her hand on the counter to steady herself.

"You're never well. You are always making excuses. I don't know what has come over you," he shouted again.

No more Mrs Nice Guy.

Victoria rarely lost her temper, but something snapped within her.

"I'm pregnant," she yelled. "I'm pregnant with your child."

She walked towards him, gave him a look of hatred, and then slammed the palm of her hand on the counter beside him.

"That's why I don't feel well, but what do you care? As long as you go on your sodding date." She walked along the corridor and left the ward.

There was total silence at the nurses' station. If eyeballs could leave their sockets and roll, a few pairs would have rolled down the corridor. Everyone was shocked, including Sami.

He stood there with a face like thunder and did not say a word. Then he spun around, entered his office and slammed the door behind him, making all the walls shake.

Victoria drank peppermint tea to settle her stomach and bought some shortbread biscuits to increase her sugar. All she needed was ten minutes. Why did Sami have to be so unreasonable? She suddenly thought of the scene she'd left behind in the Haematology Ward and smiled. At least she had announced her pregnancy, and Sami now knew. Although it wasn't how she had wanted it to be.

Sami sat at his desk, with his head cupped in his hands. He was reeling from the news Victoria had just given him.

Pregnant. PREG-NANT.

The word bounced around in his head, looking for a way out, but it wasn't able to escape. He should have realised.

No wonder she has piled on the weight. So, what now? Goodness, what a total mess this is. I am going to have a child. I will be a father, yet Victoria is no longer my girlfriend. I need to speak to my mother.

Victoria re-appeared on the ward, feeling more refreshed but was still somewhat dizzy. She would need to phone her doctor.

"OK, let's get started. Who will accompany me?" she asked.

"Victoria, are you all right?" asked Bernie.

"Much better," she replied. "Now, let's get started."

The ward round began but Victoria had to take it steady as she kept having dizzy turns. She sat on the seat beside one of the patients as she prescribed her a pool of platelets. She got up from her seat to move on to the next patient but, as she did so, the room began to spin. There was a sudden clatter, then everything went black.

73

"Victoria," Bernie said, tapping on her shoulder. She noticed that Victoria had a bleeding head injury.

"Josie, bring the wheelchair over," she shouted.

Sue hurried over with the trolley and cleaned the wound with distilled water. The bleeding continued, so she applied steri-strips and put on a bandage. Margaret Rose had gone to get Dr Turnbull, and he strode over at that moment. Victoria opened her eyes and looked at everyone.

"What happened?" she asked.

"You fainted," said Bernie.

"That's a nasty cut on her head. Take her to Accident and Emergency," said James.

"Where's Prakesh?"

Margaret Rose took him to one side and explained what had happened earlier. He dialled the number and told Accident and Emergency to expect a pregnant member of staff who needed immediate treatment. Victoria stood up and, assisted by Bernie, climbed into the wheelchair that Josie had brought.

"I'll finish the ward round," said James.

Bernie wheeled Victoria down the corridor and out of the ward. Dawn telephoned the laboratory to inform Carol.

Chris Rogers was waiting for a pregnant staff member with a head injury and was surprised to see Victoria.

"What has happened?" he asked.

"She fainted and bumped her head on a patient's bed as she fell," said Bernie.

"Let us get you sorted," said Chris, taking her into a side room, while Bernie headed back to the ward.

"I shall order some blood tests first. I need to know why you fainted. Did you feel hot or dizzy at all?" asked Chris.

"I've been having a few dizzy spells."

As Chris was taking the blood, Carol entered the room and asked, "What happened?"

"This is my mum, Carol," Victoria introduced them. "Mum, this is Dr Chris Rogers."

"The pleasure is mine," Chris smiled. "She fainted and caught her head when she fell, so I have taken some blood tests. We need to find the cause."

"As long as you're OK, Victoria," Carol said, kissing her forehead. "I'll get them fast-tracked back in the laboratory."

"Victoria is in excellent hands," said Chris.

"Thank you," said Carol, and she left the room.

"So, how does old Prakesh feel about becoming a father?" Chris asked. Victoria shrugged.

"I don't know," she replied. Chris walked around the bed with a smile on his face.

"Don't tell me. You haven't told him yet."

"Yes, he knows. I announced it to the whole world while we were having a dispute. He was rabbiting on about me being late, and something within me just snapped."

"Never a dull moment on your ward," he laughed. "This will need stitches."

Sami phoned his mother and told her the news. She was delighted about becoming a grandmother as it was the best news she'd had for a long time.

"You need to get Victoria back," Anne said.

"I don't think she wants me. Besides, I am dating someone else."

"Date whoever you want, Sami, but you must support her. Your new girl will have to accept it too. All this is such a mess. If only your father hadn't interfered."

"Exactly," he replied. "I would have had my own family."

Sami sighed. He knew that he needed to apologise to Victoria and talk to her. His phone rang again. It was James.

"Victoria has collapsed on the ward. She has gone to Accident and Emergency. I'll do the ward round. Maybe it's time to go and talk to her."

"OK, thanks," he said, and he dashed out of the side room like a rocket.

"You're iron-deficient," Chris said, as he looked at the blood results.

"Goodness!" Victoria exclaimed. "No wonder I feel so bad."

"So you will need iron tablets." Chris was stitching her when Sami entered the room.

"Victoria, are you alright? I came as soon as I found out."

He took a seat beside her bed and took her hand, clasping it tightly.

"I'm fine. Chris is looking after me."

"She's iron-deficient. It's no surprise that she felt dizzy," said Chris.

"What happened to your head?" asked Sami.

"I knocked it as I fell to the ground," she explained.

"I'm sorry. I shouldn't have yelled at you like that."

"No, you shouldn't have," she replied.

"If I had known you were pregnant, I would never have behaved like that."

"I tried to tell you, but you wouldn't meet me outside work."

Chris finished inserting the stitches and then said, "I'll go and sort the iron tablets," and he left the room.

"I should have realised," said Sami. "You have gained weight. Suddenly you didn't like coffee and started drinking healthy fruity teas. I should have seen it."

"It doesn't matter. We're here now," said Victoria.

"Where do we go from here? We need to talk," he said.

"I'm having the baby," she told him.

Chris entered the room again and handed her a prescription for iron tablets, and said, "For completeness, I will refer you to the Maternity Unit. You have taken a fall, so we must ensure the baby is OK. I'm also giving you a sick note for the remainder of this week and next week. You need complete rest." He handed the sick note to Sami.

"Thank you for looking after her," Sami replied graciously.

"My pleasure," said Chris before leaving the room again.

"I need to get back," said Sami.

"I'll phone when I get to the Maternity Unit. I'll likely have another scan, so you may get to see the baby."

"I'd like that," he said, then left the room.

Victoria was sitting in the waiting area of the Maternity Unit when Sami joined her. They waited around five minutes, and then her name was called.

"Victoria Pemberton, please," said the sonographer.

She made herself comfortable on the bed and opened her blouse. The sonographer placed ultrasound gel on her tummy and then began to pass the probe around her stomach, examining every part. As pictures of their baby appeared on the screen, Sami took Victoria's hand as he gazed at the image.

"Wow!" he said. "That's amazing."

The sonographer continued his examination for around twenty minutes, then said, "Everything seems to be fine. The baby is doing well and has not been affected by the fall." Victoria felt relieved.

"Would you like a photograph?" he asked.

"Yes, please," said Victoria. She gave the photograph to Sami, who placed it in his wallet.

Sami sat at home that evening contemplating the day's events. Not only had he discovered that he would be a father, but then Victoria had that fainting episode and, as a result, he was holding a picture of his beautiful baby.

He felt so many emotions simultaneously. He felt immediate love for his baby and so much love for Victoria, who was nurturing it. And yet so much hatred for his father and Zarina, who had been the cause of their separation.

He needed to break things off with Pauline as he didn't feel any love for her, not in the way he had for Victoria. He cancelled the date for the following day, as he needed more time to absorb everything, and he would meet her the following week. Instead, he invited Victoria for tea as there was a lot to discuss.

Victoria received a text from Chris, 'Are you feeling better tonight? x'

'A lot better, thanks. What did you put in those tablets? I feel like I want to dance now. V x'

'They do work quickly. You and Prakesh seemed closer. x'

'We're on speaking terms now. V x'

'Good to hear. You don't need the stress. x'

74

Victoria knocked at the door promptly at six o'clock. Sami was cooking her a meal. He had bought steaks and vegetables to ensure she ate healthily. He blamed himself for her collapse in the ward.

She sat at the table while he plated the food.

"You didn't need to go to all this trouble," she said.

"You need to eat a proper diet, and I will ensure you do. I want all that steak eaten."

"I don't often eat steak," said Victoria.

"You are tonight and every piece," he retorted.

"So, what are we discussing?" she asked.

"You're pregnant with my child. There's a lot to discuss. To begin with, you will need support, both emotionally and financially. I want you to know you will have that, and I shall be there for you."

"I don't want your money," said Victoria. "I had planned to bring the baby up on my own."

"So you have it all sorted then?" he shrugged.

"We had broken up, Sami. I had a lot of thinking to do. I found out that I was pregnant, and then was cast aside for someone else. I was distraught."

"It wasn't like that. Why didn't you tell me sooner?"

"I'd planned to tell you that night. Then I found Zarina in your bed."

"I didn't sleep with her," he sighed. "I was never interested in her. I tried to be polite, taking her out to places, and then she began to try that for a few nights. She thought that if I saw her body I would want sex but that wasn't the case. I was in a happy relationship with you. I wanted her to go home so that things could return to normal."

"You said early on in our relationship that you couldn't offer marriage. I accepted that, yet marriage was offered to her. Why was she good enough for that and not me?" asked Victoria.

"That was my father. I was never going to marry her," he replied.

"I felt used," said Victoria. There was a silence between them.

"I didn't realise you felt that way," Sami replied.

"I didn't originally, but I felt dirty and used after that evening." Sami reached for her hand across the table.

"I never intended for you to feel that way. I always loved you. I still love you."

"You say that, but you are dating someone else!" she shrieked. "You couldn't wait to tell me how well it had all gone and that you would be meeting her again. It's all such a mess." Victoria burst into tears, and continued, "I never wanted this. I don't want to be pregnant under these circumstances."

Sami listened, cupping his head in his hands. He took a deep breath.

"I'm going to break it off with her."

"Don't do that on my account," snapped Victoria.

He squeezed her hand and said, "It's only been one date, Victoria. I exaggerated to make you jealous. I was supposed to meet her tonight but cancelled it because I wanted to see you."

"I want you to love me, not just my baby."

Sami realised that it would be a challenging task to win her back. He had betrayed her trust and now had to earn it again. He decided to change his tactic. If he could be a supportive friend and get their friendship back on track, maybe then she could rebuild her trust in him.

"Look, you have my support and friendship. I will be a proper father to our child. I want to be an active part of their life."

"Of course. I want that too," she replied.

She had eaten all her steak, and it had been delicious. Sami then made her some tea, and they sat in the lounge.

"We can still be parents, share parental duties, decision making, and responsibilities. We need to put the child first, like responsible adults. We can still be friends, I hope," Sami said.

"Of course," replied Victoria. "I'd like that."

75

Sami offered to work Victoria's on-call shifts the following week while she was on sick leave. He had foolishly ignored the advice Richard had given, that he had been rather hasty to date Pauline so soon after Victoria, and he knew that he now had to end the relationship.

He hadn't counted on becoming a father. That had changed everything. He wanted to be the best father possible to this child and didn't want anything to stand in the way. He arranged to meet Pauline on Saturday evening. He would buy her a meal and tell her gently.

They went to Giovanni's, the Italian restaurant in town. He remembered taking Victoria there once. As they sat down, he ordered drinks and then took a deep breath.

"Pauline, I'm sorry, but this is the last time we can meet." He was relieved that he had told her but she looked across at him in surprise.

"Why? What have I done? I thought we were having a good time," she said tearfully.

"It's not you. My ex is pregnant. I'm going to be a father," he said gently.

"So you're going back to her then?" Pauline snapped.

"Not exactly," replied Sami. The waiter brought over the drinks and asked if they were ready to order.

"Not yet," replied Sami. "Can we have a bit longer?"

Pauline stood up.

"I've suddenly lost my appetite," she snapped, pushing the menu to one side. Her eyes were brimming with tears, and she just wanted to escape.

"I thought you were different, but you are no better than the others," she said, as her voice got louder. "You've used me. Last week you were all over me like a rash. Now I'm dumped. Well, I'm not just some rag doll you can pick up when you want and throw aside when you've had enough."

At that point, they had an audience.

"I'm a person with feelings."

"It's not like that," sighed Sami.

Pauline picked up his beer, tipped the contents over his head then slammed the glass back on the table.

"Have a nice life!" she yelled at him and stormed out of the restaurant.

So much for letting her down gently.

The waiter came over and took his glass.

"I'll fill this up again, Sir. Will you still be eating?"

"Yes," he shrugged.

Other members of staff came to clean the table and the surrounding floor. He ordered a meal and sat alone for the rest of the evening, deep in thought, wondering why he bothered with women. All they did was cause him strife. Then he realised that he smelled of beer. He picked up his phone and sent Victoria a message.

'I've just ended the relationship with Pauline. I'm sitting here covered in beer. S x' Victoria giggled when she read the text, and then replied.

'I can't say I have much sympathy. You can't play with people's feelings. V x'

'Would you mind giving me a lift? I don't want to get a taxi, stinking of beer. S x'

'Give me a few minutes. V x'

This is a sight I don't want to miss.

At the end of the following week, Victoria felt much better. The morning sickness was beginning to wear off, and she had more energy following the iron tablets and the break. Before returning to work, she had a follow-up GP appointment for a further blood test, and her results had improved.

The following week, she spent more time with Sami, and their friendship grew. However, she did not want him to take precedence over her mother and Chris, as they had been her loyal support through the previous weeks when they had met for lunch during Sami's absence. Sami was very jealous.

At twenty-weeks pregnant, Victoria had an appointment for a sexing scan, and Sami accompanied her. They discovered that they were having a baby girl.

Sami was delighted at the news.

76

Sami was eating lunch with his mother the following Saturday. It had become a regular outing since the fallout with his father. As they chatted, he told her about the sexing scan and revealed that Victoria was having a baby girl.

Anne had been delighted by the announcement of the pregnancy and felt the same with the news of a little girl. However, there was an air of disappointment since Imran did not share her excitement.

"Does Father know about my baby?" asked Sami.

"Yes, he knows," replied Anne.

"What is his reaction?"

"He isn't certain it belongs to you," said Anne.

"Typical," spat Sami. "He can't even be pleased for me. He knows that, if he hadn't stuck his nose in, this would have been everything he ever wanted."

"He thinks it's been a while since you and Victoria were together."

"Victoria didn't want to come near me for six weeks after the fiasco."

"Well, that's what he thinks," said Anne.

Things were a lot calmer between Anne and Imran. She stayed at her mother Rosy's place for a while, but dutifully cooked and cleaned the family home. One day, he visited Anne bearing an apology and a bouquet, so she relented and returned home permanently.

Victoria spent the following weekend converting the back bedroom into a nursery. She chose wallpaper with a pink pig design, in a lovely pastel-pink shade, and coated the other two walls with plain cream. She bought matching curtains and had some laminate flooring laid. Sami came round to assist with the decorating, and they had fun preparing the room.

She wished that they were still together as a couple, but was happy that they were at least able to maintain a friendship. Everything had seemed so perfect until the Ahmeds arrived and ripped her world apart. She remained haunted by the vision of that girl in Sami's bed and, as much as he had sworn nothing happened, could not erase that image from her mind.

Sami was still trying to earn Victoria's trust. It seemed an uphill struggle, but he felt things had improved since they were spending time together outside of work. The main problem was Victoria's friendship with Chris Rogers, as Sami suspected that he still had a romantic interest in her.

Chris saw an advertisement for a Foundation Year 2 Doctor on the NHS jobs website. He was ambitious and wanted to apply for it but needed to update his curriculum vitae and project himself more to have any hope of being a successful applicant. He messaged Victoria to ask for her advice, and they arranged to meet one lunchtime in her office.

Sami purchased his sandwich and a latte for lunch and took them back to his office, as he wanted to study the patient files before his clinic. As he approached the door, he heard Victoria's raucous laugh. He sighed, wondering who was with her.

He opened the door and saw Chris Rogers sitting close to her at her desk, studying something on the screen. He was not pleased.

"What is going on?" he asked abruptly.

"I'm just helping Chris with his curriculum vitae. He's applying for another job," replied Victoria, seeing the displeasure on his face. "I didn't think you would mind."

"Well, I do mind," he snapped. "In the future, would you mind asking if you want to bring someone in here? I had wanted to get on with some work."

"We'll try not to make any noise," she replied.

"So it was a ghost I heard laughing before?"

Sami became angrier. He didn't like that man and didn't want him in his office.

"Oh, for goodness sake," sighed Victoria.

"Look, I'll just leave," said Chris quietly to Victoria, not looking at Sami.

"Yes, I think you should," snapped Sami.

"Do you have to be so rude?" asked Victoria, showing annoyance.

"This is my office. I came here wanting a quiet lunch, and it's filled with people gossiping, laughing, and making a noise."

"We share this office, Sami," Victoria retorted as she stood up, saved Chris's work, and removed the flash drive from the computer.

"Come on, we'll go elsewhere," she said to Chris.

"I should go back to work," Chris replied.

"OK, we'll arrange for another time."

"Don't come back here," Sami barked as Chris left the office.

"Was it necessary to be so rude?" Victoria snapped angrily.

"Don't bring people into my room, especially him. Sitting there looking cosy behind your desk. Are you sure this baby is mine?"

"How dare you" Victoria shouted. "Do you think I would lie about my child's paternity? If that's how you feel, then don't have anything to do with her. I don't need you in my life." She was furious.

Just then, the door swung open and James Turnbull stood there, looking like thunder.

"I want you both in my office, NOW."

Sheepishly, Victoria headed out of the door and walked to James's office, followed by Sami. They all sat down.

"Right. Practically the whole ward heard your argument, so what do you have to say for yourselves?" There was silence for a while then Victoria spoke.

"I must apologise for raising my voice on the ward. That was unacceptable." She paused for a few minutes, trying to hold back her tears.

"I was helping Dr Rogers with his CV in the office during lunch when Sami entered. He wasn't happy at someone else being there. I apologise for not asking permission first. It won't happen again."

There was silence again.

"Then Sami asked if my baby was his, so I lost my temper. I'm very sorry."

"Victoria, please make sure you ask in the future. Now I need to speak to Sami alone." Victoria left the office.

James didn't expect an apology from Sami so he flicked through various pictures on his monitor as they both sat silently. He then stopped at one image.

"Victoria officially announced her pregnancy to me on Monday 7th March. I knew about it long before you did." Sami rolled his eyes and continued to sit in silence.

"It doesn't take a mathematician to calculate that she must be almost twenty-two weeks pregnant. When is her due date?" asked James.

"I don't know," shrugged Sami, realising he had made a huge mistake.

"I think maybe you should apologise and then talk to her. Then make sure you apologise to Chris Rogers."

"I will. Thanks."

Sami spun around and left the office. He had messed up with Victoria just as things were on a sound footing. He realised that James Turnbull had tried to help him.

He didn't know why he blurted that out, as he'd never doubted the paternity. It was his father who had mentioned it. Then, seeing them sitting nice and close, and giggling, just got him riled. He needed his lunch and cold latte.

Sami noticed that Victoria's belongings had gone when he returned to the office. He sent her some text messages, and even tried to phone her mobile to apologise, but no replies came that evening.

Victoria made a detour into town to collect flowers from the florist. It was 11th June and Neil would have been twenty-nine years old that day. She took the flowers to his grave and laid them in the usual place. She sat there for a while, enjoying the peace and tranquillity of the surroundings. It gave her a chance to gather her thoughts. She realised that things between herself and Sami were not working out.

Why is life so unfair? There was Neil, who had longed to start a family and had his life so cruelly cut short. Then Sami, who has a baby developing within me, wants to deny that she belongs to him.

"You should never have died," she sobbed, grasping his gravestone. She sat and let her emotions spill out.

When she returned to her car, she saw the texts and missed calls from Sami, but she was not in the mood to answer them.

Another text had been sent by Chris.

'Have you kissed and made up yet? Chris x'

'No, I am nowhere near that point yet. When are we rescheduling to? V x'

'Tomorrow night after work? Chris x'

'Sounds good. Where? V x'

'My place. I'll throw in a pizza for tea if you fancy. Chris x'

'Sounds perfect. V x'

This guy does know how to cheer me up. Maybe it's time to move on.

The following day, Victoria avoided the office and left her belongings in the side room of the laboratory, near where her mother worked. At nine o'clock, she went straight to the nurses' station and got herself organised. The ward round was uneventful and, afterwards, Sami asked her to step into the office. On her desk was a lovely bouquet. She opened the attached card.

Sorry. Love from Sami. xx

She looked up at him and said, "You don't get it, do you? It's one thing to hurt me, but quite something else to hurt my baby."

"What do you mean?" he replied, confused.

"What do I tell her when she asks about her father? Am I to say you refused to be her father because you didn't think she was yours?"

"That's not true," he replied. "I want to be the baby's father."

"That is not what you said yesterday," Victoria snapped. "I don't want these flowers. You can no longer win over my affections with flowers." She picked them up and placed them in the waste bin.

"You need to make up your mind, mean what you say, and earn my affections," she replied, storming out of the office, leaving Sami bewildered.

When Sami finally left the office, he could see that Victoria had started with the bone marrow procedure, so he disappeared to the doctor's suite to have his latte alone.

Later, Bernie asked Victoria if she could use the flowers to put in vases around the ward, to make things more cheerful for the patients.

"Of course, you can," Victoria replied. "I'm sorry, Bernie. Things have been rather difficult lately."

"Don't worry, Love. We all admire how you have stood up to him," she said and gave Victoria a friendly wink.

"Thanks."

That evening, Victoria arrived at Chris's flat around seven o'clock. It was a lovely compact residence, consisting of stairs up to a lounge, kitchen, bathroom, and two bedrooms.

He ordered pizza and they decided to make the adjustments to the curriculum vitae and then go through the job application form before eating. When the pizza arrived, they sat on Chris's sofa and hungrily tucked in.

"So, old Prakesh now doesn't think the baby is his?" laughed Chris.

"It seems that way," replied Victoria, "though he keeps trying to apologise. We seemed to be doing so well. Our friendship was back on track, and he had stepped up to fatherhood. He even helped me decorate the nursery. Then suddenly, that outburst. I'm not sure why he wanted to do all those things if he thought the baby wasn't his."

"Absurd, isn't it?" Chris said, shaking his head in disbelief. "I think you are far too good for him. You deserve better."

"Like you?" Victoria asked.

"Of course." They giggled.

"My offer still stands, now that you know where I live."

"I'm still not ready for a new relationship. There is too much happening, and there's a baby involved. I don't want to hurt anyone's feelings."

"I know you still have feelings for him but I don't know what you see in him. I would still like to sleep with you. Will you stay the night? At least allow me to have a memory. It may even help you decide."

Victoria took a deep breath and shrugged, before saying, "I don't know."

Before she could say, or do, anything else, he had taken her into his arms and kissed her long and hard. She enjoyed his kiss and responded. He moved his hands around her body, feeling her smooth skin and inhaling her sweet perfume.

Then he led her into his bedroom and began to undress her. Her baby bump was protruding and was very noticeable.

"I have never made love to a pregnant woman before," he smiled, as he pulled off his clothes. He took her in his arms and began to kiss her passionately, enjoying the feel of her soft skin and bare breasts against his flesh. He gently laid her on his bed as their night of passion began.

After their lovemaking, they lay with their bodies entwined, breathless with passion. As their breathing slowed, Chris leaned over to set his alarm before falling asleep with his arm wrapped around her waist.

The alarm rang at eight o'clock. Chris needed to get ready to start work as his twelve-hour dayshift started at nine.

Such is life when there is a beautiful woman in my bed.

Victoria was still sleepy, so he made her a cup of tea and said, "Stay for as long as you want. Help yourself to breakfast cereal or toast." Victoria smiled up at him.

"Thanks," she replied.

"Come back tonight if you want. Just come to work, and I'll give you the key. The door slams on the way out. I finish at nine o'clock."

"I'm not sure about tonight. We are going cot shopping tomorrow. Sami was supposed to be coming, but I'm not sure I want him there."

"I'm working the same shift tomorrow too. The offer is there if you change your mind."

Chris felt disappointed, as he thought that she wouldn't hesitate after the previous night. He leaned over and gave her another long kiss.

"Goodbye, gorgeous," he said, leaving her with a playful wink.

"Goodbye, flatterer," she laughed, and he left the flat.

At work, he couldn't help but mention that he was sleeping with a registrar.

77

Victoria dosed off to sleep again and didn't wake up until ten-thirty. *Goodness, I must have needed the sleep.*

She got up and helped herself to some of Chris's breakfast cereal and another cup of tea. As she ate her breakfast, her thoughts turned to the events of the previous night. She had come to help Chris with his curriculum vitae and had ended up staying overnight.

Undoubtedly, he was a good lover. However, she couldn't help but feel something was missing. She didn't want to feel that way as she had considered starting afresh with him, but that was the truth.

The first night she had pizza with Sami, there had been a series on television, conversations around that, and fun. There had been none of that with Chris. Then she remembered Mitzi defaecating in the cat litter tray on her first night there and Sami's embarrassment. It was so funny. She smiled at those memories.

Chris had made love to her three times last night but had woken her up to do so. She hadn't been keen on that. She also knew that, if she loved him, she wouldn't have hesitated in coming back that night. Victoria realised that she didn't love Chris. She still loved Sami.

Later that evening, Sami sent a text message asking, 'Are we still going to buy a cot tomorrow? S x' Victoria was still feeling annoyed by his outburst the previous week and replied, 'I'd prefer it if you didn't come. V x'

She could be very unforgiving.

'Could you, at least, let me know the baby's due date? S x'

'5th October. V x'

Sami decided to begin alterations in his spare room as he wanted to change it into a nursery. He dismantled the single bed and stored it in the hallway. He had promised it to Richard as Sarah was ready for a bed. Then he went to the DIY store to buy paint and some rolls of unicorn wallpaper. He returned and got to work. He glossed the skirting boards, windows, and door. Already, the room looked brighter.

Later, he took a small axe and demolished the old wooden wardrobe. It gave him great pleasure as it was his father's. He no longer wanted it and felt that his daughter deserved something better. The broken planks of wood were stored in the backyard, awaiting a trip to the local recycling centre.

Monday came quickly, as always. Sami was already in the office, getting himself prepared for the week ahead. Victoria decided to use the office that day as she needed to discuss things with Sami.

"Good morning, Sami," Victoria said as she entered.

"Good morning," he replied, continuing with his work.

"I think we need to organise DNA testing. As you think this child may not be yours, we must confirm the genealogy. I am happy to provide a sample as I have nothing to hide."

Sami stopped typing and looked across at her and said, "It won't be necessary. I do not doubt that the child is mine."

Victoria was astonished, and replied, "That's not what you said last week."

"I know. I was wrong, and I'm sorry." She shrugged.

"Look, I was jealous, OK? I saw that man sitting there with you, looking cosy. My father has never believed the baby was mine. That was all on my mind when I saw you with him. I just got riled."

Victoria took a deep breath.

"I should have guessed your father was involved."

She got up from her chair and showed him a photograph of the cot she had chosen when they shopped without him yesterday. He then explained how he had begun decorating the small room and how he had disassembled the old wardrobe belonging to his father.

"It will make good firewood," he laughed. Victoria giggled with him. *Things appeared to be back on a better footing.*

Sami took a day of annual leave on Wednesday. He had not mentioned it to Victoria, so she got on with the work as usual. She did wonder if everything was all right, so she sent him a message.

'Hi, Sami. I see you're off today. Is everything OK? V x'

It was a while before she got the reply, 'Everything is fine. Just resting. S x'

Sami was sitting on the train when Victoria's message arrived. He stared out of the window at the passing fields, full of cows and sheep grazing. How simple their lives were. If only his was that simple. A fresh start somewhere new may be best for him now. Nobody liked him at Lady Margaret's Hospital, other than Verity. James Turnbull had mentioned that week that he was offering the position of Training Officer to Andy Bartholomew, so Sami wouldn't be mentoring any more new registrars. It didn't bother him. He owed them nothing.

Also, if rumours were true and Victoria was with Chris Rogers, it would create a difficult scenario for him to face at work. He would prefer to be a 'holiday daddy' and have the child visit him during holiday times. He couldn't bear going to wherever they lived to collect his daughter at the weekend, knowing that idiot would be more of a father to her than him. Then there was that irritating smirk Chris often had on his face.

There are times when I could punch that man he thought.

Then there is my father. I am finished with him too. He has destroyed the only chance I had of having a family. I need to get away, to live my own life without any interference from anyone.

He read Victoria's text. He didn't think she would even miss him, so he chose not to mention the interview.

I can just be resting like anyone else.

Andy Bartholomew spoke to Victoria about a particular rumour that he had heard. To say that Victoria was furious was an understatement.

She had a list of patients to attend to on the different wards. She prioritised the one in the Accident and Emergency Department where Dr Nigel Cameron was assessing the patient. He suspected that it was an intracranial bleed; the patient was on warfarin, so it could be dangerous. Victoria suggested that he contact the lab and request some Beriplex.

As she left the area to head to the next ward, Nigel noticed that she stopped further along the corridor to speak to Chris Rogers. They seemed to be having a rather heated discussion. No doubt it was about the stories Chris was spreading. Nigel turned to go to the telephone, with a wry smile.

The next day, James Turnbull called a meeting with Sami, Victoria, and Andy. The seminar at Telford was drawing close, and he needed to know that his colleagues were amicable enough to travel there together.

"After all, you are representing Lady Margaret's Hospital, so I will not tolerate any argumentative displays like those witnessed in this ward. Victoria, as the registrar, you should attend. Do you feel well enough to go? What do you think about Sami accompanying you?"

"I feel fine in myself," Victoria replied. "As for Sami, he is my mentor, and I think we are both professional people. I will undoubtedly conduct myself professionally, as would be expected."

She also thought that it would be a good opportunity to have a good conversation with Sami and clear the air.

"How about you, Sami? Are you happy to travel with Victoria and treat her as a well-respected member of this team?" asked James.

"Of course," he replied. "As Victoria said, we are professionals."

He secretly wanted to discuss things with her too.

"Now, how do you all propose to travel to the venue? Shall I purchase rail tickets?"

"I'll just take my car," said Victoria. "It's a people carrier and very comfortable for long journeys. It will save the hospital money, as only I will need reimbursing for travel expenses."

"Is everyone agreeable with this?" asked James.

Andy nodded in agreement.

"As long as you clean it before we travel," said Sami. "It's not the tidiest vehicle I've ever ridden in." He gave her a wink and smiled.

"Are you offering to clean it for me, as you did once before?"

"I'll do it for a price."

"OK. You clean my car and I will make Sunday lunch for us."

"Sounds like a deal," said Sami.

"I'll add you to my insurance policy, too, just in case you need to drive."

"Great! It sounds like we have it all sorted," said James, thinking that the meeting had gone more smoothly than he had expected. He was relieved that Sami and Victoria seemed to be getting along better again.

The week before the Telford Seminar, Victoria arranged to meet Sami on Sunday to cook him lunch in return for his excellent services on her car. He also showed her the newly-decorated spare room, which she loved.

The Saturday before, he had had lunch with his mother.

"Hopefully, you can persuade her to return to you," Anne said.

"Mother, I must face the fact that Victoria will never be my significant other. She cannot forget what she saw in the bedroom that day, and we have had constant disagreements ever since. I've tried everything. Besides, she is seeing someone else now."

"Who?"

"Chris Rogers, the guy from the party. She didn't tell me. I heard it from someone else."

"Are you sure about that?" asked Anne. "I was always certain Victoria loved you."

"The news is circulating the ward."

"Ask her outright, Sami. You know what gossip can be like."

"I'm scared of what the answer may be."

"Why don't you propose to her?" asked Anne.

"Propose," Sami laughed. "I can't even get her to be my girlfriend."

"She thinks you don't want marriage, doesn't she?"

"Probably. I did tell her that once."

"What about this Chris?" Anne asked. "Will he be serious about her once someone else's baby comes along?"

"I doubt it. Chris has always been keen on Victoria, but he plays the field."

"I think a proposal may do the trick," said Anne, hopefully. "It would be the one thing which would express your level of love and commitment to her. Believe me, if she loves you, in any way, she will accept."

Sami sighed and said, "I don't know, Mother. I wish I shared your optimism."

Later that evening, Sami realised that his mother could be right. It was the one thing he could do that Chris wouldn't. It would wipe that smirk from his face.

Now, he needed to buy a ring. A diamond. How would he find out her size? Perhaps Paul Reed, Victoria's stepfather, would be able to help?

78

The Telford Seminar weekend finally arrived. Victoria, Sami, and Andy finished work early, and Victoria arranged to collect them so she could be on the road by half-past two. James Turnbull had been left in charge of haematology, so he and Verity would tend to the patients and finish the work that afternoon.

Victoria headed down the motorway, stopping only once on the journey for a bathroom and coffee break. They arrived at Telford early in the evening. The hotel reception was busy with clients waiting to check in, perhaps for the seminar too. It was a spacious reception with plush red seating, gold decor on the walls, and a large glass chandelier.

While waiting in the queue, Victoria spotted Dr Anthony Quigley from Central Hospital. She had met him during her sandwich year at university when she had a placement in the Central Hospital Laboratory. Her mother had worked there too and was a good friend of Dr Quigley's. She dropped her belongings and dashed across the reception to greet him.

"Tony. How lovely to see you," she said, giving him a big hug.

"Victoria, the pleasure is all mine," he replied. "How are you?"

"I'm doing fine. How are you?"

"I'm good, thanks. Your mother messaged me and told me you were coming here. She is very proud of you for becoming a registrar. These are my registrars, Diane and Jonathan," he said, indicating to the two people on his left.

"Great to meet you," said Victoria, shaking hands with them.

"How is the training going?" asked Tony.

"It's going great. I love the job and have a good team," Victoria replied. "Anyway, I'd better go and get checked in. We must catch up later."

The queue kept advancing, and Sami moved Victoria's luggage forward as she chatted with her friend.

"Who is she talking to?" asked Andy.

"I have no idea," replied Sami, "although he looks familiar."

She must know him quite well to put her arms around him, Sami thought.

Victoria returned to the queue and said, "That is Dr Tony Quigley from Central Hospital. My mother knows him well from her time there, and I met him during my placement there."

They checked in, and their rooms were on the second floor. Sami and Victoria had adjacent rooms, and Andy was further along the corridor.

"Should we all freshen up and meet in half an hour for dinner?" asked Sami.

"That sounds like a good plan," said Victoria. "I'm hungry. I'll knock at your door as I pass, Sami, and then we can all go down together."

Victoria hung up her maternity dresses which were bought specially for the occasion and had a quick wash. She chose a casual, but smart, look for the evening meal.

As arranged, they met and headed down in the lift together.

In the reception, a woman came over and addressed Sami.

"Sami Prakesh. Goodness, it's been a long time." She was smartly dressed in blue and had dark hair, very nicely shaped into a bob hairstyle.

"Wendy," said Sami in surprise. "It's lovely to see you."

"Likewise," she replied. "And who are these lovely people?" She spied Victoria and noticed that she was pregnant.

"This is Dr Andrew Bartholomew, Consultant Haematologist, friend and colleague. The lady is Dr Victoria Pemberton, my registrar."

"It's lovely to meet you all. We must have a drink later," she said, with a big smile, then swiftly disappeared towards the lift. Victoria noticed that Sami was feeling uncomfortable.

"Who is that?" she asked him directly. "You didn't introduce her to us."

"Wendy Bartlett," he replied.

"So, how did you meet her?" persisted Victoria.

"At university. She's an ex-girlfriend."

"Ah," replied Victoria, understanding why he felt so uncomfortable.

They were seated at a table and ordered their meals. Victoria kept wondering about Sami's ex-girlfriend and why he seemed so secretive about her. She hoped that the woman wouldn't be a thorn in the side on the trip. As Andy was present, she decided to keep things light-hearted and fun between them, so she teased Sami about his past.

"Come on, Sami. Tell me more about Wendy then. How long were you dating her?"

"Stop being so nosy. It's none of your business," he replied, giving her a wink before looking at Andy.

"I'm curious."

"It was nothing. Wendy was my girlfriend for two months, and then I left her for a pretty blonde. I'm surprised she even spoke as I wasn't particularly nice to her."

"Sounds like you were quite the Romeo in those days," laughed Andy.

"There were indeed a few in my university days," Sami replied with a snigger.

"So what happened?" asked Andy.

"I went and got married," he laughed. "Then life took a nosedive."

They decided to retire early as they had a long weekend ahead. Sami had been in his room for five minutes when he heard a knock at the door. He opened it and was surprised to see Wendy with a wine bottle and two glasses.

"A drink for old time's sake?" she asked.

"I'm not really in the mood tonight. I've had a long journey."

"Oh, come on. Just a quick drink or it could be more if you want?"

"Certainly not," he said in a firm voice.

Just then, there was another knock at his door. It was Victoria.

"Hi, Sami. Can we talk?" she asked, before catching sight of Wendy, with the wine and glasses. "I see you are busy. It doesn't matter." She turned and walked out. Sami went after her.

"What do you want to discuss?"

"It doesn't matter," she said, as she went into her room and shut the door.

Shit.

Victoria listened to the sound of laughter in the next room. Then, suddenly, it stopped. She lay on her bed and sobbed.

"So, what did she want?" asked Wendy when Sami returned to the room.

"She's my girlfriend, Wendy. We've had a few problems, and now that she's seen you in here with wine, she'll get the wrong idea," he said, exasperated.

"Oh, sorry, I hadn't realised. You introduced Victoria to me as your registrar. So, Sami, you are going to be a father? My goodness," she laughed and poured the wine.

"One drink and I'll go. I'll talk to her tomorrow."

Sami took out the diamond ring he'd purchased before the trip.

"Sami, you shouldn't have," she laughed.

"I had hoped to propose this weekend," he said.

"It's beautiful. She's a lucky girl. I'll tell her that."

After chatting about their university days and laughing over some memories, Wendy took her wine bottle and left the room. Sami decided against knocking at Victoria's door then as she might have been asleep.

Victoria woke with a start and rubbed her eyes. She had forgotten to set her alarm but saw that it was only a quarter-past seven, so she decided to make a cup of tea. She'd arranged to meet Sami and Andy to go for breakfast at half-past eight but was undecided about whether to go alone.

She was annoyed with Sami.

Why did I ever want to get back with him? Baby Jasmine and I are better off without him.

A couple of weeks previously, she had started calling her bump Baby Jasmine.

She decided to wait for breakfast because of Andy and she watched for him coming down the corridor. Then she locked her door and went to knock on Sami's. She was intrigued to see if anyone would come out with him, but he came out alone.

"Good morning," said Andy as he called for the lift.

"Sorry I didn't knock last night," said Sami to Victoria, "as I thought you would be sleeping."

"It was difficult to sleep with all the noise," snapped Victoria.

Andy looked at Victoria and then at Sami, sensing the tension between them.

"Sami had a woman in his room last night," Victoria explained. "His ex-girlfriend."

"She was only there for a while, then she left," said Sami, embarrassed in front of Andy. "We're not together, so it's none of your business."

"You're right. It's not," Victoria said, leaving the lift ahead of them.

"I've heard you haven't kept your legs closed much either," Sami called after her.

People around the reception turned their heads to look at him, as he hadn't realised that he'd raised his voice. Victoria continued to walk in front, keeping herself aloof from him, but tears were pricking the back of her eyes. She helped herself to breakfast and then went over to Tony, Diane and Jonathan, who were already sitting at a large round table.

"Good morning, Tony. May I join you?"

"Of course," he indicated with his hand to one of the spare seats.

"I don't think you should have said that," Andy said to Sami, as they were selecting their breakfast. Sami shrugged.

"Maybe not, but she makes me so cross. She always sees the worst in me." He paused while he rummaged in his pocket.

"I have this ring," he said, and discreetly took it out to show Andy. "I had hoped to pop the question this weekend."

"There's still time," replied Andy. At that moment, Sami made another critical decision. "No. I'm tired of the arguments. I will return it to the jewellers and get a refund. She's with Chris Rogers now."

79

Andy and Sami walked towards the same table. Victoria stood up and politely introduced them all, and then they took their seats and quietly ate breakfast.

Victoria got another drink but needed fresh air, so she walked outside. She went to the hotel garden and sat on one of the seats. It was sunny, and it seemed a shame to be stuck indoors. She could do with walking the dogs as it was always good for her mental health and well-being. She allowed her emotions to spill over. Maybe after that, she would feel more assertive, be able to grit her teeth and allow Sami's comments to bounce off her thick skin. She was absorbed in her thoughts. She hadn't seen someone approach and sit on the bench beside her.

"Victoria, isn't it?" said the woman in a friendly voice. "Are you all right, dear? Should I go and get the men?"

"No thanks," she replied, trying to be strong.

It's Wendy! I am annoyed with her for being in Sami's room last night. Maybe I would have told Sami how much I loved him if she hadn't been there.

"Men problems?" she asked. Victoria was still very tearful and didn't reply.

"I must apologise for being in your boyfriend's room last night. I know you may have gotten the wrong impression, but I had no idea you were together. Once he told me, we chatted about old memories, and then I left. All he did was speak of you and how much he wants to be with you," Wendy said, as she put her arm around Victoria and offered her a tissue.

She continued, "I never thought he was father material, but he is looking forward to your daughter being born. If you have the love and support of a man, you need to embrace it, as it's scarce in the world today. I loved a man once, but he left me for another woman. So I just concentrated on my career."

Victoria felt calmer listening to Wendy and hearing what Sami had told her, although it seemed like she was speaking about a different man.

"You need to go and make up with him," Wendy said. "Well, I must go as I need to prepare for my speech."

She stood up and disappeared into the hotel.

Victoria remembered looking at the programme of events and had seen that the first speech was to be made by Professor Wendy Bartlett. She decided to go back in and join her party.

She went straight over to Sami, and said, "I owe you an apology. I've spoken to Wendy, and she explained what happened last night. I'm sorry for jumping to conclusions."

Sami was surprised to hear her words but was still angry about their discussion earlier.

"Why do you always think the worst of me?" he asked.

Victoria didn't know the answer to that question and began to feel guilty. She didn't reply but went to take her seat. As far as she was concerned, she had apologised. Maybe too much water had flowed under the bridge. She needed to face the fact there would probably never be a reconciliation with Sami.

The day passed without event as Victoria sat and made notes on the various topics discussed at the seminar. It finished at four o'clock, and then everyone chatted excitedly about the evening ahead.

"What's happening for our evening meal then? Should we book a table?" Andy suggested, as he got out of his chair and stretched.

"I fancy going out," said Victoria. "We've been stuck in here all day, and I could do with some fresh air. Besides, I don't think the cuisine is that good here."

"We could go out somewhere, I suppose," said Andy.

"I'm staying in," muttered Sami in his usual unemotional voice. Victoria wasn't surprised that he wanted to do the opposite to her.

Let him be miserable and stay in.

"What about you guys?" she turned to look at Tony and his registrars. "Would you like to go out? I know this great little pub tucked away in the village of Criggion. My parents took me there when we came this way on holiday once. It's called the Admiral Rodney Inn. They serve lovely food."

"That sounds delightful," said Tony.

"I'm up for it, too," said Jonathan, "as long as you don't mind our company."

"How do you propose to get there?" sighed Sami, rolling his eyes.

"By car, of course," replied Victoria. "I can adjust the seats so that there's room for everyone. I must call and see if I can reserve a table."

She took out her mobile phone, and they heard her saying, "Hello, Stuart. It's me, Victoria. Do you remember me? I had lunch at your pub while on holiday with my parents, Carol and Paul." Her voice trailed away as she left the table and walked into the reception.

"I'd like to go," said Andy. "It sounds nice, and to be honest, I wasn't keen on the food here either."

"You go," said Sami. "I'll just dine alone."

"With the greatest respect, Sami, Victoria is carrying your child. Do you not think you should go along and make sure she's alright?"

Sami sighed and rolled his eyes, and said, "Alright. As you wish."

They all agreed to meet at the reception at six o'clock. Victoria had changed into a lovely black floral maternity dress for the evening. She went down early to reorganise the car into its seven-seat facility to accommodate them all. By the time she got back into the reception, they were assembling.

"Your taxi awaits," Victoria said, smiling at them. She was looking forward to getting out.

"Victoria, I was wondering where you were," said Sami. "I knocked but, as usual, you didn't answer."

She looks stunning.

"Sorry, I came down early as I had to reorganise the car. Let's go."

They all got in and Victoria typed the postcode into the satellite navigation system before driving off.

"So, how far is this place?" asked Sami. He was sitting in the front passenger seat with Victoria as everyone else had made a beeline for the back of the car.

"It'll take about half an hour," she said.

"What was everyone's favourite topic today?" asked Andy, breaking the silence.

"Oh, let's not talk about work. We've come out to enjoy ourselves," said Tony in a cheerful voice.

Victoria took a left turn at the roundabout.

"Mid Wales," exclaimed Sami, seeing the signpost. "For goodness sake, where on earth are we going? The back of beyond?"

"Stop complaining. It's a mystery tour," Victoria laughed, and she decided to switch the radio on.

A catchy tune came on so everyone, except Sami, did the actions and sang along to the music. He just glared out of the window.

"Wow, look at the monument," said Tony. "I wonder what it is?"

"That's Admiral Rodney's Pillar," said Victoria. "It commemorates his victory over the French in 1782."

"It looks great. I bet it would be a great walk up there. A lovely view."

"I believe it takes two to three hours," said Victoria. Eventually, she pulled into the pub's gravelled car park and made sure she entered the pub first.

"Stuart!" she called over to the bar and gave him a wave.

Stuart came over to greet her. She introduced him to her friends and colleagues. He pointed to a table on the left, which he had set earlier to accommodate them, and then brought a menu for everyone. As they read it, Stuart took the drinks order.

"What are faggots?" asked Victoria. Everyone erupted in laughter, including Sami.

"They are meatballs made from minced offcuts," said Tony giving her a friendly wink.

"Sounds nice. I think I'll have faggots."

The others ordered a mixture of Whitby scampi, pie, gammon, and Hunters Chicken. Everyone was hungry and thoroughly enjoyed their food.

"Now, who wants dessert?" asked Victoria.

Tony and Jonathan were too full, but everyone else ordered. Victoria enjoyed a chocolate arctic roll with berries.

"What a great idea of yours to come here, Victoria. I've thoroughly enjoyed my meal," said Tony.

"Me too," agreed Andy. "It's far better than the hotel."

Victoria asked for the bill and worked out how much everyone had to pay, then added additional money as a tip for Stuart's excellent service.

"It's been great seeing you again," she said to him as they left. "Hope I'll be here again on holiday soon."

As she drove home, she felt a headache coming on. It had been a long day and stressful too, with the tension between her and Sami. However, he seemed a bit calmer and more pleasant that night. She rubbed her head with her fingers.

"Are you OK?" he asked.

"I have a bit of a headache, and the baby's kicking harder than usual."

Back at the hotel, Sami wanted to open the adjoining door between the two bedrooms so that he could keep an eye on Victoria. They had to sign a form of agreement to make this possible.

In the bedroom, Victoria changed into her pyjamas and poured herself a glass of water. Sami appeared at the adjoining door.

"Are you OK?" he asked.

"I'm fine thanks, just tired."

"All right, I'm just next door. Give me a shout if you want anything." She pulled the covers back and climbed into bed, taking a sip of her water. Sami hovered nervously at the door. He needed to tell her of his decision.

"Victoria, I have something to discuss, and now may be a good time." She had closed her eyes, wondering what bombshell he was about to drop.

"Can't it wait? I'm very tired."

"I'm leaving."

"Leaving?"

"Lady Margaret's Hospital. I have a new job in Manchester."

"Manchester!" she exclaimed, as she sat up in surprise.

He sat on the edge of her bed.

"Is that because of me?" she asked.

"Partly, but I think it's for the best." Tears began to sting the back of her eyes.

"What about the baby?"

"I'm sure you'll do a brilliant job raising her to be a beautiful, intelligent young woman, just like you are. I have every faith in you."

"So you don't even want to see her?"

"Yes. Manchester isn't far. I can have some weekends or holiday visits."

"OK, fine, if that's what you want."

"I wanted to tell you first, so I would appreciate it if you kept it quiet until I give in my notice."

"When are you going?"

"I don't have a start date yet."

He got up and walked back into his room.

"I'll let you get some sleep."

As soon as he had disappeared, Victoria quietly began to sob into her pillow.

Sami lay on his bed watching the TV with the volume turned down. He wished that he hadn't decided to go, but he was through with all the arguments and upset. Then there was the reality of seeing her with Chris Rogers. He couldn't face that every day. He was sure that he could hear sniffing next door. Maybe his news had upset her.

It was as though the baby in Victoria's stomach had understood the conversation, as she started to retaliate. She kicked her belly with some power.

"Ouch," she groaned.

Sami jumped up.

"Is everything all right?" he asked.

"Sami, would you please make me a cup of tea? She's kicking really hard."

He went to boil up the kettle and then gave Victoria her tea.

"Do you need to go to the hospital to get checked out?" he asked.

"No, I'm too tired," she replied, taking a mouthful of tea. It was noticeable that she had been crying.

"I suppose I should wish you luck," she said, staring at her cup.

"I didn't think anyone would miss me, never mind cry over me," he said with a smile.

"Sami, will you lie on the bed?"

"Is that wise?"

"Please. Just for one minute."

He did as he was asked and lay beside her. Victoria turned to face the opposite way. She took his hand in hers and placed it on her belly. He could feel his baby moving.

"My goodness," he remarked. "Was that a kick? It was powerful."

"Yes."

He felt it again and again.

"Wow. I think you're carrying a footballer."

"Seems like it."

Boom. Boom. Boom. The baby continued to kick.

"I've called her Jasmine Rose," she said. "I probably should have discussed it with you. We can change the name if you don't like it."

"It's perfect," he replied.

That was the first time Sami had touched his baby. Seeing her on screen, in a photograph, or as a bump didn't have the same impact. He could feel his little child, and there was a connection. It was an extraordinary moment and it made him feel emotional, but he had to remember that she was with someone else now.

Victoria rolled onto her back and lifted her pyjama top, revealing the complete bump. Sami touched her stomach with his fingers. He continued to lie there and feel Jasmine's movements.

"Hello, little Jasmine," he said. "I'm your daddy. Nice to meet you."

As he'd decided to go away, he wouldn't see much of his baby. He felt tears sting his eyes and turned to kiss Victoria's stomach.

"Jasmine, you are beautiful like your mummy," he said and kissed what he thought was the baby's head again, before lying down and holding her some more. He had a huge lump choking the back of his throat.

How he hated his father. *This was his family, the family he had taken away with his selfish actions.*

Victoria happily allowed him to bond with his baby and continued to look the other way.

"Why did you choose to take the job, Sami?"

"I need to stand on my own two feet," he replied. "I need to be away from my father and live my own life. My mother still does my housework, for goodness sake. I need to cut those ties and get away. Live my own life and be independent."

He sighed.

"What about me?" she asked. "Do you need to get away from me?"

He took another deep sigh before replying.

"You are with someone else now. It's for the best," he said, gulping deep breaths to hold back his tears. He felt Jasmine kick his hand again.

"I'm not with anyone. Where did you hear that rubbish from?"

"It's been general gossip."

He turned to face her, with his hand still firmly on Baby Jasmine.

"I thought you didn't listen to gossip."

"Is it not true?"

"No. I slept with him once, that's all and regretted it immediately. It suddenly became clear it was you I loved."

"I love you too, Victoria, but I can't do all the fighting anymore," he said, as he took another deep breath. "I love you. You and Baby Jasmine are my whole world."

That time, his tears flowed. Victoria turned and put her arms around him. She stroked his shoulder gently to soothe him.

"Ssshh. It's OK," she whispered. "Baby Jasmine doesn't want to hear Daddy crying." As he calmed down, he got the words out.

"I felt I needed a fresh start, somewhere else, where you are not around." There was silence for a while, and then Victoria said, "I'm so sorry."

"I've loved you since the day we met," he said. "There's never been anyone else. I know it didn't look good that evening with Zarina. I don't know what else to say or do to convince you, but nothing happened. I could never have done that after the time we had in Aviemore. Remember that wild sex we had there?"

Victoria nodded. She had often thought about that day. Strangely enough, she believed him. She felt that she should have trusted him more, and suddenly the words of the lucky gypsy entered her mind.

'If you can lose the anger and let it wash away, everything will become very clear.'

That moment had arrived and it suddenly all seemed so very clear.

"I love you, Sami Prakesh," she said, flinging her other arm around his neck. She looked up at him with those baby blue eyes he loved so much.

"I love you too, Victoria Pemberton," he replied and, before she could say another word, his lips were upon hers, and his tongue was searching her mouth deeply, making up for the lost time. She felt comforted by his touch, and his kisses tickled her face. She ached for his touch.

He pulled off her pyjama top, exposing her maternal breasts. He teased her nipples gently with his tongue as she moaned beside him.

"I've missed you so much, my darling. I will never let you escape again."

It was slow, tender, and passionate when they made love that night. Afterwards, they lay in each other's arms, and Sami could still feel the movements of Baby Jasmine. Victoria nestled her head on his chest. It was the most content either of them had felt in a very long time.

The next day, Sami woke up to find Victoria sitting on the edge of her bed.

"Good morning, Sweetheart," he said, smiling at her.

"Good morning," she replied. He sensed that something wasn't right.

"What's up?" he asked.

"We made beautiful love last night. Then I remembered you are going away and leaving us." Sami got up and placed his arms around her.

"For God's sake, woman, it's only a job. Of course I'm not going now, not after everything that happened last night. You and Jasmine are my world." He kissed her.

"I was a bit worried," she said, smiling.

On the way down to breakfast, they walked hand in hand, much to Andy's surprise. "I see you've made up," he said while they were helping themselves to breakfast. "We did a lot of talking," Sami said.

"Congratulations," he replied.

80

"Good morning, everyone," said Victoria, as she sat to eat breakfast, with Sami at her side. It was clear for all to see that they had reconciled.

"Congratulations! I'm pleased for you both," said Tony.

"Thanks," replied Victoria.

The morning seminar got underway with a short morning break, then an hour for lunch, as everyone had long journeys home later that afternoon. Sami felt the box in his pocket, wondering if he would find an opportune moment.

Wendy Bartlett spoke to him during the lunch hour and asked, "I see you've both made up; have you proposed to her yet?"

"No. I haven't found the right moment."

"Come with me," she said and escorted him to the stage area. She then chatted with one of the organisers before returning to where Sami stood.

"OK. Everything is sorted. You can go on stage and propose to her."

"What!" exclaimed Sami, aghast. "I can't do that."

"Yes, you can. Victoria will love it. I'll go and find her."

Wendy disappeared, and the organiser came over and handed Sami a microphone, saying, "Good luck. The stage is yours."

Sami felt horrified.

"Victoria, have you got a moment?" asked Wendy, as she approached the table.

"OK," she replied.

"Come with me."

Wendy headed off, and Victoria followed. She saw Sami beside the stage and wondered what was happening.

"What is he doing?" she asked Wendy, in a panic. "I hope he doesn't expect me to do a talk. I am only a registrar and I don't have the experience of many people here."

"You'll be fine," said Wendy.

Sami stood on the stage, with all eyes upon him. His legs turned to jelly, and he felt sick to his stomach.

How have I managed to get into this situation?

He saw Victoria approaching the stage, looking puzzled. Wendy ushered her onto the stage. Sami knew he would have to grit his teeth and do it, as so many people were watching.

"Hmmm," he said, as he cleared his voice into the microphone to check that it was working. He wasn't a public speaker and didn't like speeches at all. He was shaking when he introduced himself.

"Good afternoon, ladies and gentlemen. I am Dr Sami Prakesh, a haematologist at Lady Margaret's Hospital in North East England. My colleague is Dr Victoria Pemberton, my registrar." His voice remained surprisingly steady as he continued, saying, "Victoria came to work for me last September. I wasn't keen on sharing my office with a woman."

He paused as it had raised some laughter from the audience.

"However, Victoria and I soon became good friends. We had a real connection." Victoria stood with a smile painted on her face.

Where is all this leading?

"Later, we started a relationship and, as you can see, she is expecting our baby in October. I know we have had some ups and downs, but the one thing which hasn't changed is my love for her. That has always been rock solid, and I am excited about our baby. So I have a question. Victoria, will you marry me?"

There were gasps from around the room.

Victoria stood rooted to the spot and couldn't believe her ears. She could feel the tears choking at the back of her throat and couldn't find her voice.

Did he really say that?

"Maybe I should do this properly," Sami said, as he approached her and knelt on one knee.

"Victoria Pemberton, will you do me the honour of becoming my wife?"

He took the box from his pocket and removed the lid to reveal a diamond ring.

She looked at the sparkling diamond he was presenting.

"Yes," she said in a choked voice.

Sami held the microphone closer so that everyone could hear.

"Yes, I will marry you."

Huge applause erupted around the room as Sami placed the ring on Victoria's finger. Then she flung her arms around his neck and kissed him. They returned to their seats, having been congratulated several times on the way back.

"So, who else knows?" asked Victoria.

"What do you mean?"

"The ring fits perfectly, and I have fat stubby fingers. That is not pure luck."

"My mother knew," replied Sami, as he placed his finger on his nose as if to indicate someone else was involved, but it was top secret. Victoria suddenly cottoned on.

"Paul," she announced. "It was Paul. He had the ring sizer out at home one night, and we were all measuring our fingers. Does Mum know?"

"No," he replied. "We made a gentleman's agreement."

"I really can't believe what you just did," she exclaimed. "The man who never socialises, and could never offer marriage, stood up on stage. He declared his love for me and proposed. It's a moment I'll never forget. My ring is beautiful too." She looked down at it and twiddled it around on her finger.

"Thank you, so much."

"Thank you. You have made me the happiest man on this planet," he said, as he squeezed her hand beneath the table.

The final talks continued until four o'clock, and then the seminar closed. Victoria said her goodbyes to Tony and his registrars, then also to Wendy and they set off homeward bound, stopping only once for a coffee and bathroom break.

81

After dropping Andy off, Victoria took Sami home and went inside for refreshment. She felt so happy and content, but there was something she wanted to ask him.

"I don't understand why you told me about your new job."

"I wanted you to know before everyone else."

"Why did you announce you were going, at the same time as carrying an engagement ring?"

"I bought the engagement ring hoping to get the opportunity to propose to you. Then I learned about your alleged relationship with Chris, so I decided I would return it to the jewellers. I took it with me to Telford, as the last resort, hoping that we would get closer over the weekend. Then, when you got upset about Wendy being in my room, I decided I would accept the job. But when I lay on the bed that night and felt Jasmine kicking, I became emotional and realised what I would be leaving behind. We talked, we made love, and then I decided to propose."

"Why did you propose when you never wanted marriage?"

"My life is more unhappy when you're not in it. The divorce traumatised me financially, taking all my savings and more. I felt such a failure. I never wanted to let anyone else down but I realised that I needed you to be part of my life. Knowing you has changed everything."

"I never realised the divorce had affected you that way," Victoria said, sympathetically.

"I grew my beard, and became untidy, to hide from the world and to avoid love. I hid behind a mask and became a recluse. Then you came into my life. You were the only one who saw the person underneath and brought me back to life again. That's why I want to marry you."

Victoria felt very humbled.

"I'm sorry that I didn't trust you more."

"We shall put it behind us and start afresh."

"So when are you marrying me? Is it to be a Muslim celebration?"

"No. It's on your terms. You choose. Just let me know the date, and I will be there."

"As much as I would love to stay, I need to go home and do my unpacking and washing."

"I want you to move in," said Sami. "At least, before we have Jasmine."

"I will," she promised and kissed him passionately before leaving.

Carol and Paul were thrilled at the news of the engagement, and Carol admired the ring.

"That's gorgeous," she said, looking at the sparkling diamond. "Whatever made him change his mind?"

"We did a lot of talking during the trip, then at lunchtime, he went on stage and declared his love for me."

"Really? I can't imagine it," said Carol.

"I was astonished," said Victoria.

Sami telephoned his mother later that evening.

"Guess what happened?" he teased. Anne thought her son seemed very light-hearted, and asked, "What?"

"It worked."

"What did?"

"I asked Victoria to marry me, and she said 'Yes'. We're engaged."

"Oh, that is fantastic news. I'm delighted. We must have a celebratory dinner."

"We're going to arrange an evening out," he said.

Once Anne had hung up, she shared the news with Imran. He merely grunted and continued watching TV, showing no interest whatsoever.

Sami and Victoria had decided not to put it on social media that night. Instead, Sami called all the staff members together at the nurses' station the next morning.

"OK, I have an announcement to make," he said, as he tenderly placed his arm around Victoria's shoulder. "I want to inform you all that Victoria and I are now engaged." Victoria then displayed her shining diamond for them all to see.

They were surprised as they were under the impression that she was dating Chris Rogers, but they all smiled and congratulated the happy couple. Typically, Dawn hugged Victoria.

"Congratulations," she said.

The staff's surprise proved to Victoria that it was Chris who had started the false rumour that they were dating.

How dare he! When he finds the news on social media, he will realise how irresponsible and immature his behaviour has been.

That evening, Victoria searched the different wedding venues online. There were some lovely places, but with waiting lists of up to two years. She had hoped for something earlier than that.

"Does it matter?" asked Sami. "You'll have plenty of time to prepare."

"The places have wedding fayres. Maybe we could go and have a look and take our parents along."

"My father isn't coming. I don't want him at our wedding."

"You can't be serious. Can you not try and reconcile now?"

"I'm very serious. It's Dad's place to apologise so, unless he does, there will be no reconciliation. I'll never forget how he looked at me when Masood was here. It was like I didn't exist. It was pure hatred. Then all the stress he's caused with us splitting up. It was all his fault, the interfering old sod. He won't spoil things again. You were right. I should have stood up to him sooner."

"I'll bring Mum and Paul. Your poor mum will miss out if it's on a Sunday."

"Let's try and arrange a Saturday, as I usually meet her for lunch then.

It's going to be difficult arranging a wedding without him knowing. It will only end in tears, thought Victoria.

She flicked onto another page, which showed the Gretna Wedding Bureau. She searched through the different packages and saw that they arranged classic wedding cars, flowers, a Scottish piper, and photography. It looked amazing.

"Would you like a Scottish wedding, Sami?"

"Where? Aviemore?"

"No, in Gretna Green, just over the Scottish border. The place where forbidden couples eloped to get married following the Marriage Act in 1754. Furious fathers had many pursuits overnight, often arriving too late after the weddings had gone ahead. I think it is so apt. I have a vision of your father chasing us there, but arriving too late." They both laughed, as Sami looked at the website.

"The luxury package looks good," he said.

"We will need your decree absolute," Victoria pointed out.

"Oh goodness," he panicked. "I've no idea where that is."

"There's plenty of time. I'll phone them tomorrow and make some enquiries."

After the ward round the following morning, Victoria went into the office and telephoned the Gretna Wedding Bureau. Everything seemed perfect, and she knew Sami would agree with her wishes.

They gave Victoria a date, 31st August that year! It was only six weeks away. If the bureau arranged everything, they could be ready for then.

She telephoned her mother.

"Check your diary for 31st August. Are you free?"

Carol checked her diary and said, "I'm off. It follows a night shift on the Bank Holiday Monday, so I have three days off. Why?"

"It's a possible wedding date."

"What! You're not wasting any time."

"Don't say anything yet. I haven't spoken to Sami."

"OK, let me know if that's definite."

Victoria waited until lunchtime to speak to Sami. She dropped it into the conversation as they sat in the doctor's suite.

"How about 31st August for our wedding?"

"Yes, fine," he said very calmly as though he had not understood.

"This year. In six weeks."

"What?"

"The wedding!"

82

S ami almost choked on his latte.
"This year?" he exclaimed.

"Yes. Why not?"

"You're pregnant, for starters."

"That doesn't make any difference. There will be plenty of time before Jasmine makes an appearance. Besides, I'm not losing you again."

"You won't lose me. If it's what you want, my darling, then book it." She jumped off her seat and threw her arms around him, before kissing him passionately.

"Thank you," she said. "Now you need to tell your mother."

Anne Prakesh was delighted at the news, but one thing dampened her spirits. She had hoped that now he was back with Victoria, Sami would have been the one to hold out the olive branch, but he was as determined as ever that his father needed to do that, and he didn't want him spoiling things with Victoria again.

She knew that Imran regretted the part he had played in their breakup. He had tried to stop the Ahmed family from coming, but he was just as adamant that he was acting in his son's best interests. He hadn't shown any interest in the news of the engagement. Neither Sami nor Imran would apologise and bury this silly feud. They were a pair of stubborn fools.

Since Sami didn't want Imran at the wedding, Anne had to keep it to herself. It was a very delicate situation, as she wanted Sami to marry the woman he loved after years of unhappiness, but also to share that moment with her husband. She felt that she was betraying him by keeping his only son's wedding a secret. So instead of being ecstatic, as she should have been, she shed a few tears. It was an awful dilemma to be in.

"I'll need a hat and a whole new outfit, Sami. I can't buy one without him wondering where the money has gone."

"I'll buy one for you. We can go through to Newcastle and hit the shops there. You can hide it in your wardrobe or leave it at my place."

Victoria sympathised with Anne's dilemma but agreed with Sami that she didn't want Imran turning up and spoiling her big day.

She telephoned the Gretna Wedding Bureau and confirmed her booking.

At home that evening, Sami and Victoria wrote their guest list and ordered their personalised wedding invitations online. Victoria chose an elegant gold and white calligraphy font for the design and ordered three unique blank cards to arrive in the following two days.

"I want Richard to be my best man," said Sami.

"I want Dawn to be my maid of honour and Paul to give me away," said Victoria. "We must arrange an evening meal with them to ask them properly."

"What about Friday?" asked Sami. "Let's see if everyone's available. We'll keep the wedding date a secret until then."

Everyone concerned received a message and they agreed to meet on Friday evening. Victoria booked a table at Giovanni's restaurant for half-past seven.

"I hope the cards and invitations arrive on time," she said, crossing her fingers, "and we must save Saturday for taking our mothers to Newcastle for their outfits."

Friday arrived, and everyone was very excited about the evening meal, especially Dawn, who had been told by Victoria to keep everything top secret from the other staff members.

They ordered their starters, and then Victoria distributed the special cards, saying, "Open them one at a time, so I can get photographs. Dawn first."

Dawn opened her envelope, and her eyes were wide as she read the words, 'Save the day. I would be delighted if you would be my maid of honour. The wedding of Sami and Victoria takes place on 31st August.'

"My goodness," she said, surprised. "Congratulations to you both. I'd love to be your maid of honour, Victoria. I'm thrilled. I've never been a bridesmaid before." Tears streamed down her face and Carol handed her a tissue.

"Your turn, Richard," said Sami.

His card was the same, except it said, 'my best man'.

"Of course. I'd be delighted," Richard said, giving Sami a friendly slap on the shoulder. Victoria handed him the invitation for Janice and Sarah.

Paul then opened his card, to which he replied, "Yes, Love. It would be my pleasure to give you away."

The following day, Anne arrived at Sami's at ten o'clock. It was an excellent opportunity to shop in Newcastle, and she felt very excited. Victoria and Carol arrived soon afterwards, and they all ventured to the shops in Victoria's people carrier.

Once there and parked, they headed to the department store to browse the fashions. There were many dresses of different colours and styles, and Carol and Anne chose various ones to try. After examining each in the mirror, Anne finally selected a deep royal blue lace embroidered midi-dress with a half-sleeved chiffon jacket-like shawl, which suited her. Carol preferred an off-the-shoulder knee-length chiffon and satin lace dress in cream and tan.

After purchasing their dresses, it was time to visit the millinery department to find matching hats. Neither Anne nor Carol liked wearing hats and tried a few different ones, laughing at the designs which didn't suit them. Anne bought a lovely hat with a faux pearl and flower design, in royal blue, which matched her dress. Carol purchased a chic hat with a bow at the back.

After lunch, they visited the shoe, hosiery, and underwear departments. They then purchased other accessories; matching bags and earrings to complete their outfits for the wedding. In the meantime, Victoria and Sami went to choose their wedding rings.

Laden with bags, everyone returned to the car and headed back to Sami's house. Anne left her outfit in Baby Jasmine's room to ensure that Imran wouldn't see it. After more refreshments and more exciting wedding chatter, she went home.

Victoria and Carol also went home to pack and transport some of Victoria's belongings, ready for a permanent move to Sami's after the wedding.

Imran was in an irritable mood when Anne returned home.

"Where have you been?" he snapped when she entered the house. "Was my son's house so dirty that you had to stay all this time?"

"We go for lunch on Saturday, Imran. You know that."

"It must have been very grand for you to take this long," he muttered.

"Oh, shut up, Imran. You were the cause of it all. It's about time you held out an olive branch to Sami and stopped this ridiculous nonsense, once and for all."

"Never," he replied. "Not over my dead body."

83

On Sunday evening, Victoria looked at wedding and bridesmaid dresses online. She found a shop on the outskirts of Newcastle which had styles she liked, so she decided to call them the next day to make an appointment for herself and Dawn to try the dresses on.

There was a lot of chatter and excitement in the air as the news spread at work of Sami and Victoria's forthcoming nuptials. They needed to discuss annual leave with James. They were also excited about handing out the wedding invitations. Of course, they knew not everyone would be able to attend as some would have to cover the shifts, but that was up to their colleagues to decide. Dawn, being the maid of honour, was given immediate dispensation.

James offered to cover the ward rounds and on calls for anyone who wished to attend the wedding. However, he needed another person to cover the Outpatient Ward. Maria Bright volunteered, so everyone else was able to go.

It was a long meeting that day with James and Andy but even that didn't dampen Sami's mood.

"Don't forget that it's my 28-week scan at one o'clock today," Victoria had reminded him.

"OK. We'll have a quick lunch before the afternoon clinic," he replied.

Victoria then went into the office to make a telephone call.

"Dawn, are you free this Saturday?"

"Yes, why?"

"We're going to try on some dresses."

Victoria had her blood taken at the clinic and was about to have her scan. The sonographer placed ultrasound gel on her tummy and examined each part of the foetus. She held Sami's hand as the probe circled their baby. Those strong little feet, that kicked her so hard in Telford, looked very prominent now.

"Everything seems fine," said the sonographer as he finished the examination and gave them a new picture of Baby Jasmine.

After the clinic, Dawn spoke to Victoria on the ward, and asked, "What do you want to do for your hen party? It's my job as Maid of Honour to arrange things."

"Goodness," she replied. "Nothing too wild as I have the baby to consider."

"What do you want to do then?"

"Maybe a spa day, with a cream tea would be nice. I'll settle the bill and pay for everyone."

"Sounds good to me," said Dawn. "My job tonight will be looking for a lovely spa."

Sami went to do his workout at the gym with Richard that evening, while Victoria went back to his place to make a meal. At home, she often liked to make a pasta dish with cheese, bacon, and beans, and Sami was keen to try it. After the workout, Sami went for his usual drink and chat with Richard.

"How are wedding arrangements going?" Richard asked.

"We've given out the invitations, and the rest is up to Victoria. I shall turn up on the day," he laughed.

"Don't you think you should help her? After all, she's pregnant."

"She's like an excited child, and I love to see her happy. I'm here if she needs me."

"So what are you doing for a honeymoon?"

"I'm going to book that cottage in Aviemore for a few days, then take her somewhere abroad next year after the baby has been born."

"Have you thought about a stag night?"

"Oh no, I can't be bothered with all that," moped Sami. "You know me. I'm not a social butterfly."

"Don't I know it," laughed Richard. "But I'm arranging something, even if it's just a night out in the pub!" As Sami went to the bar for more drinks, Richard messaged Victoria.

'I'm trying to arrange a stag night for Sami. Any ideas?'

'Good luck with that then,' she messaged back with a smiling emoji. 'A night in the pub, perhaps? Maybe a round of golf, then a night in the pub. I know other friends that could join you.'

'Sounds good. I'll sort a date.'

The following day, Dawn spoke to Victoria about her hen party plans.

"I've found a nice hotel with a spa at reasonable prices. Bernie, Susan and I will come. Is there anyone else?"

"Anne, my mum, Cathy and Helen, my two skating friends. Sandra cannot make it from America.Can we sort it here over lunchtime?"

"Sounds good."

Victoria booked the spa for Saturday, 6th August. At least that was her hen party sorted. She knew that Sami was on call that weekend, so it seemed the best time.

She then thought about Richard and wondered how he was getting on with Sami's stag night. She would ask Andy and Nigel if they were able to go but needed a date to give them.

'Any ideas for the stag night,' she messaged Richard.

'Not a clue,' he messaged back.

'The best date would be 13th August, as I'm on call.'

'I'll go with that. Who else will come?'

'Andy and Nigel. I will ask them.'

After the clinic, Victoria headed towards the Accident and Emergency Department, as she needed to speak to Nigel. He was a consultant there and one of Sami's golfing friends. He seemed very surprised about the news of the marriage. He had a shift on 13th August but would try and swap it so that he could attend the stag night.

As she walked down the corridor to leave the department, she bumped into Chris Rogers.

"Congratulations on your recent engagement," he said.

"Thank you," she replied. "I am getting married on 31st August."

"Really? Are you sure you're not rushing into things?"

"No. We have had long chats, and I've never been more certain of anything."

"Listen, I'm sorry I upset you. I hope we can remain friends."

"Friends don't spread rumours about people they care about," Victoria replied sharply. "I thought better of you."

"I got the F2 doctor's job, so thank you for your help with my CV and application form."

"That's great! Congratulations. You know where I am if you need any further help and advice." She then disappeared up the corridor and out of the ward.

A huge wave of disappointment spread over Chris as, deep inside, he was still very much in love with her.

Andy was also keen to attend the stag do. Victoria informed Richard, who then booked a nearby hotel where Sami often played golf. They would have a round of golf in the afternoon before having a meal; then hit the town for drinks in the evening and return to the hotel to stay overnight. Victoria knew that Sami would like that.

Carol decided to buy Paul a new suit for the wedding and asked Victoria for her colour scheme. She told her that Sami wanted a new grey suit and thought it might be good if he, Paul and Richard went together to choose them. Carol arranged for the following Saturday, the same day as Victoria and Dawn were attending to their dresses.

The Saturday soon came around. Victoria arranged to collect Dawn and they headed for the shop on the outskirts of Newcastle. She found it easily, following the satellite navigation system.

Victoria tried on an ivory A-line sleeveless, knee-length wedding dress with a jewel neck and lace bodice. It fit her perfectly, and she looked stunning in it. The assistant found a matching veil for her to try on.

"It is the perfect dress!" she said, delighted. "I thought that I would have to try loads of them to find one that suited me."

Dawn tried three outfits and decided on a dusky pink V-neck bridesmaid dress with an empire waist and flutter sleeves. She looked gorgeous. Again, the assistant produced a matching floral comb. Victoria purchased them all, delighted with their choices.

After dropping Dawn at her flat, Victoria took her wedding dress to her parents' house to hang it in the wardrobe so that Sami wouldn't see it. Meg and Reggie were delighted to see her and she took them out for their usual walk in the fields at the back of the house.

The three men sorted out their new grey suits in town that day. Both Sami and Paul found suits that fitted perfectly. However, Richard's needed a slight alteration and could be collected later. They also bought matching shoes.

It was a successful day as everyone had their wedding outfits. The only thing still to organise was a trip to Gretna Green village to see the wedding coordinator.

84

The following weekend, Sami and Victoria travelled to the Gretna Wedding Bureau to meet their wedding coordinator and finalise the wedding plans.

Alice, the wedding coordinator, introduced herself and invited them into a private room to go through the legalities and paperwork before confirming the finer arrangements.

Victoria wanted two wedding cars to transport the men and the ladies to the venue separately. She wanted a videographer to film the wedding and photo session afterwards, and she ordered a photo storybook album from the photographer.

A local florist would arrange lilac, pink, and cream flowers for the wedding posy and bridesmaid flowers, as well as three matching buttonholes for the men. All to be ready for collection on the morning of the wedding.

The beautician would arrange everyone's hair and makeup at eleven o'clock.

Alice also explained that a piper would serenade them into the wedding ceremony, and on their exit from Anvil Hall. He would accompany them for the photography session. Doves would be released following the ceremony. Everything seemed surreal for Victoria and her big blue eyes widened with excitement, like a child. Sami loved seeing her like that.

On the way back, they visited the hotel to confirm their room bookings: three on the first night and seven on the second night.

Everything seemed in order. They would be back, in less than two weeks, to do it all for real.

Sami got up on the morning of his wedding. He had slept alone in the luxury bridal suite. Victoria, a traditionalist, wanted to sleep separately and shared a twin room with Dawn. Richard, Janice, and Sarah had also travelled the previous day and were sleeping in a family room.

Sami brushed his fingers through his hair, contemplating life. He was getting married for the second time. He had vowed that he would never do it again after the first time but, that day, he felt differently. He didn't feel worried and couldn't wait to marry Victoria. She was his world.

Victoria woke on her wedding day and was like an excited child.

"Today's the day," she sang. "Single woman, no more."

"Aren't you nervous?" asked Dawn. "I'd be feeling jittery if it was me."

"Not at all."

"No last-minute doubts? It hasn't been precisely plain sailing for you two, has it?"

"I have none and never felt so certain about anything. Come on. We've arranged an early breakfast."

Dawn and Victoria had planned to eat early as it was important that she didn't see Sami until the wedding.

It was going to be a busy morning. Victoria had arranged to collect the flowers from the local florist at ten o'clock, and the beautician would arrive at her bedroom at eleven o'clock. She was expecting her mum, Anne, and Rosy to get changed in her room, and they would also need their makeup done and hair styled.

Carol arrived early after breakfast, and Paul was immediately banished to the men's room, along with the three buttonholes.

Anne got up and, as usual, put on her dressing gown and made her husband his breakfast. It was another day at the surgery, and she hoped that he would leave early, as she had a busy morning too.

She had to collect her mother, Rosy, and then call into Sami's house on the way to get her new outfit before she could set off on the journey. She knew that Victoria had booked a beautician to do her hair and makeup, so she wanted to get there as soon as possible.

Imran stood up and collected his belongings.

"Goodbye, Darling. See you tonight," he said, as he left the house.

Anne felt dreadful about keeping the wedding a secret from him. Sami was his only son, and she knew that deep within he would want to be there despite their silly feud. Family values were important to him. Sami hadn't wanted him there because he feared that Imran would spoil their day. She felt she had to follow her instinct, so she dressed, sat down, and wrote a letter before leaving the house.

Having given Imran enough time to settle into his office, Anne called into the surgery reception.

"Good morning, Mrs Prakesh," said Doreen, a senior receptionist who had worked there for many years. "Dr Prakesh is in his office. You can go straight through."

"Actually, no, I don't want to disturb him," Anne replied. "Would you mind handing over this letter to him for me, please?"

"Not a problem. It's nice to see you."

"And you. Goodbye." Anne left the surgery to make her calls before setting off for Gretna Village.

Imran sat in his office, studying patients' test results on his computer before surgery when there was a knock at his door.

"Come in." Doreen entered his office.

"Your wife called and asked me to give you this letter."

"I'll come through and see what she wants."

"No need, Dr Prakesh. She's left already."

"Oh, right. Thank you," he said as Doreen left the room.

That's strange. My wife is bringing in letters. What the hell is going on with my family?

He threw the letter aside to look at later and continued with his work. Curiosity got the better of him so, a few minutes later, he picked it up and looked at it. Another few minutes later, he grabbed his belongings and hurried to the surgery reception.

"Doreen, please cancel all my appointments for today and rearrange them. Something has come up and I have to leave," he said and disappeared through the door in a flash, leaving bewilderment and chaos behind.

He drove home and saw that Anne's car wasn't there.

She must have left already.

He entered the house, took the suit and shoes she'd left out for him, and then placed them in his boot before locking up. He needed petrol for his journey.

Victoria went for a loose-flowing hairstyle, as she knew Sami liked her wearing her hair down. The sides were swept around the back and clipped into a floral hairpiece into which the veil could slot later.

Dawn's hair was sassier, with a pre-styled hairpiece attached and blended into her hair, with a floral comb attached.

Then it was Carol's turn to have her hair styled and, just as she had sat down in front of the stylist, Anne phoned to say that she and Rosy had arrived. Within a few minutes, they were all together in Victoria's bedroom.

When the beautician had finished all the hairstyling and makeup, it was almost time for the wedding cars to arrive. The men would go in the first car, and Sami agreed to call Victoria after they had set off, which would signal them to assemble in the lobby for their vehicle.

Victoria put on her wedding gown, and the beautician attached the veil to her hair.

"Wow! You look stunning," said Carol with a lump in her throat, feeling so proud of her daughter. "I want to cry already."

"Oh, Mother, you've just had your makeup done."

Just at that moment, Sami phoned.

"We're on our way, Darling. See you soon."

The bridal procession left the room and waited for their car.

Imran arrived at the venue. He knew they would still be at their hotel but, if he found his way to Anvil Hall, he could wait patiently in the bar. It was important that they didn't see him, so he would have to sneak in quietly behind the wedding procession as a latecomer.

85

The men arrived first. Sami and his best man, Richard, took their places in Anvil Hall, while Paul waited outside for Victoria.

The ladies' car soon arrived. Sami's Auntie Susan, Beverley, Karen, Mark, and Chloe were already there. As Victoria climbed out of the car, she could see her other guests entering the building, Bernie, Susan, Andy and his family, Verity and family, Tony Quigley and his partner, then Cathy and Helen, her ice-skating friends. It was a shame Sandra wasn't there.

Anne, Rosy, and Carol took their seats at the front of Anvil Hall. Once everyone had settled, the minister indicated for the bridal procession to enter. The piper played as Victoria, her stepfather, and Dawn walked down the aisle.

There were lots of gasps as Victoria walked in. She made a beautiful bride, radiant and ethereal. Sami caught a glimpse of her as she drew closer, and his heart melted as she smiled across at him.

"You look stunning," he whispered.

"You're not so bad, yourself," she replied.

Imran looked at his watch. The wedding should be ready to start, he thought, as he gulped down the last drink. He got up and left the bar.

"Dearly beloved, we are gathered here today to join Sami Imran Prakesh and Victoria Louise Pemberton in holy matrimony. If anyone can show just cause why they should not be married, speak now or forever hold their peace," the minister said. At that moment, someone entered the room.

"Me. Me," a male voice spoke. "I don't want this wedding to go ahead."

A look of horror spread across Sami's face when he heard the voice. It was his father. Determined that Imran wouldn't spoil the day for Victoria, he turned and scowled at him.

"What are you doing here?" he boomed down the length of Anvil Hall. "You were not invited."

"Please," Imran said in a weak, shaky voice. "I haven't come to spoil your day. I want to see my only son get married. Is that so wrong?"

"You've just objected to my wedding," Sami shouted. Anne looked at the floor and wanted it to open and swallow her up.

"Only if I cannot be present. I have no objection," he said, as he turned to look at the minister. "Please, Mr Minister, I want to be here to see my only son get married. I have no objection." He shed a tear as everyone's eyes were directed at him, giving him angry and dirty looks.

The minister nodded and asked, "Shall we proceed?"

"Come on," Victoria said to Sami. "Let's get married. We can talk to him later." Sami turned to face her, held her hand, and the ceremony continued.

"Do you, Sami Imran, take this woman, Victoria Louise, to be your lawfully wedded wife, to have and to hold, in sickness and in health, in good times and bad, for richer, for poorer, keeping yourself unto her for as long as you both shall live?"

"I do," answered Sami.

Victoria said her vows and they exchanged rings to symbolise their love and future life together.

"I now pronounce you man and wife. You may kiss the bride."

Sami enveloped Victoria in his arms and gave her a passionate kiss. She was his, forever.

They went to sign the register and, while in the private area, he said, "Victoria, I'm so sorry about my father. I don't know how he knew we were here."

"Don't worry. We are married now, so he can't spoil anything for me today. He did look upset, though."

"So were our mothers. I think they both had their tissues out."

They laughed.

The bride and groom left Anvil Hall as man and wife, with the piper playing by their side. Once outside, two white doves are released as a symbol of their love. As they walked around the grounds in the various places allocated for photographs, Imran was included in all the family shots.

"You will regret it if you don't," Victoria had said. "I think it's time you made up with him. Today, he has reached out an olive branch."

Sami sighed and said, "He could have done it differently, instead of barging into our wedding."

"Imran, why the hell did you come barging into the ceremony like that? I was horrified," Anne scolded when she saw him outside. "You should have phoned me to say you were coming, and you could have mingled with the congregation."

"I was worried that they would see me," he replied sheepishly.

Later at the wedding reception, Victoria reorganised the seating to accommodate her father-in-law so that he could sit with the family. In the hallway outside, Imran approached Sami and spoke to him.

"Son, I want to apologise for everything. I know I've made life difficult for you."

"Difficult? My life has been unbearable these last few months, and then you barged into our wedding."

"In the end, you got your woman. She is a good woman," he said, patting Sami's shoulder, and gave a parting comment as he walked into the hall, "It was a good test for the strength of your love."

Sami gave a deep sigh.

That man is unbelievable!

During the speeches, a very unprepared Imran gave his, apologising for the abrupt intrusion of the wedding ceremony, then welcoming Victoria and her parents to the Prakesh family. Victoria and Sami were surprised. It was still the early days of reconciliation but things were heading in the right direction.

Later, after the celebrations, Victoria and Sami thanked all their guests for coming and sharing their special day. They returned to their luxury bridal suite, where Sami had slept alone the night before.

"You should have seen your face when your father entered the hall," Victoria giggled. "It went a darker shade of giemsa."

"What?"

"It's a private joke between Mum and me."

"What is?"

"Your face when you are in a bad mood. It turns a darker shade of giemsa."

"Really? Is this what I must tolerate for the rest of my life?"

"Yes," she giggled.

As they made love that night in the bridal suite, Victoria wore her basque. It was the beginning of a journey of a happy life together.

The next day, they travelled to Aviemore for their honeymoon.

"I wonder if the Jacobite train runs in September," Sami pondered.

"I'm certain that it runs until the end of October," Victoria replied.

"I wonder if the rhododendron bushes are still there."

Victoria pulled over into the next layby and kissed him.

"Life with you is going to be one big adventure."

"I promise you a longer and warmer honeymoon abroad somewhere after Baby Jasmine is born."

"Can we beat Aviemore?" she asked.

"Perhaps not," he said as he stroked her face and pushed a strand of hair behind her ear.

"Well, let's continue with this honeymoon for now," Victoria said, pulling out of the layby and back onto the open road ahead.

"Aviemore, here we come!

Acknowledgements

I have received incredible support and encouragement from all family, friends, and colleagues during my book-writing journey, all of whom have been enthusiastic about following my progress.

I am forever indebted to my dear partner Peter Orr, whose love and support throughout my writing journey have been second to none. He has shown great patience with my endless hours of writing, and he has provided lovely meals to encourage me to eat. He has tolerated things through difficult times when I have grown frustrated and grumpy and supported me through times of self-doubt. His IT skills have been pivotal in helping me build my website and many other IT-related necessities, many of which I have little knowledge of. Without his tremendous support, this journey would not have been possible.

I want to express my sincere thanks to Michael Heppell, the leader of the Write That Book pop-up course and Masterclass course, without which my dream may not have come true. These courses opened up a new meaning to the land of book writing, and Michael's enthusiasm, drive, tips, and encouragement have been a total inspiration. Through the course, I have met many inspirational people ready to help and support me when needed.

I want to express my sincere thanks to the Consultant Haematologists:

Dr. Mari Kilner
Dr. Christopher Tiplady
Dr. Alex Langridge

For their expert medical advice and guidance, which has made this storyline possible, also

Dr. Christopher Williams
for giving me an excellent idea for the book title.

I would also like to thank Sue Dunhill and Karen Ward for their guidance in the operation of the haematology and transfusion laboratories.

Heartfelt thanks to Matthew Bird for generously giving his time for the preparation, typesetting, and publication of this book.

I sincerely thank Christine Beech for generously giving her time for her meticulous editorial revision, an essential part of this book.

Thanks to Eleanor Baggaley, my writing coach, for her helpful advice and guidance.

Thank you to Ferhana Jabeen Watson for the helpful advice on aspects of the Muslim faith.

I want to thank the Gretna wedding bureau for permission to use their venue for the wedding storyline.

Thanks to Karen Scott for permission to use her beautiful cottage as part of the story.

Thanks to Stuart Anderson for permission to use his public house as part of the story.

My sincere thanks to my WTB accountability group "Penfluence" for all their generous help, support, and advice given during my book writing journey.

Thank you to all members of "Team 17" and members of "How to be brilliant" for all help, advice, and support offered during my book writing journey.

I would also like to thank the following websites for their useful information:

www.google.co.uk
www.dictionary.com
www.bloodcancer.org.uk
https://westcoastrailways.co.uk
https://visitforres.scot
www.theforthbridges.org
Wikipedia

About the Author

A J Donovan was born and raised in Sunderland, Tyne, and Wear. She has a long-term partner, one daughter, and two grandsons. In her youth, she was a competitive Ice skater, Junior Champion in 1977, Senior Silver medallist in 1982, and International and World representative. She was an ice skating coach, first at Bournemouth, then Peterborough before returning to her home town Sunderland, but was never completely happy.

She studied Biomedical Science at Sunderland University and graduated in 1999 with a 2:1 degree. She became a qualified Biomedical Scientist in 2001 and continues to practice in this field. In her childhood, she loved to write short stories in notebooks; however, life and work commitments took over, and her hobby took a back seat.

After a clear-out, she recently came across one of her old exercise books with some stories she had written over 40 years ago. She was inspired to start writing again and created an idea for the current story. This is her first romantic fiction novel, and she has an idea for a second book in the near future.